HE WAS RÁFAGA

Whose gun fed a hungry people . . . whose passion fed a woman's hungering heart. . . .

A man as proud and fierce as the lions that roamed his mountain retreat.

SHE WAS SHEILA

As cool, beautiful, and unyielding as the modern towers that stood as bastions of the fortune that would one day be hers.

Now she was Ráfaga's captive prize, held for a ransom in gold, struggling against the fire he set in her blood.

She called her captor every name, and lived to take back all but one: Lover.

Books by Janet Dailey

Night Way
Ride the Thunder
The Rogue
Touch the Wind

Published by POCKET BOOKS

Janet Dailey

Touch the Wind

PUBLISHED BY POCKET BOOKS NEW YORK

Another *Original* publication of POCKET BOOKS

POCKET BOOKS, a Simon & Schuster division of
GULF & WESTERN CORPORATION
1230 Avenue of the Americas, New York, N.Y. 10020

Copyright © 1979 by Janet Dailey

ISBN: 0-671-43668-6

First Pocket Books printing May, 1979

15   14   13   12

POCKET and colophon are trademarks of Simon & Schuster.

Printed in the U.S.A.

Touch the Wind

Chapter 1

A trio of gold bracelets jingled as Sheila Rogers closed the door of her blue Thunderbird. She turned toward the hotel where Brad worked, sleek, tawny hair swinging freely near her shoulders.

There wasn't a whisper of a breeze. Beyond the towering hotel structure, the waters of the dammed Colorado River were mirror-smooth. On its downward path, a Texas sun was leaving a long, yellow trail across the surface. The February afternoon air was cool against Sheila's cheek.

Her amber gaze flicked to her wristwatch as she started toward the hotel entrance. It was nearly five o'clock. She had cut it close again. Her shoulders lifted in a typical I-don't-care shrug that revealed she was accustomed to having people wait for her. It wasn't a conscious gesture.

Sheila didn't admit to being spoiled, although she would concede that, as an only child, she had been indulged by a pair of loving parents.

But not by Brad. She couldn't wrap him around her

1

finger as she had the other men she dated. Perhaps that was one of many reasons why she was so fascinated by him. Now Brad would be angry with her for being late, but Sheila was confident she could make him forget his displeasure.

At the thought, a faint smile curved her sensuous lips, glossed a dusty-rose shade. Combined with the promising sparkle of her gold-flecked eyes, the movement gave a look of secretive pleasure to her expression, tantalizingly mysterious to a casual onlooker.

Sheila had nearly reached the entrance door when she saw Brad standing to the side of the building with another male member of the hotel staff. The brown light of his eyes was roughly accusing as he met her gaze. He had to have seen her walking from the parking lot to the entrance, yet he hadn't called out to her. He would have let her waste precious minutes looking for him inside to punish Sheila for her tardiness.

Poised near the door, Sheila gazed at him, her breath caught in her throat. Blonde hair fell with masculine carelessness across his tanned forehead. Blatant virility was stamped in the handsome lines of his face, a suggestion of arrogance in the set of his jaw. Tall, well muscled, his sun-god looks would have set any girl's heart beating faster. The hotel uniform of a camel-tan blazer over a white pullover with dark slacks accented his male physique.

Each time Sheila saw him, her reaction was the same. First there was a vague sense of surprise that she could have forgotten how stunningly handsome he was, followed by a sense of guilt that she had kept him waiting, however unintentionally.

True, her steps were unhurried, graceful, almost leisurely strides carrying her forward. Her lips parted into a smile, beguiling and faintly apologetic. The bracelets jingled again as Sheila tucked golden-toast hair behind her ear.

"I'm sorry I'm late, honey." Her voice was low and warm, designed to soothe his irritation.

Brad Townsend didn't return the smile. He nodded

briefly to his co-worker and took Sheila's hand in a finger-crushing grip. She breathed in sharply at the pain as he pulled her after him to the side of the building.

"Brad, you're hurting my hand," Sheila protested when they stopped, uncertain if he was aware of his own strength.

He released her numbed fingers immediately, his hands grasping her shoulders as he pulled her roughly against him.

"I don't like being kept waiting," Brad growled beneath his breath, its warmth moving hotly over her lips a split second before his mouth smothered them.

The kiss was a combination of bruising punishment and mastery. Sheila struggled against his attempted domination even as she thrilled to his possession. His arms encircled her to crush the minor rebellion, the heat radiating from his embrace. Conquered, Sheila tipped back her head to let his hard mouth explore the sensitive cord of her neck and the hollow of her throat.

"I'm sorry," she murmured, her eyes closed as a fiery weakness spread through her limbs. "I didn't mean to be late."

"That's what you always say," he muttered, nipping an ear lobe.

Her fingers slid inside the unbuttoned blazer to curve her arms around him, feeling the burning warmth of his body and the flexing muscles in his shoulders and back. His roving hands were moving over her waist and hips to mold her closer to him.

The musky scent clinging to his smoothly shaven jaw was intoxicating. Sheila breathed it in deeply as she exclaimed, "I was asked to stay for a few minutes after my last class, and the time just slipped away from me."

He lifted his head. "Which professor was it this time? Not that it matters. You are every professor's pet," Brad said with a slight curl to his lips.

"It was Benton." Sheila ignored the faint jeer. "He had some suggestions to make on the outline I had submitted for this semester's theme."

"And you kept me waiting while you talked to that dried-up old prune," he accused.

"I said I was sorry."

"Maybe I should find out how truly repentant you are." Brad said it lightly, the dark light of desire in his brown eyes.

With a breathless laugh, she withdrew her arms from around him, letting her hands rest on his chest to wedge a slight space between them. She felt the strong beat of his heart beneath her fingers.

"But you have to be on duty in just a few minutes," Sheila pointed out, partially aware that she hadn't exactly told him "no."

"Yes," Brad agreed, lowering his head to let his mouth brush the sensual curve of her lips, "and making love to you isn't something I would want to hurry."

An inner heat warmed her cheeks. Not from shyness. It came more from the age-old temptation and fear to explore the unknown.

"Don't say things like that," she murmured.

"I could always be late for work," he added suggestively, and her pulse leaped in that odd combination of fear and excitement.

"No." But Sheila wasn't certain what she was denying.

His mouth continued to teasingly trace her lips until they quivered with longing for his kiss. Deliberately, Brad ignored their message. Unable to bear the tormenting nearness of his mouth without receiving his kiss, Sheila curled her fingers into his sun-gold hair and forced his head down.

The initiative was taken from her as he claimed her willing lips. The kiss hardened with fiery passion until Sheila felt engulfed by the flames. Her lips were forced apart by the rough demand of his tongue. His sensuous exploration of her mouth fanned the flames into a raging inferno that seemed to isolate them from the world, but it wasn't so.

"Come on, Brad!" A voice called out, low and impatient. "It's a couple minutes after five now."

Cold reality washed over Sheila like ice water as Brad abruptly ended the kiss, lifting his head. Shaken that someone had witnessed her abandoned behavior, Sheila willingly accepted the support of Brad's arms, letting him shield her from any knowing looks.

"I'll be there in a few minutes. Tell the boss I'm here but that I'm helping somebody start their car."

"I'll cover for you," the voice assured Brad in an unmistakably suggestive tone. "Call me if you need help."

"I won't need any help," Brad said with an arrogant laugh.

The footsteps faded behind them. A vague sensation of revulsion twisted Sheila out of Brad's arms. Yet the weakness from the overwhelming passion he had ignited moved her only a foot away. Her back was turned to him as he stepped after her, his hands settling familiarly on her waist.

The warmth of his breath stirred her hair. Sheila stiffened in spite of the unsatisfied ache in the pit of her stomach. The light touch of his hands seemed to burn through the material of her clothes to her skin.

"Embarrassed?" he mocked softly. "Tom only saw us kissing. That's all."

"It's not that." Sheila moved her head to the side to deny his assumption.

Brad immediately took advantage of the gesture to bury his mouth in the silken tangle of her hair along the outer curve of her neck. Her senses leaped in answer to the caress as his hands spread across her stomach, drawing her back against his muscular chest.

"I don't think you realize what you do to me," Sheila whispered.

"What I do to you?" Brad laughed shortly and paused to push the hair away from her ear. "You are nothing but a tease, Sheila Rogers," he accused roughly, his arms tightening around her waist until she could no longer ignore the burning imprint of his male need pressing against her flesh. "You promise with your kisses, but when it's time to come across, you back down. I should drag you into one of the hotel rooms and take you now." His hand cupped the swell of her breast.

"No."

"I won't do it." Brad turned her around to face him, his expression hard and slightly frightening. "But there have been several times in the last few weeks when you would have let me seduce you with only a token protest, so don't deny it."

An angry flush filled her cheeks. His arrogant confidence that he could take her whenever it suited him irritated Sheila, because she was all too aware that it was probably true.

"Then why haven't you seduced me?" she challenged.

"Because, my spoiled little brat," mocked Brad, "I'm not going to dance on your string the way your other boyfriends have. When we make love, it's going to be at your invitation and not because I've overcome your resistance. When we go to bed together, it's going to be because you asked for it, literally. I don't care if it's before we are married or after, but you will invite me."

"Of all the—" Sheila sputtered at his arrogant presumption that, in time, she would beg him.

Brad laughed and covered her defiant lips with his mouth. Sheila resisted for a few minutes before his kiss worked its magic and she was clinging to him again, momentarily forsaking her pride.

Finally he lifted his head, a complacent gleam in his brown eyes as he gazed at the bemused expression on her upturned face. He flashed her one of his devastating smiles.

"Tell me you love me," Brad ordered, locking his arms around her waist.

"I love you," she responded dutifully.

"And you will promise to love, honor, and obey me," he recited.

Her mouth opened to respond to his command, but the beaming light faded from her eyes as she remembered the discussion with her parents.

"I will," Sheila managed to answer after several seconds.

Brad had noticed her hesitation and the slight change in her expression. He drew his head back to study her, his gaze narrowing.

"I talked to Mom and Dad about us."

"And?" His mouth tightened into a grim line.

"They thought we were being a bit premature about wanting to get married," Sheila stated.

He released her abruptly and stepped away, his volatile temper surfacing. "I'm not good enough for you. That's what they said, wasn't it?" he demanded savagely and didn't wait for a response. "What's the matter? Am I too poor for their darling daughter? I suppose they hold it against me because it's taken me seven years to get through four years of college. Is it my fault I wasn't born with rich parents like yours and have had to keep taking time off to work and earn the money to go back?"

"Brad, please." Sheila tried to stop his bitter tirade. "It is nothing like that. They just think it's unwise for us to get married right now. You won't receive your degree until this spring and—"

"—and they are afraid that if we get married now, they will have to support us . . . or, more specifically— me! I suppose they think I'm marrying you for your money. You know what they can do with their money, don't you?"

"It isn't the money exactly." Sheila was painfully aware that talk of money struck a raw nerve with Brad. "They think we should wait a year before getting married so you can finish your degree and get a job without the responsibility of a wife. A year isn't so long, not when we love each other."

His dark gaze pinned her. "Tell me honestly, Sheila, do your parents approve of me as your future husband?"

Unwillingly, she hesitated. Her father had made his disapproval of Brad obvious. Only the influence of her mother had obtained the concession to a year's wait.

Sheila knew her father had agreed in the hope that she and Brad would part before the year was up.

"That answers my question, doesn't it?" he declared grimly.

"They don't exactly disapprove of you, either," Sheila rushed. "They just don't know you as well as I do. Besides, they still think of me as their little girl. It's hard for them to see me as a wife to some man who is practically a total stranger to them."

"Do you want to wait a year?"

"Of course I don't," she said.

"You don't look very upset about the idea." His hands were on his hips, pushing the jacket open.

Sheila lifted her hand in exasperation, bracelets jingling. "What do you want me to do? Beat my chest and wail?"

"I suppose they accused me of being a fortune hunter." His voice was thick with sarcasm.

"My parents accused you of nothing." Sheila controlled her rising temper with effort. "I admit my father doesn't exactly trust you, but my mother is willing to give you the benefit of the doubt. It isn't an endorsement, and neither is it a condemnation."

"Am I supposed to be grateful for that?" jeered Brad.

"You are supposed to understand their side of it!" she said.

It was obvious by his expression that Brad didn't agree. "What would you have done if they had told you not to marry me?" he demanded, his gaze narrowing.

"But they didn't!" Sheila protested.

"But if they had," he persisted.

Gritting her teeth, she answered, *"If* they had, I would have married you, anyway."

"I'll bet you would!" A bitter sound, only faintly resembling laughter, came from his throat. "I knew it would only be a matter of time before you'd admit that you're having second thoughts about marrying me."

"If I'm having second thoughts, it isn't because of

anything my parents said to me." She pivoted to walk away. This was a side of Brad she despised.

He caught her arm and spun her back around, tightening his grip when Sheila strained to break free. His fingers were nearly digging into the bone as he forced her to face him.

"Don't you ever walk away from me again!" Brad ordered.

Sheila met the rage blazing in his expression without flinching. "Let go of my arm and you'll see me walk away again."

"I'm not letting you go." A strange light glazed his eyes. "You're mine, and I'm not letting you go."

A shaft of cold fear plunged into her stomach. "You're hurting me, Brad." She tried not to let the panic creep into her voice. "Let go of my arm."

"It's the money, isn't it?" He relaxed his hold slightly, the glazed look leaving his brown eyes. "You've decided that after having everything you've ever wanted all your life, you don't want to live on a budget, scrimping and saving for every little luxury. That's why you don't want to marry me, isn't it? Because I can't keep you in the style you are accustomed to."

"Money is all you ever think about, isn't it?" Sheila accused. "I am not going to spend the rest of my life apologizing for the fact that my parents are wealthy. I didn't choose it to be that way. I had no control over it whatsoever."

"You've never had to go without it." He breathed tightly. "I've never had it. I've had to fight and claw and sometimes even steal to get what I wanted. Nobody has ever given me anything. They're always trying to take what little I have. Now they're trying to take you."

Sheila frowned. "No one is trying to take me from you."

"Aren't they?" Brad mocked bitterly. "Now that your parents know we want to get married, they're going to try to poison you against me. They'll pay people to tell you lies about me until you believe them. Wait and see."

"That's not true. My parents aren't like that."

"I suppose they are as pure and lily white as you are." Scorn was etched in the line of his mouth, contemptuous and vaguely savage.

"They certainly aren't the monsters you are painting them to be." Sheila snapped.

"You are either blind or incredibly naïve. I—"

The sentence wasn't finished as an impatient male voice called, "Brad!"

Brad didn't attempt to disguise his annoyance at the interruption. "What do you want, Tom?" he glared at the intruder, the same co-worker as before.

"I can't cover for you all night," he said. "You'd better get in there before you are fired."

"I'll be right there," Brad agreed with an irritated sigh.

"You'd better be," came the parting shot.

Sheila was glad for the interruption. She couldn't bear Brad's sarcastic comments and his unjustified accusations against her parents. She felt sick at heart and wanted only to get away and sort things out for herself.

"Go on in, Brad," she murmured dispiritedly. "It's time I left, anyway."

"Don't go, Sheila." He held her fast and placed a hand on her other shoulder to turn her back to him.

She continued to avoid his gaze. "There isn't any point in staying. There is nothing left to say."

"Sheila." He seemed to search desperately for a reason, then laughed shortly. "I think we've just had our first real quarrel."

"I certainly didn't start it." She could find none of the twisted humor that Brad had in the discovery.

"It's miserable, isn't it?" he said. Releasing her arm, he started to stroke her cheek in a soothing caress, but Sheila drew away from his touch, unable to make the same sudden transition from anger to affection. "I never meant for us to quarrel like this," Brad murmured apologetically. "I just lost my head, that's all."

"That was enough," she answered tightly.

"Sheila, look at me." When she didn't obey, he caught her chin and forced her to comply. His handsome, golden features pleaded for her forgiveness. "How can I make you understand the way I feel?"

"You have," Sheila assured him. "You've made it clear that you don't believe I really love you and you think my parents are conspiring against you."

"No, that's not it at all. Don't you see?" Brad gazed earnestly into her wary eyes. "You are the only thing in my life that means anything to me, Sheila. I'm afraid of losing you. I—"

A frown of concern creased his forehead, disappearing beneath a lock of blond hair. His sincerity reached out to invisibly touch Sheila.

"Brad," she whispered, responding to his plea.

Amusement born of self-derision glittered briefly in his velvet-brown eyes. "You don't understand, do you? You think I'm wrong to feel that way."

"No one can take me away from you." A half-smile curved her lips.

"I've asked you to be my wife, Sheila," he began.

"And I have accepted," she reminded him.

"Yes." Brad nodded. "But I don't have anything to offer you except my love. I'm asking you to give up everything for nothing."

His thumb was caressing her collarbone in rhythmic circles. Sheila felt the magic of his touch begin to take effect.

"It isn't such a bad exchange, darling." She smiled.

"Love can't put a roof over our heads or food in our mouths," he reminded her. "It takes money, which I haven't got."

"Ssh!" Sheila pressed silencing fingers against his lips. "I don't want to hear that word again."

Brad kissed her fingertips, then held them lightly in his hands. "I don't want to say it again, but money is one of the unchangeable facts of life. It can't be avoided simply because it's unpleasant."

"I don't care." Sheila slipped her fingers from his

hand and softly brushed the hair from his forehead. "Tell me you love me, Brad."

"I love you." He kissed her long and hard to reinforce his words. "A year," Brad groaned when he lifted his head. "I can't wait a year."

Sheila rubbed her forehead against his jaw in a feline gesture and sighed. "I know." Reluctantly, she strained against his embrace. "And you can't stay out here any longer or you will lose your job."

He withdrew his arms from around her, briefly kissing her once. "If it's not busy at the desk, I'll call you tonight."

"I'll be home," Sheila promised.

"And you'd better be there alone." Brad growled the mock threat.

"I'll think about it." She laughed and moved away without kissing him again. It would only have prolonged a moment that had already stretched too far.

As Sheila slid behind the wheel of her Thunderbird and started the motor, Brad was still standing where she had left him. He raised his hand in a good-bye when she reversed out of the stall. Sheila waved back, feeling very contented.

Driving onto the street, she was surprised to discover she was humming the tune of a sad love song. The melancholy lyrics were about a love that had gone wrong. Sheila gripped the steering wheel in irritation, blaming the song for reminding her of the argument instead of its satisfactory conclusion.

Money. What a stupid thing to argue about, she thought. Sheila wondered if poor people were naturally prouder, or if Brad was simply obsessed by it. For a few minutes during the quarrel, she had thought he was paranoid and had felt a twinge of uncertainty.

The car windows were rolled down and Sheila shook her head, leting the wind play over her face. Everything was going to be all right. She was positive of it. Brad was a rough diamond in need of some polishing to fit into her world. That was all. Once she accomplished that, they would make such a stunning couple. With her money and her parents' connections, the sky would be the only limit to their future. Bright, shining, and cloudless.

Chapter 2

Stepping through the front door, the heels of her sandals sank into the thick pile of the cream-colored carpet. By most standards, her parents' ranch-style house was a near mansion, but to Sheila, it was simply her home.

A maid quietly appeared in the foyer. Sheila handed the woman her purse and the expensive leather case containing her college books and papers.

"Would you put them in my room, Rose?" she requested, expecting the affirmative nod before it was made. "Is my mother home?"

"Mrs. Rogers is in her sitting room."

"Thank you."

The thick carpet silenced Sheila's footsteps as she walked to the wide hallway leading to her parents' bedroom and its adjoining sitting room. Outside the door, she knocked once, then walked in.

"Is that you, darling?" came her mother's questioning voice from the bedroom beyond.

"It depends which darling you mean—me or Dad?" Sheila laughed.

"I was referring to your father." Constance Rogers appeared in the connecting doorway, belting the long, desert-sand robe she wore. "We are hosting that political dinner this evening and I asked him to be home early. But you are equally welcome, Sheila, although I did expect you home sooner."

Constance Rogers was an older, more elegant version of her daughter. Her blonde hair was styled in a shorter, more sophisticated cut, its shade lightened by the invasion of strands of white. Her figure, too, was slender and firm, but it lacked the ripeness of Sheila's curves.

"I stayed for a while after my last class," Sheila explained.

Shrewd, almond-brown eyes swept over her, missing nothing. "Your lipstick needs freshening. You also saw Brad before you came home," her mother concluded with a hint of displeasure in her voice.

Sheila moved farther into the room, avoiding for the moment her mother's astute gaze. She never made the mistake of underestimating her mother. While seeming to stand in her husband's shadow, Constance Rogers was a power in her own right. It was her intelligence and social acumen, as well as her flair for public relations, that had enabled her husband to become so successful and powerful.

"Yes, I saw Brad," Sheila acknowledged, sitting down on the velvet-covered loveseat. "I'd like you to talk to Dad about him."

"Why?" her mother countered with a beguilingly curious smile that didn't fool Sheila for an instant.

"To persuade him to give up the idea that Brad and I have to wait a year before we get married," she answered smoothly.

"But I see nothing wrong with the idea." Constance Rogers walked to the wing-backed chair near the loveseat, spreading out the long skirt of her robe as she sat down.

Crossing her legs, Sheila challenged, "Are you against my marrying Brad, too?"

"Darling, I wouldn't dream of driving you into that

man's arms by forbidding you to marry him," her mother declared with a throaty laugh. "For the life of me, I can't understand what it is that you see in him. There are so many men in Texas who could offer you much more and would be much more suitable. And you could have any one of them you wanted."

"I don't want them. I want Brad," she insisted. Her fingers impatiently plucked at the corner of a throw pillow.

"Why, when there are so many others, do you want him?" Constance sighed, the corners of her perfectly outlined mouth turning upward in a sad smile.

"Because he's a challenge to me." Sheila blurted out the truth without thinking.

She was never entirely sure of him. He would not indulge her every whim, nor treat her with the adoration she was accustomed to receiving almost from birth. Their relationship had been a constant struggle between two equally strong personalities with either the certain winner. This provided the spice, but it wasn't the reason Sheila wanted to marry him.

"What I don't understand," Sheila continued, "is what you and Father have against Brad."

Her mother hesitated, then answered with equal frankness. "He is overbearing and abrasive."

Sheila relaxed against the cushions, a gleam in her cat-gold eyes. "Isn't that what your parents said about Dad before you eloped with him? He lacked culture, social refinement, and political insight, and look what influence you have had on him. You made Dad the man he is today."

"You can't compare the two," her mother insisted.

"Why?" Sheila argued. "Brad is ambitious."

"I think the correct adjective is money-hungry." Just then Sheila's father entered the room, pausing beside his wife's chair to kiss her upturned cheek.

Recovering from her momentary surprise at his appearance, Sheila flashed a reply. "I don't believe that is a bad trait. After all, Dad, aren't you always looking for a means to turn a profit?"

"The difference is that I'm willing to work for it. Your boyfriend prefers to get it the easy way," he responded calmly.

"How can you say that?" Sheila smouldered indignantly. "Look at how he's worked and struggled to obtain his degree."

The character lines in her father's sun-tanned face crinkled in an absent smile. "Yes, I've often wondered why a political science major would be working in a hotel. Since he lives here in the state capital, it's always seemed to me that if he were truly interested in his proposed profession he would be working in a government office."

"An excellent point, E.J." Constance Rogers patted her husband's hand that rested affectionately on her shoulder.

"Brad has worked in government offices before, but the hours conflicted with his classes," Sheila defended.

"Really?" her father drawled in dry disbelief. "I pride myself on my ability to judge people, and you are seeing qualities in this man that simply don't exist. I don't like the idea of my little girl being hurt."

Elliot John Rogers was a strong-willed man, and Sheila was in every way his daughter. Standing, she faced the pair without flinching.

"Neither of you understands Brad," she accused. "You simply don't know him the way I do. Furthermore, you don't want to know him, in case I prove that you are wrong."

"Sheila, that is not true," her mother protested, but Sheila was already leaving the sitting room.

There wasn't any point in continuing the discussion, not with her father present. Sheila could reason with her mother, but her father was positively rigid in his opinions, listening to no one, with the exception of his wife. Sheila retreated to her room to think. Obtaining her parents' approval was not going to be easy.

The problem was at the back of her mind all evening, through the meal she ate alone and the textbook pages of her reading. She waited for Brad to phone, almost needing the reassurance of his voice. When she slipped between her silk sheets around midnight, he still had not called. Sheila closed her eyes, hoping sleep would provide an answer.

Something was trying to awaken her. Her head moved against the pillow in protest, but the sensation persisted. Drowsily, Sheila opened her eyes, fighting through the waves of sleep trying to drag her back.

The bedroom was pitch-black. The only item her eyes could focus on was the luminous dial of the travel clock next to her bed. The glowing hands pointed to a few minutes past three o'clock, which drew a groan of tiredness from Sheila as she snuggled deeper beneath the covers.

A light rapping disturbed the silence. It sounded like someone tapping on glass. Propping herself up on an elbow, Sheila listened, every sense alert, uncertain whether she had heard the sound or simply imagined it.

It came again. Someone was tapping on the sliding glass door leading from her bedroom onto the backyard patio. No criminal would knock before entering. Sheila tossed back the covers and slid from the bed, knowing it had to be Brad. No one else would be knocking on her door at that hour of the night.

Barefoot, Sheila padded to the glass door and pulled the cord to open the floor-to-ceiling drapes of jade-green. Moonlight bathed the tall figure standing outside, blond hair gilded in the silvery light. Snapping off the lock, Sheila slid the door open to admit Brad.

"What are you doing here?" she whispered as he entered. "It's three in the morning."

The same moonlight that had outlined his masculine form now streamed through the glass door to illuminate Sheila. Her bare legs gleamed with a silken sheen, the red material of her mock nightshirt ending just above her knees. Brad's gaze made a sweeping inspection, drawing Sheila's attention to her ample, if suggestive, attire and the gaping, unbuttoned front of the shirt-gown. Her fingers moved immediately to clutch the front.

"I know what time it is," Brad answered, smiling as he moved toward her. "I just got off work and I had to see you."

"You could have phoned."

His hands settled on her shoulders and Sheila tensed. It didn't seem right for Brad to be in her bedroom at this hour, even if she was planning to marry him.

"You can't do this over the telephone." His mouth claimed hers in a long, sweet kiss, but he didn't attempt to draw her into his arms. "Do you still love me, honey?"

"You don't think I would stop loving you so soon, do you?"

It suddenly seemed romantic that Brad had come halfway across Austin on his motorbike to see her and assure himself she still loved him.

"Have you?" Brad persisted, wanting to hear her speak the words.

"No," Sheila answered with a small shake of her head. "I still love you."

He swept her into his arms, holding her tightly, his chin resting atop her dark gold hair. The embrace made her feel cherished and safe. There was no demand for passionate kisses. He seemed to want only to have her in his arms.

With her head resting at the base of his throat, Sheila fingered the lapel of his blazer. A bliss-filled sigh slid through her lips while her lashes fluttered down in contentment.

"You took such a risk coming here at this hour," she murmured as his chin rubbed the top of her head. "My father doesn't trust you as it is. You really should have called, instead."

"It's worth it just to hold you in my arms and know you still want to marry me. You do, don't you?" His mouth moved against her tousled hair.

"Yes, I want to marry you. Or do you think I make a habit of admitting men into my bedroom in the middle of the night?"

"I hope not," Brad answered with mock gruffness,

then continued in a more serious tone. "I probably should have called you, but your parents would undoubtedly have heard the telephone ring and picked it up to see who was calling. I couldn't take the chance that they might overhear our conversation."

Her eyebrows drew together in a puzzled crease. "Why?"

Brad didn't answer immediately as he lifted a hand to cradle the side of her face in his large palm.

"You are very beautiful, do you know that? Having you for my wife isn't going to be so bad after I teach you a few things."

"Mmm, and you might make a fairly decent husband," Sheila said, countering his jesting comment, "but you're getting off the subject. What did you want to talk to me about?"

"Maybe I should have phoned." There was a flash of white teeth as he smiled. "It's too difficult concentrating when I'm holding you in my arms. I keep getting sidetracked by the soft shoulders and dangerous curves." His hands glided over the silky material of her long sleeves to grasp her hands. "Come on. Let's go over and sit down where we can talk."

Retaining a light grip on her left hand, he led her to the bed. Sheila sat near the foot, curving her legs beneath her. Brad released her hand to switch on the small lamp on the bedside table. Its soft glow cast a small pool of light over the bed.

"You're making this all seem very mysterious." Sheila masked her bewilderment in a teasing murmur as Brad sat on the edge of the bed an arm's length from her.

"I don't meant to." A rueful smile curved the firm line of his lips. "It's just that ever since you left this afternoon, I've been thinking about what we said. Sheila, I can't wait a year to marry you."

"It seems like forever," she agreed with a wistful sigh.

Brad leaned forward, transmitting a sense of urgency. "We don't have to wait to be married. You're twenty years old. You don't need your parents' consent."

"I know I don't, but—"

"What will waiting a year accomplish?" he argued in a persuasive tone. "We don't have to prove anything to your parents—and definitely not that we love each other. As for their blessing, I wish we could have it, but if they choose to withhold it or attach conditions to it, like this year's wait, then we can do without it. Once we're married, they'll have to accept me."

"Are you suggesting that we should elope?" She nibbled at her lower lip.

"Yes. I don't want to wait a year, six months, or even a week," he declared.

"But what about college, your job? Where will we live?" Sheila found herself arguing.

"I know it isn't practical or logical to get married now," Brad admitted, raking his fingers through his thick blond hair. "We should at least wait until summer, when I get my degree, but when was love ever practical or logical? It's a physical and emotional need." He breathed in deeply. "I don't know." He released the breath in a long sigh. "Maybe it's not the same for a woman as it is for a man. Maybe you don't feel these needs as strongly as I do."

"That's not true," she denied quickly. "I do feel them."

He searched her face for a silent span of seconds. "Do you know how much I want to proclaim to the world that the beautiful woman at my side is my wife, Mrs. Sheila Townsend?"

"As much as I want to hear you say it." She never guessed that Brad was so romantic, masterful—yes, and even possessive, but she had not glimpsed this traditionally romantic side of him before tonight. It seemed out of character.

"Then let's run away and get married tomorrow, or no later than the day after. We can drive to Mexico and be married in a matter of hours."

"I want to, yes—" The upward lilt of uncertainty in her voice kept it from being a total agreement.

"But what?" He spoke the qualifying word that she had only implied.

"I—I need time to think." Elopement was the obvious solution, but Sheila wasn't positive it was the only alternative, although it had been the one her mother had chosen.

He captured the hands twisting together in her lap and held them firmly. "If you are worrying about your parents, honey, you are going to have to choose. You either hurt your parents, or you hurt me. They have each other, but I have only you."

When he put it that way, there was really only one choice she could make. He pulled her forward onto her knees, then slipped his hands around her waist. Sheila's fingers curled over the muscles of his broad shoulders as she gazed at him.

"Elope with me, Sheila," he ordered, reverting to the commanding Brad she knew best.

"Yes." Her acceptance needed no elaboration.

The hands on her spine exerted pressure to draw her down. His mouth closed moistly over hers, tasting the sweetness of her surrender in a tenderly passionate kiss. Sheila warmed to the loving ardor of his caress, its glow spreading through her veins. Never had she dated anyone who was so adept at arousing her desire as Brad was.

His exploring lips trailed over her cheeks and the fluttering gold tips of her lashes. Following the graceful curve of her temple, he nuzzled the lobe of her ear and and the sensitive skin below it before hungrily returning to her mouth. Her senses clamored in a heady response.

Twisting her halfway around, Brad pressed her backward until her head was nestled on the pillow. He continued to plunder the vulnerable softness of her lips while the wayward caress of his hands excited a feverish longing.

When Sheila felt his fingers loosening a button of her scarlet nightshirt, she realized she was losing what little control she had over the situation. The unmade bed was too intimate a setting for a long series of passionate kisses to remain unfulfilled.

"Brad, don't," she protested and tried to check his actions.

"Yes," he insisted and ignored her interfering hands to expertly free the rest of the buttons. He raised his head to look at her, smouldering fires of desire brightening his dark eyes. "I can't help wanting you, Sheila, and wanting to make love to you."

All the while he was talking to her in a seductive murmur, his hand was insinuating itself beneath the satin-smooth material of her nightshirt. It slid slowly and instinctively across her ribs to the rounded curve of her naked breast. Sheila felt it swell to his touch as she was unable to control the response of her flesh.

"No." She pushed ineffectually at his hand.

"Don't deny me, honey." His mouth brushed over her lips, teasing with them, while his hand continued to caress the thrusting roundness of her breasts. "You have such beautiful, firm breasts. I want to touch them and see them and know that soon they'll be mine alone to caress."

His thumb circled her nipple, then circled it again and again until it was button-hard. She shuddered, the tantalizing caress draining her will. The nightshirt slid to the side, a scarlet backdrop for her naked torso, and she couldn't force herself to object.

The lamplight illuminated the porcelain globe of her breast and the rosy bud of her nipple to Brad's burning gaze. He plucked lightly at the hard button, stimulating the nipple to a higher point. Sheila moaned unwillingly, his teasing touch driving her senses wild.

"You like that, don't you, my spoiled little brat?" His gaze glinted back to her face, his mouth crooking in satisfaction at the feverish glow in her cheeks and the trembling moistness of her panting lips. "It feels good, doesn't it?"

"Yes, yes," she breathed in tortured longing.

Her head moved in agitation against the pillow as his fingers stopped playing with her nipple and cupped the underside of her breast to push it upward. Her half-closed eyes saw his head bending toward the rosy point.

"Brad, no, you mustn't," Sheila protested and groaned when his lips encircled the pink nib.

His darting tongue licked its hardness, rolling it around, as if savoring the sweetness of a grape. When Brad bit into it lightly, Sheila gasped at the pain, which was strangely pleasurable. Immediately, his mouth opened over the nipple, taking it and its surrounding pink base into his mouth. As he erotically suckled her breast, Sheila felt the aching throb in her loins worsen, the burning emptiness pulsing to be filled.

Unexpectedly, he diverted his attention from her breast to return to her lips. Hard, punishing kisses bruised her mouth, bewildering Sheila as she wasn't permitted to respond with the passion that was consuming her. Finally, Brad lifted his head, breathing hard, a dark gleam in his eyes that suggested anger.

"I should make love to you," he said thickly, "here in your own bed, right under your father's nose. That's what he deserves."

His hand glided down the side of her ribs, his exploring fingers encountering the elastic waistband of her panties. He lifted it just enough to slip the tips of his fingers beneath the band and followed its straight line across the quivering muscles of her stomach.

"Brad, no." This time her denial was definite. The look in his eyes frightened her into protesting in earnest.

His knee forced its way between her legs while his weight pressed her suddenly struggling body against the mattress. Sheila was aware of his superior strength and knew that he could overpower her if he chose to.

Brad laughed softly in his throat. "I'm not going to make love to you—not until you ask me, remember?" He eased his weight from her slightly, no longer pinning her down. "Besides, even if I possessed your body, I'll never be convinced you are mine until we're married. Maybe your old-fashioned rules are contagious. Do you have a white dress to wear for the ceremony, my virginal Sheila?"

She relaxed, no longer feeling threatened by him. "I have a white dress. It's very summery, though." The dark glow she was accustomed to seeing returned to Brad's eyes.

"We aren't going to worry about fashion." He kissed her cheek and rolled to the side to lie next to her. Self-consciously, Sheila pulled the front of her nightshirt together, missing the mocking twist of his mouth. His finger crooked under her chin and turned it toward him. "You will marry me in Mexico tomorrow, won't you?" Immediately, he grinned. "Not tomorrow, I guess, since it's already today, but tomorrow's tomorrow."

"No one could stop me," murmured Sheila with a languorous smile.

"I did some checking tonight while I was on duty. All we need to get married in Mexico is identification and a tourist visa," Brad explained.

"I have tons of identification," she assured him, "student card, driver's license, credit cards, passport. We're going to be happy together, darling," she sighed and snuggled into the crook of his arm, gazing dreamily at the ceiling. "I know we are."

"Before we can make that a reality, we have to be married. And that means we have to make some plans." He gently pushed her away and sat up. "This is one case in which a prone position is not conducive to thinking."

Reluctantly, Sheila raised herself up into a half-sitting position against the pillows while Brad sat on the edge of the bed facing her. Flicking a wayward lock of hair from her cheek, she wrapped the nightshirt more securely around her.

"What are the plans?" Sheila asked, certain that he had considered everything before presenting this proposal to her. Brad was thorough in just about everything he did.

"First is the matter of transportation," he began. "My motorcycle would get us there and back very economically, but traveling almost halfway across the state of Texas would not be very comfortable, not with you and me and our luggage. As much as I hate the idea, logic suggests we should take the car your parents gave you. Is the title in your name? I wouldn't want us to have any trouble crossing the border with it."

"It's solely in my name," she nodded in assurance, "title, registration, insurance—everything."

"If we're going to drive that distance to get married, it would be foolish not to spend a couple days in Mexico on our honeymoon, right?"

"Absolutely." A wide smile of agreement beamed across her face, topaz eyes sparkling with pleasure. "Where are we going in Mexico?"

"Juárez."

"Juárez?" Sheila repeated in astonishment. "But that's a day's drive from here. Why not cross at Laredo or Eagle Pass? Any place would be closer than Juárez."

"Keep your voice down." Brad frowned. "I am well aware of the geographical distances, but there are other considerations to take into account. If your parents do happen to find out what we're planning and try to stop us, they'll immediately assume that if we're crossing the border, we'll pick one of the closer places you just mentioned. I'm sure it would never occur to your father that I could be so 'stupid' as to drive clear to Juárez. It's a case of reverse psychology," he finished with a faintly smug quirk of his mouth.

"You might be right." But it seemed to her that Brad was taking unnecessary precautions. She didn't like the way he insisted on regarding her parents as villains.

"I know I'm right," he said decisively, and she didn't try to argue. Brad reminded Sheila of a little boy playing a game, and she smiled secretly at the thought. "Anyway," Brad continued, "I know my way around Juárez better than the other border towns."

"I haven't been to Cuidad Juárez since I was a child. This time you can act as my tour guide and show me the sights," she suggested.

"Be glad to." There was a provocative gleam in his eyes as he ran his gaze over her length, taking in the feminine curves accented by the tightly wrapped scarlet nightshirt and the bare expanse of her long legs. "Providing we don't spend most of our time pursuing other pleasures."

Strangely, the implications of his remark didn't stimulate her desire. It made Sheila feel vaguely uncomfortable.

"We can't spend all our time in a hotel room." She attempted an off-handed shrug. "We have to come out sometime to eat."

"Maybe." Brad conceded with a faintly leering curl of his lip. He straightened from the bed and took two steps from the edge, his back to Sheila. "But that brings up another matter."

Sheila tipped her head to the side. "What?"

"Money."

She stiffened. Their afternoon quarrel was still too recent for her to forget his bitterness and sarcasm on the subject. She stared down at her fingers clutching the front of her gown.

"I thought we weren't going to talk about that anymore," Sheila said with taut quietness.

"Believe me, I don't want to bring it up." Brad massaged the back of his neck, a grimness in his tone. "This isn't going to be easy for me to say. I'm practically broke." He sighed heavily. "This week's paycheck had to go for rent. I have only a few dollars left to get me by until next week's payday."

"Oh." There was a wealth of understanding in the small word.

"God, I hate this," Brad muttered beneath his breath, then squared his shoulders. "Sheila, do you have any money of your own—I mean, besides the trust fund you'll get when you're twenty-one? I don't want you going to your father to borrow any money. It would tear my guts out to elope with you on 'his' money."

Sheila felt an initial astonishment. He was actually asking her for money. He had always been adamant, almost neurotically so, about not taking any money from her, regardless of how strapped he was. Now he wanted to use her money for them to get married.

It was a good sign. It meant that she would be able to persuade Brad to use her money and inheritance to further his career without him feeling guilty that he was living off of her. The future looked rosy-bright. Her parents would be upset by the elopement, but Sheila knew they would be won back to her side when her marriage to Brad was presented to them as a fact.

"I have my own money," she told him, "a savings account my father set up for me with almost ten thousand dollars in it. It's supposed to be a practical lesson in the value of money to be used for my living expenses this year."

Brad half-turned to look at her. "But is it yours?"

"Completely my own, with no other signature on the account," Sheila assured him.

"Good." He nodded crisply. "We'll use that, then. You can draw it out tomorrow and we'll have that obstacle out of the way."

"What about your job and classes?"

"The classes will have to be skipped and I'll arrange for Tom to call in sick for me. There isn't any problem there." He raked a hand through his thick blond hair. "We both have things to do today. I'd better be leaving so we both can get some sleep."

"Do you have to go?" Sheila sighed.

"This time." He nodded. "I'll meet you this afternoon at four in front of the hotel and we can decide on what time we'll meet and where." His mouth touched hers briefly. "And, remember, not a word about our plans to anyone. I'm not going to take any chance of it filtering back to your parents."

"Yes," she agreed reluctantly.

"Remember to lock the door," he said, then smiled broadly. "Just think, honey, in a little more than twenty-four hours we'll be on our way to Mexico."

A brief smile touched her lips. When he withdrew his arm from around her shoulders, Sheila felt cold. The disquieting sensation increased as Brad slipped into the night and she closed and locked the door behind him. She was shivering as she crawled into bed. Bridal nerves, Sheila told herself.

Chapter 3

In a Juárez hotel room, Sheila smiled at the telephone receiver. "Yes, that is what I said, Mother." And she repeated the statement she had made seconds ago. "Brad and I were married twenty minutes ago by an official of the Civil Registry."

Brad stood beside her, his arm curved possessively around her shoulders. Sheila directed her smile to her husband's handsome face. His touch was warming the confusing coolness that had plagued her all day. In retrospect, her apprehension seemed silly.

"Don't be so upset, Mother. Brad and I are going to be very happy. We're going to have a two-day honeymoon in Juárez; then we'll be home. We simply loved each other too much to wait."

When the explanations were over, she turned into the circle of Brad's arms, his hands locking together near the small of her back.

His mouth moved over the thick mane of tawny hair near her forehead. "Were they angry?"

"No," Sheila answered as she studied the plain gold

band on her ring finger. "There weren't any heavy recriminations, just an unspoken disappointment that we didn't tell them before."

"I'm glad." Brad drew his head back to look at her. "I am glad for you," he elaborated to remove any indication of hypocrisy that he cared himself.

"So am I," she agreed before he kissed her.

"The next thing we should do"—he nuzzled the corner of her lips—"is to go down to the hotel lounge and have a couple of margueritas to toast our wedding. From there, we can go to the restaurant and have an intimate dinner by candlelight. I noticed you hardly ate anything when we stopped for lunch, and I don't want you fainting from hunger later on tonight, Mrs. Townsend."

"That's me, isn't it? Mrs. Townsend," Sheila realized with a twinge of sobriety. "I'll have to get used to that."

"You'd better," he warned with mock gruffness, tightening the circle of his arms for a threatening instant before releasing her completely. "Put some lipstick on and we'll go down." He gave her a playful slap on the rump as Sheila turned to obey. "Wait a second." Brad called her back, a rueful twist to his mouth. "My pockets are empty. If you don't want me to spend our wedding night washing dishes to pay for our dinner, I'll need the money from your savings account. Give me all of it. There is no sense in taking the chance of someone swiping your purse."

"Whatever you say, Mr. Townsend." She reached in her purse for the bank envelope containing the money and handed it to him.

With the tube of lipstick from her purse, Sheila walked to the mirror and applied pale strawberry gloss to her lips. Brad was visible in one corner of the mirror. She absently watched him rip open the envelope and begin to count the money.

Sheila smiled faintly at his action. "All ten thousand is there," she assured him.

"What?" His blank gaze met the reflection of her look in the mirror.

"I hope you don't intend to count it all." There was a trace of gloss at one corner of her mouth and she touched a finger to it to wipe it away. "I am getting hungry."

"No . . . no, of course not," he agreed absently and turned away from the mirror.

His attention immediately returned to the wad of bills in his hands. As if mesmerized, he continued to count it. Sheila smiled in silent understanding at his reflection. It was probably more money than he had ever seen at one time. Her gaze slid to his hands and she felt a twinge of uneasiness at the almost reverent way he fingered the bills. She turned slowly to stare at him.

Brad glanced up and quickly stuffed the money deep into the pocket of his slacks The trance-like expression had left his face and he smiled quite naturally.

"You look very beautiful, Sheila," Brad said.

Her imagination must have been playing nasty tricks on her. "I'm glad you think so," she responded warmly. "Shall we go?"

After two margueritas on an empty stomach, Sheila started to feel light-headed. Brad had downed twice that number without seeming to suffer a similar effect; in fact, he appeared to grow more expansive and outgoing with each sip of the potent tequila cocktail.

He ordered a fifth and pulled a generous tip from the wad of money to place on the waiter's tray. Sheila couldn't help feeling uneasy at his uncharacteristic behavior.

"I've never known you to drink so much," she said with forced casualness.

"A man doesn't get married every day." His detached, smiling glance was arrogant. "This occasion calls for some celebration." And he lifted the glass containing the ice-cold concoction to his lips.

In the hotel restaurant, Sheila cringed at the show Brad made of tipping the maître d'. He drank his sixth marguerita while they were consulting the menu. Sheila suggested a glass of wine with their meal and Brad ordered the most expensive bottle in the house.

During the meal, a strolling duo of guitarists paused beside their table to serenade them. Brad immediately reached into his pocket and pulled out the money, peeling a large-numbered bill from the others. Again he made a project of tipping ostentatiously and not discreetly slipping the bill to the musicians.

When the two guitarists finally moved away from their table, Sheila gently commented on his tasteless extravagance. "You don't need to be so generous, Brad."

"I'm happy," he defended with an uncaring shrug. "And I want everyone else to be happy." He lifted his wineglass in a toast. "To you, Sheila, and our glorious future."

Her smile was forced as she raised her own glass to her lips. The wine tasted sour and unpalatable. She tried to dismiss the apprehensions plaguing her, and her father's remark that Brad was money-hungry. He was merely happy, she thought in an attempt to rationalize his actions. It had nothing to do with any exhilarating sense of power at having so much money in his pocket.

When the waiter removed their dinner plates, Brad asked Sheila, "Would you like some brandy with your coffee?"

"No," she refused. And she couldn't keep from adding tensely, "I wish you wouldn't drink so much, Brad."

"I'm not drunk." His eyes widened at her censure. Then a smile of supposed understanding spread across his handsome face. "Ah, it's our wedding night. That's what's bothering you, isn't it?" A faint smirk lent an unattractive line to his mouth. "Are you concerned that I won't be able to perform in bed tonight? I assure you there have never been any complaints on that score, drunk or sober."

His coarseness flamed Sheila's cheeks in revulsion. She lowered her gaze to the table, hating whatever it was that was changing Brad into a stranger.

"Maidenly blushes from my virginal bride." Brad laughed.

"Brad, please," Sheila hissed angrily, wishing he would lower his voice.

He shrugged. "Sorry, my love." But he didn't sound it.

The waiter returned. Sheila nearly sighed aloud when Brad asked for the check instead of brandy and coffee. Yet, again, he overtipped when paying the bill, flashing the wad of money for all to see as he did it. Sheila tried to pretend it didn't mean anything.

Once inside their hotel room, Brad kissed the side of her neck and whispered huskily, "I believe it is traditional for the bride to have the bathroom first—so, after you, my lovely."

Her luggage was on a stand near the bathroom door. Picking it up, Sheila hesitated. This wasn't the way she had envisioned her wedding night. Brad was acting more like a stranger than her lover, but it was too late now for second thoughts.

Once out of the tub, she retouched her makeup and fluffed her dark gold hair. There was only one night garment in her suitcase. Her hands trembled as she lifted it out and slipped it over her head. The filmy gown was richly embroidered with lace at the bodice, two thin straps over her shoulders holding the see-through veil of turquoise-blue.

Fighting the fluttering of her stomach, she opened the bathroom door and stepped into the room. There Sheila paused, frozen, unable to move. Brad was slouched in a chair, a bottle of tequila in one hand and a glass in the other. His jacket and tie had been discarded. His shirt was half-unbuttoned, revealing a cloud of curling blond hair. Her gaze was riveted to the bottle in his hand.

"Where did you get that?" Sheila knew there had been no liquor in the room.

"Room service." Brad studied her through half-closed eyes that still appeared alert. "Come over here," he commanded. "I want a closer look at you."

Woodenly, Sheila obeyed, her legs moving almost on their own volition. A foot in front of his chair, she stopped and stood motionless for his inspection. His gaze moved slowly from her face to her naked shoulders, trailing across the lacy bodice to the shadowy cleft between her breasts, then over their full, thrusting curves to the gauzy material blurring the flesh of her waist, stomach, and hips.

"Turn around," he ordered.

Again, Sheila found herself obeying, her heart hammering like a snared rabbit. The skin along her spine seemed to crawl with the downward path of his gaze. She felt like a piece of merchandise that was being inspected for flaws. There was the thumping sound of the glass and bottle being set on the table beside the chair.

"Not bad," Brad murmured. His hand stroked a rounded cheek of her bottom and Sheila flinched from his touch. It carried none of his previous arousing magic. "Don't worry." He laughed softly in his throat and turned her around. His hands rested on the sides of her ribs, pulling the thin lace of the gown's bodice taut across her breasts. "I still prefer your beautiful breasts."

"Brad, don't." Her voice wavered, sickened by the wine and liquor that saturated the breath blowing hotly over her face.

One of his hands moved to the point of a breast where a sleeping nipple was outlined by lace. He lifted the fabric away from it and fingered the lace as Sheila hunched her shoulders, recoiling her breast from his touch.

"This piece of sexy, blue nothing probably cost a fortune," Brad remarked idly.

"Do you like it?" Sheila breathed in deeply, attempting to hide her curious dislike of his closeness.

"Like it? I'll say I do." Releasing her, Brad walked to the table to refill the glass sitting beside the tequila bottle. A saucer of lemon wedges was on the table. "I'm going to buy you one of those for every night of the week."

"It really isn't necessary," she protested, flinching inwardly at his bragging tone.

"You're probably right." He took a swallow from the glass before biting into a lemon wedge. "It's better if you don't wear any clothes at all."

Sheila walked to the table and took the glass from his hand. "Don't drink anymore, Brad," she insisted tightly.

For an instant, he bristled. Then his arms were winding around her, pulling her close. "You're right again. Why should I drink that fiery liquid when I can taste the intoxicating sweetness of my wife."

His face moved closer to hers, his revolting breath filling her nostrils. She turned her head at the last second so that his mouth missed her lips and brushed her cheek, instead. But Brad didn't seem to notice.

His arms tightened around her as he sighed into her ear. "You have no idea how happy I am tonight, honey."

"Are you?" she returned frozenly. No matter how much she tried, she could not relax in his embrace.

"When I slipped that ring on your finger this afternoon, a whole new world opened up for me," he mused. "You don't know what it's like not to have money, Sheila. All my life I've had to kiss somebody's ass to get ahead, do somebody else's dirty work. I'm tired of hustling broads for those rich bastards at the hotel." Sheila blanched at his absent announcement. "Now, with you, that whole way of life is behind me. I'll never have to do things like that again."

The blood drained from her face, then raced back to fill it, staining her cheeks with red as surely as if he had slapped her. Sheila was beginning to realize there was a great deal about Brad that she didn't know.

"No, you won't." She choked on the agreement.

His hand roamed over the fine angles of her shoulder blade before straying to her slender waist and the curve of her hip. "You not only have a beautiful face, but a gorgeous body, as well. It has been a temptation not to wait until tonight to take you," Brad declared roughly.

Her arms had been rigidly at her sides. Now Sheila lifted them to wedge a space between them, then twisted free of his embrace.

"Brad, I want to talk," Sheila insisted.

"There is no more time for talk." He ran a mocking eye over her barely clothed body. "This is our wedding night—what we both have been waiting for and wanting. I have never met a girl who was so anxious to lose her virginity as you have been. I can't believe you are getting cold feet."

"It isn't that. I just think we should talk." She tried to keep her voice calm and reasonable, fighting the doubts raining in her mind.

"What's the matter with you?" He frowned, his hand circling her elbow to turn her around. "You've been wanting me to make love to you for weeks."

Sheila strained against his hold. "Nothing is the matter with me," she protested.

His gaze flicked to her arm, studying her attempt to twist away from his grip. "But you like for me to touch you," he reminded her. "It excites you. Remember?"

The face that Sheila had once considered handsome had somehow changed. She felt no excitement, no stimulation in his caress. She didn't understand this change in her reaction any more than she understood this change in Brad.

"Bridal nerves." Sheila tried to laugh off her apprehensions. "Just be a little patient with me, Brad."

"Oh, no." His mouth twisted in an unattractive line. "You aren't going to play one of those numbers of 'not tonight' with me. You've been teasing me for too long now."

Roughly, he yanked her back into his arms. His hand curled over the rounded curve of her bottom to squeeze the soft flesh of her cheek. He forced her hips to mold against his male hardness, the thin material of her gown acting as a second skin. Revulsion rose in her throat, a nauseous lump that nearly gagged Sheila.

"That's what you really want, isn't it?" Brad murmured thickly. "But you don't think it's ladylike to admit it, do you?"

"It isn't that," Sheila insisted. She was completely aware of her passionate nature and remembered Brad's previous ability to arouse it. Only this time he didn't seem concerned about arousing her desire.

The fragile strap of her gown slipped from her shoulder at the touch of his fingers. A side seam ripped as Brad pulled the lacy bodice downward to reveal the plump ripeness of her breasts. The one nearest to his hand he kneaded roughly while the loose-fitting gown fell to the floor around her feet.

"Brad, you are hurting me." Sheila protested the painful massaging of her breast.

It stopped as an encircling arm flattened both of them against his chest, his curling hairs scraping her sensitive skin.

He grabbed a handful of blonde hair, pulling at the tender roots until Sheila gasped. Her lips were still, an easy victim for his ravaging mouth. Brad took them, hotly and moistly, bruising their softness. Sheila was incapable of repulsing him as his tongue explored the inner reaches of her mouth. She forced herself not to resist him and managed a weak response to his ardent demands.

Swinging Sheila off her feet into the cradle of his arms, Brad carried her to the bed and laid her on the turned-down covers. Her breath was coming in deep, uneven spurts. He loomed before her, staring at her naked length on the bed. Sheila lay motionless. Her eyes watched him undress, the message transmitted to her brain in a blur of unreality. It was a nightmare, something that was happening to someone else, not her. If she closed her eyes, maybe she would wake up and find the Brad she had thought she married instead of this indifferent stranger.

Her lashes fluttered downward for a fraction of a second, snapping open when the bed sagged to take his weight. She swallowed the choked cry that rose in her throat as he settled his naked body on the bed beside her, a hand closing over the jutting roundness of her breast.

Nipping briefly at a white shoulder, he buried his face in the curve of her neck. But he soon abandoned any attempts to tease and tantalize Sheila into desire. And her attempts to fake it were pitiful. Her arms were stretched spreadeagled above her head as he shifted his length on top of her.

"Please," she requested stiffly, refusing to beg, "be gentle with me."

He forced his way between her legs to mount her. "Relax, damn it," he ordered tersely.

At the searing stab of pain, Sheila started to cry out, but his mouth covered hers to smother the sound until she could hardly breathe. He took her like a rutting boar, rolling off when he was satisfied.

Tears of shame and an odd sense of degradation drenched her cheeks, already moistened by the initial tears of pain. She felt used and abused, cheapened somehow by an act that should have been a consummation of their love. Weakly, Sheila tried to move away from the male form beside her, but her aching, trembling muscles wouldn't obey.

Propped into a half-sitting position by an unsteady elbow, Brad studied her with a cynically amused look. "What the hell are you crying about?"

If he had been kind to her, if he had said one gentle word to make up for the callously indifferent way he had used her, Sheila might have forgiven him. She might have blamed it all on his heavy consumption of alcohol.

Instead, she briskly wiped the dampness from her cheeks with the back of her hand, pride surfacing to conceal her longing for a soothing hand, even Brad's.

"Nothing," Sheila retorted in a husky, throbbing voice.

"Good." He rolled onto his side. "God, I'm tired," he muttered in a sigh.

Within minutes Brad was snoring away, the liquor

finally taking its toll. Sheila wished the tiredness would have claimed him earlier, before . . .

She slid from the bed, ignoring the fiery, aching soreness in her loins. Unaware of her nakedness, she walked to the hotel window overlooking the street below. There were people on the sidewalks and small boys hustling and begging.

Sheila had always considered herself a realist. She had never expected birds to sing or bells to ring. She had never thought she had any romantic illusions about love. Now Sheila realized that she had.

Her system was shocked, her emotions appalled by the carnal knowledge of a man, a man who was her husband. Sheila had anticipated pain and a certain amount of displeasure, but not this disgust and rejection that coursed through her. Sex was not an intimate union of two lovers. It was a violation, a demanding act of subservience to a man's will.

Brad had taken her selfishly for his own pleasure and satisfaction. The niggling question remained: Was it because of the liquor he had drunk? Would it be different when he was sober? How much of the revulsion she was feeling now was overreaction to a traumatic experience? And how much was justified?

The coolness of the night air wafted over her bare skin. Sheila turned away from the window, confused and uncertain. Her filmy nightgown lay on the floor. She hesitated, then picked it up and drew it over her head. Maybe by morning the memory of her experience would dim and everything would be all right again.

Chapter 4

Brad awakened with the sun the next morning. At his first stirring, Sheila feigned sleep, something that had been denied her as her mind kept replaying her wedding night.

He made no attempt to awaken her when he rose and began dressing. Through the slit of her long lashes, Sheila watched him tucking his shirt into the waistband of his trousers. He reached into his pocket and took out the wad of bills. Money-hungry, her father had called him, and now Sheila was half-convinced he was right. Brad had not sought out his new wife the first morning after their marriage. His first interest was her money.

"Come on, sleeping beauty, wake up," he ordered crisply without glancing at her.

After a brief debate whether or not to obey his command, Sheila slowly opened her eyes, keeping them expressionless of her inner thoughts. He had not bothered with a greeting, and neither did she.

"What is it?" Her thighs were still cramped and sore, protesting any movement.

41

"I've decided we should go to Acapulco," Brad announced, looking quite pleased with himself.

"You've what?" Sheila asked.

"This overcrowded border town is no place for a honeymoon." His gaze flicked to the hotel window, where the morning turmoil of traffic and people filtered through the panes. "My pampered wife deserves a more exotic locale."

When his brown eyes glanced back to her, Sheila could tell he wasn't the least bit interested in what she wanted. Brad was the one who had decided that Juárez was not good enough for him. Juárez was for the tourists, and Acapulco was the resort spot for the moneyed class. And Brad had elevated himself to that group by marrying her.

"I don't care about going to Acapulco," she said tersely.

"You are forgetting, my love—whither thou goest, I will go," he quoted mockingly. "Come on. It's going to be a long drive. You get up and get packed while I go check us out of this dump."

"There is nothing wrong with this hotel," Sheila insisted, but Brad was already walking to the door.

"Don't be ridiculous." He laughed at her, his hand poised on the doorknob. "I want to give you a real honeymoon. So don't argue."

With my money, Sheila thought as he stepped into the hallway. A bubble of hysterical laughter welled in her throat. She choked it back and threw off the bedcovers to rise.

In the bathroom, Sheila washed quickly. She took no pains with her makeup, applying brown mascara to the curling sweep of her lashes and a dusty-rose shade of gloss to her lips. A quick brushing to rid her streaked hair of its tangles, and she was finished. The bathroom mirror showed that the minimum of makeup did not lessen her natural beauty.

Emerging from the bathroom, she searched through her suitcase for clothes, wanting to be dressed before Brad returned. As quickly as her throbbing muscles would allow, she pulled on a pair of panties and stepped into brown slacks. The door opened and Brad walked in, eyeing the soft curves of her figure.

His interest waned in a surge of impatience. "You aren't even dressed yet," he accused.

With a toss of her head, Sheila faced him, a brassiere in her hand, her fingers curling into a lacy white cup. "Brad, we don't have time for a honeymoon now. We both have classes to get back to, and you have your job."

"We have all the time in the world," he insisted.

Sheila frowned. "But what about college? Your degree?"

"Who needs it? There isn't anything those professors can teach me. Besides, it's not what you know—it's *who* you know and how much money you've got." He patted the bulge in his trousers pocket. "And we have enough to live like royalty here in Mexico."

Her mouth opened, although Sheila didn't know why she was surprised by his statement. There had been a lot of clues. She had just not been as willing to see them as her parents had.

"That money won't last forever," Sheila reminded him stiffly. "Sooner or later, it's going to run out, even in Mexico."

Lazy, strolling strides carried Brad to stand in front of her. "It will last us easily until you receive your inheritance. You'll be twenty-one in a few months."

"Do you think I'm just going to hand it over to you?" The cat-gold flecks in her eyes flamed brightly.

Brad seemed to find her display of anger amusing. "We're married. What's yours is mine. And what's mine is mine, too," he joked.

But Sheila didn't find it laughable. All her glorious plans for their future were disintegrating one by one. She was beginning to realize that they had always been "her" plans. Brad had simply endorsed them, probably because he knew it was what she wanted to hear.

"Don't you have any ambition?" There was a sarcastic curl to her lip even as her chin trembled.

"It's going to be a full-time occupation being married to you." He fingered the strap of the bra in her hand, his eyes touching her breasts as they returned to regard her face. "For a while, at least."

"Then what?" Sheila challenged.

"I'm sure your father can find me a position that will be suitable employment for his son-in-law." Brad smiled complacently.

"Something that pays very well but doesn't take up too much of your time," she concluded, widening her eyes with false innocence.

"That's the idea exactly." He grinned. "But that's later. Right now we are off to Acapulco for some lazy days on the beach." Brad wound his finger around the bra strap and pulled it from her hand. "You won't be needing this," he declared, holding it out of reach.

"Give that back to me." Sheila refused to try to grab for it.

"It's going to be a long, boring drive today." He tossed the bra into her suitcase and closed it. "I'm going to want a little diversion from time to time. And I know my bride will want it, too."

Sheila shuddered away from the abrasive touch of his fingers. His hand hovered in the air as he gave her a long, level look.

"There's no need to be shy. We're married. Come back here. I don't have the time to be patient with you now as I was last night."

"You were patient last night?" She breathed tightly.

"More patient than I am now. You like the caveman technique, anyway." His hand closed over her breast, fondling it briefly before Sheila stepped away. Brad chuckled. "You can put your blouse on now. I'll pack the suitcases while you get your things from the bathroom."

Numbed by the unveiling of the true Brad Townsend, Sheila did as she was told. When she emerged from the bathroom, Brad was ready to leave. With a hand at her elbow, he hurried her down the hallway to an exit door.

"Aren't we going to have breakfast, or at least

coffee?" Sheila tried to slow her steps as he pushed her toward the door.

His gaze disdainfully swept around him. "No, I want to get out of this place. We'll stop somewhere later on."

There was no one in the small parking lot of the hotel. Sheila climbed into the passenger seat of her blue Thunderbird while Brad stowed their cases on the rear seat. When he slid behind the wheel, he leaned over to kiss her. Sheila turned her head at the last second and he kissed the corner of her mouth, instead.

"Still hung up about displaying affection in public?" he taunted her. "We'll see if we can't free you of some of your inhibitions during our drive." He winked and started the motor.

While Brad drove the car through the city traffic of Juárez, Sheila huddled in the seat corner nearest the door. Tired and dispirited, she felt trapped by fate. The cream-yellow silk of her blouse was cool to her naked flesh, a physical reminder of the type of man Brad was.

The outskirts of Juárez, with their squalid, hilltop shanties, were soon behind them. A road crew repairing some minor damage to the highway forced Brad to slow the car temporarily. Then they were speeding along.

With each rotation of the wheel, the certainty grew within Sheila that she had made a terrible mistake. She would arrange for an annulment, a divorce, anything that would bring this farcical marriage to an end.

The decision made, an exhaustion that was both mental and physical began to overpower Sheila. Soon she was drifting off to sleep, lulled by the steady rhythm of the engine and the turning of the tires. It was a heavy, dreamless sleep.

Hours and miles sped by before the uncomfortableness of the car seat began to prick Sheila awake. Her neck was stiff and sore and her head was bouncing against the backrest.

Rubbing the crook in her neck, Sheila slowly opened her eyes. With difficulty, she focused her gaze on the countryside. It resembled the west Texas landscape in many respects, but the looming range of the Sierra Madre Mountains in front of them confirmed they were in Mexico.

They were no longer traveling on the modern highway. A rutted dirt track stretched through the bush before them, the rough road jolting them. Sheila glanced at Brad in confusion.

"Where are we?" Her throat was parched and cottony, thickening her voice to a husky sound.

The set of his jaw was grim and angry. He couldn't spare a glance from the uneven track to look at her. "We are supposed to be on a shortcut through the mountains to the west coast, but I don't think the stupid Mexican who told me about it knew what he was talking about."

"It's quite impossible that you could have taken the wrong turn," Sheila remarked with dry sarcasm.

His gaze slashed to her for a brief second and the steering wheel was nearly wrenched from his hands as a front tire bounced into a pothole.

"This is probably his idea of a good road, but it's going to ruin this car," Brad muttered.

It was nice of him to be concerned, Sheila thought cynically, considering it was her car that he was driving. But she kept silent. There was a chill in the air. She looked again to the fabled mountains and guessed that the higher elevation had caused the temperature to drop. Suppressing a shiver, she hugged her arms around her.

"It's getting cold. Can't you turn the heater on?"

"It isn't working," Brad snapped.

"Somewhere there is heat because the warning light on the dashboard is lit," Sheila observed caustically. "Is that steam rising from the hood?"

Brad barked out a string of savage imprecations. Stopping the car and leaving the motor running, he charged out, slamming the door. Steam billowed into the air when he raised the hood.

With the same volatile impatience that had marked his departure, he returned to the driver's seat and angrily switched off the motor. He sat there for a charged minute, his hands clenching the wheel.

"Damn!" He pounded his fist against the wheel.

"What's wrong?" Sheila was deriving a peculiar kind of satisfaction from his frustrated rage.

"A broken water hose," Brad growled.

"Can you fix it?" Her eyes were rounded and blinkingly innocent of any deliberate provocation. He abhorred manual labor.

His face was livid with fury. "Oh, sure, I always carry around spare parts."

"I didn't know." She shrugged. "I just thought that you might have foreseen the possibility of a breakdown and planned for it."

"Just shut up, Sheila," he snarled.

"What are we going to do now? Sit here and wait for someone to come along? This is such a well-traveled road that—"

With the swiftness of a striking cobra, his hand encircled her throat, choking off the rest of her words. The handsome face was mottled with rage as he brought it close to hers.

"Don't open your mouth again until I tell you," he ordered. His fingers slightly tightened their grip, causing Sheila to gasp for air.

Sheila managed a short nod of understanding, breathing deeply when the strangling pressure was removed. Tears of pain smarted her eyes. Sheila turned her head to the side window, wiping away the traces of tears with her fingertips.

"You certainly can't take a joke, can you?" She choked out the retort, but Brad didn't respond.

A dust-devil whirled beside the car and danced into the brush. Sheila followed its flight into the emptiness of the land. It seemed a wilderness.

Dust was whipped into a hazy cloud by a gust of wind. Her gaze sharpened as she detected movement in the haze. The air cleared slowly to reveal horses and riders. In the obscuring thickness of the brush, it was hard to tell how many there were, a half dozen, maybe more.

Sheila didn't alert Brad to the presence of the riders until the small band spotted the stalled car and stopped to stare curiously. A blue Thunderbird in the middle of nowhere was not a common sight.

"Brad, someone is out there," she said finally.

"What?" He leaned toward her. "Where?"

"There." Sheila pointed, plagued by a fear she couldn't explain. "On horseback. Do you see them?"

"Yes, I see them," he answered.

"Who do you suppose they are?" She continued to watch them, finding it strange that they hadn't ridden forward to investigate.

"Mexican cowboys, by the looks of them," Brad concluded. "I've heard there are a lot of ranches in this area. It's supposed to be cattle country."

A frown of uncertainty knitted her eyebrows. "Yes, that could be."

"Don't worry. I'm not going to take any chances."

He leaned over the seat back and opened his travel-worn suitcase. Sheila glanced over her shoulder to see what he was doing. Her eyes widened in surprise at the sight of the snub-nosed revolver he took from beneath a pile of clothes.

"What are you going to do with that?"

Brad ignored the question. He checked to make sure the gun was loaded before tucking it into the waistband of his slacks and buttoning his jacket closed.

As he opened his door, he ordered, "You stay in the car."

Her gaze returned swiftly to the band of riders, approaching the car at a sedate walk. When Brad stepped out, one of the riders separated from the others to ride forward.

"Hello!" Brad called to him, walking around to the raised hood.

"*Buenos días, señor,*" the man returned. He stopped his horse and dismounted, his bulky shape concealed by a dirty, brightly striped poncho.

"Do you speak English?" Brad asked.

"No hablo inglés." The man shook his head sadly.

"Look"—Brad breathed in deeply and released an irritated sigh—"my car has broken down." He motioned the man to come to the front of the car. "See? The water hose is busted."

The man said something in Spanish that sounded suitably sympathetic to Brad's problem. He was shrugging his helplessness when he moved away from the hood.

The other riders had clustered around the man's horse, watching the proceedings. Sheila counted eight of them, nine including the man talking to Brad. She couldn't shake the eerie sensation that sent chills down her spine. It was as if some primitive part of her had caught the scent of danger. Ignoring Brad's command, she stepped out of the car.

"The car won't run until it's fixed. What I need—" Brad stopped at the sound of the car door shutting and glared at Sheila. "Get back in the car."

Her gaze never left the riders. "I'm staying here."

It was a motley group of men. A powdering of dust dulled their clothes, an assortment of ponchos and pants. Their horses were small and narrow-chested, nondescript compared with the powerfully muscled quarter horses common in Sheila's home state.

Combining pantomime with an attempt at sign language, Brad endeavored to communicate with the Mexican. Sheila was aware of his action out of the corner of her eye.

"Is there a town or village close by where I can have the car fixed?" Brad said the words slowly, acting them out when he could. "I must find someone to fix the car —repair it so it will run again. *Comprendez?*"

The man listened and watched him earnestly, but in the end he shook his head regretfully and lifted his hands. *"No entiendo, señor."*

Brad muttered an aside to Sheila. "Why can't these damned Mexicans learn how to speak English?" He started all over again. "Is there someone out there somewhere who can fix the car?"

Sheila's gaze traveled warily over the group of riders, always being drawn back to one man, although on the surface there was nothing about him to distinguish him from the others. Wearing a dust-covered, Western-crowned hat with a wide brim, he was slouched in the saddle, a gloved hand resting on the protruding horn. Yet Sheila sensed an animal alertness behind the indolent pose.

Like the others, there was a shadowy darkness to his cheeks and jaw to indicate he hadn't shaved recently. It gave him an unkempt, and vaguely disreputable, appearance. But this one man did not have the broad flatness to his face that hinted at the Mexican-Indian extraction of the other riders. His features were angular and lean. And the obsidian dark eyes staring back at Sheila were hard and cold.

"Damn it! There has to be a mechanic somewhere around here!" Brad's patience snapped at his inability to communicate successfully with the Mexican.

"*Mecánico? Si, si.*" The man nodded in sudden understanding and followed with a spate of Mexican as he pointed back the way they had come.

"Now we are getting somewhere," Brad murmured grimly.

A puff of wind blew shimmering strands of brown-gold hair across Sheila's face. She reached up to tuck them behind her ear, unaware that the action stretched the silken material of her blouse across her breasts. Her gaze was compelled to return again to the dark rider.

"Will you ride your horse to where the mechanic is and bring him back?" Brad pantomimed the question. "I'll pay you for your trouble. Pay you—have you got that? Pesos. Many pesos. Don't tell me you don't know what pesos are?" he added cynically.

"Pesos? *Sí, sí.*" The man assured him of his understanding and waited.

"How much do you want?" Brad asked, reaching into his trousers pocket. "Fifty pesos?"

As he pulled out the wad of bills Sheila had given him, she went cold all over. She wanted to scream at

Brad for his stupidity in showing the man all that
money, but nothing could get past the lump of fear in
her throat. The Mexican laughed with undisguised delight, revealing chipped, yellowed teeth, and said something to the others.

She couldn't believe that Brad didn't feel the subtle
change in the atmosphere—that charged feeling in the
air that precedes a violent storm. Sheila faced the riders,
her eyes darting to the faint smiles appearing at their
compatriot's announcement. Only the one compelling
rider seemed untouched by the news. Every muscle in
her body was tensed for flight.

"Fifty pesos isn't enough, huh?" Brad muttered beneath his breath, "Greedy bastard." And he began peeling off more bills. "How about a hundred pesos?
Would that persuade you?"

Sheila wanted to laugh hysterically at Brad. His
singleminded desire to show how wealthy he was made
him blind to the situation, and she couldn't force the
words through her mouth to warn him. The whole
scene was building toward a climax, and she was powerless to stop it.

The Mexican's left hand emerged from the folds of
his poncho and reached toward the money. "I've found
your price, have I?" Brad declared and started to separate some of the bills from the rest.

The man didn't wait to be given the money. Instead,
his hand closed over the whole amount. Too late, Brad
realized the danger that Sheila had sensed from the
beginning. Swearing, Brad fumbled inside his jacket for
the revolver tucked into his waistband.

As the butt of the gun emerged in his hand, Sheila's
horrified eyes saw the muzzle of the Mexican's gun
protruding from the right side of his poncho. A deaf-
ening explosion followed. When her eyes focused again,
Brad was crumbling to the ground, the snub-nosed revolver slipping from his fingers.

You stupid fool, Sheila thought.

She wanted to run to him, but the Mexican was already kneeling beside him, prying the wad of money from the tightly clenched fingers.

Sheila took a faltering step toward Brad, staring at the small red hole in his chest. There was no gory, spurting of blood such as she had seen depicted in movies—just a small, deadly hole and a slow-spreading scarlet stain to betray the mortal wound.

The crack of saddle leather and horses' hooves penetrated the dazed mist of her mind. The scent of warm horseflesh was mixing with the acrid smell of gunsmoke. As her gaze widened to encompass the scene beyond Brad's motionless body, Sheila saw that the band of riders had moved in. Two had dismounted to join the man going through Brad's pockets.

Her gaze swept over the menacing group. Her heart stopped beating for a second, then pounded madly in fear. They were all staring at her. Sheila flattened herself against the car door.

Two more riders dismounted and began walking toward her. There was nowhere to run. They had killed Brad and she knew she could expect no mercy, certainly none before they had killed her.

Survive! The word screamed through her veins. Survive! The panicked beat of her heart slowed instantly and the stranglehold of fear was removed from her throat. She must survive.

Chapter 5

Sheila faced her attackers boldly. "I know how you can get a lot more money," she said calmly. "Do you understand? *Mucho dinero.*"

Her statement was met with silence. They were all looking at her, their expressions unchanged. The two men had halted their approach. Sheila knew she had their attention.

"*Mucho dinero,*" she repeated

The two men started toward her again. One was tall, his face shadowed by the wide brim of his hat. The other was short and stocky, a leering smile on his mouth.

"My name is Sheila Rogers," she began again, ignoring the fact that her name had been legally changed to Townsend. "My father is very rich. He would pay someone a lot of money if I am returned to him *unharmed.*" Sheila emphasized the last word. "He would pay a lot of money."

No one seemed impressed by her words. Her gaze swept the riders, ricocheting away from the hard, lean features of one, the dark rider. Instinct said he was the most dangerous of the lot.

"One of you here must understand what I'm saying." An angry, desperate ring entered her voice. "My father would pay a great deal of money to have me back."

Sheila was struck by the irony of her plight. She was here in this godforsaken stretch of land, married, and now a widow because of Brad's lust for her money. Now, perhaps her only chance of surviving was hinged on that money.

A low voice said something in Spanish, breaking her train of thought. Her gaze swiftly sought the owner of the quiet tone. It belonged to the lean, dark rider, who was watching her with a hooded look, his horse restlessly stamping the ground.

A second voice jerked Sheila's head around. "How much?"

It came from the tall, broad-shouldered man approaching her. Sheila found herself staring into a pair of clear blue eyes, emotionless and cool. The accent had been unmistakably American.

"You're American," Sheila almost gasped.

He ignored her observation. "How much will your father pay?"

"Thousands," she assured him. "Enough for all of you as long as you don't hurt me in any way."

Without taking his eyes from her, he directed a few sentences in Spanish over his shoulder to those behind him. It was obviously a translation of her answer. Her gaze slid to the compelling rider who had spoken first to see what effect the words had on him. His chiseled features were an impenetrable mask. He spoke again in that same low voice and Sheila's attention returned to the American.

"Who is your father, and where does he live?" he asked flatly.

"His name is Elliot Rogers, and he lives in Austin, Texas," she answered simply, knowing there was no point in elaborating.

"Never heard of him," was the indifferent reply.

"I doubt if you were ever invited to the same parties."
Her cat-gold eyes made a pointed sweep of the marauding band. "You don't travel in the same circles."

The man chuckled softly and didn't translate what she had said. He walked toward her. Sheila steeled herself not to flinch as he reached out and fingered the material of her blouse. He smelled of dust, sweat, and horse.

At closer quarters, Sheila could see a trace of boyish good looks behind the stubble of beard and the sunhardened features. She tried to judge his age, but the lines of experience made it difficult. He could be in his thirties, yet Sheila had the feeling he was even younger.

His blue eyes ran over the length of her, missing nothing, yet Sheila didn't feel disturbed by his thorough and knowing inspection.

"Those are expensive clothes," he observed.

"That's what my father thought when he paid for them," Sheila answered to enforce her position as an heiress.

Smiling slightly, he released the material of her blouse and took hold of her hands, lifting them up where he could see them. His attention focused on the gold wedding band.

"Him?" His head bobbed sideways to indicate Brad's body.

"Yes," Sheila admitted. "My married name is Sheila Rogers Townsend. We were on our honeymoon."

"What were you doing here?" he asked.

"Brad was told there was a shortcut across the mountains. He was trying to find it when the car broke down."

"This isn't it," he told her.

Without altering his position, he said something in Spanish. The familiar low voice that answered caused a murmur of dissension to ripple through the group. Sheila held her breath as she glanced at the frowning expressions of disagreement. The dispute was silenced by the firm ring of authority in the low voice.

"You're in luck," the American said. "The boss believes your story." Although his mouth curved upward at the corners, there was nothing warm in the smile. "You do know there are ways of finding out if your father really has any money, don't you?"

"I'm not lying," Sheila responded calmly. "Did you think I would?"

"You might," he said, nodding, "to save that lovely neck of yours."

Releasing one of her hands, he turned to take a short rope from one of the riders. The action seemed to be a signal for the others to resume their looting.

"There's no need to tie me up," Sheila insisted as he looped the rope around one wrist.

"It's just a precaution." He tugged the rope tight and wound it around her other wrist.

The fibrous strands bit into her tender skin, the rope's snugness permitting little circulation to reach her fingers. Any attempt by Sheila to flex them chafed the rope against her skin.

Her gaze slid to the man who had believed her story. Somehow she had known from the beginning that he was the leader of this band.

As she watched, he gave an order in Spanish and the men slowly began to climb back into their saddles. Her eyes wavered to the body lying on the ground. She should feel shock or sorrow at the sight of him, Sheila thought. It was wrong not to mourn the passing of a life, especially when the man was her husband. But fear and the fierce will to survive had pushed all other emotions from Sheila's mind.

There was a tug on her hands to pull her forward. Sheila resisted, and the rope immediately bit into her flesh as pressure was applied to make her obey.

"Wait," Sheila pleaded. The American stopped, looking at her with a quizzical lift of an eyebrow. She cast a darting glance to Brad's body. "You aren't just going to leave him there like that, are you? Where the animals can—" Sheila couldn't finish the sentence, unable to voice the horrible picture that flashed through her mind.

A harsh light glittered in the blue eyes. "We just

killed him," he reminded her, his mouth crooking cynically. "You don't really expect that we'll turn into Christians and give him a decent burial, do you?"

Sheila closed her eyes at the bitter logic and opened them to stare at the lifeless figure. "It isn't right to leave him here like that," she repeated lowly.

A jerk of her bound wrists sent Sheila stumbling forward. One of the riders was holding the reins of the American's horse as she was half-dragged to the left side of the empty saddle. Before she could recover her balance, a pair of hands gripped her waist and she was lifted astride.

Gripping the horn to steady herself, Sheila glanced at the American. His hand was resting on the leather saddle skirt near her leg. He gave her a long, hard look, then said something in Spanish to the man holding the horse.

Without a word to Sheila, he turned and walked to the body lying in the sandy dirt. Lifting the dead weight, he heaved it over his shoulder, carrying it like a bulky sack of potatoes to the passenger door of the car.

Magnetically, her gaze was pulled away from the scene, drawn to a pair of eyes that were as black and hard as nuggets of coal. They compelled her to look at the man, the leader of the band of renegades. Her pulse accelerated in vague alarm.

A flurry of movement and an angry Spanish voice released Sheila from the pinning gaze as his attention was directed elsewhere. Unconsciously, she had tensed in those brief seconds, and now she felt the constricted muscles begin to relax. Her gaze swung to the cause of her release.

The Mexican with the yellowed teeth, the one who had killed Brad, was astride his horse in the center of the half-circle of mounted riders. A stream of demanding Spanish was issued to the man who seconds ago had chilled Sheila with a look. The Mexican's horse moved restlessly beneath him, reacting to his rider's anger.

He gestured to Sheila and brought his hand back to

possessively tap his chest. At that instant, Sheila realized he had positioned his horse to block the American from returning to her. Although she couldn't understand what he said, his purpose was clear. He was claiming her as his property.

Cold fear raced down her spine. Surely they wouldn't make her ride with the man who had murdered Brad! her mind cried in terror. At least the American had retained a streak of compassion.

Her widened eyes sought the carved face of the leader. The decision was obviously his. He didn't even look at her as he gave an indifferent shrug of his shoulders and reined his horse away from the circle. With a triumphant shout, the Mexican spurred his horse toward Sheila.

He reined the horse in beside her, pulling savagely on the bit. Her gaze darted to the American, hoping he would protest, but there wasn't a flicker of opposition on his face. The arm that circled her waist snapped the grip of paralysis.

"No! No!" Sheila was dragged, kicking and screaming, from the saddle.

Her cries went unheeded as she was drawn sideways across the saddle. The iron band of his arm tightened around her waist, nearly squeezing Sheila in half. He touched his spurs to the flank of the horse. It bounded forward, throwing Sheila against the man's chest. With each stride of the horse, the saddle horn poked her thigh.

The murderer laughed at her struggles, knowing, as Sheila did, that she couldn't writhe free and was wasting her energy trying. Catching back a sob of frustration and self-pity, she quit fighting and stiffly held her body rigid across his lap.

The horse had slowed to a jarring trot. Her sullen, accusing eyes swept the band that had begun its exodus from the crime scene. Two stragglers were cantering to rejoin the loosely gathered group. The gold fire in her eyes flashed their resentment when the blue-eyed Amer-

ican loped by. He didn't even glance at her as he guided
his horse to the leader's side.

Her tied hands and the sidesaddle position forced
Sheila to rely on the support of the man's arm and
chest. Her shoulder rubbed against his chest, the coarse
weave of his poncho scratching through the silken
material of her blouse. His breath was foul and Sheila
turned her head to avoid inhaling it.

Saddle leather creaked as the band put distance between themselves and the dirt road. Their route through
the rugged terrain paralleled the looming mountain
range. An invisible command seemed to pass through
the group. Almost simultaneously they all slowed their
horses to a walk.

The saddle horn applied steady pressure, no longer
jabbing her thigh. The man said something to her in
Spanish, his tone low and suggestive, his hot breath
fanning her face. Sheila flicked him a poisonous glance
and tensed as she saw his gleaming eyes looking downward.

Her hunched position against his chest had caused
the buttoned front of her blouse to billow out while her
arms pushed her breasts together to form a deep cleavage. Sheila raised her forearms to let her tied wrists
protectively hide her plunging front.

"No, no, señora," he denied with a leering smile
and grabbed the rope to pull her hands down.

Twisting in the saddle, he wedged his elbow between
her wrists, applying pressure to the knot and holding
her arms away. At the first brush of his fingers on the
satin-smooth material outlining her breasts, Sheila drew
away, straining backward over his arm to elude his
lecherous hands. The action thrust the fullness of her
breasts against the thin material. His hand covered the
rounded swell of one breast.

"Get your hands off me!" Sheila cursed angrily.
"You filthy, ugly beast!"

He laughed again and punishingly squeezed her
breast. Two riders rode closer to watch, offering words
of encouragement and snide suggestions to the man they

called Juan. Sheila kicked at his leg, her feet flailing in
the air in an effort to find their target. The blows landed
on the stirrup leather of the horse.

His fingers moved to the buttoned front of her blouse,
tugging at it impatiently until the button threads ripped.
As her ripe breasts were revealed, he shouted to those
looking on, as if showing off the richness of his prize.

Shamed and degraded beyond description, Sheila now
struggled even more wildly than before. His exploring
hands investigated his prize, his callused finger roughly
caressing her flesh until Sheila gagged in revulsion.

"My father won't pay you a cent!" she choked in
humiliation. "Not a cent! Do you hear?" She screamed
her warning to the man riding at the front and the
American at his side.

The horse pranced sideways beneath the struggling
pair on his back, tossing its head and snorting nervously.
Sheila realized there would be no rescue. She had been
given to this beast masquerading as a man, and she
knew she would rather die than be used again.

The horse skittered again in frightened agitation.
There was only one way to escape the repulsive hands,
and Sheila began aiming the blows of her feet to the
horse's shoulders and neck. Whinnying its alarm at the
attack, the horse half-reared, checked by the sudden
sawing of the reins and the punishing jab of a spur. But
Sheila kept kicking, panting, and sobbing with determination to save herself.

The horse threatened to bolt in panic. It was requir-
ing all of the rider's skill to hold the animal in. With
the others laughing at his predicament, Sheila could see
the mottled red of rage growing in his face.

Her heel hooked one taut rein. She kicked at it,
jerking the horse's head around. Its nervously shifting
hooves tried to turn with the action, but the sudden
change of direction was impossible. Sheila felt the
horse's legs buckling before it fell heavily to the ground.
She twisted loose from the imprisoning arm as they
fell and staggered free of the horse's flailing hooves.

Off balance, Sheila stumbled forward, trying to run.

She had barely covered ten feet when she heard the heavy footsteps behind her. A hand grabbed her elbow and spun her around. Her feet went out from under her and she fell to the ground. Brad's murderer stood above her, his broad features ugly with the look of revenge. Two riders reined their horses to a stop on either side of Sheila and dismounted.

Scooting backward, Sheila's frightened eyes never left the man called Juan. She scrambled to her feet while he moved menacingly toward her. Instantly, the other two men moved in, grabbing her arms to hold her. She kicked wildly, biting at their hands.

Unexpectedly, she was released. Sheila didn't question why; she just turned to run again. During her struggles the rest of the riders had formed a circle around her.

Breathing heavily from her panicked exertions, Sheila pivoted back, wary and on guard, not knowing what to expect next. Her gaze fastened on the lean-faced man who commanded the group, his expression impassive and aloof. His shuttered black eyes slid to her heaving breasts, her creamy-silk blouse hanging open. Immediately, her arms lifted to cover herself.

The slashing line of his mouth quirked at the defensive action that came too late to conceal what all eyes had seen. Dismounting, he untied something from his saddle. It looked like a blanket and a lariat. Sheila quailed inwardly, but she refused to give ground as he walked toward her.

His leanness was deceptive, she discovered. He was much taller and broader than she had first thought. He moved with the supple grace of an animal, a predatory beast. The fathomless dark eyes never left Sheila's face, mesmerizing her almost to the point where she couldn't have run if she tried.

Stopping in front of her, he shook out a serape. He lifted it above her, pulling the slashed opening over her head. He tucked the end through the circle of her arms, drawing her hands and arms to the outside of the coarse fabric.

His low-pitched voice said something to her in Spanish, a mocking inflection in the quiet tone. The blood was racing hotly through her veins, her nerves raw and stretched taut at the sensation of danger in his nearness.

The loop of the lariat was drawn over her head. Her heart stopped in terror as the rope brushed the side of her neck, but he pulled it down around her shoulders.

"What are you going to do to me?" Sheila gasped, unable to bear the suspense any longer.

He said nothing, not that she would have understood his answer if he had given it. Fear quivered through her as she tried to guess his intention. When the loop circled her waist, he pulled it tight, the rope acting as a belt to hold the narrow width of the serape against her body.

Her questioning eyes left the impenetrable mask to seek the lone man who could explain. "Why is he doing this?" she asked the American.

"You were so anxious to run," came the indifferent reply, "that he's decided to oblige your desire for some exercise."

Her head jerked back to the glittering pair of ebony eyes. Holding the coiled rope, he turned and walked back to mount his horse. He sat for a motionless instant in the saddle gazing at Sheila's pale face. Laying the rein alongside the horse's neck, he started forward at a walk. The rope began to stretch taut. Sheila had the choice of walking at the end of it or being dragged.

Either one was preferable to the repellent touch of Brad's killer, but Sheila chose to walk. Her tied hands clasped the length of the lariat tugging her along, using it for balance.

A mile, two miles, more. Her legs were leaden weights to be dragged over the rough, uneven ground. Dust choked the air she had to breathe, kicked up by the horse and rider she followed. Perspiration made her hair cling to her neck. Her face was streaked with the mixing of dirt and rivulets of sweat.

She pushed herself onward, beyond what she had thought was the limit of her endurance, stumbling more often as each step jarred her teeth. She was driven on by hatred for the wide-shouldered man who held the rope.

Tripping over a clump of grass, Sheila fell to her knees. The rope pulled her over the rough ground. A muffled cry of pain was torn from her lips as she was dragged nearly the length of her body before the rope went slack.

Struggling, she managed to get to her knees, too exhausted to stand. Sobbing with her bone-aching tiredness, Sheila sat on her heels. Her lungs felt as if they would burst before she ever recovered her breath. A threatening blackness reeled in front of her eyes. Any moment she expected to feel the tug of the rope, but she didn't care. She wouldn't take another step.

A pair of dusty boots came into view of her blurred vision. Wearily, Sheila raised her head. It lolled weakly to the side. The masculine, beard-shadowed features of her tormentor swam before her glazed eyes.

He towered above her, a round, canvas-covered canteen in his hand. Unscrewing the lid, he offered it to her. Her throat was rasping-dry, her mouth woolly, and her lips parched and swollen.

Sheila stared at the canteen for a long moment. Raising her gaze to the lean, hard face, she searched her mouth for a tiny drop of saliva and tried to spit. It was a puny gesture of hatred.

He stared at her silently, then shrugged and lifted the canteen to his lips. The gurgle of liquid in the container tormented Sheila to near madness. Her thirsty body screamed at the moistness of his lips when he lowered the canteen. Pride was forgotten. If he had offered her the canteen a second time, Sheila would have accepted it greedily.

Instead, he screwed the lid back on and walked to his horse. Holding back a sob, Sheila stared at him. She had nearly surrendered her pride to this renegade leader, her ruthless captor. Sheila had never looked into a pair of eyes that were as black as hell and completely devoid of emotion.

She was hovering on the brink of hysteria. Her exhausted brain and body needed only the slightest push to tumble over the edge. She was being driven by the survival instinct, the same instinct that kept her propped upright.

Her weary gaze swept the small, brush-covered clearing. The other riders had stopped, dismounting to give their horses a rest. The corners of her mouth twitched briefly as she panted to fill her nearly bursting lungs with air. The break had not been called because she couldn't walk another step, but because the horses needed a rest.

Lifting her eyes, Sheila looked at the serrated outline of the mountains against the horizon. A blinding sun stood guard above them, shadowing their slopes until they seemed dark and forbidding. They appeared nearer than they had before. Or was she just imagining it in her exhaustion?

Her blurring gaze veered to the east and looked down. They had been climbing, probably steadily since they had left the road to the south. The thinning air explained why her breathing was so labored. Sheila was too enervated to find consolation in that.

Bowing her head, she let her eyes close. She was too tired to think. It seemed to require all her effort to keep her lungs and heart working. In a trance-like stupor, she listened to the hammering beat of her pulse.

No other sound penetrated her hearing—not the low murmur of voices conferring in the language that was foreign to her, not the stamping of the horses or the swishing of their tails as they kept the flies at bay . . . nothing but the reassuring sound that she lived.

Chapter 6

The creaking of saddle leather and the jangling of spurs were an alarm to break Sheila's trance. Forcing her head up. she stared dully at the fathomless black eyes gazing at her from atop the horse.

The rest stop was over. The band was mounted and ready to move on. Sheila stared into the hard, chiseled lines of the dark-eyed rider, her new devil-master.

Reaching into the dregs of her reserve strength, Sheila staggered upright to sway unsteadily on her feet. The slipknot had loosened to let the rope hang limply around her waist. She waited for it to tighten, for the horse to move forward and stretch the rope wrapped around the saddle horn.

Instead, a gloved hand picked up the rope lying across a black-clothed leg. With an expert flick of his wrist, the loop around her waist slid to the ground. The horse was nudged toward her. Groping through her dazed senses, Sheila tried to take in what was happening, but it was too much for her.

Leaning over in his saddle, he scooped her up in the

steel curve of his arm, lifting her as if she weighed no more than a child. Indeed, Sheila felt remarkably weightless, floating in a suspended state.

When he turned her in his arms to sit across his lap, she remembered the revolting and degrading treatment she had received at the hands of the one called Juan, who had shot Brad. Her listless muscles could not fend off another such assault.

Still Sheila tried. "No, please." The words croaked from her parched throat as she strained against his arm. The tiny surge of energy was soon spent, leaving her limp and conquered in his arm. Not a gram of resistance was left. "Please," Sheila helplessly begged in a whisper, "not again."

No longer holding her, merely supporting her with his arm, he ignored her pleas and began coiling the rope that had pulled her the last miles. When it was again tied to the saddle, he adjusted her position so that her shoulder was tucked into the hollow under his left arm and her head rested against the solidness of his left shoulder.

The left hand gathered the reins looped around the saddle horn, then rested lightly against her hip as he urged the horse into a walk. The other riders followed in a loose group. In this position, Sheila didn't have to exert any effort. His arms and chest supported her completely.

Through weary eyes, she peered at his face under the concealing sweep of her gold-tipped lashes. The dark stubble of a black beard forcibly accented the strong, powerful lines of his jaw and chin. There was a cruel thinness to his mouth, ruthlessly set. Slashing grooves were carved on either side of his mouth. The suggestion of patrician fineness in his nose was repeated in the jutting cheekbones rising from the lean hollows of his cheeks.

Outlined by thick, spikey lashes, the flat, black eyes moved relentlessly over the land the riders were traveling through, an ever-ready alertness which mirrored nothing of his inner thoughts. Thick, masculinely arched eyebrows of black marked the beginning of his forehead slanting into the brim of his dust-stained hat.

It was a compelling face, too aggressively male and too bluntly carved. It commanded attention. His presence would dominate a group even if he didn't speak a word, as it had when Sheila had immediately singled him out from the rest.

Aloof and hard, he was a man to be feared. Yet she was resting quite comfortably against him, the rippling muscles of his chest and arm cradling her. The musky male scent of him filled her senses. It seemed to drug her fatigued brain and lower all her defenses Her eyelids drooped and closed.

Something touched her cheek. A low voice, velvet-smooth and husky, murmured unintelligible words in an ordering tone. Her lashes fluttered and slowly opened, fighting through the sleep-drugged mists that clouded her vision. She was leaning against something hard and unyielding. Or was it someone?

Her eyes focused on the gloved fingers moving away from her cheek. As recognition flashed at where she was, the support was withdrawn from her. Muscles that were stiff and sore reacted slowly to keep her balance as he dismounted and reached back to lift her down.

Sheila's knees buckled, but the hands on her waist steadied her until her legs stiffened to support herself. Immediately, he let her go and walked around to unsaddle his horse. Not trusting her ability to walk yet, Sheila glanced around.

A golden twilight was purpling to dusk. A chill seeped into her bones. They were camping for the night. She looked around the naturally formed hollow of ground serving as a campsite. Tall grass grew densely where a small spring trickled. A horse was already tearing at the thick shoots while its rider pulled the saddle off.

The murmur of water pulled at Sheila like a powerful magnet. Thirst burned her tongue and throat. She stared at the sound, her feet rooted to the rough soil.

A canteen was thrust under her nose. At the moist

scent of water, her tied hands greedily reached for it until her eyes recognized the gloved hand holding the canteen. Her gaze traveled up the poncho-draped arm to the saturnine face of her abductor.

Her parched body quivered with longing for the water, but she couldn't bring herself to drink from his canteen. Lowering her hands, Sheila defiantly met his hooded look, knowing she would be the one to suffer from this self-destructive display of rebellion, yet not caring.

A black eyebrow quirked, permitting her a second to think it over before the canteen was withdrawn. Half out of her mind with thirst, Sheila pivoted away to encounter the thoughtful blue gaze of the American. She took a faltering step to the side, away from all of them, but was halted by a commanding Spanish voice, the one she was beginning to recognize.

"I'm too tired to run away. All I want to do is to sit down." Her voice was hoarse and rasping, hardly recognizable as her own. "Can you understand that?"

Evidently, her message was understood, either by interpreting the weakness of her voice or from the unsteadiness of her legs. No one attempted to stop her as she started forward again, her protesting muscles providing litle coordination.

A carpet of green grass offered Sheila a cushion. She crumpled to it gratefully, not wanting to move or think. But she needed to concentrate on something other than her thirs. She tried staring at the darkening sky to find the first evening star. Her searching eyes found a man squatting beside her and holding a canteen in his hands. She breathed in sharply at the tormenting sight of it, her accusing gaze flying to the pair of blue eyes.

"Go away." Sheila demanded huskily.

"I thought you were a survivor, Mrs. Sheila Rogers Townsend." he mocked, "but here you are, trying to die of thirst. Have you always had these suicidal tendencies?"

"It's none of your business." Closing her eyes to

avoid seeing the canteen, she turned her face into the grass beneath her head.

"But it is my business. It's everyone's business here," he pointed out. "You claim to have a rich father who will pay a lot of money to have you returned to him. And here you are, trying to kill yourself before we can oblige him."

"Money." Sheila tried to laugh, but it came out as a choked sound.

"Back there on the road, you talked a pretty good argument about why we should keep you alive. You never panicked, never lost your head. So why don't you be smart now and have a drink?" He unscrewed the lid of the canteen and she quivered at the sound. "You don't really want to die, Mrs. Townsend."

Sheila flinched. "Don't call me that." What she was really thinking was that she didn't want to die.

A hand curved under her neck, lifting her head. The coolness of the canteen's metal opening touched her lips. The sweet scent of water filled her senses.

"Come on. Drink up." He tipped the canteen, sending a slow trickle of water between her lips.

Sheila lifted her hands to tip the canteen higher and let more of the refreshing water fill her parched mouth. She couldn't swallow fast enough and began to choke.

"Take it easy," the American cautioned and held the canteen back. "Drink it slow—a little at a time."

Sheila forced herself to take slow sips when she wanted to gulp it down by the gallons. There was still water left in the canteen when he took it away. She could have drunk it all and more and said so.

"Later," he assured her, then laid her head back on the grass.

Her head moved against its pillow of grass so she could look at him more easily. She studied him silently for a minute, still wrapped in the comfortable cocoon that temporarily protected her from the reality of her situation.

"What's your name?" Sheila asked.

His hesitation was obvious as he made a pretense of

securely fastening the lid of the canteen. When it was done, he glanced with seeming indifference at the rest of the band. There was a coolness in the blue gaze that returned to Sheila.

"They call me Laredo," he said, indicating with a nod of his head the other members of the group. Sheila waited expectantly for him to confide his full name. His mouth thinned in grimness. "That's as good as any," he concluded.

Curiosity glittered cat-like in her eyes. "Are you from Laredo?"

"Not exactly," he denied and offered no more.

"You are an American?" Sheila persisted.

"I was born there." He glanced to the north, a far-away look in his eye. He made it sound as if he were never going back or couldn't go back.

"Who are they?" Shadows were lengthening through the campsite, making dark shapes of the men moving about.

"Their names? Their occupations? They've probably forgotten. It's better this way," said the man who had assumed the name of Laredo. "It makes it easier."

A small fire had been started. Its flickering light touched the malevolent face of the man named Juan. Chipped, yellowed teeth were exposed by the sullen snarl splitting his lips. He was watching Sheila intently. Her body remembered vividly his filthy, groping hands and the foul smell of his breath.

"Easier for you and your friends to steal, murder, and rape," Sheila challenged with bitter hatred.

He had followed the direction of her gaze. His expression was bland when he looked back and tossed the canteen to the ground beside her.

"I'll leave this with you," he said. "I'd wait a bit before drinking more." And he started to walk away.

"Laredo." Sheila called him back, levering herself onto an elbow, her wrists still bound in front of her. He turned and waited for her to speak, his manner expectantly polite, yet remote. "Am I—" She found herself choking on the words, then began again. "Am I to provide the night's entertainment for you and your friends?"

"You said your father wouldn't pay a cent if you were harmed." But his answer neither confirmed nor denied her fears.

"I know what I said," Sheila retorted. "That doesn't answer my question."

Shrugging, Laredo turned and walked to the campfire, leaving her to imagine the worst. No longer blinded to her situation by exhaustion and thirst, Sheila pushed herself into a sitting position.

There was nothing to stop them from raping her and still demanding ransom from her father. By his actions, Laredo had made it plain he would not stand against his friends to protect her, and this marauding band had no scruples. Tied and stiff with soreness, Sheila was powerless to help herself.

Food was being dished out from a pot hanging over the fire. Beans, her nose told her, and she felt the gnawing pangs of hunger in her stomach. It had been nearly twenty-four hours since her last meal. It seemed much longer. Nightmares always seemed to last longer, and hers had only just begun, Sheila thought.

Several yards away, Laredo sat cross-legged on the ground, eating from the dish in his hand. A tin cup filled with steaming coffee was balanced on his knee. Sheila watched him ravenously, her stomach growling in protest.

Outlined by the firelight, a tall figure walked toward her. Sheila recognized the lithely moving man instantly as the leader, her captor. Only when he had nearly reached her could she see the dish of food he carried in one hand and the cup of coffee in the other.

Bending, he set her meal on the ground beside her and then straightened up. Hunger blinded Sheila to the unappetizing sight of a sticky glob of beans, a strip of dried meat, and a hard chunk of bread. She eagerly held out her wrists to be untied so she could eat. He merely stared down at her, his hard features hidden in the night's shadows.

"Untie me," she demanded.

He made no move to free her hands. Sighing impatiently Sheila glanced over her shoulder to Laredo. "Would you please translate in Spanish to this ignorant leader of yours that I can't eat with my hands tied?"

Hesitating, Laredo lifted his head to look beyond Sheila to the man standing beside her. There was a brief exchange in Spanish in which she heard neither "*sí*" or "*no*" spoken by the low-pitched voice. Before she could decide which way the decision had gone, she was sitting alone and the man was walking back to the fire.

Her frustrated gaze swung back to Laredo. He was rising to his feet, dish and cup in hand, and walking toward her. Sitting on the ground beside her, he set aside his food to loosen the knotted rope and unwind it from her wrists.

"Thanks." Sheila flexed her numbed fingers and wrists. There were raw red circles where the tight rope had chafed her skin, but her hunger was too overpowering to feel any discomfort at the moment.

"I only followed orders." He shrugged indifferently and picked up his plate.

With unsteady hands, Sheila followed suit. For the next several minutes, she concentrated on filling her empty stomach, scooping up the thick beans with the chunk of bread and tearing off bites of the leathery meat with her teeth.

Not a crumb was left on the plate when she finished the meal off with a swallow of coffee Replete, she curled both hands around the tin and stared at the dying fire.

Laredo did likewise, drawing her glance. In the soft glow of the waning light, he looked younger, a touch of loneliness in his haunted blue eyes. Sheila's curiosity was aroused again.

"You don't really belong here with them," she told him quietly.

His sideways glance was cynical and mocking. "Don't I?"

"You're not like them."

"Why?" His mouth crooked. "Because I can speak English?"

"No, of course not." Tipping her head to the side, Sheila studied him. "Why are you with them? I can't believe it's by choice."

"You don't want to believe it," he corrected her.

"Are you with them by choice?" She was determined to get a straight answer to her question.

"Yes." There was absolutely no regret in his voice. "They're my friends."

"Even though they killed a man and made you a party to it?" Sheila couldn't accept that he actually meant what he was saying.

"You're referring to your husband? He was killed by his own stupidity. If he hadn't reached for the gun, he would have been unharmed and just minus some money —that's all." His blue eyes glinted in quiet speculation. "I notice you're not overly grief-stricken by his death."

Sheila ignored the last comment deliberately. "Because he defended his property, he provoked his own death?" she said, rephrasing his words in a taunt. "Is that the way you rationalize his murder?" Her fiery gaze slid to the renegade leader standing a few feet away. "Or are you mouthing *his* words? Your boss, who mercifully spared my life so he could hand me over to the same mauling pig who murdered my husband!"

Sheila hadn't spoken softly or tried to disguise her poisonous contempt. Laredo sipped at his coffee and didn't respond.

"What's the matter? Are you afraid I'll remember that you didn't argue at all when your boss turned me over to your fellow outlaw? I can't blame you for that, can I?" Sheila jeered. "All you do is follow orders."

"That's right," he acknowledged calmly.

"Regardless of whether you think they are right or not," she added in disgust. "Who is he? The devil reincarnated?"

"Names aren't important around here." It seemed impossible to provoke Laredo into anger; he neither defended his boss, nor denounced him. "I told you that before. Drink your coffee."

"What do you do? Just bow very low and call him boss?" Appealing to him seemed useless, but it was her only hope. "You've got to help me, Laredo. You're an American and I'm an American. You can't let them do whatever it is they plan to do with me. Please.

"Oh, my God." Sheila swallowed a panicked sob. "Can't you feel them watching me, watching us?" Her skittish glance encompassed the circle of men sitting closer to the campfire. It was not her money that kept drawing their looks. "Help me get away; help me escape."

"So you can go to the *soldados*, the *policia*, and tell them what happened?" Laredo scoffed at her request, hard amusement pulling at the corner of his mouth. "You forget I was there with them. The noose would go around my neck, as well as theirs."

"I wouldn't tell them anything, I swear. Please help me."

"Forget it," he said, draining his coffee cup.

Hot tears scalded her eyes. Sheila widened them, hardly daring to breathe for fear her breath would turn into broken sobs. It was several minutes before she could regain her poise.

"Where are you taking me?" Her husky voice grouped Laredo with the others now.

"Tomorrow?" His gaze touched her briefly, then looked to the west. "Up there."

Sheila turned, catching the red glow of a cigarette tip, a reminder of how close the bandit leader was to them. Her gaze shifted to the looming, black outline of the Sierra Madre range.

"Into the mountains?" she asked for confirmation and received a curt nod.

It explained their reliance on horses for transportation. Vast stretches of the northern range were accessible only on horseback or on foot. This forbidding, primitive land would offer a perfect hideout for the outlaw band. Her heart sank lower in despair.

"How will you contact my father?" she asked, fearing for the first time that she might never be allowed to leave.

"There are ways."

"What will happen to me when you get the money?"

"That's not up to me." He shook his head, apparently unconcerned about her fate.

"Him, I suppose." With a jerk of her head, she indicated the silent figure standing a few feet away. "Do you jump whenever he says so, or do you first ask how high?" Sheila snapped with an acid bite.

"You talk too much." There was a hint of impatience in his voice to indicate he wasn't as impervious to her tiny barbs as he appeared to be. Rising to his feet, he offered a hand to help Sheila up. "Come on. It's getting late and it's time we turned in."

She had reached out to accept his hand, but the rest of his words checked the movement. Her fingers were suspended in the air, inches from his open palm.

"We?" Sheila repeated, every nerve end instantly alert.

"You're sleeping with me tonight." Laredo nodded.

Rage billowed in a red mist before her eyes. She had appealed to him for help, made known to him her fears of what might happen to her in the dark of night.

Had he thought she would offer no resistance? Because he was an American and had talked to her, did he think she would be grateful it was to be him and not one of the others?

His extended left arm held the loose poncho away from his waist and hips. In the dim light, Sheila saw the hilt of a knife protruding from the leather sheath hooked to his belt. The securing flap wasn't snapped.

Pretending a bitter resignation, Sheila took hold of his hand with her left one and let him pull her onto her feet. Under the cover of stumbling forward, she grabbed for the knife and pulled it from the sheath before Laredo realized what she was doing. She twisted free and retreated two steps. The knife blade flashed menacingly in the flickering light of the campfire.

"Don't touch me," she hissed.

"You little fool, give me the knife," he muttered in a low, angry voice.

"Come near me and I'll ki——" A sharp cry of pain ripped through her throat.

Steel talons circled her rope-burned wrist from behind, twisting it until the knife slid from her paralyzed fingers. Instantly, Sheila was jerked around, her arm bent high in the middle of her back as she was pinned against the solid wall of a man's chest.

Another set of fingers grabbed a handful of hair and yanked her head backward. Her lips parted in a second gasp of pain while her rounded eyes looked into the lean, hard features of her captor's face. The glittering black coals burned first her eyes, then blazed a fiery trail down her cheeks to her lips, moist and trembling.

Any moment Sheila expected the ruthless set of his mouth to brutally smother hers. Every pulsing fiber in her body felt the savagery of his kiss, although he had not yet claimed it. But her mind reeled in shock from his imaginary possession.

As roughly as she was crushed against him, she was cast away, staggering to the ground near his feet. Reaching down, he picked up the rope that had bound her wrists and tossed it to the silent Laredo, snapping a low order in Spanish.

Laredo's mouth was grim as he began retying her hands. "You crazy fool," he muttered. "Why did you pull a stunt like that?"

"I'll do it again," Sheila vowed, but her voice shook. "He knows it."

When Laredo straightened up, a blanket was thrown over Sheila, accompanied by a crisp flow of Spanish. She wanted to cower beneath the blanket, but she couldn't take her eyes away from the towering man watching her. Laredo walked away and returned within seconds to set his saddle next to Sheila. Shaking out his blanket, he lay down on the ground beside her and pulled it over him, tipping his hat forward to rest his head on the saddle.

"Get some rest while you can, Mrs. Townsend. It's going to be a long day tomorrow," Laredo said coldly. "Someone will be on guard all night, and I sleep very light."

Catching back a defeated sob, Sheila watched the tall figure carry their cups and dishes to the fire and return to stand a few feet away in the darkness. A match flared, cupped by a pair of hands to a cigarette. Then she couldn't make out his shape at all, but she knew he was there, her new devil-master.

There was no sensation of safety or relief that Laredo was merely lying beside her and not forcing himself on her. She was still quivering from the punishing arms that had held her. Closing her eyes, she doubted if sleep would come.

The knotted rope irritated the raw skin of her wrists. Beneath her, the hard ground poked at her sore, aching muscles. Sheila caught the scent of burning tobacco. Survive, she thought, and she wanted to laugh.

Chapter 7

Her knees were quivering from gripping the horse's flanks. The stiff leather of the saddle skirt had rubbed sore spots on her inner thighs. Sheila's tied hands no longer had the strength to hold onto the cantle for balance. She longed to rest her head on Laredo's broad back, knowing it would bounce like a ball if she tried. The dark leader was beside them. He'd been in the saddle all day, yet he looked fresh and alert, not bone-tired and half-deadened with pain, as Sheila was. Her gaze hurled gold-tipped daggers at the seemingly indefatigable man.

The ground rose sharply and Sheila had to concentrate her energies on staying astride the horse and not sliding off its rump. Rising before dawn, they had reached the mountains shortly after first light.

Following no trail that Sheila could discern, the riders had snaked up mountains where it seemed only a mountain goat would go, then down through valleys and mountain passes and up again.

It appeared they were solely guided by their leader's

instinct. In a moment of bitter hatred and resentment, Sheila hoped he was lost. The feeling didn't last long as she started to slip back on the horse's haunches.

"Help!" Sheila gasped.

Laredo reached an arm behind him to pull her back. It stayed half around her waist for support as the horse began galloping to the top of a steep rise. Sheila sagged against it. Atop a narrow ridge, the horse again resumed its trotting pace.

"Can't we stop and rest?" Sheila protested wearily. "Or at least slow down?"

"Hang on. We're almost there," he promised without sympathy.

"Where is that? Hell?"

It seemed an eternity later that they turned to ride through a mountain corridor. Twisted, stunted brush clung tenaciously to the rocky walls closing in on the riders. The horse quickened its stride, pulling at the bit as it sighted home.

Looking over Laredo's shoulder, Sheila tried to catch a glimpse of their destination. The mountain corridor emptied into a small, narrow canyon carved deep in the bowels of the Sierra Madre range. A visible trail wound down to the canyon floor, where loosely clustered adobe huts dotted one side of the canyon.

It was in front of one of these that Laredo reined in the horse. Swinging a leg over the saddle horn, he stepped to the ground. Sheila swayed into the arms that reached to lift her down. Absently, she noted the other riders were heading off to other adobe structures, dimly hearing cries of greeting and figures hurrying to meet the returning band.

Laredo's arm stayed in a supporting curve around the back of her rib cage as he escorted her into the shadowed interior of the adobe building. They paused inside and Sheila disinterestedly inspected the room.

A primitive kitchen and eating area occupied half of the room. She supposed the crude furniture in the nearest half depicted a living room. An arched opening in one wall led into a hallway, suggesting rooms beyond.

A familiar Spanish voice spoke behind Sheila. She turned as Laredo's arm dropped from her back to meet the shuttered dark eyes of her captor. Cold metal slid between her wrists and she glanced down as Laredo cut the rope that bound her hands.

A word of thanks started to form on her lips until she remembered what Laredo had told her before. He was only following orders. So she flexed her stiff fingers and said nothing. Sheathing his knife, Laredo walked to the door.

"Where are you going?" she asked with a slight toss of her head, trying not to show her apprehension at being left alone with the renegade leader.

Laredo paused, glancing from Sheila to his boss, then back again to her. "To take care of the horses."

He walked out and her gaze ricocheted from the pair of glinting, dark eyes. She had the uncanny sensation that he was reading her mind and pivoted away. Her spine prickled with awareness. Sheila wasn't surprised when she heard him speak only a foot behind her.

"Señora." The low, commanding tone was accompanied by a hand appearing alongside of her to motion her toward the hallway.

It branched into two rooms. He indicated with a gesture for Sheila to enter the last room. Surveying it, she guessed it was to be her new prison. The monk-like cell consisted of an uncomfortable-looking cot, a crude dresser with a basin and water urn on top of it, and a chair. A coarsely woven curtain in a dull orange material hung at the lone window.

Her sweeping gaze stopped at the rectangular mirror hanging above the dresser. Sheila stared at her reflection in shock. She looked like a haggard tramp. Her face was streaked with grime and sweat. Her hair was matted and straggly, its glossy sheen hidden beneath clotting layers of dust. The dusty serape covering her made her figure seem shapeless.

Unconsciously, Sheila touched a hand to her cheek, as if to be certain the reflection she saw really belonged to her. She felt the grit that coated her usually creamy-smooth complexion. It awakened the rest of her senses to the filth that soiled the rest of her body and the stench of perspiration and horse odor that clung to her skin and clothes. She barely looked human and turned from the mirror in distaste.

"Is there somewhere I can clean up?" Sheila asked quickly.

Not a flicker of understanding crossed the carved mask of his features. Sheila sighed impatiently, wondering how she was going to get her request through to him.

"I want to wash. Do you understand?" She rubbed her hands together in a cleansing gesture. "Wash. Take a bath."

He studied her miming action and walked to the dresser to pour water from the urn into the basin. A wave of his hand indicated Sheila was to use it to wash.

"No No." She shook her head determinedly. "Look, *Señor*—whatever your name is." She hesitated before filling in the blank with a disinterested shrug.

"Ráfaga," he interrupted blandly. Not a whisper of emotion was evident in the lean, masculine face or the flat, black eyes.

Sheila stared at him curiously, not certain if he had actually furnished his name. Considering the way Laredo had avoided giving it, she had almost decided it was going to remain a secret.

"Seño Ráfaga?" she repeated to determine if it was his name. There was a faint, slightly arrogant inclination of his head in acknowledgment. "Seño Ráfaga," Sheila began again, "I don't want to just wash my hands." She again repeated the rubbing gesture. "I want to wash all over—my hair, my clothes, all over. Do you understand?"

His expression was inscrutable. Surely he could understand what she meant, Sheila thought in irritation. She wondered if he wasn't deliberately being obtuse when he waved a hand again toward the washbasin.

"It's too small," she snapped and sat down in the

middle of the floor, pretending to splash water and wash. "I want to take a bath—in a big tub of water. Do you understand?"

Laughter came from the door. "What are you doing?" Laredo asked with obvious amusement, his blue eyes silently laughing at Sheila.

Her cheeks flushed red in embarrassment. Stiffly, she scrambled to her feet, dusting the seat of her pants as she tried to regain some measure of dignity.

"Would you explain to this Spanish-speaking imbecile that I want a bath?" she demanded coldly.

"The plumbing around here is strictly the outdoor type," replied Laredo, his mouth still twitching in silent laughter.

"Surely there has to be something around here bigger than that stupid washbasin. Where do you bathe?" Sheila challenged. Then she added caustically, "Or don't you?"

An insertion in Spanish kept Laredo from answering her question as he responded instead to his boss. Their exchange was brief, musically fluid, and low.

"My bath?" Sheila reminded Laredo when their conversation appeared to be finished.

"*Baño,*" came the low Spanish word.

"That means 'bath.'" Laredo supplied the translation.

"At last my message has gotten through," she sighed impatiently.

"As I said before, the facilities around here are primitive," Laredo continued, "but there is a spring we use for bathing."

"Am I allowed to use it?" she asked stiffly.

Her answer came from the leader, who had identified himself as Ráfaga. A dresser drawer was opened and a folded cloth was removed. Ráfaga carried it to Sheila, a used bar of soap atop the coarse fabric of a towel.

Warily, she took it from his hands, tensing under the aloof appraisal of his dark gaze. He motioned her toward the hall to indicate Sheila should lead the way while they followed.

Outside the adobe house, a man lounged against a pole supporting a porch-like roof, a rifle in his hand, the muzzle pointed toward the ground. At Sheila's appearance in the doorway, he straightened, the muzzle swinging toward her as he took a step to block her exit.

When the other two men appeared behind her, he relaxed his alert stance slightly. He didn't look familiar to Sheila. She was almost positive he hadn't been a part of the band that had just ridden in moments ago. Ráfaga stepped ahead of Sheila, signaling her to wait while he spoke to the stranger.

"Who is he?" Sheila watched the two curiously while Laredo waited with her. "What's he doing here?"

"He's the guard. There'll be someone outside the door as long as you are here."

"For whose protection?" she retorted. "Is Ráfaga afraid I'll steal another knife and attack him?" She caught the flicker of surprise in the blue eyes upon her use of the bandit's name. "He told me that was his name," she explained coolly.

"Ráfaga? Yes, that's what he's called."

"You seem surprised." Her head tipped to the side in a challenge.

"Only that you got the message across, considering the difficulty you had with 'bath.' " Amusement glittered in his blue eyes again.

" 'Me, Tarzan, you, Jane' is much easier to act out." Sheila shrugged, knowing it had been even simpler than that. "I don't suppose that is his real name any more than Laredo is yours."

"No, it's a name given to him by the men."

"What does it mean?" Sheila looked at Ráfaga. A panther perhaps, she thought, considering his animal grace and that feline aloofness with a touch of predatory ruthlessness thrown in.

"I think it translates into"—Laredo frowned as he searched for the English equivalent—"a gust of wind or a flash of light."

The descriptive term suggested something fleeting,

something that was elusive and volatile. Considering his occupation, it was probably appropriate, Sheila thought wryly, and she wondered if it was true or wishfully portentous.

"What is his real name?" she asked curiously.

"I don't know." Laredo removed his hat to run his fingers through the thick brown of his hair and then put it back on, pulling it low on his forehead. "It isn't a question that a man likes to be asked around here."

The guard was listening to what Ráfaga was telling him, but watching Sheila intently. She seemed to be the object of their discussion. She realized that yet again Laredo had avoided giving her a direct answer to her question about the guard.

"You never did explain what the man was guarding," she reminded him. "Me or Ráfaga?"

"Diego will be there, or someone else, to make sure you don't decide to take any long walks." Tipping back his head, he peered at her from beneath his hat brim.

Her gaze swept the mountains ringing the canyon. "Where would I go?" Sheila sighed bitterly.

"There isn't any place you could go," Laredo agreed, "but Ráfaga thinks you would be foolish enough to try."

"Do you?" she countered.

"You forget. I'm the one you stole the knife from. Yes"—Laredo nodded—"I think you would try to run, but you won't be given the chance."

Sheila realized she was well and truly trapped. Her prison came complete with walls, guards, and a warden. The only thing lacking was the bars at her window. She felt her frustration mount and knew it was only the beginning.

His conversation with the guard concluded, Ráfaga turned to rejoin them. Sheila's eyes shimmered with bitter resentment as he motioned her to the left side of the adobe building. Laredo touched fingers to the brim of his hat in a mock salute and walked in the opposite direction.

"Do you trust yourself alone with me?" Sheila flashed

at Ráfaga's hooded expression. She knew he didn't understand a word she said, but she had to release some of her temper or choke on it. "Aren't you afraid I'll do something desperate like scratch your eyes out?"

As if he knew how impotent her venom was, he didn't blink an eye at her poisonous tone. He used hand signals to guide her beneath the shading trees behind the clay-colored building. Subtropical growth hid the dammed pool below the spring until they were nearly on top of it.

The sun-kissed surface of the water glittered cool and inviting. Birds flitted from branch to branch, crying out alarm at the human intrusion. Sheila forgot her anger of a moment ago, abandoning it in the surging desire to feel her body cleansed of the grit and grime from the last two days.

Laying the towel and soap on the bank, she started to pull the dirty serape over her head, then remembered the man behind her and turned. He stood watching and waiting.

"Would you please turn around?" She made a circling motion with her hand.

His dark gaze remained shuttered and unrevealing, but it didn't leave her. Stubbornly, Sheila made no move to undress, determined not to be the one who ended this staring contest.

"*Baño*," Ráfaga said crisply and motioned to the pool.

"I am not getting into the water until you turn around," Sheila insisted with a flash of temper.

He took a step to a tree near her and indolently leaned a shoulder against its trunk. His dark gaze didn't waver from her face. Speaking in Spanish, his hand pointed to the pool, then over his shoulder the way they had come.

Sheila caught the words "*baño*" and "*casa*." The latter she knew meant "house." She guessed he was telling her if she didn't bathe, they would return to the house. Fuming inwardly, she realized her choice was either to remain dirty or undress while he watched.

Turning her back to him, Sheila tugged the serape

over her head, fingers trembling with her inner rage.
"If you were hoping for a private performance, you're
going to be mistaken," she ground out savagely. Holding the torn front of her blouse together, she turned
and threw the serape at his impassive face. He caught
it with one hand. "My clothes are just as dirty as the
rest of me."

Sheila sat down to remove her shoes, then slid from
the grassy bank into the pool. The shock of the ice-cold
temperature of the water drew a sharp gasp of surprise.
But there was no turning back as Sheila immersed herself completely in the pool. Surfacing with a toss of her
wet mane, she smoothed the strands away from her
face, her teeth chattering from the cold.

Half-sitting and half-floating on the shallow bottom
of the pool, immersed up to her neck, Sheila fought
her way out of the entangling looseness of her blouse
and tossed the sodden garment onto the bank. She
tugged free of her slacks, as well, leaving her under-
pants on. Inching her way to the edge of the pool, she
deposited her slacks beside her blouse and reached for
the soap. The water was too cold for Sheila to waste
time congratulating herself on successfully thwarting
Ráfaga. She soaped down briskly, feeling the dust and
grime float away.

By the time she had rinsed the lather from her hair,
her arms and legs were becoming numb from the frigid
temperature of the water. Awkwardly she moved to
the bank and reached for the towel. Shaking out the
fold, she held it in front of her breasts with one hand
as she scrambled out of the icy pool and wrapped it
around her.

Briefly she looked at Ráfaga. His shoulder still rested
negligently against the tree trunk while he watched
Sheila. Tucking the ends of the towel beneath her arm,
she knelt beside the water to scrub her blouse and
slacks clean. She shivered uncontrollably, a mountain
of goosebumps covering her naked skin. Wishing for
clean, dry clothes to put on, Sheila settled for clean,
wet clothes.

Keeping her back to Ráfaga, she tugged on her slacks before abandoning the towel. The blouse was minus its buttons, so Sheila tied the loose front in a knot. The plunging vee exposed the cleavage between her breasts while the saturated, clinging material emphatically outlined every curve of her breasts. Its coverage was dubious, but Sheila couldn't bear the thought of putting on the dirty serape.

Wrapping the towel in a turban, she straightened up and turned to Ráfaga. Her shoulders were squared, the lift of her chin proud, as she tried to control the shivers of cold racing over her skin.

Indolently pushing himself away from the tree trunk, Ráfaga made a low comment in Spanish and glanced pointedly at her shoes. A flush of pink briefly colored her cheeks as Sheila bent over to put them on. She felt the touch of his gaze and realized how much she revealed when she leaned over like that. She quickly turned away to squeeze her wet feet into the shoes.

Her toes were squishing noisily with each step by the time they retraced the path back to the house. The guard stared curiously at her shivering, besodden state, but Sheila was too chilled to feel self-conscious. Without waiting for him to motion her toward her room, she hurried there on her own. Entering it, Sheila began sneezing. Ráfaga disappeared from the doorway.

"What's the matter?" she taunted after him. "Are you afraid of catching cold?"

Kicking off her wet shoes, Sheila walked to the bed, intending to remove the thick blanket and wrap it around herself for warmth. Ráfaga returned, carrying a man's white shirt. He handed it to her, speaking in low, rolling Spanish. Unable to suppress the shivers that quaked through her cold body, Sheila accepted it.

"*Gracias.*" Sheila doubted that the gesture had been motivated by anything more than a selfish wish not to have a sick female on his hands.

"*Por nada,*" was the crisp response he gave before he pivoted and left the room.

Hesitating only a second, Sheila quickly removed the

wet clothes and tugged on the warm, dry shirt. Her shaking fingers had just fastened the last button when Ráfaga reappeared, his dark gaze skimming her from turbaned head to her bare toes, dwelling briefly on the bare length of her shapely legs. The trails of the shirt ended at mid-thigh.

He said nothing as he tossed a comb onto the bed and picked up her wet clothes lying on the floor. He left the room, taking her dripping clothes with him. Sheila started to protest, then sighed at the futility of it, and she began combing the snarls out of her hair.

The crude cot looked remarkably inviting She slid beneath the blanket, the coarse fabric rough against her freshly scrubbed skin. But it was warm, and soon Sheila drifted into a light sleep.

The sound of a woman's voice awakened her. The sun was still up, so she couldn't have dozed for long. She listened for several seconds to the lilting Spanish voice, the woman's tone happy and faintly teasing.

Curiosity made Sheila push the blanket aside and she rose. With barefoot quietness, she wandered into the hallway, pausing in the archway of the main room of the adobe house. Her inquisitive gaze looked for the source of the attractive voice.

Ráfaga was standing in the kitchen. Heat waves stirred the air above the cup he held in his left hand. His right arm encircled a slender brunette. Large, sparkling, dark eyes were gazing laughingly into his face, provocative and playful as the woman leaned against him. Her hands were spread inside the front of his shirt half-unbuttoned to give her access to his naked chest and the vee-shaped cloud of curling dark hair.

The stubble of beard had been shaved from his strongly carved jaw and cheeks. No wide-brimmed hat covered the ebony blackness of his hair growing with rakish thickness away from his forehead The slashing lines on either side of his mouth had deepened into sharp grooves, hinting at an amused smile. His enigmatic dark eyes were looking at the girl, accepting her attention as if it were his due.

A hard, male vitality now over-stamped the powerful and ruthless set of his masculine features. And it made him seem, to Sheila, more dangerous than before. Her heartbeat quickened, sending her pulse hammering in her throat.

She hadn't moved since halting in the archway, yet something betrayed her presence to Ráfaga. His dark gaze swung to her, its rapier thrust pinning Sheila where she stood.

The vivacious brunette turned to see what had distracted his attention. Her eyes widened at the sight of Sheila standing in the hallway, semi-clad in a man's shirt. She noted the dark honey color of Sheila's hair.

The brunette's eyes began snapping with black fires of hatred. She stepped angrily away from Ráfaga's side, turning on him with a vengeance. A spate of rapid-fire Spanish burst from her lips. Her hand gestured at Sheila in Latin temper.

Unaffected by the raging outburst, Ráfaga offered a low comment, which didn't pacify the girl's anger. She stormed over to Sheila, a vitriolic flow of Spanish spewing forth again. She was obviously incensed to have Sheila in the house, especially so scantily clothed.

From the contemptuous tone and the sharpness of the girl's dark gaze, she surmised that the brunette was making derisive comments about her. Unconsciously, Sheila let a smile touch her lips, amused by the unnecessary jealousy.

The action caused the already enraged brunette to draw in her breath with a hiss like a deadly viper. The next second she was spitting in Sheila's face. All amusement at the situation vanished at the wet drops on her cheeks. Sheila reacted without thinking, hot anger surging through her veins as her opened palm struck the brunette's face.

There was a momentary shriek of pain and surprise as the girl cupped her stinging cheek. Then she was flinging herself at Sheila, pulling at her hair and hurling words of Spanish abuse. Stunned for only a second, Sheila retaliated instinctively, fighting and clawing while fending off the brunette's scratching fingers. The sharp command from Ráfaga had no effect on either of them.

"Sweet Jesus!" Laredo's startled voice sounded through the barrage of Spanish.

The kicking, hair-pulling fight had barely begun before the two men intervened to break it up. An arm circled Sheila's waist from behind and forcibly dragged her out of reach of the other girl. Her feet flailed the air a few inches above the floor.

"Put me down!" Sheila pushed uselessly at the muscled forearm across her waist.

Ear-splitting shrieks came from her opponent, held fast in Laredo's arms. Sheila stiffened as she realized who held her. Ráfaga's voice barked an order near her ear and the brunette stopped struggling, although the fire of jealous hatred blazed as brilliantly in her eyes now as before.

Sheila was half-turned in his arm, his thumb and forefinger gripping her chin and twisting it up so he could see her face. She strained away from his chest, her amber eyes flashing their loathing of his touch. His expression was masked. Faint mockery gleamed in his fathomless eyes.

He said something in Spanish to the brunette. Sheila sensed by his tone that it was uncomplimentary to her. Seething, she wrenched her chin from his fingers.

"What did he just say?" she demanded of Laredo.

"He was reasoning with Elena," he answered after a hesitant glance at his boss, "asking her why he would take a clawing wildcat with yellow eyes to his bed when he could have an eager, purring kitten instead."

The explanation snapped the slender thread holding Sheila's temper in check. "Pig! You filthy animal!" She struck at his implacable face, but the blow was blocked by an upraised arm. "As if I would ever let you touch me! Murderer!"

Her raining blows fell harmlessly on his arms and shoulders, never reaching the face that was their target. Growing tired of her struggles, Ráfaga swung her into his arms.

"Your bed?" Sheila spat. "I would sleep in a snake-pit before I would lie in your bed!"

His gaze narrowed at the glowing hatred in her eyes. The line of his mouth thinned as he turned, carrying her in his arms, and walked to her room.

Stopping beside the cot, he dropped her unceremoniously and stood above her for several seconds. He didn't say a word, but everything about him seemed to cry that if he wished, he could force her to lie in his bed. As the color washed from her face, he left the room.

Chapter 8

Nearly an hour later, Laredo had come to her room, announcing it was time to eat. She was hungry, but she had no desire to return to the main room of the house, where Ráfaga and his hot-tempered woman were.

"Nobody is going to wait on you or carry trays of food to your room," Laredo stated calmly. "If you want to eat, you have to come to the table or go without."

He, too, had washed and shaved, his appearance decidedly American now, but Sheila knew he felt no special bond with her just because they shared the same nationality. He was a member of the band. He belonged to the opposite side.

Sheila stood at the small window, holding back the curtain to watch the sun hovering on the point of a mountain peak to the west. Letting it fall, she turned to look at Laredo, the sensual outline of her lips grimly tight.

"All right, I'll go to the table to eat, but you keep that little Mexican cat away from me," she warned.

"Ráfaga has calmed her down."

Sheila remembered the angry banging of the pans and doubted it. "He better have, or he might find himself sleeping with a dark-haired girl whose face is all scratched."

"It would more likely be you who would come away from a fight all scarred up." A bemused smile lifted one corner of his mouth. "Elena fights dirty. You wouldn't stand a chance against her in an all-out brawl."

"You'd be surprised at what I've learned in the last few days," Sheila said, then stalked past him into the hallway.

When she entered the main room, Ráfaga was seated at one end of the table. His dark gaze noted her presence, although Sheila deliberately ignored him. The young Mexican woman was dishing food onto the plates, made of pottery.

There were four chairs around the table, three empty. Sheila chose one that put her back to the living area and on Ráfaga's right.

The atmosphere crackled with tension. Sheila knew the volatile brunette was not reconciled to her presence. Her eyes hurled daggers each time she looked at Sheila.

The animosity emanating from the girl across from her was almost tangible. It tainted the food, making it nearly impossible to enjoy the meal. Exasperated, Sheila set her silverware on the table.

Turning to Laredo, she demanded, "Will you explain to this jealous little witch that I am not interested in her lover?" She darted an irritated glance at the girl. "You can also tell her that if she'd give me a knife, I'd make sure he'd never get any closer to me than he is right now."

Hiding a smile, Laredo flashed a brief look at his boss, then translated what Sheila had said. Skepticism mixed with malevolent dislike as the brunette made her reply.

"She thinks you are only saying that because you are afraid of her." Laredo repeated in English what Elena had said. There was a wicked glint in his blue eyes. "She says that only a woman who is too old and crippled would drive a man such as Ráfaga from her bed. She says you look neither old nor crippled."

The praise for Ráfaga's expertise as a lover acted as a red cape to Sheila's temper. Since it had been first rendered in Spanish, he had obviously heard it. Her cat-gold eyes flashed to him, seeing the deliberate blankness in the look he returned to her.

"Of all the——" Sheila sputtered in helpless rage before she checked her exploding temper and clamped her lips tightly shut. She turned roundly on Laredo. "Tell her that he had my husband murdered and that my only wish is to see him suffer the same fate!"

The brunette's pointed chin lifted at the information translated by Laredo. Finally, she nodded her understanding and the sparkle of battle left her eyes as she dismissed Sheila as a potential rival for Ráfaga's attention. But there was still a wariness about her when she glanced at Ráfaga, as if she didn't trust him where Sheila was concerned.

The truce permitted Sheila to finish her meal in relative peace. The minute she was done, she excused herself from the table and returned to her room.

Her thoughts kept returning to the same questions. How long would it be before her parents were contacted and the ransom demand made? How long would it take to raise the money and pay it? Most disturbing of all—would she be released when the money was paid?

Darkness came with the setting of the sun. Crawling beneath the blanket on the hard cot, she hoped sleep would come quickly and help her forget the unanswerable questions.

Laredo left the adobe house soon after Sheila was in bed. A low murmur of voices continued to come from the main room, intimacy implied by the soft tones and punctuated by moments of pregnant silence. Sheila tried to concentrate on the night sounds outdoors, but she found herself straining to hear the couple in the main room.

Footsteps brought the voices closer, to the bedroom

adjacent to Sheila's. An embarrassed heat burned her skin at the sound of clothes being discarded in haste. The lilting caress in Elena's soft voice was abruptly silenced and Sheila closed her eyes against the image of the ruthless male's mouth closing over the brunette's.

The wall separating the two bedrooms was not thick enough to deaden the creaking of the cot or the sighing moans of ecstasy from female lips. Sheila covered her ears with her hands, trying to block out the sounds of their lovemaking. With nauseous persistence, it kept hammering at her eardrums.

Endless minutes stretched sickeningly together without a hint of either of them being satisfied. Sheila moaned at the repellent thought that the sounds might continue off and on all night as Ráfaga proved his prowess in bed.

A scream of disgust was rising in her throat when the silence came. Sheila pressed a hand to her churning stomach and waited to see if the storm of their passion was over, or if it was merely a lull. There was a creaking of movement on the cot and she swallowed quickly at the sickening lump threatening to gag her.

But the expected resumption didn't occur. There were rustling sounds of clothing being put on, followed by a whispered, caressing comment from Elena. Then Sheila heard the light tread of the woman quietly leaving the room and eventually the house. Shuddering with distaste, Sheila wondered how many nights she would have to listen to their bestial coupling.

She stared at the ceiling, violently hating all men and their carnal desires. None of them could be trusted. They were insensitive, selfish animals, caring only about their own physical needs. Love was a trap, devised by man to enslave woman to his will. Sheila vowed never to be caught in it.

Silence filled the house. A surge of restlessness claimed Sheila, agitating her into movement. Tossing the blanket to the foot of the narrow cot, she rose and moved quietly into the hallway.

The confines of the main room grated. A full moon

sent silvery light cascading through the windows, darkly
shadowing the corners of the room and restricting
Sheila's restless pacing to the area of its light. The back
of her neck prickled in warning and Sheila pivoted
toward the hallway.

Ráfaga stood in the opening, a silvery sheen to his
ebony hair. Naked to the waist, his golden-brown torso
gleamed in the moonlight, dark trousers molding his
lean hips and thighs, while emphasizing the length of his
legs. Paralyzed, Sheila stared at his saturnine features.

An eyebrow lifted in query. *"Señora?"*

She stood there, staring, knowing he was asking why
she was unable to sleep. But, seeing him like that, half-
clothed, Sheila could only remember that minutes ago
he had lain naked with a woman, performing the most
intimate acts with her.

Frowning slightly, he tipped his head to the side,
watching her alertly. An overwhelming desire to escape
gripped Sheila. She wasn't certain what kind of threat
he was posing. She only knew she had to escape from
him, and she bolted for the door.

"Sheila!" His use of her name carried the command
to halt.

She ran faster, reaching the door and starting to
yank it open. His hand slammed it shut before he
seized her arm and spun her around.

"Let go of me!" She struggled desperately. "Pig!
Animal!"

She heard the demanding ring of his low voice and
paid it no heed. Kicking at his shins with her bare feet,
she twisted like a mad animal to break his hold. As if
sensing Sheila was teetering on the edge of hysteria, he
grabbed her shoulders and shook her hard until she
thought her head would snap off.

"Pig!" Sheila breathed brokenly when he stopped
shaking her. Blackness reeled in front of her eyes and
she had to cling to the hard flesh of his naked shoulders
to keep her balance. "You're a depraved monster! Was
Elena too easy a conquest? Have you decided to rape
me now?"

Her eyes blazed with the yellow fires he had described to Elena. His mouth tightened grimly, a muscle leaping convulsively in his jaw as the smouldering black coals in his eyes gazed down at her. Before she could draw another breath, her hands were twisted behind her back and she was crushed against his bronze chest.

The musky, male scent of him was heady and strong, drugging her senses with its potency. Driven by desperate fear, Sheila writhed futilely against him, her heart hammering in her throat.

The breadth of his shoulders seemed to dwarf, following her as she bent backward over his arms. His voice hissed an angry command in Spanish near her ear. Sheila twisted her head to avoid the sound, making the mistake of turning her face toward his.

The accidental touch of his male lips froze her into immobility. She couldn't move as she went cold all over, then fiery-hot. Time was suspended as their lips maintained the feather touch. Sheila waited in breathless fear for the bruising possession of his mouth.

Remembering Brad's brutal assault, Sheila closed her eyes. "Not again," she sobbed in a whispered plea for mercy.

The fragile link was broken. Ráfaga straightened up, lifting his head as Sheila blinked at his obsidian eyes. There was a faint flare of his nostrils, a suggestion of proud arrogance. His arm slid down the back of her bare legs to swing her off her feet and into his arms.

"No!" she gasped in protest and struggled wildly. Her efforts were easily blocked as he carried Sheila to her bedroom. Letting her feet slide to the floor, he turned her into his chest. Sheila used her arms to try to wedge a space between them and thwart his attempt to crush her again in his unyielding embrace. She realized too late that he had allowed her to succeed in pushing him away, as he pinioned her arms between them.

His hand half-encircled her throat, pushing her chin up. Sheila stiffened in shock as his mouth captured hers, closing over it warmly and firmly. Rigidly, she tried to recoil, but the pressure on her throat was increased to effectively check the attempt. He forced her to endure his kiss until he decided to end it.

When he did, he pushed her roughly away. Sheila staggered backward at the unexpected rejection, falling down hard on the cot. His stance indicated he could take her if he chose to, but he didn't want her, and her fears to the contrary were groundless. Without a word, he turned and walked out of the room.

Shivering at his coldness, Sheila lay down on the cot and curled herself into a tight ball. Her eyes burned, but no tears slipped from her lashes. Sleep was a long time coming.

For two long days, Sheila kept to herself, retreating to her room whenever Ráfaga was in the house. Her blood simmered near the boiling point each time she saw him, hating him with an intensity that left her shaken.

Yet Sheila was powerless, his prisoner, subject to his punishment should she provoke him. There was no one to intercede on her behalf. She was alone with only her own instincts of survival to guide her.

By the afternoon of the third day, the empty, dragging minutes and the rooms that seemed to grow increasingly smaller were tearing at Sheila's nerves. She felt she would go mad if she had to spend another hour inside the house.

Walking to the door with long, agitated strides, she pulled it open. Immediately the guard turned, the rifle in his hands held across his chest to bar the way. Sheila stopped, her head lifting like a doe scenting danger.

The guard smiled, chipped, yellowed teeth leering at her. It was Juan, the man who had murdered Brad and tried to rape her. Waves of revulsion washed over her as his gloating dark eyes traveled her length. He seemed to strip away her clothes while her flesh shuddered violently at the almost physical touch of his gaze.

"Baño, Señora?" he inquired with a lewd gleam in his eyes.

Sheila tried to swallow the lump in her throat and

shook her head. The negative movement swung the tawny mane of hair about her shoulders, the paler streaks catching the sunlight.

He shifted the rifle in his hands, pointing the barrel at Sheila. The muzzle prodded the knotted front of her blouse, nudging her backward into the house. She retreated a step and his gaze focused on the rise and fall of her breasts, straining in deep breaths against the silky material of her blouse. Panic rose, but she tried not to show her fear.

His attention was diverted by a sound behind him. He glanced over his shoulder, the leering grin leaving his expression. Sheila's vision was blocked by the door frame, preventing her from seeing what or who had caused his broad features to be covered by a dutifully bland mask.

The authoritative ring of a familiar Spanish voice provided the answer. Juan replied, his gaze returning to Sheila. The gleaming black light in his eyes seemed to promise that they would meet again—alone, without interruptions.

Sheila paled at the silent, ominous threat. Ráfaga came into view with Laredo at his side. Juan stepped away from the door, lowering the rifle muzzle to the ground. Briefly impaled by Ráfaga's gaze, Sheila turned stiffly into the house, her limbs shaking from the encounter with Brad's murderer.

"What were you doing?" Laredo queried.

What could she say? That she had wanted some fresh air, but the animal on guard had stopped her? Should she tell him that Juan had been about to force her into the house and attack her? They wouldn't believe her.

Juan was one of them. They would accept his word before hers. Sheila guessed that orders had been given that she wasn't to be touched, so Juan would never admit that he planned to harm her in any way, only prevent her from leaving the house.

"I'm going crazy locked up in this house!" Sheila screamed. "I wanted some fresh air, but the dog you have guarding the door wouldn't let me out!"

"It's better if you stay in," Laredo said.

"For how long?" Her voice cracked shrilly on a note of hysteria. "You can't expect me to stay inside this miserable hole forever! I'm nearly climbing the walls as it is now!"

Ráfaga made a comment in Spanish, drawing Laredo's look. Some silent message passed between them before Laredo glanced back to Sheila.

"I'll take you for a walk," he announced.

"Thanks," Sheila retorted with bitterness.

Stepping to the side, Laredo made no response to her sarcasm Juan's short, stocky hulk waited outside. He straightened from the porch post to bar her way again, but a quiet order from Laredo made him shift to the side.

Sheila lowered her head as she walked by, letting the length of her dark blonde hair swing forward to veil her face from his eyes. But she sensed him watching her, silently menacing.

Laredo's hand at her elbow directed her away from the scattered collection of adobe buildings and toward the tree-shaded side of the canyon floor. Again she was being isolated from the other inhabitants of the canyon.

Behind her, Sheila could hear children playing. Birds sang gaily in the trees and bushes while horses and a few cattle grazed contentedly in the sunlit meadow, tails swishing at the flies. It all seemed so incongruous, considering her plight.

Laredo had released her arm to let her walk freely. Sheila clasped her elbows in a nervous warming gesture. She stared straight ahead, her eyes wide, a glimmer of apprehension in their depths.

"Talk to me, Laredo," she said urgently. "Tell me who you are and how you came to be here. Tell me lies—I don't care. Just talk to me so I won't be able to think."

He paused, studying her silently, then resumed his strolling pace. "Where would you like me to start?" he asked.

"I don't care." Sheila shrugged indifferently and breathed in shakily. "How did you come to be here—to join up with this band of renegades, or whatever they are?"

"I was smuggling marijuana across the border. The man I was dealing with tried to change the terms, up the price on what I wanted. We fought. He pulled a knife and I took it away and killed him. Unfortunately, the Mexican police arrived before I could run." His voice was flat, without emotion. It was a bald statement of facts, nothing more.

"It sounds like self-defense," Sheila murmured to keep the conversation going, "or, at the most, involuntary manslaughter. What were you convicted of?"

"It never came to trial."

"What?"

His mouth crooked in a semblance of a smile. "The judicial system in Mexico is not the same as in the States. It's the old Napoleonic Code, under which you are guilty until you prove otherwise. You're jailed until you come to trial, which can be a long time. Keeps the criminals off the streets."

"That's why you're here, then, hiding in the mountains, because you're wanted by the police," Sheila concluded. She felt quite blasé about the fact he had killed someone, regardless of the circumstances. "How did you escape?"

He stopped to light a cigarette and offered one to Sheila. She accepted it, hoping the nicotine in the tobacco would soothe her raw nerves. He exhaled a thin trail of smoke and watched it curl and dissipate in the clear air.

"There was a raid, a well-organized assault on the jail where I was being held. It happened so fast that I wasn't even sure what was going on," he recalled absently. "Cell doors were being opened. Everybody was running in all directions, trying to escape. But I saw this one Mexican raider, icy cool and controlled. He had three other American prisoners with him and he looked like he was guiding them out of the confusion. I figured he knew what he was doing and where he was going—which was more than I did—so I tagged along."

"Ráfaga." Sheila said, identifying the leader.

"Yes." Laredo nodded and studied the tip of his cigarette. "Someone on the outside had hired him to bust the three American prisoners out of jail and get them back across the border to the States. I just hitched a ride that's all."

"But why didn't you go back to the States with the others?" she frowned. "Why did you stay here with him?"

"The others were just facing minor drug charges. Mine was murder," he reminded her. "I would have been extradited to Mexico to face trial. Besides, I killed a guard during the escape, so even if I could have gotten out of the other charge, they would have had me on the second one. The American government might have looked the other way if I had done something minor. but for the good of international relations, they would have had to search for a murderer. My family would have been notified. There would have been headlines in the local paper. Now they don't know where I am or what I've done or if I'm alive. It's better if I stay on this side of the border."

"But wasn't your family notified when you were arrested the first time?" Sheila questioned.

"I was jailed under a phony name with a phony passport." Laredo inhaled deeply on his cigarette and shook his head, blowing out a cloud of smoke. "The Mexican police found out who I really was, but the wrong name is still listed with the American consul. So my family doesn't know."

"How can you be sure?"

"There are ways," he answered, retreating to the mysterious phrase that implied connections.

Sheila started walking again, wandering aimlessly toward the grazing horses. "How long have you been with Ráfaga?"

"Nearly three years."

"He seems to spend a great deal of time with you, more than with the others," she commented idly.

"I suppose you could say I've become his left-hand man." Laredo smiled lazily.

"Left-hand?" She glanced at him curiously. "Who's his right-hand?"

"Nobody. He doesn't trust anybody to be on his right." Laredo paused to crush his cigarette butt beneath the heel of his boot.

A cold chill raced down Sheila's spine. She tossed her own half-smoked cigarette into the long grass beneath her feet.

"What's going to happen to me, Laredo?"

"I don't know what you mean."

She lifted her head to eye him warily. "Have my parents been contacted yet?"

A mask was drawn over the vaguely boyish features, making them hard and unrevealing. "I can't answer that, Mrs. Townsend," Laredo replied stiffly.

"For God's sake, call me Sheila!" she declared in agitation. "I don't want to be reminded of Brad!"

"I didn't intend to, Sheila." Laredo relaxed slightly.

"When the money is paid, will I be released?" she asked, quickly taking advantage of the hint of compassion in his tone.

"I don't know why you wouldn't be, if the money was paid." He shrugged and began walking.

It was hardly a satisfactory answer, and Sheila sighed dispiritedly. Far off in the distance there came a lonely wail. She stopped, listening intently to hear the sound again.

"What was that?" she murmured.

Laredo glanced to the south. "A train—the Chihuahua–Pacific railroad, which runs from the Mexican side of Presidio, Texas, through the Sierras and Copper Canyon to the Pacific coast. When the wind's right, you can hear its whistle echoing through the mountains."

"How far away is it?" An eager note crept into her voice.

"As the crow flies, I don't know, maybe not far, but

a hundred miles of rough terrain if you tried to get there on foot. You wouldn't make it, Sheila," he remarked dryly.

Her mouth tightened. She refused to acknowledge that it had crossed her mind to try to reach it should she be provided with the opportunity to escape. Laredo stopped.

"Let's try changing the subject," he suggested, striving to lighten the brooding atmosphere. "Tell me, are there any more at home like you?"

"I'm an only child," Sheila retorted, "which is good for you, since my parents would pay anything to have me back safe."

Laredo let her sarcasm sail over his head. "I have a younger brother. He's a natural athlete—basketball, track. His junior year in high school he made the All-American list as a quarterback. His coach thought a college scholarship was almost guaranteed when he graduated." Laredo became pensive. "I wonder if he got it."

"You miss your family, don't you?" Sheila commented softly, suddenly feeling an accord with him.

For a moment she felt him start to withdraw, preparing to deny her assertion. Then he smiled, a mischievous light dancing in his blue eyes.

"Do you know what I miss?" He seemed to laugh at himself silently. "A hot butterscotch sundae with mounds of whipped cream, nuts, and a cherry on top. I dream about it at night. Sometimes I get such a craving for it that I think I'll go out of my mind if I don't have one."

"That is a severe case of sweet tooth, I think." Sheila smiled.

"Yeah." Laredo nodded in agreement, his sparkling eyes holding her gaze. "It's gotten worse since you came here." As if he had suddenly realized what he had said, he turned away, letting a space widen between them. They were walking among the horses now and Laredo slid a hand over the rump of a chestnut. "So you are an only child?"

Sheila hesitated, then let him change the subject. "That's right. Spoiled and pampered, one of those rich little brats, as Brad used to say." His name slipped out before she could stop it.

"Meaning it affectionately, of course." Laredo smiled.

"No." She caught the gleam of her wedding ring in a downward glance. "Meaning it enviously, I think."

"Is that part of the reason why you aren't exactly grieving for him?" He studied her profile.

"Brad was really more interested in my money than he was in me. He enjoyed the sense of power it gave him," Sheila answered flatly.

"Why are you telling me that?"

When Sheila glanced up, he was watching her with a hint of skepticism in his look. A breeze teased her hair and she pushed it away from her face.

"I don't know. Maybe because you told me about your family. Or maybe because I had to admit it out loud and hear the words," she answered slowly. "Maybe I want you to be my friend."

"Why?" Laredo persisted.

"Because I remind you of hot butterscotch sundaes, I suppose." She tried to tease him out of his interrogative mood. "Does it matter why?"

"It could." He ran an eye over her. "You might want to twist me around your finger."

"Could I?" Sheila tipped her head to the side, deliberately provocative.

There was a mocking quirk to one brow before Laredo looked away. "You have the ammunition in all the right places."

Behind his dry tone, Sheila sensed his reluctant acknowledgment. She wasn't surprised that he found her attractive.

But it was something he only implied that interested Sheila. Although Laredo had tried to sever the ties with his family and his country, he hadn't succeeded in cutting all the threads. And Sheila represented a link to home, regardless of how much Laredo insisted that he belonged here.

How she could forge the link stronger and persuade him to transfer his loyalties from the band to her? Using sex was the likely answer, but she shied away from it violently.

Their strolling pace had carried them to the far edge of the meadow. A movement on Sheila's left caught her eye. A small boy was scurrying to his feet, a mop of black hair falling into his dark eyes. The rusty-brown poncho he wore seemed to drown him, as did the baggy tan trousers.

Hesitantly, he dipped his head in an uncertain greeting. *"Buenos tardes, señora, señor."*

"Buenos tardes." Sheila repeated the phrase with a faintly curious smile.

Laredo added his greeting to hers. "We have come far enough," he said, changing their direction to recross the meadow. "We'd better start back."

"Are there many children here? I've heard them playing outside." She gazed toward the scattered collection of adobe brick houses, seeing movement but unable to distinguish figures at this distance.

"A dozen or so, all tolled, I guess, counting the Indian children," Laredo shrugged.

"Indians?" Sheila frowned.

"There were a couple of families of Tarahumara Indians living here when we came," he explained. "They keep pretty much to themselves."

Sheila didn't ask for conversation as they retraced their path. He had told her as much as he was going to. She supposed she should congratulate herself for getting Laredo to open up as much as he had, although the information certainly didn't benefit her.

Chapter 9

A new guard was on duty when they reached the house. The broad, flat features were blandly carved. He tipped his head downward in a deferential nod of respect as Sheila walked by him. It was the first gesture of courtesy she had received since arriving at the canyon hideout.

The bemused light in her eyes drew a comment from Ráfaga when she entered the house. Immediately, she felt her fur ruffle and turned to Laredo.

"What did he say about me?" she demanded.

"He merely commented that you looked better for the walk," Laredo answered.

"You can tell him that all prisoners need a little exercise," Sheila retorted. "And you can also tell him that I'd like a bath this afternoon while the sun is still high enough to warm the pool. I'll get my soap and towel so you can take me. I'm sure he wouldn't trust me to go there by myself."

She stalked toward her room, the moment of good humor vanishing the instant she had come in contact again with Ráfaga. Slamming the dresser drawer, Sheila heard the low murmur of voices in the other room. The voices stopped their Spanish exchange when she returned.

"I'm ready," she announced.

"I have a couple things to do," Laredo replied, setting his Stetson atop his head. "Ráfaga will take you."

The fuse of her temper igniting, Sheila flashed, "Who doesn't he trust? You or me?"

"Maybe both." Laredo grinned. "He knows it's a hell of a long time since I've been with a blonde."

"Isn't it enough that I have to suffer the indignity of not being allowed to bathe in private? Can't I be permitted to choose who has to watch me?" she fumed.

Laredo glanced at Ráfaga's expressionless face and shrugged to Sheila. "Orders." The one word was his only explanation.

The knuckles on the hand clutching the towel stood out clearly as Laredo gave her a brief and mocking nod before he walked out the door. Sheila glared at the bronze mask concealing Ráfaga's thoughts, tremors of primitive rage quaking through her.

"Well, peeping Tom, are you ready?" she challenged sarcastically.

Compressing her lips in a tight line, Sheila turned and walked through the door left open by Laredo. Ráfaga followed two paces behind, letting her retrace the path to the spring-fed pool without his assistance.

At the pool, he moved to the same tree that had supported him before and leaned a shoulder against it. Her breathing was labored, constricted by her temper. She had no desire to put on wet clothes again when she finished bathing. Turning her back to him, Sheila began tearing at the knotted front of her blouse.

"Do you have some perverted kind of libido that gets turned on watching a woman undress and bathe?" she demanded huskily in frustration. "Or do you just get a kick out of humiliating me?"

She pulled the blouse off and tossed it to the ground. Her creamy-white shoulder blades felt the touch of his gaze as it traveled down her tapering back to her slender waist. Her finger trembled with the zipper of her slacks.

"You are a sadistic monster to put me through this." Her voice quivered. "You should be quartered and hung out for the buzzards to eat. I wish you could understand what I'm saying so you'd know what an inhuman savage I think you are . . . obnoxious and vulgar and loathsome and—" Sheila ran out of words to describe her hatred.

The zipper freed, her slacks slid down around her ankles. She stepped out of them, her nakedness staining her cheeks crimson-red. A second later, Sheila dived shallowly into the pool. She surfaced almost immediately, the icy temperature of the water stealing her breath.

Pushing the wet strands of hair from her eyes, Sheila glanced back to the tree. Ráfaga was sitting at the base of it, his stained brown hat pulled low over his eyes. Sheila could feel his disturbingly intent look as she moved to the bank and the bar of soap in the grasses at the water's edge.

When her bath was finished, she walked boldly out of the water, not attempting to cover herself with her hands. Picking up the towel, she quickly began rubbing herself dry, feeling the warmth of embarrassment and refusing to give in to it.

"Take a good look." She had a strong urge to throw the towel in his face. "Maybe it will help stimulate you for your nightly visit from Elena."

At the sound of his mistress's name, Ráfaga rolled to his feet, amusement glittering in his eyes, but he didn't approach her. Fighting a sudden attack of nervousness, Sheila stepped into her slacks, half-turning away from him.

The silky material of her blouse clung to her damp skin. As he moved toward her, Sheila's poise was shaken. Her fingers began struggling to draw the material into a knot.

Before she could succeed, he was calmly pushing her hands aside and pulling the front together with his steady fingers. As he tied the knot, his knuckles brushed the swelling curves of her breasts. Sheila flinched at his touch. The grooves on either side of his mouth deepened in mockery.

"Can I help it," Sheila murmured tightly, her air of bravado overshadowed by his closeness, "if your touch makes me feel I should wash again?"

Her flesh was tingling from the contact. Indifferent to her acid tone, Ráfaga studied the yellow tongues of flame lighting her eyes. They stood silently, the air crackling between them, with Sheila almost daring him to touch her again.

She longed to push him into the icy pool. He seemed to read her thoughts, because his dark gaze darted to the glass-smooth surface of the pool, then back to her face, amusement glinting again in the ebony-black depths of his eyes.

Irritation seethed near the surface as they started back to the solitary adobe house set apart from the others. Sheila led the way, aware of Ráfaga directly behind, despite the animal silence of his footsteps. Sheila controlled her temper. She knew he was dangerous.

The afternoon walks with Laredo became a daily routine. She looked forward to them as eagerly as a child looks forward to a candy treat. They offered a break from the suffocating boredom of the house and the disturbing presence of Ráfaga.

Never in her life had Sheila been so idle. There had always been something to do to fill the minutes. Here, there was nothing to do but wander through the house when she was alone and wait for the afternoon walks with Laredo. After a week, the monotonously empty existence had stretched her nerves thin.

At the end of a walk, Laredo commented, "You look exhausted, Sheila. Haven't you been sleeping well at night?"

"Not particularly." A fine tension honed her answer.

The blame rested with Ráfaga. Elena's visits to his bed weren't necessarily nightly, but it was almost worse for Sheila to listen to his steady breathing through the thin wall of her bedroom.

"Why don't you lie down and take a nap?" Laredo suggested "You look as though you could use one."

"I don't need a nap!" Sheila stalked through the door he held open for her.

The air around her seemed to vibrate like a tuning fork. Her agitation increased at the sight of Ráfaga sitting at the table cleaning his rifle.

"What I need is to get out of here! How much longer is it going to be before you hear from my parents? Or have you already?" Sheila demanded, turning to Laredo.

"I can't answer that."

"You can't answer that." Her hands rested on her hips as she mocked him. "You can't answer anything unless *he* pulls your string. Why don't you ask his permission to find me a new set of thumbs to twiddle? I'm getting tired of the old ones."

"You're bored, is that it?"

"Bored? My God, is that the understatement of the year." Sheila breathed disgustedly and pivoted away, encountering the aloof appraisal of Ráfaga's dark gaze.

"The walks—" Laredo began.

"—occupy maybe two hours of the day," Sheila interrupted. "What am I supposed to do with the other twenty-two? Sleep them away?"

There was a grim look about his mouth as Laredo breathed in deeply and glanced at Ráfaga, as if asking for his advice. Sheila listened impatiently to the exchange in Spanish.

"What proposal has Solomon of the thieves and murderers made?" Sheila demanded.

A half-smile touched Laredo's mouth, as if he found her kitten claws amusing. "He agreed that you have too much time on your hands. Since you have to stay in the house, he's decided you should take care of the cleaning and help Elena with the cooking."

"*He's* decided!" Sheila choked indignantly. "It's not

enough that I'm a prisoner here; now he expects me to be his maid, too!"

"You have to admit it will pass the time." Laredo's mouth twitched with amusement. "And you do live here, too. You should contribute something to the housekeeping chores."

"I should, should I?" she challenged angrily. "If this place was spotless, it would still be a dumpy hole. And as for cooking, I don't know how, at least not in these primitive conditions! Besides, any food I set in front of him would be spiced with poison!"

"He'll take his chances." Laredo dismissed her threat with a shrug.

"Elena won't like having me in the kitchen," she flashed.

"He's made his decision. You'll help," he concluded.

When Elena learned of Sheila's change of status, her Latin temper exploded with spontaneous combustion. Ráfaga refused to listen to her stormy protests and silenced her with a threateningly low comment.

The fragile truce that had existed between the two women was destroyed. Again there was the hatred born of jealousy in the brunette's eyes as she put Sheila to work doing menial tasks, berating her in Spanish when she didn't understand.

During the preparation of the evening meal, the two men took ringside seats at the kitchen table. Laredo watched with undisguised amusement while Ráfaga merely observed with disinterest.

Simmering at the abusive tone constantly snipping at her, Sheila slammed the plates on the table, glaring at Laredo when he chuckled softly. "So help me," she muttered tightly, "if that bitch doesn't stop yelling at me, I'm going to ram a tamale down her throat! You better tell your boss to do something about shutting her up before I do it for him!"

"Temper, temper," Laredo mocked quietly.

"In about two minutes, you're going to find my temper, because I'm going to lose it!" Sheila retorted.

A torrent of more unintelligible orders rushed from

Elena. Sheila pivoted, her hands clenching into tight fists at her side. A sharp word from Ráfaga closed Elena's mouth with a snap. Resentment snapped in her malevolently dark eyes as she thrust a plate of boiled meat and a knife into Sheila's stomach.

Setting them on the table, Sheila gripped the knife handle. "I can't make up my mind who to use this on," she murmured.

"I don't think Elena knows you aren't to be trusted with a knife." Laredo commented with a crooked smile.

Sheila returned the smile with false sweetness. "On second thought, I know *exactly* who to use it on—your implacable boss. I would like to carve out his heart and have it here on this plate instead of the meat." The gleaming blade hovered about the stringy-looking meat. "Then I could cut it in thin pieces, or maybe it would be so hard I would have to chop it up in large chunks."

"You are bloodthirsty." Laredo laughed as Sheila laid the knife blade on the meat to cut it thin, then moved it to slice a larger chunk.

Bronzed fingers closed over her hand. Sheila tensed as Ráfaga shifted her hands so the blade rested on the thinner cut. She realized he had merely been directing her on how to cut the meat.

"*Gracias.*" She gave him a saccharine smile. "I would rather cut your heart in thin slices. It would take longer." Starting to slice the meat, she glanced at Laredo. "Why didn't you translate what I really said?"

"And spoil your fun?" He laughed silently.

"I'm sure he alreadys knows that I think he's a ruthless, contemptible bastard," Sheila retorted evenly.

"Careful," Laredo warned.

"Why?" she countered. "He doesn't understand a word I say. I can call him anything I like."

"But that particular word doesn't sound so very different from the one in his own language." The smile that curved his mouth had lost much of its amusement.

"Really . . . ?" Sheila widened her eyes in false amazement and innocence. She turned her gaze to Ráfaga, veiling the dislike glittering in her eyes with a demure sweep of her lashes. "I didn't mean to call him a bastard, then. I'm sure it would be more accurate to refer to him as a son-of-a-bitch."

It became an amusing game to insult him while concealing it behind a facade of polite comments. There was never a flicker of interest in his inscrutable features, and Laredo didn't volunteer a translation.

Chapter 10

The newness soon wore off the game. By the third night, Sheila's sweetly coated insults no longer brought her a sense of elation. Instead, they left a bitter aftertaste because of their impotence. It had been a childish display of rebellion, Sheila realized, understood only by Laredo.

It hadn't changed anything. She was still a prisoner, never left unguarded for a minute. Elena was still insanely jealous of her. Her revolt had only been a verbal one, since she was helping in the kitchen and doing odd things around the small house. The alternative was idle hours, and Sheila had had all she could stand of those.

Outside her window, drizzle alternated with a sheeting downpour, trapping Sheila inside the house. Yellow tongues of lightning scorched the mountain peaks, licking across the sky, electric and blinding. Ominous dark clouds blackened the sky, adding to the dreary gloom of the stark interior of her bedroom.

In the midst of a cloudburst, Sheila heard the clumping hooves of a horse plodding over the water-soaked earth, approaching the adobe building. The sound stopped outside and someone pounded on the door. She couldn't help wondering who would be venturing out in this weather.

Her curiosity was heightened when she heard Ráfaga give an order to the guard on duty. The man abandoned the shelter of the porch roof to slosh through the rain toward the distant collection of adobe buildings.

For several minutes there was only the low murmur of voices in the main room, where Ráfaga and the rider were. Sheila lifted aside the curtain to stare at the sheeting rain. No one was guarding the door. Everyone was inside, sheltered from the storm.

Only a fool would be wandering about in weather like this, Sheila thought—a fool or someone wanting to escape under the cover of the rain. Quickly she levered herself onto the windowsill and swung her legs around to slide to the ground.

Her feet splashed in a puddle of water and her hand sought the solid wall of the house to regain her balance in the slippery footing. Lightning split open the sky as Sheila hurried toward the concealing trees behind the house.

Before she could reach them, she was drenched to the skin. The driving rain plastered her hair to her head, and water ran into her eyes to blur her vision. Each breath she drew was laden with moisture.

The thick branches of the trees abated some of the rain's force, the stinging spray no longer pelting her cheeks. Sheila paused once, blinking through the water clinging to her lashes, to glance back at the house.

Two men were hurrying toward it, heads bent against the driving rain. For a paralyzed instant she thought they might have seen her and ducked behind a rain-darkened tree trunk. But neither looked in her direction as they dashed for the shelter of the porch. The taller figure, in a yellow slicker, Sheila recognized as Laredo. The other man had to be the guard, evidently sent by Ráfaga to fetch Laredo.

At any moment someone could discover she was gone. Sheila began running, keeping to the concealing cover of the trees. Out of sight of the house, she felt more secure and slackened her pace.

Lightning crackled, searing the air, followed immediately by a resounding clap of thunder. The ground beneath her feet seemed to tremble from the sound. Sheila was tempted to leave the shelter of the trees and take the shorter route across the meadow to the canyon pass. A whole new torrent was released and she changed her mind.

Bending her head against the slanting sheets of rain, she hurried onward. The sound of her squishing footsteps was muffled by the steady downfall of rain beating through the leaves of the trees.

"Sheila."

Nearly deafened by the downpour, she wasn't certain she had actually heard someone call her name. She stopped, a hand shielding her eyes. A horse snorted on her left.

Sheila's heart pounded in alarm as she pivoted toward the sound. Laredo was calmly walking his horse through the trees, the brim of his hat pulled low on his forehead. Water ran from the pointed crease in front like an eavespout.

Her hearing was suddenly acute, catching other sounds. Sheila's gaze darted to the thinning trees on Laredo's left. Three other riders were spread out in a search line. One of the riders was Ráfaga. Sheila knew it even before his forbidding features could be seen beneath the shadow of his hat brim.

The horses stopped, forming a half-circle around her. Running was futile, so Sheila stood her ground. Tipping her head to a proud angle, she refused to let them see how bitterly her failure to escape tasted. Rain streamed over her face.

"What are you doing out here?" Laredo knew the answer to his question. It was in the cool mockery of his blue gaze.

Sheila gave him the answer such a question deserved.

"I wanted to go for a walk, so I did. Unfortunately, I didn't realize it was raining so hard."

"Isn't that odd?" Laredo shifted in his saddle, leaning slightly forward over the horn. "When I saw you running from the house into the trees, my first thought was that you were trying to escape."

He had seen her and rushed to alert Ráfaga. "That was silly of you," she commented tightly.

"It just goes to show you how easy it is to get the wrong impression about something like that." He smiled mockingly.

"Yes, it is," Sheila agreed, seething with anger but fighting to keep it in check.

Lightning crashed, a blinding fork of electric flame. Laredo glanced around as if suddenly becoming conscious of the deluge pouring down from the sky.

"Either way"—he nudged his horse to Sheila's side— "I guess it's lucky I happened to see you. You might have caught pneumonia if you had walked too far." A yellow-slickered arm reached out to help her into the saddle. "We would have been here sooner, but it took a little time to saddle the horses. We weren't sure how far we might have to go before we caught up with you. Unlike you, none of us was looking forward to a long walk in the rain."

His needling jibe drew a flashing look of resentment from Sheila. He had kicked a foot free of the stirrup nearest her. She stepped into it and let Laredo pull her aboard.

Sheila was soaked to the bone and shivering when Laredo set her down in front of the adobe house. She hurried inside, not waiting to be ordered or led. Laredo, Ráfaga, and the third rider quickly followed, and the guard could be heard leading the horses away.

"You'd better change into some dry clothes right away," Laredo advised.

Sheila was halfway to the hall. She stopped, turning, her teeth chattering uncontrollably as she hugged her arms around her. "In case you've forgotten, my wardrobe is very limited. It consists of what I'm wearing and

a shirt. I washed that this morning. I don't have any
dry clothes to put on."

Most of her sarcasm was negated by the chill that
shook her voice.

Turning on her heel, she again started for her bedroom, stiff and angry and sorry for herself. She heard
Laredo say something to Ráfaga in his fluent Spanish
and receive a reply.

As she entered her room, there were footsteps in the
hall, the familiar ones she heard every night. Tensing,
Sheila turned to face Ráfaga when he entered her room.

The heavy poncho that had protected him from the
rain was gone. His shirt, opened at the throat, was dry,
although it damply clung to his leanly muscled chest
and shoulders. His trousers were darkly wet from the
knees to his boots. The look in his eyes was as harsh as
a frigid winter night.

Water dripped from Sheila's saturated clothes, forming a small puddle on the floor. More dripped from the
matted wetness of her hair, running in glistening trails
down her face and neck. The sodden material of her
blouse almost lewdly molded every curve of her breasts,
including the nipples, hardened by the chilling wetness.
His raking gaze missed nothing.

"What do you want?" Sheila realized her nervous
challenge was as puny as the belligerent hissing of a
half-drowned kitten.

He clipped out an answer and gestured in a dismiss-
ing fashion at her clothes. The implication was obvious
that he wanted her to take them off.

Sheila bridled. "Just because I'm forced to bathe in
front of you doesn't mean I'm going to undress whenever you want so you can watch!"

The hard lines of his mouth thinned forbiddingly.
Lithe strides carried him to her before Sheila's numbed
body could react. His lean fingers started tugging at
the knot of her blouse, where tiny rivers of water joined
to run down the valley between her breasts. She knocked
his hands away.

"I'll do it!" she muttered through clenched teeth.

With an aloof nod, Ráfaga walked to the dresser and removed the towel from its peg near the washbasin. Walking back, he waited until Sheila's slacks had joined her blouse on the floor. She was painfully conscious of her nakedness as she reached for the towel he held, but his disinterested gaze didn't look beyond the whiteness of her moist face.

While her shaking hands began drying her skin, he walked to the bed and pulled off the blanket. The towel had barely absorbed the excess moisture when he began wrapping the blanket around her middle, drawing it tightly across her breasts. He tossed the trailing width over her left shoulder in a makeshift sari.

His gaze lifted to her hair, reminding her of its dripping wetness. Slightly dazed by his ingenuity, Sheila raised the towel to the saturated strands. Snugly tucked, the blanket didn't slip at all when she moved. She felt warmly wrapped, as if in a rough cocoon.

Sheila began briskly rubbing the towel over her hair as Ráfaga left the room. There were footsteps again in the hall. This time they weren't Ráfaga's. Sheila didn't lower the towel from her head as Laredo appeared in the doorway.

"Hasn't the guard come back from putting the horses away? I suppose Ráfaga is afraid I'll slip out the window again if I'm left alone for a minute," she declared tightly.

"He wants you to come into the other room," was the level answer.

"Where he can keep an eye on me." Her sarcasm was poisonously dry.

"No, where you can get warm. There's a fire in the fireplace," Laredo explained patiently.

"It's unbelievable how thoughtful he is," Sheila flashed. "I'm sure it's an order and that I have no real choice in the matter."

"None," he agreed.

A hissing sigh slipped through her white teeth. "I expected as much. Let me get my comb."

"Sheila?" The half-question, half-command in his voice caused Sheila to pause beside the dresser.

"What is it now?" she murmured with disguised irritation.

"Don't try it again," Laredo said.

"Try what?" Sheila asked, being deliberately obtuse.

"Running away—as if you didn't know," he elaborated.

"Oh? And why shouldn't I?" She picked up her comb, asking the question with seeming idleness.

"Because you were lucky today."

"Lucky?" A cold laugh came from her throat. "How was I lucky?"

"You didn't make it out of the canyon. It wouldn't have been very pleasant if you had," he said soberly.

"Why?" she challenged. "Because I might have gotten lost in the storm? Or maybe I would have been eaten by wild animals? Forgive me if I find your pretended concern for my welfare just a little bit sickening."

Laredo ignored her jeering questions. "Nobody leaves the canyon without Ráfaga's permission, Sheila—nobody," he emphasized.

"That sounds like a threat." She tilted her head to a defiant angle.

"Call it a threat, a warning, whatever you like," he replied evenly. "It's a rule for the safety of all of us in the camp. This place wouldn't be a secret if everybody was coming and going at will. Someone outside could discover its existence. So, nobody leaves here without Ráfaga's permission—and, most of all, you."

Her hand tightened around the comb, its teeth biting into her fingers. She understood the logic behind Laredo's explanation, but as far as she was concerned, she wasn't obliged to obey the rules.

"He rules with an iron hand, doesn't he?"

"If he didn't the canyon would have been discovered before this."

"More's the pity that it hasn't been." Sheila breathed thinly. "None of you would be here, and neither would I."

"I know the circumstances aren't the same for you," he said. "But understand that it's different for the rest of us. We prize our freedom as highly as you do. Here, we're safe and free. Ráfaga does everything he can to keep it that way."

"I'm sure he does," she snapped.

Laredo sighed, "You won't understand."

"I understand." Her eyes flashed her angry frustration. "I understand I'm a prisoner here . . . that I'm not allowed a moment of privacy . . . that you're all a band of murderers and thieves and you don't deserve to be free."

His mouth tightened into a grim line. "Come on, let's go in by the fire."

For a moment, Sheila remained stubbornly where she was. With a faintly regal tilt of her head, she finally swept past Laredo into the hall.

Chapter 11

A fire crackled cheerfully in the fireplace, competing with the pelting raindrops on the roof. Ráfaga was seated at the table with the third man, the stranger whose arrival had precipitated Sheila's escape attempt. Both glanced up as she entered the room and followed her with their eyes as she walked to the hearth.

She knelt in front of the fire, the slit of the blanket revealing a shapely calf and a hint of a bare thigh. The constricting wrap of the blanket forced Sheila to curl her legs to the side to sit on the warmed stone floor in front of the fire.

Laredo moved to the table, taking a chair nearest the fireplace. The silence that had greeted Sheila's entrance was broken when he sat down. Sheila wondered why they kept their voices down. She couldn't understand a word they said, anyway.

Briskly, she began rubbing the towel through her hair, scattering droplets of water. The ones hitting the hot stones inside the fireplace sizzled into nothingness.

When her hair was damp-dry, Sheila began running a comb through the sleek, honey-dark strands.

The stranger seemed to be imparting some kind of information to them. The responses from Laredo and Ráfaga seemed to be yes's or no's or questions.

She wondered at the subject. Undoubtedly, it was important for the man to arrive in the middle of a thunderstorm and for Ráfaga to dispatch the guard for Laredo upon the stranger's arrival.

She turned from the fire to let its radiating heat finish drying the thick mane of hair in back. The comb continued its rhythmic separation of the strands, aiding the drying action. Her hair was molten gold against the backdrop of the flickering flames.

Some magnetic force compelled her to look at Ráfaga. His brooding gaze seemed to be staring past her and into the fire, mesmerized by the dancing flames. Then Sheila realized he was watching the play of the firelight on the creamy bareness of her right shoulder and her collarbone.

With disturbing intentness, his gaze slowly traveled up the slender curve of her neck. The fathomless blackness of his eyes studied the gracefully feminine line of her cheeks and jaw, the classic straightness of her nose, before moving on to the luxurious length of her gold-tipped lashes. Retracing his route, his gaze made a detour, coming to a full stop at her lips.

The almost physical possession of his gaze sent her pulse pounding with a trip-hammer beat. Unexpectedly, his shuttered, yet compelling, eyes shifted their attention to capture her look. Sheila had the craziest, overwhelming sensation that some force was pressing her backward, laying her down beside the fire to be seduced, willingly.

Shaken by the vividness of the impression, Sheila heard him respond to a comment from Laredo, yet his concentration didn't seem to waver from her. With effort, she broke away from his magnetic look, her breathing shallow and uneven.

Laredo rose from his chair and walked to the fireplace. Swiftly she averted her head to the flames, hoping that if he noticed her flushed skin, he would attribute it to the heat of the fire.

Squatting, he added another log and stirred the red-hot lumps of burning wood. Balanced on the balls of his feet, he slid her a sideways look, calm and questioning.

"Have you dried out yet?" he asked.

"Yes." She nodded stiffly and stole a wary glance at the table. She suddenly had the feeling they were talking about her, perhaps all along. "Laredo?"

His hands were on his knees, ready to push himself up, but he waited, cocking his head to the side. "Yes?"

Her gaze flickered to the man at the table. "Who is he?"

"A friend," he answered noncommittally.

Sheila looked again at the Mexican. "Is he one of your connections?"

"He's a friend," was all Laredo would admit.

Sheila turned to study him. "He's here about me, isn't he?"

"What makes you say that?" he asked.

"It's a feeling I have. Is he?"

"Sheila"—there was patience in his tone, calm and controlled—"you are asking questions that you know I can't answer."

"Why not? It concerns me; therefore, it's my business, too," she reasoned stubbornly. But Laredo shrugged and said nothing. "Surely you have contacted my father by now. Is that why this man is here? To tell you what he said?"

Laredo breathed in deeply, a brief glitter of impatience in the look he gave her. "Don't push it, Sheila." He sounded very calm. "When there is anything definite, you will be informed." With that, he pushed himself to his feet to end the conversation.

"Tell your boss that I would prefer to go to my room now," she requested, fighting the trapped, helpless sensation.

His blue gaze bounced to Ráfaga and ricocheted

back to Sheila. "The rest of the house is too chilly and damp. Stay here by the fire, where you'll be warm and dry."

"What would happen if I went, anyway?" she challenged.

"You'd be brought back," Laredo stated and turned away.

Frustrated, she began combing her hair again, listening to the crackle of electricity that matched her own nervous tension. Again Sheila felt the disturbing absorption of Ráfaga's gaze, but she didn't let it capture her.

Short minutes later, the stranger rose from the table. Ráfaga walked the man to the door, giving an order to the guard. The man left his post to accompany the stranger into the rain. With the guard gone, Sheila knew she wouldn't be allowed to go to her room until he returned.

The departure of the stranger signaled the beginning of another discussion between Laredo and Ráfaga. Certain that it had something to do with her, Sheila listened, catching a note of dissension in Laredo's tone. He was obviously disagreeing with some decision that had been made.

When Elena arrived to cook the evening meal, Sheila didn't get up to help. No one objected, certainly not Elena. However, the brunette's appearance halted the discussion between Laredo and Ráfaga. Judging by Laredo's disgruntled expression, Sheila guessed that he hadn't succeeded in changing Ráfaga's mind.

Nibbling at a corner of her lip, she wondered if her father had offered less money than had been demanded for her release. Perhaps Laredo was willing to settle for less. Or maybe it was the other way around.

All through dinner Sheila considered the possibilities. If her absorption was noticed, it drew no comment. No one at the table appeared to be in a very talkative mood, although Sheila noticed Elena was making subtle attempts to make up to Ráfaga.

When the meal was finished, Elena brought coffee

to the table. Sheila saw the way the brunette leaned across Ráfaga, deliberately brushing her breasts against his shoulder and arm. A shudder of disgust ran through her at the blatantly suggestive action.

Immediately she felt Ráfaga's gaze. It sliced over her, sharp, yet strangely aloof. Sheila stared at the darkly mirrored surface of her coffee, as black and inscrutable as his eyes.

Ráfaga looked away and said something to Elena. Whatever it was ignited her temper. A vituperative stream of Spanish was directed at him. The brunette's hands gestured contemptuously at Sheila. Somehow, again, she was the subject of their quarrel.

After two calming replies that had no effect, Ráfaga snapped out an order. Flashing him a poisonous look, Elena turned on her heel and stormed out the door.

Sipping at her coffee, Sheila stared at the dirty dishes on the table. With a sigh of resignation, she stacked and carried them to the basin, leaving the men to finish their coffee at the table.

Sheila had barely begun washing up when the door burst open and Elena swept in, her dark hair covered by a shawl. She hurled the bundle in her hands at Ráfaga and walked out. Sheila glanced at the brightly colored cloth bundle. His dirty laundry? she wondered, and a wry smile teased the corners of her mouth.

The door had slammed shut as Ráfaga straightened up from the table and began walking toward Sheila, carrying the clothes. She stiffened irately. If he thought she was going to do his washing, he was in for a surprise.

Before he handed her the bundle, he shook it out. Sheila stared at the embroidered front of a blouse and the crimson fullness of a skirt. There were obvious signs of wear, the material thinning at the creases of the hems. They were castoffs of Elena's, grudgingly and angrily given.

Sheila didn't care. The prospect of wearing clothes that hadn't had their buttons ripped off or ended suggestively at mid-thigh was altogether too appealing to refuse because of pride.

The coarse blanket of her makeshift sari suddenly began to scratch her naked skin. She took the clothes eagerly from his hand and hurried to her bedroom, forgetting all about the dishes in her haste to change.

The blouse was a little tight around the shoulders and the skirt was short. It didn't matter. As far as she was concerned, they were a perfect fit.

Her attitude changed with the donning of the clothes. Sheila felt suddenly, if temporarily, buoyant and care-free. Gliding back to the main room, she was unconsciously motivated by a desire to show off her new clothes. They gave her a confidence she hadn't been aware was lacking.

Ráfaga was the first to look up when she reentered the room. His inspecting gaze traveled over her from head to toe in a clinical appraisal that was hardly the reaction her ego wanted. Sheila found Laredo halfway to the door with his rain slicker on.

"You can't go, Laredo," she protested and hurried to him.

He smiled at her indulgently. "It's getting late."

"Stay a while," Sheila coaxed.

She was unaware of the alluring picture she made. Her face was aglow with enthusiasm, a natural smile parting her lips, her eyes sparkling with pleasure. Her hair glistened antique-gold in the firelight. The creamy whiteness of her skin contrasted perfectly with the crimson skirt flaring about her legs.

"I . . ." Laredo hesitated, his blue eyes running over her with obvious approval and a glint of something more.

"Come on." With carefree abandon, she took hold of his arm with both hands. "I have a whole new outfit and I want to celebrate the occasion before the newness of my secondhand clothes wears off."

"All right." Laredo grinned and shrugged out of his slicker.

Sheila took it and hung it back on the hook near

the door. As she turned back, the skirt swirled about her legs. Framed by the firelight, her hands were on the snug waistband, her stance faintly provocative.

"You haven't said how I look," Sheila reminded him. "I admit it isn't exactly chic, but—" She let it trail off, smiling up at him warmly, in the midst of a friendly and playful mood.

"It's more than you usually wear," he commented with mock sadness, "but it's a definite improvement on the slacks."

"Chauvinist!" She laughed.

His eyes darkened to an intense shade of blue. "You are stunningly beautiful, Shcila," Laredo said quietly.

She hadn't set out to deliberately charm him, but she readily basked in the ardent admiration of his look.

"I certainly feel more comfortable." She smoothed a hand over her skirt, absently studying the contrast of her fair skin against the vivid red material.

"Tell me"—Laredo reclaimed her attention—"what kind of celebration are you planning for your new clothes?" Gentle mockery veiled the dark blue fire of his eyes.

"I feel like dancing," she declared.

"Sorry." A smile of mock regret briefly curved his mouth. "I'm afraid the musicians have the night off."

The scrape of a chair leg jerked Sheila's head toward the sound, suddenly reminded they had an audience. Ráfaga's features were drawn in a harshly cold mask, dark and dangerous and decidedly Spanish.

Sheila did not need to be told that the blood of cruelty ran in his veins. It was in the ruthlessly molded line of his jaw and mouth, faintly arrogant and savagely noble. He was walking toward a rain-darkened window and Sheila followed him with her eyes.

The unwelcome reminder of his presence chilled some of her pleasure in the moment. She glanced back at Laredo. Determination shimmered in her eyes.

"We can dance whether we have music or not," Sheila declared.

"You'll remember." Placing her left hand on his

head in disagreement, the firelight glistening over his brown hair.

"You'll remember." Placing her left hand on his shoulder, she forced him to take hold of her right hand and began humming a ballad.

Hesitating for a fraction of a second, Laredo smiled a crooked smile of amused indulgence and rested a hand on the curve of her waist. His initial, leading steps were awkward and out of tempo, but Sheila persisted until he found his coordination.

"See!" She smiled at him, pausing in her humming of the familiar tune. "You haven't forgotten."

"I guess not. At least you still have all your toes." He grinned. "You were taking quite a chance, dancing with me barefoot. I could have stomped all over them."

"I wasn't a bit worried," Sheila assured him.

They circled the small open area of the main room. The swirl of her skirt flamed scarlet in the firelight. The flickering light lent a magic atmosphere to the room, blocking out reality. Laredo whirled Sheila around in a tight spin, his hand shifting to the small of her back as she laughed and clutched him for support. He slowed his steps, smiling down at her.

"And you were trying to convince me you had forgotten how to dance," she teased.

"I guess I was wrong." He shrugged briefly.

"I guess you were."

"It's crazy, but do you know what this reminds me of?" Laredo held her in his arms, his steps slowing to an absent swaying.

The arm around her waist tightened and Sheila let herself be drawn against him, contentedly nestling her head against his shoulder. His strength was comforting.

"No. What?" she questioned, smiling against his shirt.

"The dances—the proms I used to go to." His hand absently caressed her back. "Holding you like this, it doesn't seem so long ago."

Sheila tipped her head back to see his face, handsome with an engaging boyish charm. She saw his downward gaze slide to her lips. She only had to make the slightest move to invite his kiss. But that wasn't what she wanted.

His reference to home and the way things were swept away the few moments of enchantment. Suddenly the new clothes didn't matter to her at all. She wanted only to get away, to go back to her home, and to safety. Perhaps Laredo might provide the way and means, after all.

"When is my father going to pay the money for my release?" she asked.

Laredo stiffened. "I don't know."

"Who's going to get it?" She tried to make the question sound casual and unimportant. "It will probably be split, I suppose, with each of you getting a share."

"I imagine so." A mask stole over his face, but Sheila knew it was fragile and could be broken.

"That's too bad. For one man, it would be a lot of money."

"Yes," Laredo agreed curtly.

"You know you could have it all, don't you?" murmured Sheila.

His muscles contracted, rejected what she was saying. He would have withdrawn, put some distance between them, but Sheila remained pressed against his length.

"Sheila—" he started to protest, but she interrupted.

"No, listen," she insisted. "You could have it all, every penny. You could take me home. The money would be waiting. My father would see to that."

"It's no good." Laredo shook his head firmly.

"Yes, it is. We both would be home, where we want to be. We could go out for a walk here one afternoon and never come back." She hurried to convince him of the feasibility of her plan. "You could have a couple of horses waiting for us and we could ride off and be miles away before anyone knew we were gone."

"I can't go back. I explained all that."

"But you can this way. Don't you see?" Sheila argued persuasively. "You'd be a hero. You would have rescued me. Your family and friends would be proud of you and my father would be grateful. He knows a lot of influential people. He'd find some way to make sure you'd never have to come back here."

"I—" He was frowning, his resistance appearing to weaken.

Sheila touched her fingers to his lips, silencing his protest. Then she let her hand slide along his strong cheek to the silky brown hair near his temple. She ran her fingers through it lightly in an obvious caress. The arm around her waist tightened automatically, drawing her upturned face closer to his.

"You'd have a small fortune for bringing me back— plus my father's gratitude and help." She let her voice grow husky and soft. "And mine, too, Laredo. I know you find me attractive. And I wouldn't mind spending the rest of my life repaying you for taking me away from here. Money, respectability, and me," she promised, "all three, if you want them. All you have to do is take me away, take me home."

"No!!" Ráfaga's voice, low and ominous, like rolling thunder, ripped them apart. He was facing them, cold fury darkening his eyes. "You will not seduce him to do your bidding with words, *señora,* nor with deeds. Laredo knows the punishment for leaving here without my permission. And he knows that if he takes you with him, I will find him and kill him. When a man has to choose between money, a woman, or his life, he will choose his life. Laredo will take you nowhere until I say you may leave!"

The color drained from her face. Sheila stared at him, her mouth opened with shock—not because of what he said, but because of the fact that she had understood every word of it. He had spoken in flawless English.

"What . . . how?" In her confusion, she couldn't even word the questions. "You speak English," she managed to say lamely.

"Yes, I speak English," he agreed coldly.

"You could have told me." Sheila recovered some of her poise.

"Would it have stopped you from calling me a bastard?" Ráfaga taunted. "Or from wishing to carve out my heart with a knife and slice it into thin pieces? I think not."

Sheila recalled too well the insults she had hurled at him when she believed he could not understand what she said. She burned at the discovery.

"No, it wouldn't have made any difference," she agreed angrily. "So why didn't you tell me? Why did you pretend that I needed Laredo to translate anything I wanted to say to you? Did you enjoy making me look stupid?"

"I had no wish to talk to you, nor to be expected to answer your questions. Also"—an eyebrow lifted in cold accusation—"if you had known I understood English, you would never have spoken to Laredo in front of me as you did just now."

Her gaze darted to Laredo, standing quietly to the side. He had known Ráfaga spoke English fluently and had made no effort to warn Sheila of her foolishness. Her anger broadened to include him, too.

"You could have warned me," she accused.

"It wasn't my place." Laredo shrugged.

"No, that's right," Sheila agreed caustically. "You're with him, aren't you?"

"I told you that from the very beginning," he answered calmly.

Hatred and contempt coursed through Sheila. "I don't know which of you I despise the most." She glared. "You, Laredo, for being a traitor to your own kind, or you . . ."—she flashed a venomous look at Ráfaga's saturnine expression—". . . for being . . ."

"I do not care what your opinion of me is," Ráfaga interrupted coldly. "I only wish you to understand and believe that attempts such as you made tonight will not succeed. No one here will help you escape."

"I wouldn't be so sure about that." Sheila tossed her

head defiantly, her darkly golden mane of hair glistening in the firelight. "Money can buy a lot of loyalty."

His obsidian gaze narrowed. "You are very rash, *señora*. You speak without thinking. I will learn of any future attempts you make. And if you persist—" He let the unspoken threat hover in the already charged air. "I should not like to deny you the little freedoms you now have."

"Freedoms? What freedoms?" Sheila took an angry step toward him. "I am a prisoner here against my will!"

Ráfaga was unmoved by her anger. "I have permitted you the freedom of this house and certain liberties outside of it under guard. Would you prefer it if I confined you to your room?"

"You wouldn't dare," Sheila gasped, trembling with the turbulence of her emotions.

"I may"—he faced her calmly, his expression hard and unrelenting—"if your wagging tongue proves to be too much of a nuisance."

There was no thought to what she did. Instinct alone guided her hand toward his cold, patrician features. It was seized in mid-air by his iron fingers. Reflex lifted her left hand to complete what her right had started. It, too, was imprisoned in his grip before it reached its target.

"Let me go." Sheila refused to struggle, letting him hold her hands in front of her, as if manacled by his grip.

Ráfaga gave her a menacing look before he shifted his attention to Laredo. "You may go," he told him. "I think *señora*'s celebration is over."

At the sound of an obedient footstep, Sheila turned her head, seeing Laredo walking to the yellow rain slicker hanging near the door. A desperate anger filled her at the thought of being left alone with Ráfaga.

"No, don't go, Laredo!" she protested, calling him back. "You can't leave me alone with this beast—this sadist!"

Her cries fell on deaf ears. Laredo didn't even hesitate as he pulled on his slicker and walked out the door.

"What kind of a hold do you have over him?" she hissed, straining her wrists against his unyielding grip.

"He owes me his life," he replied unemotionally. "To you, he owes nothing."

"And how long are you going to make him pay? For the rest of his life?" Sheila accused.

"He has only to tell me he wishes to go and he may leave," Ráfaga informed her. "He stays of his own choosing. He gives me his loyalty of his own choosing. He can leave anytime—as long as he does not take you."

"Yes, you swore you would kill him if he tried." The bitter taste in her mouth coated her voice with the same acidity.

"It was a promise—one that every man here knows I will keep. Take my advice, *señora,* and do not try to persuade someone to help you leave here. I do not think you would like his death on your conscience." Unexpectedly, he released her and walked away. "Go to your room, Señora Townsend."

The compulsion was to defy his order. Sheila trembled with the force of it. With a whirl of her skirt, she pivoted and walked stiffly and proudly to her room.

Chapter 12

Thunder rattled through the house, the elements matching Sheila's own stormy disposition. As she lit the candle beside the bed, the room seemed to grow smaller.

It grated on her that what little freedom she had was only at Ráfaga's sufferance. She caught a glimpse of her reflection in the mirror and turned. Staring at the flame-colored skirt and the embroidered blouse she wore, Sheila remembered the way she had rejoiced at receiving them and now felt sickened by them.

Ráfaga had given them to her. Suddenly she couldn't bear the feel of the material against her skin. She stripped off the clothes and grabbed the blanket she had discarded earlier.

Wrapping it around her, she picked up the clothes and wadded them into a careless bundle. With head held high Sheila walked into the main room.

Ráfaga stood beside the fireplace, staring into the flames. His hand was braced on the mantle, his left knee bent to rest a foot on the wood box. The shadows cast by the firelight accented the angular planes of his face.

When Sheila entered, he slowly lifted his head. The hooded darkness of his eyes gazed at her impassively, noting the blanket she wore and the bundle in her arms. His aloofness stung.

"What is it now?" Ráfaga asked blandly. Then his mouth quirked in irony. "Have you thought up new insults to tell me since you have discovered I can speak and understand your language?"

"Here are your mistress's clothes. You can give them back to her." Sheila tossed the bundle at his feet. It landed half into the fireplace. "I don't want them."

He rescued them from the greedy flames and held them negligently in his hand. "They pleased you earlier."

"Earlier." Her voice trembled. "I didn't realize how much I abhorred anything remotely connected with you."

An ominous gleam entered his eyes. With deliberate slowness he walked toward her, pausing to drop the clothes on a chair, then continuing. Inwardly intimidated, Sheila held her ground.

"Since that is the way you feel, the blanket is mine." A smooth thread of complacency ran through his voice. "Give it to me."

"No," she denied with a frowning start. Her hand instinctively clutched the folds of the blanket, as if she expected him to tear it from her.

"But it is mine," Ráfaga pointed out again. "Since you do not want anything of mine touching your skin, I want it back."

"Very well." Sheila was having difficulty breathing naturally. It made her voice lack strength. "I will change into my own clothes and then bring it to you."

Before she could turn away, he said firmly, "I want it now."

"No," she denied, the chill of fear coursing through her veins.

"Why not?" he reasoned mockingly. "Because you wear nothing underneath it? But I am familiar with your nudity. I have seen you several times. I know the upward thrust of your round, firm breasts, the slimness of your waist, and the way your slender hips were made to receive a man."

Her cheeks flamed hotly as Sheila pivoted to run, terrified of the situation her rashness had provoked. His hand grabbed her arm just above the elbow, his fingers digging into her soft flesh to spin her around. The blanket slipped from her shoulder, aided by his other hand pushing it aside. Sheila barely managed to keep it from falling to the floor.

"I know these things that Laredo could only guess." Ráfaga slowly drew her closer to his muscular length, his voice husky and smooth like velvet.

Yet beneath it, Sheila sensed a ruthlessness. Holding the blanket over her breasts, she was able to use only one arm to try to push him away. It would have been just as futile with two. His head bent toward her and Sheila twisted hers back and away.

His mouth plundered the slender curve of her throat, searing her skin with licking tongues of fire. She lifted her hand to the hard contour of his jaw, trying to push him away and failing.

"Why do you not caress me as you did Laredo?" His breath taunted against her neck. He pulled her hand away and twisted it behind her back, lifting his head to let his dark gaze mock her futile struggles. "Perhaps I can be persuaded to let you go."

"Pig! I hate you!" Sheila spat.

The arm at her back tightened to crush her hips against the rigid muscles of his upper thighs. Arching backward to avoid contact with his chest, her breasts rose and fell rapidly in agitation. The loosened blanket slipped to reveal more of her curves.

"Yes, my lioness, you hate me." Ráfaga smiled coldly. "You would like to scratch my eyes out. You constantly try to fight me, ignoring my orders even though you know I will make you obey them. You would have fared better if you had been meek and frightened instead of so determined to defy me."

"If I had been meek and frightened, you and your murdering band would have raped and killed me when Brad was murdered!" Sheila reminded him in a savage breath.

"Now you are at my mercy."

"Mercy? You have no mercy! No heart!" she said, then tried to struggle free again, but he held her easily.

She saw the muscles along his jaw harden and knew she had provoked him again. She accused him of having no mercy, and Ráfaga exhibited none as he bruised her lips with his punishing mouth.

Caught in the violently spinning whirlwind, her senses reeled under the assault. The ever-constricting band of his arms denied breath to her lungs while he smothered her mouth with his. Blackness swirled at the edges of her consciousness. Sheila fought to keep from being drawn into the vortex of his anger.

His aggressive virility was making her lose touch with reality. The grinding pressure of his mouth became less forceful and more sensually persuasive. And Sheila was too light-hearted to resist the exploring taste of his probing tongue. She was only half-aware that he had released the pinning grip on her arms. The arousing movements of his hands across her hips and back, molding closer to the granite strength of his body, were setting off explosive charges until she was clinging weakly to him.

Only a low moan of protest escaped from her throat when he lifted her off his feet and into his arms. His mouth maintained the soul-destroying kiss as he carried her. An insidious, primitive desire was growing inside of her and Sheila felt helpless to stop it. She hated him desperately while acknowledging his mastery of the art of seduction. Compared with Ráfaga, Brad had been a bungling amateur.

He laid her on the bed, rolling her out of the blanket as he did so. Sheila reached for it instinctively, but he tossed it out of reach. Then her lover-drugged senses realized it wasn't her bed. It wasn't her bedroom.

For a moment, Sheila was too paralyzed by the discovery to move. The weight of his body was on the mattress before she could recover. His hands instinctively found her in the semi-darkness. Their firm touch sent Sheila kicking and clawing like a wild animal. He laughed throatily, fending off her arms and legs as he pinned her to the mattress.

"Scream if you wish, little lioness," Ráfaga murmured. "No one will hear you above the storm. Even if they do, they will not come."

The warmth of his mouth found the sensitive cord along her neck. Sheila dug her fingers into his skin, feeling the satisfactory sensation of his flesh giving way beneath her nails as she raked them across his shoulders. Despite his muffled curse of pain, the hands holding her down did not relent an inch.

Her frantic violence was sapping her energy. Sheila paused to catch her breath. Immediately, he claimed possession of her parted lips, pressing her head back as he kissed her. His hands cupped her breasts to explore their round firmness.

Sheila felt her nipple hardening beneath his touch and cried silently at her inability to control the responses of her flesh. Her head was spinning helplessly in the torrent of churning desires wracking her body.

These wanton, abandoned feelings were strange to her, yet she was powerless to control them. They were controlling her, taking over and making her want the physical gratification of his possession. The sensations were heightened when his mouth trailed down her neck to her breast. The touch of his tongue on her nipple drew an unwilling moan of pleasure from her lips.

There was no urgency in the languid passion of his caress, but the slow-burning fire inside her kept growing hotter and hotter. His exploring hands discovered and gently probed her secret, intimate places, touching, teasing, and releasing all her inhibitions and fears.

The heady male smell of him was an erotic stimulant, arousing her. As much as she wanted, she could never be indifferent to his touch. She was like a leaf, twisting, twisting, in the wind. Her virginity had already been lost to Brad's savagery. Now her self-respect was rapidly being lost to Ráfaga's sensuous mastery.

Beneath her hands, she could feel the naked, rippling muscles of his shoulders and the warm wetness of blood where she had scratched him. But her fingers were no longer clawing and raking his skin; instead, they were almost glorying in the feel of his hard flesh.

While she had a breath of will, Sheila pushed her hands against his shoulders, forcing Ráfaga to lift his head and end his tantalizing play with her nipple. Overpowering her, he bent his head toward her lips, but she eluded them.

"What are you waiting for?" Sheila murmured desperately. "Why don't you rape me and get it over with?"

"But that would be too quick, my lioness," he replied. "I wish to prolong the moment, the torture."

His breath fanned her cheek an instant before his mouth covered hers in hungry demand. And it was torture, sweet torture. The ache in her loins sent Sheila's nerve ends screaming with the need for his possession. In trembling caresses her hands moved over his back and shoulders. Her body writhed and twisted with the agony of her passion.

But it was some time before the full weight of his lean body moved onto her. His pulse was racing as wildly and as hotly as hers. His naked skin was fiery-hot to the touch, and the heat seemed to fuse them together. Sheila felt his male hardness and knew his need was as great as hers.

A purring-kitten sound came from her lips as his muscled legs slid intimately between hers, forcing them apart. Fulfillment was only a moment away, and a shudder of mindless ecstasy quivered through her. When it came, Sheila was enveloped in a whirling, velvet mist of sensations. Primitive tremors alternated with rapturous wonder until she lay weak and spent, and alone.

The whirlwind of strange, new emotions slowly dissipated. Its aftermath left Sheila stunned by his sensual lovemaking. Gradually she surfaced and there was self-disgust and shame that she had found any pleasure in his arms.

Ráfaga moved, his shoulder brushing her arm. A shiver of awareness danced over her skin, the banked flames within flaring to life. Her jaw tightened at the involuntary response of her body, frightened that she was unable to control it.

Sheila had to get away from his touch. Sliding her legs to the edge of the narrow bed, she started to rise, but his hand caught her arm. Sheila was unable to wrench away from his steel grip.

"Where are you going?"

"To my room," Sheila retorted stiffly.

"Why?" Ráfaga asked, detached and impersonal now.

"I was under the impression that all your whoring companions left you to sleep alone," she replied caustically rather than admit she needed time to gain control of her senses and forget the satisfaction she had found in his arms.

"You say that because of Elena, no?"

"Who else?" Sheila flared. His fathomless dark eyes were immune to the look of loathing she gave him. "Do you think I could not hear the two of you when I lay in my bed? The disgusting sounds of your lovemaking? Her whispered good night when she left?"

"If you found it so disgusting, you should not have listened," Ráfaga taunted.

"I had no choice with two rutting pigs in the next room," she declared.

He pulled her beside him, his arm forcing her shoulders onto the mattress. Sheila didn't struggle, choosing a rigid unresistance to his touch.

"The sleeping arrangement suited Elena and me, even if it did not please you," he said coldly.

"What would please me"—Sheila matched his icy tone—"is to not sleep in this bed with you."

"That is unfortunate," he murmured arrogantly.

"Why?" she stormed. Childishly, she reminded him, "Elena didn't sleep with you. Why must you force me to stay?"

"The situation is not the same. Elena wished to be home with her family and the man who is her husband. You have nothing waiting for you but an empty bed."

Sheila turned to face him, the tangled gold of her hair acting as a pillow for her head. "What? Her husband?" Disgusted shock curled her lips. "Do you mean she was married and came here—to you?!!"

The blackness of his gaze ran disdainfully over her face. "You are very quick to condemn others when it is your own mind that is vulgar and crude. César, Elena's husband, is paralyzed. He is one of the living dead—his mind is not in this world. For four years he has been this way, leaving Elena with only his memory to love and two children. She is young and has the physical needs of a normal woman. While she wanted a man's love, she did not wish to forsake her husband. I needed a woman but did not require a wife. So we came to a mutually satisfactory agreement."

"It doesn't matter how you disguise it or what rationale you use; she is still your mistress and she is still married," Sheila retorted.

His hand slid to her throat. It rested lightly on the vulnerable and exposed curve, his fingers capable of tightening to a stranglehold, but his touch remained gentle, almost a caress.

"You believe she is a hypocrite for staying with her husband and seeking physical satisfaction from me, no?" Ráfaga taunted. "And what about you, who cries murder and does not even grieve for her husband?"

"You don't know what I feel inside," Sheila said defensively.

"When I am lying in bed, I, too, hear your sounds in the next room," he told her in sardonic mockery. "Never once since you have been here have I heard you cry—not for yourself or for him."

"If I cried, would it change anything?" she demanded bitterly. Not for anything did Sheila want to admit to Ráfaga that she felt nothing for the loss of her husband. "Would it make you pity me? I doubt it." She answered the question herself. "You have no compassion. You don't know the meaning of the word. Perhaps I don't grieve where you could hear or see because I know you would mock it."

"Perhaps you do not grieve because he did not love you, nor you him," Ráfaga countered.

Sheila breathed in sharply, realizing how thoroughly he controlled everything that went on in this canyon hideout. There was only one person who could have given him that information

"Laredo told you what I said about him," she said in accusation.

"Is it true?" he persisted. "Tell me about him. I want to know."

Stubbornly, she hesitated, not wanting to obey, but she knew he would force some answer from her. So she gave him one that was meant to wound.

"There is not very much to tell," Sheila answered slowly. "The two of you would probably have gotten along famously together. You are very much the same. Brad, too, was interested only in my money. He also took me because I was available and he thought he had the right to use me to satisfy his lust."

"You were a virgin when he took you." It was more of a statement than a question as the disquieting glitter in his dark eyes roamed her face.

His hand shifted to her jawline, his thumb tracing the outline of her lips. Sheila's nerves vibrated at his closeness, lying next to her, naked, so virilely masculine and vitally strong.

"Was I?" she murmured, unable to lie convincingly when she knew he could feel the slightest change in her heartbeat.

"You said you were on your honeymoon with your husband when we took you. And I could tell no one has taught you the ways of love. Tonight you were surprised and frightened by the pleasures a woman can feel. But it is quite natural, little lioness. Perhaps as you grow to learn this, you will learn tolerance for Elena, also," Ráfaga murmured.

Grow to learn this: the words raced down her spine.

Her gold-flecked eyes widened, fear interlaced with anger as she stared at him.

"What are you suggesting?" Sheila demanded, trying to keep the note of panic out of her voice. "You aren't saying that you intend to teach me??"

"You will learn quickly, I think," he said with a considering look.

A flash of lightning splintered into the room, briefly illuminating the rough, unyielding contours of his face.

"I may be your prisoner here, but I'm not going to become your mistress," Sheila stated vigorously, "if that's what you have in mind."

"Not willingly, perhaps."

She tried to push away the hand that cupped her face, but his gentle touch turned to steel. "Leave me alone. You never came near me all this time. Why now?" she demanded.

"It is natural for a man to want to possess a beautiful and desirable woman like you. When you provoked my anger tonight, I saw no more reason to deny what I wanted," Ráfaga replied in a dispassionate tone. "Are you not sorry now that you put your proposition to Laredo in front of me?"

"I don't believe you," Sheila murmured coldly. "There is one thing I've learned while I've been confined to this house with you. You do not let yourself be carried away by emotions, not anger, or desire."

His throaty chuckle at her statement held no humor. "Your head is beautiful, but not empty, is it, *señora?*" His fingers curled into the hair near her ear. "I find your beauty tempting. Others may, too. If you offer it to them, and money, they might not be able to resist. Tomorrow morning they will learn that you are my woman. No one will help you or dare to come near you then," Ràfaga ended complacently.

"Damn you!" Frustration throbbed in her voice, making her curse sound more like a sob of despair. That explanation Sheila believed.

More angry, embittered words were on the tip of her tongue, but her head was already being lifted to meet his descending mouth. Sheila resisted, straining away from him. His mouth opened over her lips in a series of long, drugging kisses. She might have been able to be impassive and indifferent if he had been bruising and rough, like before, but this dizzying, lazy seduction undid her.

Her flesh willingly let itself be molded to his hard male contours. Sheila surrendered to the whirl of inevitability, wildfire raging through her veins. The velvet mist enveloped her again.

Later, much later, Ráfaga drew the blanket over both of them and ordered Sheila to sleep. Part of her mind wanted to argue with him, to declare again that she didn't want to sleep in his bed. But a languorous exhaustion claimed her body. She didn't even object when he possessively curved an arm across her waist.

It seemed she had barely fallen asleep when a torrent of Spanish abuse awakened her. Lying on her side in bed, Sheila had difficulty remembering where she was or what was causing that furnace-like heat down her back, hips, and legs. A weight was lifted from around her middle, the delicious warmth leaving, too.

Not fully awake, Sheila turned to seek its source. Her eyes opened when she heard Ráfaga's voice inches away. All traces of sleep fled, her senses fully alert and her memory vividly clear.

Elena stood a few steps inside the room. Her dark Spanish eyes had the look of a wounded animal driven to anger by pain. Her golden complexion had paled to a waxen hue as she glared at Ráfaga lying in the bed beside Sheila. Whatever Ráfaga had said to Elena in Spanish had not soothed her. Her voice was shrill when she replied, her tone bitterly angry and accusing.

Sheila pulled the blanket tighter around her nakedness, repelled by the jealous scene being staged by Elena. Why hadn't she awakened in the night and slipped from the room? The answer was obvious. She had been physically exhausted by Ráfaga's virile lovemaking and mentally confused by her disturbing reaction to it.

The last thing Sheila wanted was to become embroiled in a dispute with Elena over Ráfaga. She was welcome to have him. Sheila was glad to relinquish any claim Elena might believe she had. There was no quicker way to do that than by leaving the bed and the room.

"Stay where you are." Ráfaga laid a restraining hand on her arm, as if reading her thoughts.

"She wants you, and I certainly don't!" Sheila gasped.

"It is of no consequence what either of you wants," he answered sharply. "This is the way it will be."

He must have said as much to Elena in Spanish, because his following words unleashed another stormy outburst. Ráfaga seemed unmoved by Elena's angry pain. His bronzed features were masked in indifference. Sheila considered again what a heartless, unprincipled brute he was.

A third voice in Spanish, calling from the main room of the adobe house, interrupted Elena. Sheila's heart stopped beating as Laredo appeared in the doorway. He stopped short, the faintly amused expression on his face wiped away at the sight of Sheila lying in the narrow bed.

The color drained from her face, then raced back to flood it crimson-red. There was nothing in the clear blue of his eyes to reveal what he was thinking, but Sheila felt like a cockroach and wished she could scurry to some dark corner and hide. The sensation intensified as she remembered the demeaning way she had responded to Ráfaga's intimacies.

Elena turned, speaking rapidly in Spanish to Laredo, obviously trying to enlist his support. Laredo shook his head in firm refusal and started to leave, not wanting to become involved with the triangle.

"There is no need for you to leave, Laredo," Ráfaga stated. "Elena is going."

When he translated the same message to Elena, she gave him a cold, proud look and answered him in a low, savagely controlled voice. Ráfaga said nothing in return, his face expressionless. Elena turned rigidly and left. The glitter in Laredo's blue eyes plainly held a be-mused "I could have told you this would happen" look.

Unaffected, Ráfaga threw back the cover and swung his feet to the floor as he sat up. Sheila's tight hold on the blanket kept him from uncovering her, as well. She averted her eyes from his nudity as he stepped into the trousers left on the floor. A fresh surge of embar-rassed shame hotly stained her cheeks. Accidentally, she encountered Laredo's glance.

"I asked you not to leave me last night," Sheila said in an accusing fashion. She propped herself up on an elbow, the tilt of her head regally defiant. "I don't sup-pose it matters to you that he raped me after you left. After all, he's your boss, your god." The sharpness of her tongue hid her shame.

Laredo looked at her in silence. The blanket was pulled tightly across her chest, revealing her bare shoulders and arms. Dark, honey-blonde hair cascaded in rippling, molten gold over one shoulder. Her cat-gold eyes shimmered with the moistness of pride.

Ráfaga fastened the waistband of his trousers and glanced over his shoulder, his compelling gaze demand-ing her attention. She shivered at the cool mockery in his eyes.

"Do not blame him for what you provoked," he told her smoothly. "It was not rape." Sheila breathed in sharply, angry words of protest springing to her lips, but she didn't have a chance to say them. "Do not deny that you were like a she-cat in heat last night."

Her gaze slid to the congealed blood on his shoulders and the long red lines where she had scratched him. "Is that how you're going to explain those marks on your shoulders?" But Ráfaga simply ignored her, as if the marks were so trivial they didn't warrant an explana-tion.

"You should clean those scratches," Laredo ob-served.

Calmly, Ráfaga poured water from the pitcher into the basin on the dresser and moistened a cloth. "Sheila made them. She can clean them for me."

"Like hell I will!" she said angrily. "I hope you get blood poisoning and die!"

"See how bloodthirsty she is?" Ráfaga said to Laredo in mock reproval. He walked to the bed, a harsh glint in his eyes. "But you will clean the scratches, my lioness."

"I will not," she declared. "If you want them cleaned, you'll have to get Laredo or someone else to do it, because I won't."

"You will." Leaning forward, his fingers clamped over her wrist, digging into the small bones.

The blanket slipped dangerously low. With one hand imprisoned by him and the other arm propping herself up, Sheila realized she was in a precarious position. There was a malicious, dancing gleam in the dark eyes that held her gaze.

Sheila knew he would not think twice about pulling her from the protective cover of the blanket, revealing her nakedness for Laredo to see if she continued to disobey him.

"All right," Sheila agreed snappishly. "But I can't do anything when you're holding my arm that way. You'll have to let it go unless you intend to break it."

He laughed softly in arrogant satisfaction and released her arm. Bundling the blanket around her, Sheila inched to the side of the bed where he stood. When he offered her the wet cloth, she snatched it from his hand. His mouth quirked at the action and he turned to sit on the edge of the bed, offering each shoulder for her ministrations.

On her knees with the blanket clutched to her breasts, Sheila stared at the rakish thickness of his ebony-black hair and the golden-bronzed skin covering his muscled shoulders and back. If she had a knife in her hands instead of a cloth, she would have plunged it into his spine.

"The scratches, *señora*." His lazy, accented voice reminded Sheila of her purpose, while leaving her with the impression that he was reading her mind.

Her touch was deliberately not gentle as she began

wiping his dried blood from his hard flesh. She felt his muscles contract from her roughness, but Ráfaga neither flinched nor made the slightest sound, not even an indrawn breath, to reveal she was causing him any pain. His control didn't lessen the cruelty in her touch.

When the parallel scratches were exposed, Sheila discovered they were worse than she had thought. She had not just scraped the skin. Her nails had dug deep to rake furrows into his flesh. They looked sore and angry, extremely painful. Her gaze slid to Laredo, who had been watching her work. The expression on his face agreed with her assessment.

"Is there some alcohol around to disinfect them?" Sheila asked, not allowing any emotion to creep into her voice.

She told herself she didn't care that she had hurt Ráfaga. He deserved it. But she did feel a rise of compassion and consoled herself that it at least proved she wasn't as barbaric as her captors.

Laredo nodded. "I'll get it." He was gone only seconds and returned with a liquor bottle, two-thirds full.

Uncorking it, he handed it to Sheila, taking the wet, soiled cloth she held. She hesitated, glancing at the austerely carved line in Ráfaga's jaw and the coldly patrician arrogance of his profile.

"This will hurt," she told him unnecessarily.

"Perhaps you would wish to apply it in drops to prolong the torture." His smooth voice taunted her.

Compassion vanished in a flash of temper. Without warning, Sheila tipped the bottle, dousing the scratches with the alcohol, but she didn't feel any satisfaction when he winced as the fiery liquid seared the lesions.

Immediately, Ráfaga rose and walked to the dresser to remove a shirt from a drawer. Sheila wondered if he shouldn't have a bandage on the wound, but she wasn't about to suggest it. Mutely, she handed the bottle back to Laredo.

"Have you learned to cook, *señora?*" Favoring his

shoulders, Ráfaga put on his shirt, flicking an indifferent glance her way.

"No." Not *their* food with *their* crude implements— Sheila qualified the denial in her mind. "I guess you'll have to fix breakfast yourself or go hungry until lunch. Elena's temper will probably have cooled down by then and she'll be back to fix it," Sheila remarked coldly.

"Elena will not be back," Ráfaga informed her, then turned to Laredo. "Arrange for Juan's wife to come each day to prepare our meals. Tell her she is to come after her own family has been fed and that she may bring her young child with her if she wishes." A faint smile touched his lips as he gazed at Laredo. "Juan has always told us she is the best cook in Chihuahua. We will find out, no?"

There was a smile of agreement from Laredo before he left the room to carry out the order. When the front door had closed, Ráfaga turned his attention to Sheila.

"You will move your belongings to this room," he stated, tucking his shirt inside his trousers. "You will sleep here from now on."

"Will I?" she challenged without a hope of backing it up.

The slashing grooves on either side of his mouth deepened in mocking amusement, but he made no response as he walked from the room, as if he knew her protest was made merely to save her pride.

Chapter 13

After last night, Sheila had expected that Ráfaga would withdraw his permission for her afternoon walks with Laredo, not trusting them to be together. But, to her surprise, he suggested they should continue them.

Now, walking through the green meadow where the horses grazed, Sheila wished she had refused. The silence between them was heavy. Sheila was self-conscious and on edge, shamefully aware of her changed status in the house.

"For God's sake, say something," she demanded tautly. "Say you're sorry or that I deserved it—say *anything.*"

"It's not the end of the world, Sheila," Laredo placated gently.

She stopped short. "Am I supposed to be overjoyed that he has decided he wants me for his mistress?"

"Sheila," Laredo sighed with a hint of exasperation.

She began walking stiffly. "Why don't you go rob some other unwary motorist and kidnap his wife so he'll forget about me?!"

"We don't rob and kidnap motorists."

"Oh, don't you?" Sheila taunted. "Pardon me if I call you a liar."

"That was an accident." Nonplussed, Laredo stared grimly ahead. "Things just got out of hand. Motorists being robbed and killed on the highways is about as common in the States as it is in Mexico. It happens, but rarely."

"Really?" Her tone was deliberately skeptical. "If you don't obtain your money by stealing, then how do you pay for your food, clothing, ammunition, and everything else?"

"We aren't exactly living in splendor," he pointed out dryly. "And you have to remember the cost of living here in Mexico is considerably lower than in the States, especially the bare essentials which is all we have here. A lot of what we eat is grown or raised right here."

"So what do you do with all the money you steal?" Sheila challenged. "Does Ráfaga see himself as Robin Hood and give it to the poor? Or is he like Pancho Villa, with his numerous women and plundering band of raiders, hiding their misdeeds under the guise of 'la revolución'?"

"I told you before that we don't steal." His eyes narrowed into icy-blue slits. "A couple of times a year, Ráfaga raids a prison or a jail. You might say he's hired to do it."

"I see." Sheila nodded coldly, remembering Laredo's story of how he had joined the group. "This is a mercenary commando group, then. You don't rob or steal. You just break into a few jails, kill a few guards, and collect your fee. You don't do anything as bad as stealing."

"Damn it! What do you expect us to do?" Laredo demanded angrily. "Are we supposed to go out and get jobs? Work in the fields? Hell, all of us here were wanted by the law before we ever joined up together. I'm not pretending that what we're doing is right or lawful. I know I'm either in, or going to, my own hell. But maybe some of those kids we're busting out are going to get another chance before they end up like me."

"I'm sure your motives are very noble," she murmured with a sardonic bite to her tone.

"I don't give a damn what you think my motives are." His features were hardened with cold anger. "But I don't think you have the right to judge me or Ráfaga or anyone here. We're just trying to stay free and get by the best way we know how."

Sheila realized she was on dangerous ground. If she continued to deride the way Laredo rationalized his guilt feelings, she might alienate him completely. There was still a chance she might persuade him to help her escape, despite what Ráfaga had said.

"How did Ráfaga get started in this?" She subtly altered the subject in a less personal direction. "What did he do?"

"I don't know," he answered curtly.

"Surely you must know something about him," Sheila insisted. "Does he have a family? Was he an orphan? Where did he learn to speak English so well? You said you'd been with him three years. In that time, you'd have to have learned something about him."

Laredo tipped his head to the side in disagreement. "Ráfaga doesn't answer many questions, especially about the past. I asked him once and he told me he didn't live in yesterdays."

Sheila hesitated, her curiosity fully aroused by Laredo's apparent lack of information. Granted, Ráfaga was enigmatic, a law unto himself, but Laredo had to know something. It seemed impossible that he wouldn't.

"You must have heard stories about him—from the others, maybe." Her sideways glance studied the closed look on Laredo's face.

"I've heard stories," he agreed in a clipped tone. "I don't know how true any of them are."

"Such as?" Sheila queried.

It was Laredo's turn to hesitate. "Some say his mother was the mistress of a wealthy American. Other stories have it that he is the younger son of a prominent

Mexican family. Another story claims that he slipped across the border as a child to live with an uncle in the U.S., passing himself off as his uncle's son for a number of years." He paused for a few minutes, walking silently. "And there are stories that he was in prison for taking part in anti-government actions or for smuggling guns to some reactionaries. It's definite that he committed some crime. All of them convey the fact that he is educated, account for his fluency in English, and his knowledge of prisons and what they can do to a man if he's in there too long."

"Which one do you think is true?"

"None of them." Then Laredo qualified his answer. "I imagine one of them is probably close to the truth, but only Ráfaga could tell you which one."

"When?" Her voice was tinged with bitterness. "When we're alone at night in bed?"

"Look." Laredo stopped, taking Sheila by the shoulders and turning her to face him. "Basically, you haven't been treated that badly. You could have been raped and killed, with your body left beside that of your husband's. You talked your way out of that and it was Ráfaga who intervened to keep you from being raped by some of the others."

"He didn't do it to protect me," she retorted. "He did it because he was afraid my father wouldn't pay the money if I was harmed."

"Be realistic, Sheila," Laredo said grimly. "Your parents would pay the money no matter what condition you're in. I know that, and so does Ráfaga. As a matter of fact, you could be raped and killed now and chances are we could still collect the money."

Paling, Sheila realized that what he said was probably true. It could still come true. It was sobering to discover that the one person who stood between her and that fate was Ráfaga. But Laredo wasn't finished.

"You're lucky to have as much freedom as you do. Sure, there's always someone with you on guard. But, as Ráfaga pointed out, you could be confined to your room. Or"—Laredo paused for emphasis—"you could be kept tied up all the time. So Ráfaga has decided that you're going to share his bed from now on. You're damned lucky he's not a fat, slobbering bastard like Juan. You haven't been beaten or starved. In fact, you've damned near been treated like royalty. Things could be a hell of a lot worse. And it's about time you stopped feeling sorry for yourself and realized it."

His hands dropped from her shoulders to his sides. Laredo started to walk again, gazing straight ahead. Shaken by his lecture, Sheila fell into step beside him, her head slightly downcast.

"You are a survivor, Sheila." Laredo spoke more quietly, his tone firmly gentle. "You get to be one by making the best of a bad situation. I'm not suggesting that you should like it; just make the best of it."

Put that way, it sounded very much like surrender, and Sheila wasn't certain that she was ready to admit that. But she had to acknowledge there was some wisdom in what Laredo said.

"I'll think about it," she said.

The thud of cantering hooves turned Sheila's head. The casual erectness of the rider and his easy grace in the saddle instantly identified him as Ráfaga. His bay horse was loping directly toward them.

A check of the reins slowed the horse to a trot, then to a head-tossing stop in front of Sheila. With hands crossed atop the saddle horn, Ráfaga nodded briefly to Laredo, then turned the full darkness of his gaze to her upturned face.

"Would you like to go for a ride, señora?" The horse stomped and shifted restlessly beneath him.

"Yes, on a horse of my own," Sheila said.

"Come." He slid his left foot from the stirrup and offered an arm to pull her up. "We will find you a mount."

Hesitating, Sheila glanced at Laredo. His expression seemed to be telling her: "Remember what I said." Using the stirrup as a step, she covered Ráfaga's outstretched hand with her own. His sun-browned hand encircled her forearm in a firm grip. Sheila felt the steel-hard muscles in his arms flex as he pulled her astride the saddle in front of him.

Shifting the reins back to his left hand, he reined the horse in a half-circle, his arm brushing lightly against her body. Her shoulders rubbed against the solid wall of his chest as the horse sidestepped nervously under the additional weight before breaking into a canter toward the group of adobe houses.

His muscular thighs burned the backs of her legs. The earthy smell of him awakened her senses, producing a reaction that was purely physical and beyond her control. His warm breath stirred the hair at the back of her neck.

"Are you certain you wish a horse of your own to ride?" He spoke near her ear.

"I am very certain." But the husky tremor in her voice revealed her disturbed state, and she knew Ráfaga had heard it.

Nearing the cluster of crude houses, he slowed the horse to a shuffling trot. It was the first time Sheila had been permitted anywhere near them. She tried to ignore the physical contact with him and look around her with interest.

"What were you and Laredo discussing so earnestly before I rode up?"

"We were plotting how we might escape." She lied deliberately just to irritate him.

"You make a joke, *señora*." There was a mocking laughter in his tone and a suggestion of arrogance at how certain he was of his control over the situation.

"*Señora*? Don't you think such formality is a little ridiculous under the circumstances?"

Turning in the saddle to eye him coldly, Sheila found his face disconcertingly close to her own. Her gaze slid to his mouth and the deepening grooves of satyric amusement on either side. She looked quickly away as her pulse raced in sensual alarm. Rigidly, she faced the front, fighting the sudden weakness in her limbs.

"But, of course, you are right." After a slight pause, he added, "Sheila."

Something in the way he said her name added to the erotic confusion of her senses. A slight movement of his left hand brought the horse to a walk as they came to the first adobe building.

As they rode slowly between the rows of small, crude buildings, his right hand slid around her waist to rest on the bareness of her stomach just below the knotted front of her blouse. Her muscles contracted at the searingly intimate touch, her breathing shallow and sporadic.

She loathed Ráfaga completely in her mind, yet he had this strange mastery over her flesh; he merely had to touch her to make her want him.

She was painfully conscious of heads turning to look at them, men and women alike. Some of them nodded or lifted a hand in greeting to Ráfaga, an obvious sign of respect in their attitudes.

Even the few children playing outside the houses stopped to stare. Sheila knew that her blonde hair and fair skin were an unusual sight. Ráfaga's darkness was a perfect foil to contrast with the lightness of her complexion.

A dog raced forward to bark and snap at the horse's heels. His ambling walk never faltered, although the horse laid an ear back at the sound. At one house, a man sat in a chair beneath the wide overhang. He neither moved nor looked up when they drew level with him.

Sheila noticed the brightly designed blanket draped over his legs and remembered that Ráfaga had told her Elena's husband was an invalid. Her gaze shifted curiously to the door of the house to find Elena standing in the shadowy opening. Jealous hatred burned in her eyes as she stared at Sheila.

They had ridden past the house and were approaching the small corral before Sheila realized the true cause of Elena's jealousy. It hadn't simply been the sight of her riding with Ráfaga. It had been the intimately possessive arm around her middle.

That realization prompted another. Ráfaga's invitation to ride had not been made because he desired her company, nor to provide her with a diversion. He was making his statement of last night come true. "By tomorrow," he had said, "everyone will know you are my woman."

Rumor would have spread quickly through the small population concerning her changed status, and Ráfaga had visibly confirmed it by riding with her through the center of their small enclave.

When Ráfaga halted the horse in front of the fenced horse enclosure, Sheila immediately swung her leg over the saddle horn to dismount. She was eager to get away from the disturbing contact with him that had temporarily blinded her to his true purpose for the outing.

But his arm remained firmly around her waist, lowering her to the ground even though he knew she didn't want his assistance. She started to walk stiffly to the corral, where the horses were gathering to greet Ráfaga's mount.

"*Buenos días,* Señor Ráfaga. Hello, *señora.*" The heavily accented greeting in English stopped Sheila.

A Mexican was walking briskly from beneath the canopy of a shed. His strongly gentle features held an expression of deferential respect without being ingratiating. She had seen him before on guard outside the house.

"What is it that I can do for you?" he asked in heavily accented English.

"I want a horse saddled for the *señora,*" Ráfaga answered.

The Mexican looked to the five horses bunched together at the fence rail. "Which one?" He was asking Sheila's preference, but it was Ráfaga who answered.

"The bay with the star."

Sheila's gaze swept over the horses, finding the bay with a white star on its forehead, Roman-nosed and placid looking. She found little about the animal to arouse her interest.

"The bay? No, no, *señor*." The man seemed to share her opinion of Ráfaga's choice. "The *roano*." Instantly, he translated for Sheila's benefit. "The roan mare is better."

A blaze-faced chestnut marbled with white stretched its neck over the corral rail. There was a suggestion of thoroughbred breeding in the mare's long-legged, racy build, although she lacked the grace Sheila had seen in American counterparts of the breed. Her eyes were large and luminously brown, curious, yet gentle.

"No, not the roan." Ráfaga refused the suggestion.

Frowning, the man gave him a confused look, obviously believing that he had selected the best horse from the group and not understanding why Ráfaga preferred the bay over the roan mare.

"I think he means," she explained to him, "that he wants me to ride a horse that is less apt to run away with me, or vice versa."

"Run away? Oh, no, *señor,* the mare is very gentle. My son, Pablo, he rides her all the time," he insisted.

A black eyebrow was arched thoughtfully at Sheila. Coming to a decision, Ráfaga made it known in Spanish. The satisfied smile that curved the man's mouth told Sheila she would be riding the roan even before he led the mare from the corral.

"Aren't you afraid I'll try to escape?" Sheila taunted softly, keeping her voice low so only Ráfaga would hear her words.

He studied her with lazy, half-closed eyes. "You will think about it." His voice was husky, yet hard, like velvet over steel. "But you will not try."

He was right. Sheila would not attempt to get away while he was with her. Ráfaga was much too ruthless. He would stop at nothing to ensure that she didn't escape from him. It was irritating the way Ráfaga always seemed to know how she thought.

Piqued, Sheila turned away and walked to where Juan was saddling the mare. She stood at its head, stroking the velvet nose, aware that Ráfaga had followed her, but she ignored him. He leaned negligently against a fence post beside her, hooking a heel on the lowest rail. The back of her neck tingled where his gaze rested on her.

The mare nuzzled her shoulder in seeming affection. Sheila patted its neck. "Does she have a name?"

"*Sí.*" He pulled the cinch tight, expertly securing the strap. "She is called Arriba!"

"Arriba?" Sheila repeated, and the mare pricked her ears.

"*Sí.* Her mother was very old. For a very long time, the mare have no babies. Then she have this one and we say: '*Arriba! Arriba!*' So that is what we called her," he explained with a broad, friendly smile.

When the mare was saddled and bridled, the Mexican held her head for Sheila to mount. It was Ráfaga who stepped forward to give her a leg up and adjust the stirrups to a comfortable length.

Sheila found herself studying his features, so aggressively male and so forbiddingly handsome. She looked quickly away when he finished. Why did she find him so compelling?

The mare tossed her head, signaling her eagerness to be off, but she waited tractably for Sheila's command. Not until Ráfaga was mounted on his own horse did Sheila touch a heel to the roan's flanks.

Riding side by side, they skirted the edge of the dwellings, not going down the middle as they had when they arrived at the corral. The flatness of the meadow beckoned, its narrow width marked by the rising canyon wall. The two horses moved through the tall grasses at a reaching trot.

"Where will we ride?" Sheila turned her head to meet Ráfaga's gaze.

Instead of looking at her, she found him watching the bouncing of her breasts, their fullness alternately relaxing and straining against the material of her cream-colored blouse. Immediately, Sheila reined the mare in, her cheeks flaming scarlet. Ráfaga stopped his horse, too, his dark gaze sliding up to her face.

"Do not be embarrassed," he said smoothly. "It is an altogether pleasing sight."

"You invited me for a ride," Sheila reminded him with icy disdain, "not to endure any disgustingly lewd looks from you."

There was a wicked glint in his eyes, but he merely nodded once and nudged his horse forward again. "We will ride to the far end of the canyon," he said, finally answering her first remark.

At the touch of the reins, the mare immediately moved out to match the loping canter of Ráfaga's bay. "Can't we go outside the canyon?" Sheila glanced to the pass through which she had entered the canyon stronghold so many days ago.

Ráfaga gave a negative shake of his head. "Perhaps another time we will."

With the half-promise, Sheila had to be content. But the ride was a tantalizing taste of freedom. She sensed the fleetness of the mare in her long-reaching strides and perhaps the ability to outdistance his bay horse.

After cantering across the meadow to the far end of the canyon, Ráfaga turned into the trees. They wound their way through the grove, dodging limbs and thick brush at a fast walk.

Within the trees, the air was oppressively humid from the recent rain. Soon Sheila felt the clinging dampness of her blouse as disturbed branches sent minuscule showers spraying over her.

Looking through the trees, Sheila glimpsed the rear wall of an adobe building. It was the one she shared with Ráfaga. Their ride had nearly brought them full circle. Ahead there was a shimmer of silver glistening through the leaves. Minutes later, they rode into the clearing by the spring-fed pool and slowly walked their horses around it.

Sheila lifted her thick hair away from her neck, letting the small breeze cool her skin. "The pool looks inviting," she murmured unconsciously.

"Would you like to bathe here after the ride?" Ráfaga inquired blandly.

"What?" She looked at him blankly before realizing she had spoken aloud before. "Yes, I would," she answered quickly.

The brief nod he gave seemed to indicate she had his permission. Sheila bristled at his autocratic attitude, but he didn't notice as he reined his horse into the lead. Soon they were riding out of the trees, with the corral just ahead. Again the man emerged from the canopy of the shed as they rode up.

"Did you have a good ride?" He held the mare's head while Sheila dismounted.

"A very good ride," Sheila assured him, running a hand over the mare's long neck. "Arriba was a well-mannered lady."

"She behaved herself, no?" he smiled. "She did not try to run away?"

"No. She was perfect." She returned the smile.

"You like her, no?"

"I like her, yes," Sheila laughed.

"Then she is yours." His hand swept the air, palm upward, to indicate the mare. "I give her to you."

"You can't be serious!" Sheila protested. She glanced at Ráfaga, who was standing to one side, watching with distant amusement. "You're not actually giving her to me, are you?"

"*Sí, sí,*" he insisted. "Arriba is yours. I give her to you."

Bewildered, Sheila looked again to Ráfaga, uncertain what to do. Amusement glittered in his eyes. There was an almost imperceptible nod of his head. Sheila took it to mean she was supposed to accept the horse as a gift.

With a confused smile, Sheila nodded her acceptance. "*Gracias.* I don't really know how to thank you. She's such a beautiful mare."

"If she please you, that is enough," he said.

Still, Sheila hesitated, wondering if something more was expected of her. The mare butted her head against the Mexican's chest, wanting the bridle removed. The roan horse was now Sheila's. Was she supposed to see to its care?

A hand closed around her elbow. "We must go," Ráfaga stated, indirectly providing an answer to that question.

"Is he really serious about giving me the mare?" she questioned when they were out of the man's hearing range.

"Sí, he is very serious." The slashing grooves deepened at the corners of his mouth, as if concealing amusement. "But he will be surprised if you take him literally."

"I don't understand." Sheila shook her head, more confused now than before.

"It is a courtesy gesture," Ráfaga explained with an indulgent gleam in his dark eyes, "to show his generosity. It would have offended his dignity if you had not accepted it, but he also expected you to tactfully leave the gift behind or give him one of equal value."

"I see," Sheila murmured.

"It is a custom of my country, a touch of chivalry. We say 'my house is your house,' and we mean it very sincerely, but we do not expect that you will take it and sell it."

"I should hope not." She laughed briefly, glancing up to his face in time to see a faint smile touch the hard line of his mouth.

Her pulse accelerated upon seeing the way the smile changed his rough features. Sheila realized how relaxed she had become with him and immediately stiffened, pulling her arm from the light grip of his hand. How could she find him so charming?

Chapter 14

Having gathered soap and a towel from the house, they arrived at the spring-fed pool. Sheila knew it was useless to ask him to turn around while she undressed. Instead, she turned her back to him, stripping with disguised haste so that she could seek the concealing waters of the pool, where his appraising eyes couldn't see her nakedness.

A sound caught Sheila's attention. She glanced over her shoulder, her eyes rounding in surprise. Ráfaga was minus his boots and shirt, his bronzed torso gleaming naked in the sunlight.

"What are you doing?" she asked accusingly.

"Do you expect me to bathe with my clothes on?" countered Ráfaga. Not expecting her to respond to his rhetorical question, he began unfastening his pants.

Sheila quickly turned her head, the heat of anger and embarrassment flushing her cheeks. There was a second in which she was incapable of movement. She should have expected this, she told herself. After last night, she should have expected anything. Foolishly, however, she had not.

She reached for her clothes, lying on the ground near her feet. "Just because you've forced me to sleep in your bed does not mean that I'm going to bathe with you!"

Before Sheila could make the first move to put back on her clothes, strong arms were swinging her off her feet. The bareness of her soft hip felt the hard muscles of his stomach, and her nipple was tickled by the cloud of dark hairs on his chest.

Her stifled shriek of protest went unheeded as he cradled her firmly in his arms. Holding herself rigid, Sheila glared into his implacable features.

"Put your clothes down," Ráfaga ordered, "unless you wish to get them wet."

"Don't you know how much I despise you?" Sheila hissed futilely.

"Is that why you always challenge me?" The complacent glitter of his cold, dark eyes was mocking, almost daring her to fight him.

Trying to struggle would be useless. Ráfaga would simply carry her into the water, dry clothes and all. Perhaps it was overcoming her resistance that he enjoyed, Sheila thought angrily. If it was, this time she would disappoint him.

Stiffly, she dropped her clothes to the ground, neither relaxing in his arms nor trying to twist free. He carried her into the pool and not until he was waist-deep in the water did he withdraw the strong arm from beneath her thighs, letting her feet glide down to the bottom of the pool.

Sheila felt a childish urge to splash the cold water at his arrogant patrician features, but she resisted the temptation, knowing it would only provoke him into retaliation. And she knew too well his brand of retaliation.

Sheila was shorter than Ráfaga by several inches, and the cool water lapped at the upward curve of her breasts. The arm at her back was removed, his hand surfacing to offer the bar of soap to her. She looked at it for tense seconds before taking it, carefully avoiding any contact with his hand.

Ráfaga turned in the water, facing away from her. Startled, Sheila didn't understand his unexpected rejection of her, his failure to attempt to seduce her in this idyllic, sylvan setting. Not for one minute did she believe he wanted only to bathe and nothing more.

"Wash my back," he commanded smoothly.

Her head jerked, her eyes throwing daggers at the vulnerable space between his shoulder blades. A scathing denial of his order was on the tip of her tongue. Sheila sank her teeth into her lower lip to forcibly silence a retort. That was what Ráfaga expected, and she knew he would take delight in forcing her to obey.

Stifling her resentment, she began to methodically soap his back, spreading the lather over the sinewy muscles of his shoulders and ribs. The lather gave a silken feeling to his hard flesh. It became increasingly difficult to remain detached while she washed him.

Her sensitive fingers felt the slight flexing of his biceps as her hands moved over his left arm. Sheila knew the strength of those arms and hands, strength in punishment and in making love. The latter she could not forget, not with the red welts on his shoulders to remind her.

Sheila moved to his right arm to avoid the sight of the worst wound she had inflicted. The scratches looked angry and sore. She couldn't help wondering if the soap wasn't making them sting. She tried to convince herself that she hoped it did, but her mind was too busy trying to control the rising awareness of her senses to be totally vindictive.

Turning at an angle in the water, Ráfaga faced her, presenting the naked expanse of his chest for her ministrations. The aloof mask over his features made her feel like a slave girl washing her master.

His male beauty wiped every other thought from her mind. Her gaze kept wanting to slide below the water level at his waist. Sheila trembled with the effort to keep her attention focused on the curling hairs of his chest.

Then Ráfaga was taking the bar of soap from her hands. "It is my turn." His voice was velvet-soft, huskily caressing.

She was without willpower as his hands touched the bare flesh of her shoulders. The soapy lather being spread over her soft skin was an erotic stimulant to the senses that were already aroused by his masculinity.

When his hands cupped her breasts, Sheila felt her nipples hardening in his palms. The massaging action of his strong fingers ignited a fire in her loins, a flaming desire to know the fullness of his possession.

One hand slid to the small of her back beneath the water line while the other continued its sensuous caress of her breast. The buoyancy of the water made Sheila feel as if she floated against him. His hand slid farther down to spread over the softly full cheeks of her bottom. As she was arched toward him, Sheila felt the male hardness of his need.

A fluttering of resistance asserted itself and she pressed her hands against his chest. His mouth opened over her lips, tasting their sweetness to the fullest. There was a roaring in her ears at the demanding mastery of his kiss. Yet, somehow, Sheila managed to cling to her fragile resistance.

While her lips parted under the command of his probing tongue, she kept the rest of her body stiff to his touch. She could feel the beat of his heart beneath her hands and the ripple of his muscles that could so easily overpower her, but they didn't.

"Do not close your legs to me, Sheila," he whispered thickly against her lips.

He sounded so emotionless, so detached from everything but his own passion that Sheila had to object to what he demanded of her.

"No." Her protest was muffled by the incessant possession of his male lips.

"Open them," Ráfaga ordered.

The arm half-encircling her back tightened in com-

mand. She obeyed willingly and was lifted up to receive
the thrust of his hips. Her faint moan of unwilling satisfaction was blocked by his exploring tongue. The water
lapped at her skin, but it was unable to quench the fires
of their passion now blazing with one flame. Her fingers
curled into the black thickness of his hair as orgasmic
shudders quaked her body. It was like drowning, then
surfacing with a rush to new, dizzying heights.

Mindless, unconscious of time or place, Sheila let
him carry her away to the unknown reaches of desire.
She ceased to think of Ráfaga as her ruthless captor.
Never had she dreamed she could be so totally abandoned in the giving of herself, nor so selfishly eager to
receive all that was given back.

When the flames had burned themselves out, it was
several minutes before Sheila could fight through the
blackness. Opening her passion-drugged eyes, she saw
Ráfaga lazily watching her. In her mind, she acknowledged that he owned her body and soul and realized,
fatalistically, that no one else would ever hold such
power over her flesh and spirit.

She moved her head in silent protest against the fates
and discovered with a start that she was lying on the
grassy bank. She couldn't remember Ráfaga carrying
her to shore. It frightened her the way his touch could
make her forget everything.

He was lying on his side next to her, his hand resting
intimately on her stomach. Sheila noticed the smouldering look of satisfaction in his dark eyes. It reminded her
of a jungle cat that had just feasted on its prey and was
now replete.

"I hate you," she spat out weakly, knowing it wasn't
quite true.

There was a flash of white as Ráfaga smiled and
rolled to his feet. "I wish all my enemies hated the way
you do, especially if they looked like you," he mocked,
raking her naked length briefly with his gaze before
walking over to dress.

It galled her that he found her words amusing, but
it was worse knowing she had given him ample cause to

taunt her. Tight-lipped, she dressed hurriedly. Desperately, Sheila wanted to vow she would never betray herself again, but she doubted it was a promise she could keep.

Laredo's voice called Ráfaga's name as hurried footsteps approached the pool. Both turned their heads simultaneously as he emerged from the shade of the trees.

Laredo's blue-eyed gaze flickered momentarily to Sheila. Tiny rivulets of water ran down her temples and neck from the wetness of her darkly golden hair. He carried two rifles. One he tossed to Ráfaga with a clipped explanation in Spanish.

With lightning-quick reflexes, Ráfaga caught the rifle and shifted it to one hand, grabbing Sheila by the arm with the other and shoving her forward. She nearly stumbled to her knees, but Ráfaga pulled her up sharply to hurry her along the path.

"Quit pushing!" Sheila protested and tried to wrench her arm away from his hard grip. Her shoes were back by the pond. It was impossible to gingerly pick her way over the uneven ground with his hand shoving her along. "I can't run barefoot!"

Neither Laredo nor Ráfaga paid any heed to her protests. A mounted rider waited in front of the adobe house, holding the reins to two saddled horses.

"Juan!" Ráfaga gave Sheila a final push toward the house and the armed guard waiting there. He added a stern order in Spanish. It was obviously a command for the guard to stay with Sheila.

For a frightened second, the name Juan conjured up the image of Brad's murderer, with his foul-smelling breath, yellowed teeth, and leering eyes. When she was able to check her forward movement from the last push, Sheila gasped with relief at the sight of the quiet, vaguely respectful Mexican who had taken his place. It was the man from the corral.

Lifting her clinging, wet hair away from the corner of her eye, she looked over her shoulder to the trio of riders spurring their horses toward the canyon entrance. She stared after them, bewildered and curious.

"What is going on?" Absently, she murmured the thought aloud.

"Do not worry, *señora*," he comforted in heavily accented English.

"What happened?" She looked to the riders, slowing as they neared the pass. "Where are they going?"

"*Soldados*—soldiers," he corrected himself. "Close to here."

"Looking for me?" Sheila breathed in, her first ray of hope shining.

"*Quien sabe?*" The guard shook his head. "We wait."

"Yes, we wait," she sighed anxiously. Hesitating, Sheila glanced to him. "Your name is Juan?"

"*Sí, señora.*" He nodded respectfully.

"There is another man named Juan, isn't there?" she questioned warily.

"*Sí*—Juan Ortega." His dark eyes widened expressively. "He is *loco*—bad."

There were a few other, more forceful adjectives Sheila would have used, but she kept her silence. Instead, she concentrated all her thought in a prayer that the soldiers would soon come riding through the canyon entrance.

They must have found the car and Brad's body, she decided. Perhaps her parents had notified the authorities to look for her when she hadn't returned with Brad as she had told them she would.

Over an hour later, three riders appeared at the canyon entrance, the horses trotting sedately down the slope to the floor. Sheila's hopes sank into the dust.

She abandoned her post of vigil and walked into the house. She remained in her room when Ráfaga and Laredo entered the house minutes later. There was no longer anything of hers in the room. Ráfaga had supervised the moving of her few meager belongings to his room that morning.

A handful of men entered the adobe house after Ráfaga's return. Lying on the small cot, Sheila stared at the ceiling, listening to the Spanish voices in the main room. Each time Ráfaga spoke, she immediately recognized the low timbre of his voice. She closed her eyes tightly, trying to shut out how vividly aware she was of everything about him. But it was hopeless.

When the evening meal was ready, prepared by Juan's wife, Ráfaga called Sheila from her room. The men remained, refusing the offer of food but accepting coffee from Consuelo. Sheila could only pick at her food, too painfully conscious of the men looking on. She felt the piercing looks directed at her by Ráfaga, but she returned none of them, keeping her head lowered while she pushed the food around on her plate.

She would have retreated to her room again, but Ráfaga ordered her to stay. Her pride almost made her refuse, but Sheila realized that he wouldn't tolerate any defiance in front of his men. Keeping silent, she helped Consuelo clean off the dishes and remained seated at Ráfaga's side.

The discussion was obviously about something of importance, considering the serious expressions on the faces of everyone there. But Sheila couldn't understand a word of it. Ráfaga made notes on yellow paper, but they were also in Spanish.

Two pots of coffee had been drunk and the moon was high in the night sky before the meeting was concluded and the men left. Laredo was the last, tarrying for a few minutes to speak to Ráfaga alone, then nodding a good night to Sheila. While Ráfaga went over his notes, making additional notations on the side, Sheila removed the coffee mugs from the table.

Then she tried to steal silently from the room, wanting to be in bed and hopefully asleep when he came. But she was stopped before she had taken three steps toward her destination.

"Where are you going?" Ráfaga looked up.

"To bed. Where else?" Sheila answered defensively.

"Wait," he ordered. "I will be only a few minutes."

"I'm tired and I'd like to get some sleep." She wasn't

going to give in without an argument. "I don't see any reason to wait for you."

"I should not wish to disturb your sleep later."

Her temper flared as she read between the lines of his reply. "My God," Sheila gasped, "isn't once a day enough for you? Do I have to endure it again?"

Using a rear leg as a pivot point, he swiveled the chair at an angle. An arm was hooked negligently over the back as his hooded gaze met the flashing resentment of her jewel-bright eyes.

"Come here." Sheila's first impulse was to ignore the command and walk from the room. Ráfaga interpreted the cause of her momentary indecision and repeated his words. "Come here."

Her fingers curled into her palms, nails digging into the sensitive skin. Sheila walked to his chair, rigid defiance in every taut nerve even as she complied with his order. His hand gripped an arm stiffly held at her side and drew her closer to his chair.

"You endure my touch, do you?" he said with low mockery.

"Yes!" Sheila hissed in return, but a pulse was already hammering in her throat at his disturbing nearness.

"And you think that to make love once a day is enough, do you?" Ráfaga continued to taunt her, his dark eyes glittering and enigmatic, the aloofness of control in his saturnine features.

"It's *too* much!"

"You think you would not enjoy it, hmmm?"

"I know I wouldn't!" Already her senses were making a lie out of her denial.

With a biting twist of her wrist, he brought her against the chair, her legs brushing against a muscular thigh. Sheila steeled herself to ignore the searing contact. The grip on her wrist forced her to bend slightly to lessen the pain.

The breath was stolen from her lungs when his gaze shifted from her face to her breasts, straining against the confining material of her blouse and the knot that held the front closed. His free hand lifted to the plunging vee.

Wildfire raced through her veins as his lean fingers slid inside her blouse to cup the underside of a breast, pushing the material aside to expose its creamy roundness. When his mouth touched the rosy nipple, Sheila gasped in protest and delight. Closing her eyes tightly, she tried to ignore the way he licked her nipple into pebble-hardness.

It was exquisite torture to resist his arousing sucking of her breast. Sheila succeeded in not giving in to the waves of desire stirring her senses until his hand moved down her stomach to slide intimately between her thighs.

There was a jelly-like quiver in her knees and she knew she was lost. Like a drowning person succumbing to an undertow, Sheila let herself be drawn onto his lap. Ráfaga undressed her with deliberate slowness before he carried her to the bedroom with her hands locked around his neck and her lips a willing captive of his possessing mouth.

It was a seduction cycle that repeated itself over the next two weeks with changes of opening and settings and dialogues. Sheila kept trying to control her senses, sometimes holding her betraying desires at bay for a while, but always—inevitably, it seemed—Ráfaga obtained the response he was seeking.

Each rehearsal of the scene improved the climatic end, leaving Sheila little to cling to but her pride. Everything else Ráfaga had taken bit by bit.

Her life before she was brought to the canyon seemed so long ago that it might never have existed. Often Sheila would awaken in the cool of the mountain night and find herself snuggled against Ráfaga, taking advantage of the warmth of his body heat.

In those sleep-laden moments, it seemed so natural to lie beside him. It was as if she had never slept alone.

Sheila stirred restlessly on the cot, disliking the thoughts that were disturbing her half-sleep. A hand touched her arm and she twisted away from it, her pride needing to assert itself.

"No." She halfheartedly protested Ráfaga's light touch and the demand she thought it made.

"I do not have the time to change that to 'yes' this morning." His low, faintly accented voice was riddled with lazy amusement, confident of his ability to change her answer if he chose to. "Come. You must wake up and dress."

Frowning, Sheila opened her eyes. The flame from a lamp cast a circle of light over the center of the room, but through the curtained window, she could see the sky was still black with night. Confused, she looked at Ráfaga, fully clothed, sitting on the edge of the bed pulling on his boots.

Making certain the blanket still covered her nakedness, Sheila propped herself up with her elbows. "It isn't morning yet."

His dark gaze flickered to her briefly. "It soon will be." He tugged on the other boot. "Consuelo is fixing breakfast."

Sheila listened and heard the confirming sounds of someone else in the house. "But why so early?" she persisted.

Ráfaga got up from the bed and glanced at her. "I am leaving at first light."

"Leaving?" His statement took Sheila by surprise. She pushed herself into a sitting position on the bed, dragging the blanket with her, clutching it to her breastbone. "You didn't say anything about leaving last night. Where are you going? Why?"

His mouth twisted with cynical amusement. " 'Where are you going? What are you going to do? When are you coming back?' " Ráfaga mocked her barrage of questions. "You sound like a wife cross-examining her husband. I did not realize you were so concerned about where I went and what I did."

Sheila immediately regretted her impulsive questions. "I don't give a damn what you do!" she snapped and swung her feet over the side of the bed.

"That sounds more like my lioness." He laughed softly in his throat. "Scratching and spitting whenever she is not purring in my arms."

Sheila tugged the blanket from the end of the bed and wrapped it around her before she rose to walk stiffly to the dresser. The blanket dipped low in the back, nearly to her waist, her sun-streaked hair curling loosely at the top of her shoulder blades. As she reached for her blouse and slacks, she heard Ráfaga walk up behind her.

"Why do you persist in covering yourself with that blanket?" he mused. "Do you think I do not already know every inch of you?"

"I have no desire to parade around naked in front of you." Sheila tensed as his hands moved to rest on her shoulders.

He lifted aside the hair at the nape of her neck to let the searing warmth of his mouth explore the sensitive area. Sheila felt herself melting under his disturbing caress, but she knew too well her defenses wouldn't last if she didn't distract him, and quickly.

"I suppose you're leaving to break some criminal out of jail," she said with the harshness of accusation.

Her goal was accomplished as he raised his head, meeting the reflection of her gaze in the square mirror above the dresser. The arch of one dark brow was demanding, the sharpness of his dark gaze interrogating.

"Why do you say that?" His voice was almost too bland.

"Laredo told me that's what you do." And Sheila wondered if she wasn't supposed to know. "I suppose you just go charging in there on your horses and take the guards by surprise."

"The horses get us in and out of the mountains— no more." Ráfaga stepped away from her. "Outside the Sierras, we must use other transportation."

Sheila realized he had neither admitted nor denied that his destination was a prison. "Is that where you're going?" she asked again.

He studied her with a sideways look for a moment.

"We are going to see if it is possible, and if it is, when the best time to do it would be. We will be gone three, maybe four, days at the most."

"What are you going to do with me while you're gone?" she asked with cautious unconcern. "Are you going to lock me in a room and post a guard at the door?"

"Is it necessary?" countered Ráfaga.

"I don't know." Sheila shrugged. "Do you think it is?"

His mouth thinned at her evasion. "Consuelo will be in each day to cook for you. You may leave the house only with Juan. He will be responsible for you. I have left orders that if you step outside the door, you are to be stopped unless Juan is with you. There will always be someone on guard, whether Juan is here or not," he finished in a clipped, authoritative tone.

"What you are saying is that you don't trust me?"

"Right," Ráfaga agreed coldly. "I do not trust you." He turned smoothly on his heel and walked to the hall. "Get dressed so that we may eat the breakfast Consuelo has prepared."

"I'm not hungry," she murmured obstinately.

Ráfaga paused at the door, a cynical twist of mockery to his mouth, deepening the grooves carved at the corners. "Poor Sheila. Who will you sharpen your claws on while I am gone? Perhaps you will find that you miss me."

"Never!" she hissed like a pathetically vulnerable kitten.

There was a glint of laughter in his dark eyes before he strode into the hallway, leaving Sheila to dress in private.

The food was on the table when she entered the kitchen area. Ráfaga made no further attempt at conversation, and Sheila ate in silence.

As she pushed her plate away, there was the shuffling sound of several horses approaching the adobe house at a walk. The creak of saddle leather was followed by the opening of the front door.

Laredo walked in, pausing just inside. "We're ready."

Ráfaga held Sheila's gaze for a long moment, his features masked. Rising, he walked toward the door, stopping to remove his poncho from a hook and pull it over his head. Silently, Sheila watched him put on his hat, pulling it low on his forehead, and pick up the rifle propped against the wall. Then he turned back to Sheila.

"You will come outside," he ordered in a flat, emotionless tone.

It was the last order given directly from him that she was going to have to obey for the next several days and Sheila rose to accompany him.

"*Señora.*" The quiet voice of Consuelo stopped her. Sheila turned as Juan's wife walked quickly to her, saying something in Spanish and offering Sheila a heavy rebozo. Sheila accepted the Mexican shawl, smiling her thanks for the woman's thoughtfulness, and wrapped it around her shoulders.

Ráfaga stood at the door, holding it open for her to precede him outside. The low murmur of voices stopped when they walked out of the house together. There were more people than horses clustered in small groups outside.

Five saddled horses waited, with two riders already mounted, Laredo and another man. The other two riders, besides Ráfaga, were saying their good-byes to their families.

A firm hand gripped Sheila's elbow, propelling her forward to the horse Juan held. For a moment, Sheila thought Ráfaga had decided to take her along with him. He kept her at his side while he slid his rifle into its scabbard. Then he turned, taking hold of her other arm. She stiffened as he started to draw her toward him.

"This is for those who stay behind"—Ráfaga spoke in a low voice that would not carry beyond her hearing range, the same flatness in his tone now as before—"so that they will know you are my woman, and to harm you is to harm me."

Sheila didn't protest as he pulled her toward him. Her head lifted automatically, her lips meeting his descending mouth. It was a hard, sweet kiss, possessive in its intensity and brief in its duration.

Her lips trembled when he released them. But Ráfaga didn't immediately release her arms, holding her against the solid wall of his chest while his hooded gaze studied her face.

"When I ride out, you will stand here with Juan and watch me leave. You will not go into the house until the others start for their homes," he commanded.

At her nod of agreement, Ráfaga let her go and swung lithely into the saddle. Sheila stepped backward to Juan's side as Ráfaga reined his horse away from her. The other four riders joined him, loosely grouped in no particular order. Laredo tipped his hat to her and touched a spur to his horse.

A red dawn streaked the sky as the five riders turned their horses toward the pass leading out of the canyon. Sheila watched them ride away, but Ráfaga never turned around to see if she was still there.

Chapter 15

The small adobe house seemed so empty with Ráfaga gone. In the silence, Sheila could almost hear the echo of her own heartbeat. She wandered to the front window, feeling like a ghost rattling its chains.

Outside, a mid-afternoon sun was beginning its slide toward the western peaks. The crimson hours of morning seemed so far away. If the daylight hours passed so slowly, what would the night be like? Sheila wondered. She wrapped her arms tightly around her middle and closed her eyes.

"Perhaps you will find you miss me," Ráfaga had taunted her.

"Never!" she had denied. But she remembered the hard strength of his muscular body lying beside hers and the practiced caress of his hands arousing her flesh, the exquisite feeling as his mouth took her soft lips.

Most of all, there was that sensual moment when he drove in his stake of possession. A hungry fire burned in her loins at the vivid memories the thought of him had provoked. Her heart suddenly ached for the sight of him.

A beast, an animal, she had accused him of being. But was she any better, longing for the physical gratification he gave her? Sheila lifted a hand to run shaking fingers through her hair. Had she become some kind of a tramp? Would any man satisfy this lusting of her flesh?

She remembered the way she had been sickened by Brad's mauling hands and his bestial use of her body. And Laredo's touch didn't evoke any prurient sensations. Ráfaga seemed to be the only one with this special power over her senses. *Why? Why?* her mind, screamed, but it didn't really want to know the answer.

"Physical chemistry," Sheila rationalized aloud.

Breathing in deeply, Sheila opened her eyes. Her heart stopped as icy fear froze her muscles. Outside the window, leaning against a post, was the man who had shot Brad. His small, leering eyes were looking at her. There was an almost drooling laxity to his mouth.

Frightened and nauseated, Sheila backed away from the window. It had been days since she had seen him. But there he was, outside guarding the door—and guarding her.

Sheila retreated to a far corner of the room. Her trembling legs sought the support of a chair. She huddled in it, clinging to Ráfaga's words that she was now his woman. No one would lay a hand on her and risk his wrath.

For the first time it was brought home to Sheila what might happen to her if Ráfaga didn't come back. She prayed fervently for his swift and safe return. Any thought of escaping while he was gone vanished. A sixth sense told her that the man outside would somehow know her every move. In the house or with Juan, she would be safe and protected. Anywhere else Brad's killer would be waiting.

A knock on the door made Sheila jump in alarm. "Wh-who is it?" Her voice was tremulous. She tried to get a grip on herself.

"It is me, Juan," a familiar voice answered from the other side of the door.

Sheila sighed with relief, releasing the breath she had unconsciously been holding. "Come in." Her voice was considerably more steady than before.

Juan walked in, leaving the door open, as if convention demanded it. "I thought perhaps the *señora* would like to ride," he said in his heavily accented English. His bearing was dignified, his attitude courteous and respectful, as if he were a host seeing to the entertainment of a guest.

"Yes, yes, I'd like that." Sheila nodded, suddenly needing to escape the emptiness of the house and the silent menace of the man standing guard outside.

The roan mare was saddled and waiting for her, the reins looped around the post supporting the porch roof. Sheila hurried to the mare, stiffly ignoring the man on guard, but she was uneasily aware of his hot eyes following her. Mounted, she waited impatiently for Juan, not feeling clean until they had ridden away from the house and the guard's stripping look.

"The *señora* rides as if *el diablo*—the devil—is pursuing her," Juan commented when Sheila finally slowed the mare to a walk far from the house.

She hesitated, then said curtly, "The man guarding the house, the one who is also called Juan—I don't like him." It was an understatement, one that did not express the fear the man instilled in her.

"*Sí*, I understand," was the only response she received.

The ride helped to soothe Sheila's taut nerves, the ride and Juan's quiet company. She was sorry when it ended more than an hour later, but Juan promised they would go out again the following day. Sheila knew she would look forward to it.

The third day of Ráfaga's absence, the emptiness of the house was oppressive. When Juan rode up, leading the roan mare, Sheila practically burst out of the door.

The guard held the mare's head while she mounted and she smiled a quick thanks.

The man who had shot Brad had not been on duty since that first day. Although she hadn't asked, Sheila felt than Juan was responsible. He knew how violently she disliked the man.

During their afternoon rides, she had grown to admire Juan's politeness and quiet dignity, and his smile, which was always ready and friendly. Sheila returned it now as they spurred their horses into a canter across the canyon meadow. Not until they had crossed its width did they slow their mounts.

Sheila patted the mare's arched neck as the horse pranced in an eager walk. She turned her face to the wind, letting it cool the flush of excitement in her cheeks.

"It's good to get out of the house," Sheila declared fervidly. "Sometimes I think I'm being swallowed up in its emptiness."

"It is that way with me," he said with a sage nod of understanding, "each time Consuelo leaves our home to cook for you. It will not be so lonely for you when Ráfaga returns."

Her pulse leaped at the mention of his name. It was crazy, insane. But Juan would not understand if she denied his comment. Sheila knew that she missed him and that she wanted him back safely.

"How long have you known Ráfaga?" she asked, instead.

"A long time," he answered, as if he had lost track of the years.

"How did you meet him?"

"I took care of the horses on a big *rancho*. I was very good," he said proudly. "My brother was in jail with three others because of drugs. He told me a man was going to break them out. I want to help because my brother is going crazy in this place. I wait outside to help my brother run."

There was a faraway look to his eyes as he talked. His voice was more heavily accented when Juan continued. "It was hot, siesta time. Everything was quiet. Nothing was moving. I watch, thinking this man was not coming because all was so still. Then suddenly there was noise and shouts, then people running. I see my brother and shout to him to come with me. He starts to run and someone shoots. I see my brother fall down and I run to him. He is hurt very badly and I carry him away to hide. A man shows me where to hide and I stay there with my brother.

"This man comes back much later and looks at my brother. He tells me there is nothing to be done and I must leave him. But I say no, he is my brother. The man, he looks at me for a long time, then says to bring my brother and come with him. That is how I meet Ráfaga," Juan concluded.

"He brought you here?" Sheila questioned and received an answering nod. "What happened to your brother? Did he live?"

"Sí."

They walked their horses in the shade of the south canyon wall. Ahead was the sloping trail to the pass, and, for Sheila, freedom. Or was it? She gazed at it, then glanced curiously at Juan.

"Why did you stay here? You hadn't done anything wrong. There wasn't any reason to hide."

"My brother was here," he explained with gentle patience. "And later Ráfaga brought our families here. He is a good man. This is not such a bad place to live. I work with the horses. There is food for my family to eat and money to buy clothes for them. My country is poor, señora, but we live much better than many."

"But what about your children? There are no schools, nowhere they can learn to read or write," Sheila persisted. "They can't even leave this place."

"I teach them English so that one day they can perhaps go to America." Sheila saw the lift of pride to his chin and realized she had offended him by suggesting he was not providing the best for his family. "It is an important thing for them to learn."

"Yes, of course it is," she agreed with a quick smile.

Juan reined his horse away from the sloping trail leading out of the canyon and Sheila's mare followed. They rode in silence toward the east rim of the canyon.

"Do you ever go with him—with Ráfaga?" she clarified.

"Only sometimes," he answered, then mused, "but it is something to see. One minute all is quiet, then . . ."— Juan snapped his fingers—". . . he is there and he is gone. Ráfaga, like the wind," he added in explanation.

Laredo's definition sprang from her memory, when he had said that Ráfaga meant a gust of wind. Would he blow in and out of her life that quickly?

A surge of restlessness swept through her. She looked up to the canyon walls, wondering how much longer he would hold her here, his captive, his slave, his mistress.

Touching a heel to the mare's flank, she took the lead from Juan. She didn't want to talk anymore, not when the subject seemed to inevitably turn back to Ráfaga. He had said he would be gone three or four days. This was the third day, possibly the last hours she would have to herself for a long time. She should be enjoying the absence of his company.

Winding through the trees on the north side of the canyon reminded Sheila of the time she had ridden through them with Ráfaga. At the spring-fed pool, her flesh burned with the memory of the way he had made love to her in the water. There was no escaping him in her mind, just as there was no escaping from the canyon walls of her prison, complete with armed guards.

Frustrated, Sheila turned the mare around to start back to the house. They had ridden past the corral and were approaching it from the rear, a way Sheila had not gone before. Unexpectedly, the ground dipped to form a large, natural hollow. In the center were two tall posts about four feet apart. She reined the mare to a halt at the edge of the hollow, staring curiously at the red-earthed center.

"I've never seen this before," Sheila murmured.

Glancing at Juan, she saw the troubled darkness of his eyes as he gazed at the hollow, his expression sternly sober. "What is this place?"

"It is for punishment."

"Punishment?" She frowned. "What do you mean?"

"Those who do wrong, who do not obey, are brought here for punishment." He nudged his horse alongside the roan and reached down to grip the reins beneath the mare's chin. "Come. I know it is necessary, but I do not like to look upon this place."

He led her away from the hollow toward the corral. Confused, Sheila would like to have questioned him further, but it was obvious Juan didn't want to talk about it. She already knew that one of Ráfaga's rules was that no one left the canyon without his permission. The person who did was evidently taken to the hollow and punished.

That much she could surmise, but the form of punishment . . . ? Considering Juan's reaction to it, Sheila decided that maybe it was better that she didn't know. She shuddered without really knowing why.

At a shuffling walk, the horses passed the corral, Juan no longer leading the roan mare once they had skirted the hollow. They rode side by side onto the dirt path between the adobe houses. As they neared Elena's house, Sheila noticed the invalid man sitting beneath the overhang. She was faintly surprised when Juan lifted a hand in a halting gesture.

"A *momento, señora*." He excused himself to walk his horse to where the man sat.

The roan mare drifted along with his horse and Sheila didn't try to stop her mount. She listened to Juan greet the invalid and talk to him in Spanish, his tone quietly conversational. Several times, he gestured toward Sheila as he spoke. Nothing flickered in the invalid's vacant expression. He stared into space, as if he wasn't aware of their presence.

Elena appeared in the doorway, darting Sheila a fiery look before speaking sharply to Juan. She walked quickly to her husband and stood behind his chair.

Her hands rested on his shoulders. The action reminded Sheila of a mother protectively comforting her child. She felt a rush of pity for Elena and knew the brunette would not thank her for it.

Averting her gaze, Sheila reined the mare to the center of the path to wait for Juan. He joined her almost immediately. Sheila nibbled hesitantly at her lower lip. Juan noticed the movement.

"Elena was angry with me, *señora*," he said as if he thought Sheila believed the brunette's sharpness had been because of her. "She is certain my brother doesn't understand what I say and finds me foolish to talk to him."

"Yo-your brother?" Sheila faltered.

"*Sí,* César is my brother. You did not know?" he asked curiously.

"No." She shook her head, slightly taken aback at the discovery. "No, I didn't know." Another thought occurred to her and it tumbled from her mouth before she could stop it. "But Ráfaga and Elena, they—" Discretion intervened and she couldn't say aloud that they had been lovers.

"It is over now." Juan guessed the rest of her sentence and indicated that there wasn't any need to discuss it.

Juan seemed so moral and sensitive that Sheila couldn't believe he had actually approved of the liaison. "But she is your sister-in-law."

"She takes care of César." There was a closed look to his face that told Sheila, as his words hadn't, that she was prying into something that was none of her business.

Irritated, Sheila faced front. "I don't see how you can be so loyal to Ráfaga when he was your sister-in-law's lover."

"I do not blame Ráfaga." There was a faint reprimand in his level voice.

Indignation sputtered before Sheila remembered this was a male-dominated culture. It was a society of double standards, especially in the rural areas. But

Sheila was suddenly not in the mood to argue the point with Juan.

Voicing curt gratitude for the outing, Sheila dismounted at the house and handed the reins to Juan. The roan mare nuzzled her shoulder and Sheila absently stroked the blaze-faced horse.

"Sorry, Arriba, no sugar today," she murmured, then walked into the adobe house.

Sundown did not bring Ráfaga's return. She would have another night and part of another day to be on her own. Lighting a kerosene lamp, she set it by a chair and picked up one of the books Laredo had given her. She read until her eyes were too tired to see, then went to bed. After two restless nights, sleep came swiftly this time.

The closing of the front door and footsteps echoing hollowly in the empty house awakened Sheila. She opened her heavy-lidded eyes and listened to the footsteps approaching the bedroom. A lazily sensuous smile touched her lips as she rolled to Ráfaga's side of the bed. Her sleep-drugged mind was not functioning properly or it would have checked the swell of gladness in her heart.

"Ráfaga," Sheila whispered as a dark figure framed itself in the doorway.

There was no answer. Her sleepy gaze noticed a discrepancy. The figure wasn't tall enough to be Ráfaga. All traces of sleep vanished as her muscles tensed in alarm, her senses fully alert.

"Juan? Is that you?" She was breathing deeply, trying to check her rising fear.

"Sí, Juan," a guttural voice answered

But it wasn't Juan—at least it wasn't the proud, gentle man Sheila had meant. It was the other man, Juan Ortega, Brad's murderer. Her gasping cry of terror was muffled by the constricting muscles in her throat as his menacing hulk moved into the room. But there was no time for panic.

With lightning-swift calculation, her mind registered several facts at once. The guard outside the house had either been this man or a cohort of his; otherwise, he couldn't have entered the house. Her screams might bring the other man in, and right now the match was even, if overbalanced in his favor.

There was no one to save her, only herself. Naked beneath the blanket, Sheila realized the bed was not the place to make her defense. As he reached the foot of the bed, Sheila scrambled out, dragging the blanket with her, and tried to run from the room. Her legs became entangled in its folds, slowing her flight.

He grabbed for her arm and missed, his fingers curling into the trailing length of the blanket, instead. Foolishly, Sheila tried to hold onto the protective cover and was pulled within his reach. He let out a low laugh of triumph as he hauled her against his broad chest.

With all her strength, Sheila tried to push away from him, forsaking her hold on the blanket to be free of his revolting nearness. One arm was firmly around her waist to hold her while his other hand moved to her front.

The wiry hairs on the back of his hand scraped at her soft flesh as he ripped the blanket from her breasts and tore it aside from the rest of her. He clamped a rough hand on one of her breasts.

The sickening smell of his foul breath warned Sheila of his descending mouth. She twisted her head far to the side, shuddering as the repulsive moistness of his mouth found the curve of her neck. Scratching like a wild animal, Sheila tried to claw her way free, breathing with gasping sobs of terror. She succeeded in partially turning in his hold, but all it gained her was the repugnant feel of his hardness pressing against her bare bottom.

He was breathing heavily in his lust, his hot, stinking breath nearly smothering Sheila. Twisting and writhing with desperate violence, she still couldn't elude his groping hands, roughly feeling their way over her nude body.

A cry was wrenched from her throat as he propelled her backward toward the bed. The back of her knees bumped against the mattress and her legs buckled. He followed her down, his suffocating weight pinning Sheila beneath him. Unable to capture her lips, he fastened his mouth on a breast, opening wide, as if to swallow it. Digging her fingers into his scalp, Sheila tried to force his head away from her breast by pulling savagely at his hair. His teeth sank into her nipple, biting it until the excruciating pain made her let go of his hair.

While continuing to suckle her breast, he grabbed a handful of her bottom and began to shift her more fully beneath his hips. Sheila struggled frantically, but she seemed only to succeed in aiding him in his efforts. She felt him trying to force his way between her legs. She tried to raise a knee to wound him, but his driving weight was too much for her to overcome.

Her stomach recoiled at the touch of his hand as he fumbled with his pants. Sickened and terrified beyond description, Sheila lowered her hands to push at his ribs and waist, trying with all her might to roll him off. Her right hand brushed against something solid and inanimate—the hilt of a knife.

There wasn't any time to think. Her searching fingers sought and found the snap that held the knife in its sheath. Unfastening it, she pulled the knife free and began stabbing at his back. He stiffened in surprise at the first thrust of the blade.

With the second, he was straightening, twisting an arm behind him to grab at the pain. When Sheila plunged the knife into his body the third time, he suddenly realized where the pain was coming from.

His face was black and contorted with rage. He grunted like a maddened bull, but Sheila was sobbing in her desperate effort to stop him from raping her any way she could. She didn't see his swinging hand until it was too late. Lights exploded in her head as he struck her jaw with the back of his hand.

A swirling black mist of pain threatened to engulf her. Sheila fought to remain conscious, knowing she had to keep her advantage or be lost to his lechery. Her hand had a death grip on the knife, but she didn't have to use it again as his weight left her and he staggered from the room.

He took all her strength when he left. Drained, Sheila lay on the bed, broken sobs coming from her throat, tears streaming down her cheeks. Gradually the pain in her jaw eased to a bearable level. Her skin began to crawl where his mauling hands had grabbed her.

Dragging her bruised and aching body from the bed, Sheila lurched toward the dresser. She pushed aside the lamp, wanting the darkness to hide her, and laid the knife beside it. The pitcher of water beside the basin was full. Picking it up, Sheila slowly began pouring the cool water over her shoulders and hot flesh until it was half-empty.

The water streamed down her body to form a puddle on the floor. But she was mindless to it as she began rubbing the soap everywhere his filthy hands had touched her, painstakingly covering every inch.

Still sobbing, she rinsed away the lather with the rest of the water, but the repellent sensations lingered. Grabbing the coarse towel from its hook, she tried wiping them away. She rubbed her skin until it was nearly raw and would have continued if she hadn't heard the front door opening.

A murderous, primitive hatred seared through her veins. The towel slipped to the floor, falling in the pool of water at her feet. Her violent anger shook the hand seeking the knife on the dresser. This time she would kill him. Moving stealthily on tiptoes, Sheila glided into the hall.

Chapter 16

The yellow gleam in her eyes was like that of a man-killing lioness. With her back flattened against the wall near the entry arch to the main room, Sheila waited for her prey. Motionless, she listened to the approaching foosteps. A feral smile curved her mouth as the bulky figure entered the hall.

Raising the knife, she aimed it at his spine and struck. But the blade slashed through empty air, her target spinning away. All her weight had been in the killing blow that missed.

Off balance, she cried out in frustration. A steel trap closed over her wrist, slamming her hand against the wall. The impact knocked the knife from her fingers.

"No!" she gasped in rage.

"I did not ride half the night to be murdered in my own home!" snapped a familiar, growling voice.

"Ráfaga? It's you!" Sheila cried in disbelief. Her anger died as rapidly as it had flamed to life. "You're back! Oh, God, you're back!" She flung herself into his arms, burying her head in the comforting solidity of his chest. "I'm so glad! So glad!"

He slipped the saddlebags from his shoulder, letting them fall to the floor. It had been the saddlebags that had lent bulk to his figure, disguising his lean build. His arms didn't immediately go around her, although she clung to him tightly.

"Sheila—"

She heard the anger and confusion mixed in his voice and moved her head in protest. "Hold me." Her own voice throbbed with the need to feel his strength. "Please, just hold me." There was refuge in his embrace and Sheila didn't question why.

He hesitated, then let his arms close around her. His hands moved along her spine to mold her more firmly to his length. He bent his head down, rubbing his chin and jaw against the tousled silk of her hair.

The hard feel of his body was beginning to blot away the lingering traces of Ortega's touch. Her lips began pressing kisses against his chest. The steady beat of his heart reassured Sheila of the rightness of what she was doing.

Lifting her head, she let her kisses move to the hollow of his throat. Her fingers moved aside the collar of his shirt, unfastening buttons to slide her hands over his warm chest.

His mouth brushed her temple and Sheila quivered in sudden longing. She tilted her head back to see his strong features, her lips parting in a silent invitation. His gaze fastened on her mouth, soft and trembling, glistening moistly.

"Please," Sheila murmured, "kiss me."

He waited an infinite second before he lowered his head to accept her invitation. His mouth opened over hers, hard and hungry. Sheila returned the kiss with the same insatiable fire, not realizing until that moment how much Ráfaga had taught her about making love. She forced his shirt open so she could feel her breasts against the nakedness of his chest.

With practiced expertise, his hands were roaming

over her hips and rib cage, rediscovering the points of pleasure along her shoulders. His mouth moved to investigate these special passion places more fully and accidentally brushed her swollen jaw.

Pain shot through her like splintering glass. Unwittingly Sheila cried out, cupping her hand to the injured area and twisting her head away. Instantly she felt his gentle fingers touching her hand.

"I have hurt you?" There was surprise in his husky tone.

"No, I—" Sheila tried to protest.

"Let me see," Ráfaga ordered softly, but it was no less an order as he pushed her hand aside to let his fingers explore her jaw. She flinched uncontrollably as he touched the swelling lump. "What is this?" he demanded grimly. "How did this happen to your face?"

His dark features were shadowed by the dim light, but Sheila could see the ruthless set of his jaw and mouth. Tears misted her eyes as the sordid tale spilled from her lips.

"He was trying to rape me and I fought with him. I got hold of his knife and stabbed him. That's when he hit me. When you came, I thought it was him coming back to finish what he had started. That's why I tried to stab you with the knife—because I thought it was him and I wanted to kill him. I wanted to kill him!" she repeated again on a rising bubble of hysteria.

"Who?" His fingers dug savagely into her shoulders, shaking her hard. "Who did this to you? Who?"

Her momentary hysteria was replaced by anger. Sheila hurled the name of her attacker at Ráfaga. "Juan!" she cried out, spitting the venom of her hatred.

His response was just as explosive. "Liar!!" He shoved her away from him. The violent force of his action sent her reeling backward against the wall.

A moment ago Sheila had been all-loving; now she was all-hating. "If you don't believe me, go ask him yourself!" she hissed. "You'll find stab wounds in his back—three of them!"

His face was like chiseled granite, hard and unyield-

ing. His dark eyes were like blackened chips of ice,
raking her with their bleak anger, cutting to the bone.

"You will make your accusation to his face." His
mouth was a cruel, thin line.

"Gladly!" Sheila breathed hotly.

Ráfaga turned sharply on his heel, anger holding his
erect carriage rigid as he walked into the main room.
Shaking, Sheila stumbled into the bedroom. Her toe
caught the edge of the blanket lying on the floor.

She picked it up and wrapped it around her, suddenly
feeling very cold. She wanted to lie down on the bed
and die, but she could hear Ráfaga's voice snapping
orders to the guard. With her head held high, Sheila
walked into the main room.

The lamp was lit, casting an eerie glow over the
room. Ráfaga was standing with his back to the fireplace, his hands clasped behind him. His legs were
slightly apart in a stance that very much indicated he
was lord of all he surveyed.

Sheila remembered the way she had thrown herself
into his arms and brazenly invited his kisses. Of all
the men from whom to seek comfort and understanding,
he was the last she should have chosen. There wasn't
a compassionate bone in his heartless body.

He gave her a long, hard look. Defensively, Sheila
tilted her chin a fraction of an inch higher, meeting his
look with coldness. His harsh gaze slid to her cheek.
Sheila guessed that the skin was already discolored, as
well as swollen. It was beginning to ache worse now,
a painful throb that pulsed through her head, making
her feel slightly sick.

There was a knock at the door. Ráfaga curtly called
out his permission to enter. A violent shudder quaked
through Sheila. She turned as the door opened, unable
to look at the repulsive face of her attacker. Lowering
her gaze to the floor, she listened to the brief exchange
in Spanish.

"It is the *señora* who wishes to say something to
you," Ráfaga announced in a deadly calm tone.

Her head jerked to glare at him, hating the disbeliev-

ing taunt in his dark eyes. Sheila forced herself to turn
toward the door, steeling her jumping nerves to carry
out this ugly scene. First she saw Laredo, his blue eyes
narrowing briefly as he noticed the bruise on her cheek.
Holding herself rigid, she looked at the man Laredo
held by the arm.

A sleepily confused pair of dark eyes stared back at
her, questioning and uncertain. It was Juan, the man
who had been her constant companion these last three
days. He and Laredo were the only people who came
close to being her friends. Her dismay at discovering
why Ráfaga had been so certain she was lying robbed
her of speech.

Distantly, Sheila heard an order given in Spanish. A
grim frown creased Laredo's forehead as he released
Juan's arm and stepped behind him to lift his shirt. He
glanced back at Ráfaga and shook his head. Then
Sheila was conscious of Ráfaga looming beside her.

"There are no wounds, *señora.*" Behind his ice-coated
words, she heard the biting accusation that she was a
liar and worse.

Her speechlessness disintegrated in a burst of fury.
He was too quick to condemn her.

"I didn't mean *him!*" Sheila raged, her head pounding as if there were a thousand demons inside. "I meant
the murdering bastard who killed my husband—the one
you gave me to so briefly and then took back! He
obviously decided it was time you stopped having the
sole use of my body and shared the prize with him!
Laredo knows which fat, slobbering beast I mean!"

With her fury spent, she began sobbing uncontrollably. Sheila twisted her away from Ráfaga, her
shoulders hunching in shame and degradation. Hot
tears streamed from her eyes, burning her cheeks as she
wept freely and openly. Her knees threatened to buckle
and she swayed unsteadily. Strong fingers reached out
to grip her shoulders.

"Don't touch me!" Sheila recoiled wildly, her voice
hoarse and broken with racking sobs. "Pig! Animal!"
She was hysterical.

Swearing savagely in Spanish, Ráfaga issued clipped orders. In a matter of seconds, her struggling, sobbing body was pushed into another pair of arms. Something hard touched her lips and Sheila twisted away from it. The object followed persistently.

"Come on, Sheila," Laredo coaxed firmly. "Drink this." Still she fought him, weeping uncontrollably. "Snap out of it!"

He grabbed a handful of hair and twisted her head back, forcibly pouring some liquid between her lips. It burned her throat like fire. Coughing and choking, Sheila pushed the bottle away from her mouth and Laredo didn't force it back.

As the burning subsided, Sheila could breathe without feeling that her lungs were on fire. The dose of liquor had stopped her hysteria and reduced her sobs to dry, hiccuping sounds. She leaned her weary head against Laredo's shoulder, grateful for the support of his arm around her.

Her tear-moistened lashes opened slowly, her gaze drawn to the unyielding coldness of Ráfaga's eyes. Sheila had to endure his freezing regard for only a second before the door opened to divert his attention.

This time Sheila had cause to shudder. Two men were dragging and carrying a third man into the room. A wave of revulsion filled her at the sight of him. He was shirtless, his stout, naked torso exposed. Despite his fatness, Sheila knew his muscles were not flaccid. A crude bandage was wrapped around his broad waist, the material stained scarlet with his own blood.

Ráfaga could not doubt her now, Sheila thought as her embittered gaze slid to him. His features were drawn in ruthless, cruel lines, coldly remote. The lamplight caught the gleam of something metallic in his hand. Sheila glanced down to see a knife in his hand, Juan's knife, the knife she had used to stab him. Ráfaga took a slow, menacing step toward the man being held.

The look in his eyes struck cold terror in her heart. Ráfaga was going to kill him. She knew it. Sheila even wanted to see Ortega die, yet some part of her recoiled from what was happening.

When Ráfaga took the second step, Brad's murderer must have realized his intention and began babbling in Spanish. His voice was almost whining. Sheila glanced at Ráfaga, expecting to see contempt etched in his hard features. He was standing rigidly in place, his shoulders stiffened. A muscle was twitching in his jaw.

There was a subtle change in the atmosphere. Sheila felt the attention of the others in the room shift to her. Her gaze swerved upward to Laredo's face. He was looking at her, searching her features with a mixture of skepticism and grimness. A cold chill raced down her spine.

"What's the matter?" she asked warily. "What's he saying about me?" Sheila demanded a translation.

Laredo eyed her for a minute before he spoke. "He said he was on guard outside and you came to the door, motioning for him to come in. He knew he wasn't supposed to, but it was nighttime and he thought there might be something wrong."

Sheila began shaking her head, moving away from the arm around her shoulders. "No!" she denied vehemently.

"He said you began talking to him," Laredo continued. "He didn't understand what you were saying, but he thought you wanted to leave the canyon and that you wanted him to help you. When he refused, you came closer to him and let the blanket fall to the floor. Then you put your arms around him and he lost his head. That's when you grabbed his knife and stabbed him. He said he had been tricked and that you would have run away if he hadn't struck you."

"It isn't true!" she protested strongly.

"He swears by the Holy Virgin it is," Laredo replied flatly.

"It isn't true!" Sheila turned to Ráfaga. Unconsciously, she crossed the space that separated them. "It isn't true!" she repeated.

It was imperative that Ráfaga believe her. But he

was so distant, like a bronze statue regarding her with sightless eyes. She knew both he and Laredo were remembering the time she had tried to enlist Laredo's aid in escaping. Clutching the blanket with one hand, Sheila moved closer to him, curving an arm around the muscles of his waist.

"Not a word of what he told you is true!" Her voice was husky with emotion. "He came to our room while I was sleeping. He tried to force himself on me. Why do you think I begged you to hold me and kiss me?"

Something flickered in his eyes, a smouldering light that warmed Sheila. His arm instinctively circled her back to draw her to his muscular frame. The blanket slipped from one shoulder and his hand settled on the bareness of her skin, a half-caress. Then Juan, her attacker, spoke again and Sheila felt the warmth withdraw from Ráfaga's touch.

"What did he say?" Sheila pressed closer to Ráfaga, trying to breach the barrier he had suddenly erected.

"He said you wound around him like a serpent, too." His voice was flat and unemotional, but his fingers dug punishingly into her shoulder. "He said you bewitched him the way you are trying to bewitch me."

"Oh!" It was a stifled cry of protest. Sheila tried to twist out of his arms, but Ráfaga held her fast.

"You do not bewitch me," he said lowly, "nor do you escape from me." Retaining his grip on her, Ráfaga spoke rapidly in Spanish to the others.

Sheila stopped struggling. She lacked the strength to fight him, and it would have been useless, anyway. When Ráfaga finished, the two men holding Juan released him. Her attacker's reaction was a mixture of relief and fear. Everyone, including Laredo, quietly left the house.

Her head was bowed, a wet mist clouding her eyes. "You let him go," Sheila accused in a voice low with pain.

"He disobeyed an order. For that he will be punished," Ráfaga stated.

"And me?" she retorted bitterly. "Am I to be punished because I was almost raped?"

He exhaled an impatient, angry breath and abruptly let her go. "It is late."

"I'm not tired." But her voice sounded very tired. "And I'm certainly not going to bed with you!"

"Sheila—" he began angrily.

"Earlier it was 'señora.' Now it's Sheila," she interrupted with bitter sarcasm. "Why? Because you want me to lie in bed with you! Well, you can go to hell!" She was visibly trembling.

"I have been away for three days wondering if you would be here when I returned." His nostrils were flared in anger. "Now I am back and it is still hell. But you are still mine. You will lie with me—here or in the bedroom. It makes no difference."

"Don't you dare come near me!" Sheila hissed. She was breathing deeply, frightened by the hard, ruthless look to his face.

His mouth twisted in a cold smile. With calm deliberation, he began stripping, shedding his clothes and seeming to discard the cloak of civilization along with them. Sheila's heart pounded madly, half in fear and half in response to the sudden gnawing tightness in her stomach. His body gleamed in the lamplight like hard, polished bronze. When he stood before her, she shook her head in mute protest to what he demanded.

"Lay the blanket on the floor," Ráfaga ordered.

No, no, no! Sheila was screaming inside, but she felt her hands unwrapping the blanket from around her. There her compliance stopped and the blanket slipped from her hands into a heap on the floor. His dark eyes began an insolent appraisal, traveling from head to toe and back.

His hand reached out to grip the curve of her waist and draw her unresisting body against the hard contours of his. With his right hand, he cupped the back of her neck and forced her head up to his lips.

It was a hard, brutal kiss, filled with anger. Shocked by the absence of any fiery passion, Sheila tried to resist, but his arms were iron-strong and unrelenting. She couldn't escape the bruising menace of his mouth.

With a dangerous and cruel sensuality, he parted her lips. Her breasts were crushed against the wall of his chest. The male hands on her back were arching her hips to him, quivering down her backbone. Then he was pressing her backward and down until the hard floor was beneath her shoulder blades.

Afterward Ráfaga carried her to the bedroom. Bruised and slightly battered by his animal possession, Sheila didn't make a sound as he put her on the bed. She was unaware of the hurt, wounded look in her eyes, but Ráfaga studied it as he gazed down at her.

Turning, he walked to the dresser and lit the lamp. Sheila lifted a protective hand to her eyes, shielding them and her face from the light. She heard his footsteps as he left the room. He returned within seconds to cover her nakedness with the blanket she had dropped in the main room.

"Why is all this water on the floor?" It was a demand and a question.

The savage intimacy ending only minutes ago made it difficult for Sheila to assimilate his question. She frowned, trying to collect her wits.

"It's—it's from bathing," she said, finally remembering. Her troubled eyes saw him pick up the pitcher by the basin. "It's empty. I used it all."

"Why?" Ráfaga demanded with a Satanic lift of one dark brow.

"For obvious reasons." Sheila ran a shaking hand through her hair in agitation and she shuddered as she remembered the very urgent reason. "I felt dirty, contaminated from—from *him*," she said, unable to refer directly to her attacker. "I had to wash—to scrub away filthy traces of him, but I don't expect you to understand what it's like. My God, you don't even believe me!" There was a trembling catch in her voice as she hurled the last sentence at him.

Turning her face to the wall, Sheila jammed a fist against her mouth, trying to swallow the unbearable lump in her throat. Again she heard Ráfaga approaching the bed and she closed her eyes tight.

"Here," he said.

She looked at him out of the corner of her eye. He was offering his saddlebags to her. She stared at them coldly, tears burning the backs of her eyes.

"What is it?" she asked.

He tossed the bags on the bed beside her, then walked to the dresser. "I bought you some clothes since you were so reluctant to wear any castoffs of Elena's."

Sheila didn't quite believe him and unfastened the flaps to dump the contents of the saddlebags onto the bed. She stared at the clothes that tumbled out: a pair of Levi's, a skirt, and at least one other pair of slacks, as well as several blouses. Her stunned fingers singled out a cranberry-colored silk blouse for closer inspection.

"I thought the color would complement your fairness," Ráfaga said quietly. Sheila turned to him, finding herself lost in the compelling darkness of his eyes.

Even though he was across the room from her, she could feel the dominating force of his presence. Sheila broke free of his gaze.

"Where did you get them?" She glanced at the clothes on the bed, a corner of her mouth lifting with wry bitterness. "Don't tell me you raided a store?"

"I *bought* them at a store." His voice underlined the verb.

"Why?" Sheila challenged.

"Because, as you have pointed out many times, you needed clothes."

"Is this some sort of appeasement for holding me a prisoner here? Because, if it is, it won't work," she snapped. "What you would really prefer is that I have no clothes at all. That way whenever you felt a surge of lust, you could take me without wasting the time to strip off my clothes." With a sweep of her hand, she pushed the clothes to the floor. "I wouldn't dream of disappointing you." Sarcasm filled her voice.

"You are refusing them?" Ráfaga impaled her on his spearing gaze.

Her amber eyes flashed with sparks of anger. "Maybe I should throw them in your face so you'll be certain of my message." Sheila saw the thinning of his mouth. "Don't pretend you were trying to be thoughtful; if you were, you would let me go instead of holding me here!"

He turned his back to her, his hand doubled into a fist on the dresser top. "You hate it very much here, do you not?" It was a flat, unemotional statement.

"Hate?" She laughed a bitter, throaty laugh. "How odd that you should choose that word, considering that five minutes ago you didn't make love to me—you made 'hate' to me!"

"*Sí*," Ráfaga admitted, pivoting to walk slowly to the bed. "I took you in anger a moment ago." He loomed above her like a bronze god.

"Why?" Sheila felt the chill of his coldness. "Did you want to finish what Juan started? The only thing I was trying to escape from was him. The very day you left I saw him and I knew he would be waiting out there for me if I tried to get away. I thought I would be safe from him if I did as you said, staying in the house or going out only with the other Juan. I thought your word could protect me, but it didn't. When I think of the way I fell into your arms when you returned, it makes me sick. I'm not even safe with you. You proved that when you called me a liar and raped me!"

The mattress shifted beneath his weight. Sheila tried to roll away from him, but he caught her wrists and spreadeagled her arms above her head. Pinned, she stopped struggling as she waited for him to make use of his advantage.

"I believe you when you say Juan tried to rape you," he said grimly. "I believe you stole his knife and stabbed him to defend your honor."

"Then, why?" Sheila cried her confusion. "Why did you listen to him?"

"Because I think you may have invited him into the house," he answered. "You had to know tonight was your last chance of escaping before I returned. And I know you would make an empty promise of your body to any man who helped you. You have done it before with Laredo." Sheila groaned and turned her head away. "I think you asked him, believing you could control him, only to discover you could not."

"I didn't! I swear I didn't!" she protested, squeezing her eyes tightly shut.

"Not a moment ago, you said you wanted to be free," Ráfaga reminded her coldly, "that you wanted to escape. You admitted what I already knew. Perhaps there was truth in each of your stories. I could not kill him for wanting you, or I would have to kill myself, because I, too, feel the desire to possess you."

The moist warmth of his breath was against her cheek. Sheila stiffened at the tantalizing brush of his mouth over her lips. His weight was settling on top of her. She twisted her head away from his light, exploring kiss.

"Don't" she protested, aching. The blanket scratched the nakedness of her flesh as it was trapped between their bodies.

"That is one reason why there was no gentleness in my heart when I took you." His voice was muffled by her hair, its anger directed at himself. "The other reason was that I knew Juan Ortega was right when he said you had bewitched me. For three days you haunted my vision, lioness. At night, it was the remembered feel of your softness beside me."

His teeth nibbled at her earlobe, sending shivers over her skin. This was the seductive mastery Sheila remembered, this velvet over steel. She was being commanded again to take part in the lovemaking, to receive satisfaction, as well as give it.

"You have bewitched me, lioness," he murmured again against her mouth, a roughness still in his tone, "into wanting you. It is only right that I make you want me."

Chapter 17

An unnatural silence filled the house. Standing at the front window, Sheila glanced over her shoulder. She frowned as she realized Consuelo had left without her usual smiling *"buenos días."* This unnerving silence must have affected her, too, Sheila decided.

Her fingers touched the buttoned front of her blouse. Dispassionately, Ráfaga had ordered her to wear the clothes he had brought her. It was the last thing Sheila could remember him saying directly to her.

His marked indifference this morning and this noon made a mockery of his attention to her last night. Sexually, she must have bewitched him, but he certainly wasn't under her spell in any other way.

In some ways it seemed to Sheila as if the reverse were true. She wavered between love and hate whenever he was around, like a barometer trapped between two conflicting fronts. She wondered how much longer these two emotions could war with each other before one of them came out a victor.

The sound of horses' hooves turned Sheila's attention out the window. Juan rode into view, leading her roan mare, Arriba, and Ráfaga's bay. The back of her neck prickled in warning. Sheila pivoted to find Ráfaga standing in the middle of the room, his entrance made with animal silence. Her stomach twisted itself into a knot of longing as she met his hooded look, impassive and aloof.

"Juan is here with the horses." She tried to sound natural and calm. "I presume we're going for a ride." It came out brittle and challenging.

"No."

"Then, why—" She started to look out the window again.

"It is time for the punishment of Juan Ortega. The midday sun is hot and it is a long walk to the place. I thought you would prefer to ride," Ráfaga stated. A sardonic glint flickered in his eyes as he added, "Do you wish to see his punishment?"

"I—" Sheila hesitated. She wasn't certain exactly how she felt, except that she wanted to erase all memory of Juan's attack from her mind.

"You were anxious enough last night to drive a knife into his back and later to have me kill him for you. Has your stomach become weak with the rising of the sun?"

Sheila read between the lines. Ráfaga was accusing her of having a guilty conscience, of having invited Juan into the house without being prepared to face the consequences. He was suggesting that in the harsh light of day, she might feel equally to blame for what happened because of her supposed invitation.

"No, it hasn't," she snapped angrily. "I shall enjoy seeing him punished."

There was a slight inclination of his dark head in arrogant acceptance of her decision. "The horses are outside."

Sheila stalked past him to the door. A silent and solemn-faced Juan handed her the mare's reins. Ráfaga's fingers touched her elbow to assist her in mounting. She pulled away, disdainfully rejecting his offer.

Astride the saddle, her smouldering eyes saw Juan's

gaze fix on the purpling mark along her jaw. She had seen the disfiguring bruise in the mirror and knew how ugly it looked.

"*La señora* is all right?" Juan asked with gentle concern.

"I'm fine." But her response was much sharper than she had intended.

As she clamped her teeth shut tightly, a twinge of pain shot along her jaw. Reining the mare around, Sheila guided the animal toward the distant cluster of houses.

She knew their destination—that hollowed piece of ground beyond the corral. Out of the corner of her eye, she noticed Ráfaga move his bay up to ride beside her, but she didn't acknowledge his presence with a word or a look.

There wasn't a sign of life as they rode by the adobe buildings. When they neared the hollow, Sheila discovered why. Every man, woman, and child living in the canyon was at the hollow. Despite the crowd, there was little talking. Only the younger children were playing, the ones who didn't know what was about to happen.

At the rim of the hollow, Sheila halted the mare and Ráfaga did the same with his horse. Immediately, they became the cynosure of everyone there. Sheila watched the heads turn in their direction and felt the hush become more pronounced.

Laredo was standing with two other men in the center of the hollow near the two poles. She saw his head jerk as he noticed her beside Ráfaga. He separated himself from the two men, long, ground-eating strides carrying him to the top of the hollow.

"What the hell is she doing here?" He confronted Ráfaga with an angry look.

There wasn't a crack in the mask that covered Ráfaga's features. "Mrs. Townsend wished to come."

Sheila blanched at his cold formality. She had gone from Sheila to *señora,* and now she was addressed as Mrs. Townsend. If he was seeking to prove that he was involved with her only physically, he couldn't have chosen a better way.

"This is no place for her," Laredo persisted. "There isn't any reason for her to see this. Let her go, Ráfaga."

"I did not order her to come," Ráfaga answered with unruffled coolness. "She stays or leaves by her own choice."

Laredo turned to her, his blue eyes snapping. "For God's sake, Sheila, get out of here. You don't want to see this. I'll send Juan with you."

"You forget." She turned so he could see the disfiguring bruise marring her left cheek and jaw. "I have ample reason to want to see him punished, Laredo."

He breathed in deeply, lowering his head with an exasperated shake. "You are either stupid or stubborn. I just hope to hell you know what you're doing." There was a lightning flick of his blue eyes in her direction before he pivoted away.

A low command in Spanish came from Ráfaga. Laredo stopped and moved to take the reins of the bay as Ráfaga dismounted. He didn't look again at Sheila, but she felt the mocking slash of his obsidian eyes before Ráfaga moved away from the horses.

The attention shifted to the center of the hollow. For the first time, Sheila noticed two men holding her attacker. There was a definite pallor beneath his swarthy complexion, and his dark eyes kept darting nervously to the twin posts. She could almost see the sweating beads of fear running down his face. Although he stood unmoving, Sheila knew he was cowering inside. Looking at him, she still felt revulsion, but little fear.

Gradually, she became aware that everyone was watching Ráfaga, waiting. Her gaze slid to him, standing several yards away. His back was to her, but it was as if he felt her attention and had been waiting for it. The instant she looked at him, Sheila heard him begin to speak in Spanish. His voice was calm and low, yet it carried to all without effort.

Laredo was standing at the bay's head near Sheila.

She leaned forward in the saddle, her gaze not leaving Ráfaga.

"What is he saying?" she asked.

Laredo turned his head slightly, showing his profile without taking his attention away from Ráfaga. "He's explaining why Juan is to be punished."

When Ráfaga finished his explanation, he stood silently. Sheila's gaze swept over the people gathered around the hollow. They were glancing around, as if waiting for something.

"What's happening now?" Sheila questioned Laredo again.

"If anyone wants to protest his decision, they are allowed to speak now and argue in Juan's behalf."

"How democratic." she mocked dryly, then received a chastising look from Laredo.

At a nod from Ráfaga, the two men led Juan to the two posts. Positioning him between them, they began tying his arms, stretching him between the two poles. When that was done, one of the men ripped open the back of Juan's shirt.

A movement near the posts caught Sheila's eye. Her gaze widened at a whip loosely coiled in a man's hand. She wasn't certain what type of punishment she had expected Juan would receive, but somehow she doubted if she would have guessed a public whipping.

Mesmerized, she watched the man shake out the whip, letting it snake over the ground in front of him. His arm lifted. Sheila heard the whir of rawhide in the air and saw the slash it made on Juan's back.

A red stripe appeared on his flesh, halfway between his shoulder blades and the bandage circling his lower back, where Sheila had stabbed him. His body jerked convulsively at the pain.

Whir and slash. Whir and slash. It was repeated over and over again. A maze of red lines crisscrossed his back. Sheila's attention was rooted by horror to the scene. She couldn't tear her eyes away from what was happening or deafen her ears to his strangled cries.

Soon, he wasn't making any sound as he slumped life-less, his arms bound to the poles, keeping him upright.

The rawhide slithered to the ground and became mo-tionless. Its snaking, striking fury was spent. A second man walked to the poles, a knife gleaming in his hand. The blade sliced through the ropes that supported the body. She watched him tumble to the ground and lie there inert.

An inexplicable force suddenly pulled her gaze to Ráfaga. His saturnine features were looking back at her, impassively studying Sheila's face. Her stomach churned. She was going to be sick.

With a roughness unusual to her, Sheila yanked at the reins. The mare half-reared as she tried to relieve the sawing pressure on the bit. When the roan was pointed away from the hollow, Sheila dug her heels into the mare's flanks, nearly losing her seat as the mare bounded forward.

In the cover of the woods, Sheila dismounted before the mare came to a full stop and fell to her knees. The violent heaving of her stomach didn't stop until there was nothing left. Sheila knelt there, drenched in a cold sweat, weak and deathly pale.

Finally, Sheila made her shaking legs support her, but she didn't have the strength to climb back on the roan mare. Clutching the saddle for balance, she walked beside the horse, wavering unsteadily as they made their way through the trees.

I've got to get out of here. I've got to get out of here. The desperate chant kept drumming inside of her, the words hammering at her brain until the pressure was nearly unbearable.

Ahead, her glazed eyes saw the shimmering reflec-tion of the sun in the spring-fed pool. Sheila staggered into the clearing, dropping to her knees beside the pool. She wanted to splash water over her face, but her hands were shaking too badly.

Someone was beside her. She turned to see Ráfaga bending next to her. Before she could recoil, he was pressing a wet cloth to her face, wiping the perspiration from her forehead and upper lip. Her lashes fluttered down at the soothing coolness. And Sheila suddenly didn't care what kind of monster was providing this relief.

"You did not enjoy seeing him punished as you thought, no?" Ráfaga rinsed the cloth and applied fresh dampness to her neck.

"It was barbaric and inhuman," she said and shuddered as the image of shredded flesh flashed in her mind's eye.

"All punishment is inhuman," he replied smoothly and with a hint of grimness. "What is the alternative?"

"I don't know," Sheila mumbled.

"If you find a punishment that is humane, it would solve a big problem in the world."

He curled the wet cloth around the back of her neck and left it there. Taking her by the shoulders, he drew Sheila to her feet. When she opened her eyes, she found him looking deeply into them, an enigmatic darkness in his own eyes.

"Perhaps you should not have seen it," Ráfaga said lowly.

She wished she hadn't, but wishing did no good now. Still weak, Sheila swayed unsteadily. Ráfaga lifted her off her feet to cradle her in his arms. She didn't murmur any protest when he carried her back to the house.

The scene in the hollow haunted her for days. One night Sheila awoke from a nightmare about it and Ráfaga comforted her as if she were a frightened child, holding her closely and stroking her hair until the trembling stopped.

During the daylight hours, she spent more of her time in deep thought, considering life, its values, and contradictions. All the while a little voice in the back of her head kept repeating: *You've got to get out of here,* as if it knew something that she didn't.

A full week later, she and Ráfaga were out riding in the warmth of a spring afternoon. Unexpectedly, he led her up the sloping trail out of the canyon. As they emerged from the walled pass, he turned his horse at a right angle to follow a faint animal trail. Sheila gave Arriba her head, letting the mare pick her own way up the steeply climbing path.

The trail ended on a narrow, rocky plateau, dotted with stunted trees. Sheila dismounted when Ráfaga did, following his lead as he loosened the cinch of his saddle to give the bay horse a breather after the long climb. Letting the reins trail to the ground, she wandered toward the rocky ledge where Ráfaga was standing.

The ledge provided an unobstructed, expansive view of the canyon below and of the mountainous peaks of the Sierra Madre range, stretching northward. Lightheaded from the increase in altitude, Sheila sat down on a flat rock to gaze at the scenery and the canyon settlement.

Her thoughts soon turned to the ever-dominating presence of Ráfaga. He stood near the edge of the ledge, a knee slightly bent as one leg supported most of his weight. The folds of his poncho concealed much of his lean, muscled frame.

Sheila's attention slid to his profile. His hat was pulled low on his slanting forehead, covering the thickness of his jet-black hair. His dark eyes had a farseeing look. Bronzed skin stretched over his cheekbones, hollowing down to a strong jaw.

The slashing groove running from the corner of his classically straight nose to the edge of his mouth accented the straight, hard line of his masculine lips and the natural thrust of his chin. He was aggressively male, indomitable, sure of himself and what he wanted. Sheila couldn't help wondering how he came to be that way.

"Who are you, Ráfaga?" She tipped her head to the side.

He turned in her direction, an inquiring brow lifting, as though he had forgotten she was there. His hooded eyes held her look for a minute.

"I am a man," he answered simply.

It was an unpretentious statement. It struck Sheila that she knew of no one else who would have answered the question that way. Everyone she had ever known would have identified himself by his occupation or his accomplishments, elaborated to give himself importance. But not Ráfaga.

"But who are you?" she persisted. "What is your real name? Where do you come from? What did you do? Why are you here?"

His mouth quirked in amusement as if he found her questions foolish. "What tales have the others told you about me?"

"The others? You mean Juan and Laredo? They've told me several stories, each one different," Sheila admitted. "Were you ever in prison?"

"Yes." Again an answer without an explanation.

"Why?"

"For committing a crime. It is the usual reason." There was a suggestion of a smile around his mouth.

"What crime?"

"Does it matter?" Ráfaga countered. "I have committed a sufficient number of others since then to make the first pale in significance."

Sheila realized it was useless to pursue the question. He had no intention of telling her and he was much too sharp to trap.

"And you escaped?" She switched to another line.

"Sí."

"Why?"

"You have not ever been in a prison or you would not ask that." He studied her impassively. "To be caged like an animal is a torture equal to the physical agony of the whip, especially when those you love must bear the shame of your punishment, too. The condition is worse if neither you nor your family has money to buy the small liberties. Then you live like an animal. There have been improvements, but—" He lifted a shoulder in a small but expressive shrug and left the rest unsaid.

Sheila's attention had been caught by his phrase "those you love." "Do you have a family? Brothers or sisters?"

"I had a family." Ráfaga turned to the range mountains.

"Had? Are they dead?"

"For me they are," he responded with a complete absence of emotion. "I cannot go back to them without staining them with what I have become."

"You miss them." Sheila wasn't aware that she had spoken her thought aloud.

"I no longer know them, and they no longer know me." His dark eyes caught her and held them. "We cannot go back to what we once were. A moment that is gone cannot be recaptured. Only a fool would try."

"How did you become what you are? A—" She searched for the right term. Somehow "bandit" and "outlaw" did not fit him, although she knew they were partially accurate. "A mercenary?" she settled on finally, still dissatisfied with her choice.

"A twist of fate. A man who escaped with me had left a friend behind in the prison. He wanted to go back for him and offered me a small sum of money if I would help. I had no money and could not risk going to my family. I had three choices—to go hungry, steal, or help him."

"If you had to do it over again, would you still make the same choice?"

"*Quien sabe?* Life does not permit its path to be retraced and the direction changed. Today can change tomorrow, but not yesterday."

Turning, he moved away from the edge to squat on his heels a few feet from Sheila. His arm moved beneath his poncho. Seconds later it emerged, a dark, thin cigar between his fingers. After placing it between his lips, he struck a match head against a rock and used both hands to protectively cup the flame from a teasing wind. The same breeze soon carried the pungent aroma of burning tobacco to Sheila's nose.

"Are you—were you a revolutionary?" She brushed a strand of sun-streaked hair from the corner of her mouth.

His dark eyes glinted at her. "Everyone in Mexico is

a revolutionary. You can still hear the cries of *'viva la revolución!'* in the streets at fiesta time. It is the same here as it is in your country. Once the first gun is fired for freedom, the bullet becomes immortal." Ráfaga paused, inhaling lightly on the cigar, then releasing a thin trail of smoke. He rolled the thin cigar between his fingers, studying it as if he found it of interest. Sheila didn't speak, sensing that he was considering her initial question before answering it directly. "Perhaps when I came to the Sierras, it was with the dreams of a young boy to right injustices."

Sheila caught the cynicism, the dry, self-mockery in his voice. "What happened to those dreams?" she prompted quietly.

"The view from a distance, maybe. You have an expression"—his dark gaze lifted from the glowing cigar tip to her face—"about the forest and the trees."

"You can't see the forest through the trees," Sheila supplied with a nod.

"*Sí,* that is it," Ráfaga agreed. "I saw that freedom was not won at the point of a gun. It is found only when the gun is lowered. And I learned what wiser men have always known—that lasting change is slow to happen."

"And Mexico?" she questioned.

"It is happening slowly." His mouth twisted. "But we still have many men who work hard for very little and go to the nearest *cantina* to drown their frustrations while their women go to churches to pray."

The faint contempt in the last comment forced Sheila to ask, "Don't you believe in God?"

"I believe there is a god," Ráfaga acknowledged. "I don't believe a god is responsible for the way we live our lives. We each take our own steps."

Straightening, he walked back to the edge of the plateau. Cigar smoke swirled in a thin, gray trail, carried by the wind. He seemed remote. Although he hadn't answered her questions with specifics, he had confided some of his thoughts. Now he had withdrawn; the aloofness had returned.

"If the questions are over"—Ráfaga dropped the

cigar butt beneath his boot, crushing it under his heel—
"it is time we started down."

"There is one more question I've been meaning to
ask," Sheila said, her voice quiet, yet determined.

"What is it?"

"When are you going to let me go?" She watched
him intently, but there wasn't a flicker of emotion behind the saturnine mask.

Without answering, he walked toward the horses,
grazing on the clumps of grass growing stubbornly in
the rocky ground. He picked up their trailing reins and
led them to where Sheila sat. A gold light sparkled
resolutely in her eyes. She wasn't going to let him ignore
her question.

"There's been plenty of time for money to be paid for
my release," she pointed out. "Why haven't you let me
go?"

"No money has been received." He held out the
mare's reins.

"I don't believe you." Sheila shook her head. "My
father would have been able to pay almost any sum by
now. How much did you ask for?"

Unconsciously, she took the reins from his hand.
Ráfaga stepped away, walking to the left side of his
bay. He looped the reins over the horse's neck and
raised the stirrup to tighten the cinch. Sheila caught at
his arm, her fingers curling into the material of his
poncho.

"How much?" she repeated in a voice that trembled.

He looked at her, his dark eyes shuttered, reflecting
only her image and none of his thoughts. "No money
has been demanded."

Not relaxing her hold on his muscled arm, Sheila
drew her head back. The muscles in her throat constricted and she swallowed.

"What do you mean?"

"Exactly what I said," Ráfaga replied evenly. "No
demand has been made for money from your parents."

"But—" She was confused, almost dazed. She

brushed a hand across her eyes, as if to clear her vision so she could see and think clearly. "Why?"

Walking around to the mare's left side, he tightened the cinch on Sheila's saddle. He was ignoring her question, pretending not to have heard. No, she realized, he wasn't even pretending. He had heard it, but it didn't matter.

"You aren't going to let me go, are you?" Her voice was tight and choked.

His hands spanned her waist. Sheila was too numbed to protest when he lifted her into the saddle. Passing the reins over the mare's neck, he let them rest on the saddle horn. Her gaze followed him as he walked to the bay and swung effortlessly into the saddle.

"I'm not going anywhere until you answer me," Sheila warned and reined the mare away from the trail.

He turned the bay around to face her, urging the horse forward until his leg was brushing against hers. His impassive features met her wary expression.

"You will stay," Ráfaga said briskly, pausing a second to add, "for a while."

"For how long?" Sheila insisted. "Until you get tired of me? Then what will you do? Turn me over to your men? Sell me?"

His mouth tightened in an uncompromising line. "You ask too many foolish questions."

"Foolish!" Her voice cracked. "Why is it foolish to want to know what's going to happen to me when you're finished with me?"

"When that day comes, you will be free to leave," he snapped.

"Do you expect me to believe that?"

"I give you my word." His voice was cold and harsh, its pitch deep.

The ominous glitter of his eyes dared Sheila to challenge his statement. She swallowed her words, doubting that she would believe anything he told her at this moment.

"Do they—do my parents know I'm alive?" she asked instead.

"I do not know."

"Surely you must," Sheila insisted. "Your network of informants would have told you if they were making inquiries about me."

"I have heard nothing."

"Can't you get word to them?" Tears misted her eyes as she realized her parents probably believed she was dead. After all this time, what else could they think? "Can't you at least let them know I'm all right?"

"It is not possible."

"It *is* possible!" Her voice shook traitorously. "Laredo has told me countless times that there are ways to find things out. Those same 'ways' can be used to notify my parents."

"It does not work in reverse," Ráfaga told her curtly.

"My God, don't you have any feelings at all?" The constriction in her throat made breathing painful. "You must know what they're going through—knowing I could be dead, but not knowing for certain either way."

"It would also be painful for them to know you are alive and not know where you are or be able to contact you," he pointed out roughly.

"Please, Ráfaga, please get word to them," she begged.

"It is not possible." He took the reins from her hand, backing his bay and turning to lead her horse. "We will not discuss it anymore."

"God, how I hate you!" She breathed shakily, knowing it was only the black of a deeper emotion.

"So you have said many times," he mocked coldly. "Your words are beginning to pall with repetition."

Chapter 18

The soothing notes of the guitar softly serenaded the starlight outside the window. Sheila tried to ignore the song being played, her mind racing as it had done these last weeks, scheming and plotting to find a way to escape.

There was no hope with Ráfaga here. He kept her constantly at his side, taking her everywhere, aware of her every minute, as if he knew exactly what was going through her mind. Sheila had been counting on finding an opportunity when he left to raid the prison he had scouted.

As the days turned into weeks and Ráfaga had given no indication of setting up the raid, Sheila had begun to grow anxious. Tonight, at the supper table, she had finally asked with assumed casualness when he would be going.

It had taken every ounce of her poise not to react when he told her, with equal casualness, that there would be no raid. The prisoner's trial had been held and he was being transferred to an American prison to serve his sentence.

Sheila was back to square one and her every move seemed blocked. There was no way out. And there was no one to help her.

The last note of the guitar faded into silence, filling the room with pregnant stillness. An irresistible force compelled Sheila to look over her shoulder. Her pulse leaped at the smouldering darkness in Ráfaga's narrowed, watchful gaze. She felt the strongest urge to go to him, not to plead for her release but to experience the searing fire of his embrace.

It was always like this. The power he had over her body was disturbing. Each time he took her, Sheila rediscovered the pure ecstasy of his possession. Ráfaga had totally mastered her senses; he could lift her to heights of passion she hadn't known existed.

The guitar was set aside. With cat-like grace, Ráfaga rolled to his feet and crossed the space to where Sheila stood by the window. She became lost in the dark fires in his eyes. Although he wasn't touching her, she could feel his seductive prowess. Strong, lean fingers curved around the soft flesh of her upper arms. Sheila felt her bones melt as he drew her against him. Her heart was hammering crazily against her rib cage.

Its erratic beat made a mockery of her thought to escape. She was in love with him. She probably had been for a long time.

Her heart was reminded of what he was, a leader of a band of desperadoes. He held her captive, used her as his woman without regard for her wishes. But Sheila knew all that. She had known it for a very long time, and it made no difference. The heart was never logical or wise.

His hand was pushing aside the collar of her blouse while his hard lips sought the sensitive spot on her shoulder. A delicious quiver danced over her skin when he found it. The inner struggle between what was wise and what was fact ended. This time love won as Sheila

arched her spine to give him greater access to the area
he was exploring.

Soon he was lifting her into his arms and carrying her
into the bedroom. This time, when Sheila lay naked beside him, she held nothing back. In the sweetness of
surrender, she found fulfillment for her love. Tomorrow
was soon enough to dwell on the consequences of her
emotional involvement. Tonight she gloried in the passionate fires of his possession.

But cold reason did come on wings of fear. Her last
bastion of defense had been breached and Sheila was
no longer heart-whole. She lived in terror he would
discover how completely she was enthralled by him.
There was no future for her love. Sheila knew she had
to flee from Ráfaga while she still had the chance to
forget him.

Ráfaga touched her arm and Sheila jumped, her
widened eyes racing to him to see if he could tell what
she had been thinking. A dark brow was quirked in
mockery at the way she had recoiled so violently from
his touch.

"You said you wished to ride this afternoon. Juan
has brought the horses," he told her in a voice dry with
amusement.

"Good," she said tightly.

But she was trembling badly. Sheila jammed her
shaking hands deep in the pockets of her Levi's to conceal them from Ráfaga's alert gaze. She stepped carefully around him, avoiding unnecessary contact. She
was living on the raw edge of her nerves. It couldn't
last long.

The roan mare whickered as Sheila approached,
thrusting her blaze face forward to have her velvet nose
stroked. Sheila obliged, the taut muscles around her lips
relaxing into a smile.

"Hello to you, too, Arriba," she murmured, watching
the mare's ears prick at the sound of her name. "Ready
for a run, are you?"

Juan leaned from his saddle to hand Sheila the reins.

Taking hold of the saddle horn, she put a foot into the stirrup and swung aboard before Ráfaga could offer any assistance. He took the reins to his bay from Juan and walked to the horse's side to mount.

His hand closed around the saddle horn. Glancing over the cantle, Ráfaga saw Laredo striding toward them and waited. Sheila sensed the urgency in Laredo's stride and listened curiously to the low exchange in Spanish between the two men.

After an impatient nod of agreement, Ráfaga stepped from the saddle, hitching the bay to the nearest post, before his gaze flicked to Sheila.

"I have something I must do," he told her. "Ride with Juan. I will join you later."

"Of course," Sheila murmured. The smile she gave Juan was tremulous. Her stomach was twisted in knots. "Shall we go?"

"*Sí.*" He nodded with a wide smile and turned his horse toward the meadow where the horses and the small herd of cattle grazed.

Sheila clicked to Arriba and the roan mare followed, moving out eagerly. Aware of the dark pair of eyes watching her ride away, she rigidly kept her head facing front, refusing to look behind her, although she knew Ráfaga was expecting it. Juan kept his horse at a walk and Sheila didn't attempt to hurry the pace.

"The *señora* is troubled about something, no?" His heavily accented voice was gentle with concern as he studied her strained face.

"No. No, of course not." She repeated the second denial more forcefully and touched a heel to send the roan cantering across the meadow.

Cows trotted out of her path in irritation. A calf kicked up its heels and raced away, its tail high in the air. The long-legged mare had a reaching stride; even in a canter, the animal began outdistancing Juan's slower, stockier mount. Sheila glanced over her shoulder, knowing he would soon urge his horse into a gallop if she got much farther ahead of him.

In previous carefree times, Sheila might have chided

him for his horse's slowness. Today she merely observed it with an absent look ... at least her look was absent until she saw Juan's horse stumble. A full stride later, it went down, tumbling forward.

Her startled eyes saw Juan kicking free of the saddle as the horse went heavily to the ground. Immediately, Sheila reined the mare in, spinning Arriba around to race back to her fallen companion. Juan was already up and walking when she reached him.

"Are you all right, Juan?" she asked anxiously.

"*Sí.*" His answer was absent as he urged his downed horse to stand.

With kicking, flailing legs, the panicked horse finally rose, his eyes flashing white, his head tossing nervously. The horse was shifting about, favoring its right front legs.

"He's hurt," she said, but Juan had already noticed and was running an exploring hand over its leg, crooning softly to the horse in Spanish to calm it down. "Is it very bad?"

"It is . . ."—Juan hesitated, frowning as he groped for the English word—". . . —a bad sprain, I think."

Sheila sighed deeply in relief. "That's good. I was afraid for a moment—" She didn't finish the sentence.

"I will have to take him back to the corral, *señora,*" he said, his expression apologizing that the ride had to end so soon.

"That's all right, Juan. I underst——" She didn't finish this sentence, either.

It flashed like a lightning bolt through her mind. This was just the chance she had been waiting for, her opportunity to escape. Juan's horse was lamed. He couldn't possibly stop Sheila or come after her.

Without giving herself a chance to think, she reined the mare in a half-circle, pointing her toward the sloping trail leading out of the canyon. There were tears in her eyes and she didn't have the slightest idea where they had come from.

"*Señora!*" Juan called out to her in surprise. Her heels were dug into the mare's sides, but she still had a tight hold on the bit. The roan plunged sideways, leaping and rearing, not knowing which command to obey. *"Señora! Don't go! No, señora!"*

Her chin trembled as she glanced over her shoulder. She could see the desperate look of fear on Juan's face. He ran toward her. She leaned forward in the saddle, letting Arriba take the bit as she whipped the trailing ends of the reins across the mare's haunches.

"Come back!"

But Juan's shouting voice was already fading. The mare was charging up the slope, bits of rock and dirt sent flying by driving hooves. Sheila looked back once near the top to see Juan running across the meadow to raise the alarm.

Through the pass, Sheila pointed the mare down the mountain and gave the roan her head. There was a faint trail through the thickly forested mountain, winding and twisting its way down. Sheila hugged closely to the mare's neck, dodging and ducking the branches that tried to unseat her.

The obstacle course of tree trunks reduced the pace to a canter, the roan mare making fluid changes of leads with each curve of the trail. They seemed to go down forever. When the ground leveled out, the mare slowed to a trot, blowing hard, with nostrils flared wide to drink in the air.

Sheila's impulse was to whip the horse into a gallop, knowing that Ráfaga would soon be coming after her. Common sense refused to let her do it. There was still a long way to go to reach any kind of civilization. She had to conserve the mare's strength.

As she slowed Arriba to a walk, there was a reassuring spring to the roan's reaching stride. In the mountain valley, Sheila turned south, taking the avenue of least resistance. To the east, there were more mountains to be crossed, which would mean a slower pace and drain the mare's stamina. The valley stretched northward, but as far as Sheila knew, the land was rugged and barren and sparsely populated. South was the right choice. There were towns and cities, logging and mining camps in that direction. Besides, the valley floor was relatively level. It would give the fleetfooted roan a chance to use its speed to outdistance any pursuit.

Glancing over her shoulder, Sheila couldn't see or hear anyone following her. Ráfaga's image flashed in front of her mind's eye and her heart constricted with longing. She shook her head to block out the image.

Sheila stroked the roan's damp neck. They rode on, alternately cantering, trotting, and walking. Sheila had no idea how many miles they had traveled, nor how much time had gone by. The sun had begun its downward arc to the west. There were only a few daylight hours left.

Then something alerted Sheila. She turned to see half a dozen horses and riders galloping toward her at an angle. She recognized Ráfaga instantly. For a split second, she could only stare, unable to react.

Her heels dug into the roan's flanks and the mare shot forward. In two leaping strides, the horse was galloping. Ahead, Sheila saw a long and very level stretch of ground. If she could reach that, she knew the fleetfooted mare would leave the riders behind.

But Ráfaga must have already seen it and made the same deduction. He wasn't underestimating the speed of Sheila's mount. They were riding hard at an angle to cut her off before she reached the level area. It was too late to wish she had seen them a minute sooner.

Leaning forward in the saddle, she buried her face in the horse's flying mane. Sheila felt the mare flatten out, as if the animal sensed the desperate need of its rider for greater speed. Every muscle in the mare was straining, driving to win the dash for freedom.

Sheila tipped her head to the side, looking through the blur of the light mane to see how close the riders were. She saw them, still some distance away, the angle widening.

"We're going to make it, Arriba!" she cried exultantly. "We're going to make it!"

There was no possibility that Ráfaga could intercept

her before they reached the flat stretch of ground. Pain stabbed her chest. For a second, Sheila wanted him to catch her. She wanted him to take her back to the canyon. But she didn't check the mare's pace in that moment of weakness.

As she and Arriba raced past the invisible line that gave them victory, Sheila saw Ráfaga rein in his horse, admitting defeat. She glimpsed the bay's plunging and rearing movements as it slid to a stop. Then she looked quickly away. She remained low in the saddle, crouched over the mare's neck, but her hands were no longer urging the mare to top speed. Still, the roan didn't slacken its stride.

Simultaneously, an explosion ripped through the air and the mare staggered, breaking its stride. The horse tried to recover, laboring to get its balance. Stunned, Sheila tried to help, tugging at the reins to bring the mare's head up and get its legs beneath it.

But it was too late. The mare was tumbling to the ground. Sheila barely had time to kick her feet free of the stirrups and push out of the saddle. She went flying through the air. Then everything went black.

When she opened her eyes, Ráfaga's face glowered above hers. For a dazed moment, Sheila didn't know where she was or what had happened. She tried to move and pain shot through her head.

"You were a fool to try to escape," he snarled, his mouth thinning.

Sheila closed her eyes. "I know," she agreed with a tiny sob.

There was the sting of tears in her eyes. She didn't know if she wanted to cry because she had failed in caught up with her. She was a fool for many reasons. her attempt to get away or because she was glad he had

"Do you have pain?" he demanded roughly.

"Yes," Sheila moaned, her lungs burning with the effort.

"Where?" There was still no compassion in his tone, only anger.

"My head." She tried to raise a shaking hand to

touch the place and found a million other places that hurt. "Everywhere," she gasped.

"Lie still," Ráfaga ordered.

Despite his anger, his touch was amazingly gentle as his hands explored for specific injuries. Sheila took comfort from that. The numbness was beginning to wear off. Except for the ache in her head, she didn't think she was seriously hurt anywhere else, just one big bruise from the fall.

Ráfaga reached the same conclusion. "There is nothing broken."

"Arriba—" Sheila started to ask the condition of her valiant mare, but Ráfaga was slipping an arm beneath her shoulders to help her to her feet.

Her bruised body protested and Sheila had to concentrate on making her muscles obey. His arm stayed around her in support as she wavered unsteadily. Her gaze was caught by a large, roan-colored object lying motionless on the ground. It was Arriba, stripped of saddle and bridle, inert in death.

With a stifled cry, Sheila staggered to the mare, falling to her knees beside the dead horse. Her disbelieving hand touched the long neck, the dampness of sweat clinging to the horse's hair. The body was still warm, but no longer pulsing with life. She didn't know exactly when she saw the hole and recognized its cause.

Sheila glared accusingly at Ráfaga, mindless of the pain spinning through her head. "You killed her! You shot her!" Sheila's voice broke as Ráfaga loomed above her.

He reached down and hauled Sheila to her feet. "Did you think I would let you get away?"

"But you didn't have to kill her!" Sheila tried to pull free.

His grip tightened to yank her against him. The force of the sudden contact nearly knocked the breath from her lungs. Her arms could not wedge any space between them as he crushed her against his chest, her head tipped back to let him see the hurt, angry tears in her eyes.

"If there had been any other way to stop you, do you think I would not have used it?" Ráfaga growled. "Do you think when I held the rifle in my hands I was not aware I was risking your life or serious injury to you? Do you think I did not wish to call the bullet back when it had left the gun?" The line of his mouth was grimly drawn. "It is not important to me that the horse is dead." He left unsaid that it was important she was alive and unharmed.

"But it wasn't Arriba's fault," Sheila protested, the shock too fresh to find any consolation in what he left unspoken.

"No, it was my fault for letting you ride the mare in the first place." His low voice was raw and tight with barely controlled anger. "If I had not liked the picture of two long-legged beauties—" His jaw snapped shut on the rest as he glared icily beyond Sheila. "What is it?"

"There's a patrol headed this way," Sheila heard Laredo answer. "They must have heard the shot."

Sheila was turned around and pushed toward Ráfaga's bay as he clipped out an order. "Tell the men to separate. We will meet back at the canyon."

Before she could attempt to mount, Sheila was lifted into the saddle, with Ráfaga swinging up behind her. His feet hadn't found the stirrups yet as he spun the bay around, spurring the horse into a gallop. Sheila had only a fleeting glimpse of riders approaching from the south, a considerable distance away. She couldn't help thinking how very close she had come to escaping.

Ráfaga turned his horse to the northeast as the small band of riders scattered to the wind. Carrying double, the bay couldn't outrace the patrol, so Ráfaga guided the animal up the steep slope of a mountain where the bay's mountain-bred agility compensated for the lack of speed.

Once when they paused in a gap of trees, Sheila felt Ráfaga turn in the saddle to look behind them. "Are they following us?" she asked.

"We have lost them," he stated unemotionally. But there was no mistaking the slashing bitterness as he added, "That is not the answer you wished to hear, is it?"

His anger with her had not lessened. Sheila fell silent. There wasn't any way to deny his accusation, even thought it wasn't the truth. Neither spoke again as the bay horse worked its way northward, along the leeward side of the mountain ridge.

It was dark by the time they reached the canyon pass. Moonlight silvered the corridor as they rode through, the bay trotting eagerly to its home ground. Sheila felt a slight tug at her heart, as if she, too, were coming home.

Laredo was inside the house, waiting. He glanced up, unsmiling in welcome. "I see you made it," he said. "Consuelo made coffee and there's food on the table."

Sheila opened her mouth to say that she wanted only to go to bed, but Ráfaga spoke before she had a chance. "We will have coffee."

He used the tone of voice that Sheila was very familiar with. It was the one that said he would pour it down her throat if she tried to refuse it. So she said nothing and walked to a chair at the table.

Ráfaga poured two cups, adding a liberal amount of sugar to the one he set before Sheila. She sipped the strong, black liquid, unable to look at him as he sat down beside her. There was an oppresive, brooding silence in the atmosphere. She glanced at Laredo, sitting opposite her. He looked quickly away, a troubled darkness in his blue eyes.

Almost immediately he rose from the table. "I'd better go," he said curtly and walked out without waiting for anyone to say good night.

Sheila was uncomfortably aware of Ráfaga's dark gaze piercing her.

"Why did you run away, Sheila?"

Her head jerked to him, the welling tears hiding the love that gleamed in her gold-flecked eyes. "I had to try to escape. I had to try," she repeated.

He took the coffee from her trembling hands and looked at her for a long moment. His shuttered gaze told her nothing of what he was thinking, but she waited for him to pull her from the chair and into his arms, the only place she felt she belonged anymore.

Instead, he turned his head to stare into his coffee mug. "You need sleep. Go to bed."

Sheila rose numbly from the table and made her way to the bedroom to undress and crawl beneath the blanket. She lay awake for a long time waiting for Ráfaga to join her, but eventually her tired and aching body insisted she sleep.

Chapter 19

Ráfaga was not in bed when Sheila awakened, although she had a vague recollection of having felt his arm around her in sleep. There were the sounds of someone moving around in the kitchen. The bump on her head was tender, but her head no longer throbbed from the pain.

There was a cursory glance from Ráfaga when she entered the kitchen. The morning greeting on the end of her tongue stayed there. His brooding anger hung like a dark cloud over the room. It charged the air like a violent electrical storm about to break.

Sheila tried to ignore it with a quiet greeting to Consuelo. *"Buenos días,* Consuelo."

The woman's dark eyes simply flickered briefly in her direction. A smile hovered nervously on her lips as she nodded and hurriedly resumed her tasks.

A low, growled order from Ráfaga in Spanish brought a bobbing nod from Consuelo and a breathy, *"Sí, señor."* And the woman hurried out the door almost with relief.

Gold fires snapped in Sheila's eyes, her irritation mounting. Last night it had been Laredo who was uncomfortable in her presence. This morning it was Consuelo who had been afraid to look at her.

Above all, there was Ráfaga. His anger Sheila could understand, only it wasn't the right kind of anger. It was somehow inverted with another quality that Sheila couldn't fathom.

Pouring a cup of coffee, Sheila carried it to the table, where Ráfaga sat, ignoring the food Consuelo had prepared. Her appetite had faded as her irritated confusion had risen.

"There is food," Ráfaga pointed out.

"I'm not hungry." Sheila shook her head in refusal.

He offered no argument, nor did he remind her that she hadn't eaten since yesterday noon. Although he didn't move, Sheila felt his impatience as surely as if his fingers were drumming the table. It was his stillness and silence that disturbed her and the sensation that inside him a violent war was going on.

She had tried to escape before—that time in the storm. He had been angry, but not like this. She studied him over the rim of her coffee mug. His saturnine features seemed to be carved out of granite. The black, tightly shuttered look of his eyes kept Sheila from seeing what he was thinking.

Sheila clenched her teeth, the continuing silence becoming unbearable. "Why don't you say something?" she insisted. "All right, so I ran away and you caught me. It isn't the first time I tried."

"But it is the first time you made it out of the canyon," Ráfaga answered curtly.

A thought occurred to her. "You aren't blaming Juan for that?" She remembered what had happened to Juan Ortega when he had disobeyed one of Ráfaga's orders. "It wasn't his fault. His horse went lame. There wasn't any way he could stop me."

"I do not blame Juan." Again Sheila heard the steel running through his voice like the sharp edge of a knife blade. "As you say, his horse was lamed in an accident."

"Then what is it?" Sheila frowned, a surge of impatience tightening her mouth. "What's wrong?"

"You left the canyon without my permission."

"Oh, I'm sorry," she retorted with sarcastic mockery. "Maybe I should have ridden to find you so you would know I was escaping. That would really have been the smart thing to do, wouldn't it?"

A muscle twitched in his jaw. "You broke a rule."

"One of *your* rules!" Sheila flashed. "I am not bound by *your* rules! They mean absolutely nothing to me!"

"You do not understand!" he exploded, an explosion that was doubly ominous because he did not raise his voice. "When I made you my woman, I made you subject to those rules."

"That's just too damned bad!" She was openly defiant, refusing to be intimidated by his anger.

"Yes, it is," Ráfaga snapped the agreement, "because if you are subject to the rules, you are also subject to the punishment for breaking them!"

"Really? I—" The sarcastically taunting words were stolen from her throat as the full implication of his statement suddenly hit her.

Punishment for breaking rules and disobeying orders was meted out at the hollow beyond the corral. Sheila paled. A vision of shredded flesh made her stomach churn.

"You can't mean that I—" She rose from the table. Her head moved from side to side, trying to shake away the thought, as if it were a bad dream, but the reality persisted. "You wouldn't do that to me!"

Ráfaga was standing in front of her. His fingers were digging into the soft flesh of her upper arms. She was aware of the pain they were causing, but she was insensitive to it.

"If I could reverse the rule for you, I would." Were her glazed eyes imagining it, or was she really seeing the tortured look in his dark eyes? "All I can do is lessen the punishment because you are a woman and because you are new to our ways." His voice was flat and hard.

"No, you can't condemn me to that!" She tried to pull away from his hold.

He shook her hard, once. "It is the one law that is sacrosanct to us. It guards our freedom and the risk of discovery. I cannot change it."

"But I am your woman. Surely—" Sheila tried to argue.

"A rule cannot be for one and not another." Ráfaga cut her off. "It either stands or it falls."

His arms went around her, gathering her to his chest. The hand at the back of her hair pressed her head against his chest. She trembled violently from the cold fear that consumed her. She felt the strong line of his jaw against her hair as he bent his dark head to rest his chin along the side of her head.

"I cannot stand in the way of your punishment, *querida*," he said tightly. "I can argue for leniency and take measures to see that the harm to you is not severe. That is all I can do."

As she shuddered uncontrollably, his arms tightened around her, as if trying to absorb some of her fear. Sheila closed her eyes, feeling the coldness of dread freezing the blood in her veins.

"When?" she whispered.

Ráfaga didn't need to ask what she meant. "This morning. Now," he answered grimly. Sheila turned her face into his shirt, her nerves constricting. "It is better this way. There is no time for the mind to dwell on it."

"You knew, didn't you?" A terrible bitterness coated the words. "You knew last night. So did Laredo. And Consuelo knew this morning. You all knew."

"Yes, we knew."

"And you didn't tell me until now," Sheila accused.

"Everyone knew the penalty for what you had done. You did not. I found no reason to replace your ignorance with fear."

The part of her mind that could think clearly re-

membered the hours she had slept while Ráfaga had
remained awake, sitting alone in the main room. He had
been plagued by the knowledge of what awaited her
this morning. It explained the brooding anger that was
never quite directed at her.

Understanding this didn't make it any easier to accept what was to happen. She strained against his arms,
objecting to his attempt to comfort her.

Ráfaga let her wedge a space between them, an arm
remaining firmly around her waist to keep her arched
toward him. His other hand rested on the curve of
her neck and shoulder, his fingers digging into the cord
and his thumb pressing against the bone of her jaw
and chin. His dark eyes looked deeply into hers, seeing
the crackling fires of resentment and fear.

"I hate you for this," Sheila declared, her voice trembling.

"*Sí*. And you will hate me more before the day is
over." There was a knock at the door. Sheila's head
jerked toward the sound, her heart stopping its beat for
a split second. "It is time," Ráfaga announced coldly.

A stifled cry ripped from her throat. She tried to
pull free of his hold, struggling to escape, but he held
her easily.

"You are a woman, a *norte americano*." Ráfaga
spoke in a low, slashing voice. "It is expected that you
will weep and beg not to be taken, that you will swoon
at the sight of the whip, or cower and be dragged to
the posts. That is the way they expect you to behave."

Sheila stiffened, recognizing the challenge he made.
She had a vision of herself reacting in the way he had
described and knew she could not live with that kind
of humiliation. A coldness swept over Sheila to numb
her senses and freeze out the horrors of her imagination.

"You may let me go." The look she gave him was
cool. "I will not run."

"You are going to disappoint them?" There was
something of a taunt in his voice.

There was another knock at the door, more demand-

ing than the first. "You'd better answer that," she said
coldly.

His dark gaze made a considering sweep of her face.
Then he released her and walked to the door, opening
it wide. Two men stood outside, horses tied to the
post. One spoke quietly to Ráfaga while both glanced
past him to Sheila, eyeing her with undisguised curiosity.
She returned their looks, unflinching and faintly haugh-
ty.

Ráfaga turned, announcing impassively to her, "We
will go now."

Her legs were remarkably steady as she walked past
him and through the doorway, deliberately ignoring the
two men. Outside she paused, surveying the horses,
permitting herself a moment of sorrow that the roan
mare would never again be waiting for her.

"Which one am I to ride? Or . . ."—her gaze slid
icily to Ráfaga—". . . am I to walk, herded like an
animal to the slaughter?"

"You will ride the bay," Ráfaga answered smoothly.

His horse. As Sheila walked to it, one of the men untied the reins from the post. Sheila mounted and held
out a hand to take the reins, but the man kept them
as he mounted his own horse. Again she looked at
Ráfaga.

"Will you tell your man that I don't need to be led?
I am capable of guiding my horse in the right direction."

Without a flicker of emotion, Ráfaga said something
in Spanish to the man. Evidently he had relayed her
statement because the man hesitated, skeptical of the
wisdom in giving Sheila the reins. But he didn't argue.

With shoulders squared and her head erect, Sheila
turned the bay toward the houses, waiting for Ráfaga
to climb aboard his horse before nudging the bay into a
walk. Ráfaga rode at her side, the other two men
following behind them.

As before, when Juan Ortega had been brought to
the hollow for punishment, everyone in the canyon was
gathered there. A tight-lipped Laredo stood waiting,

his hands on his hips. He grabbed hold of Ráfaga's reins.

"You can't go through with this, Ráfaga," Laredo growled.

"I cannot stop it," was the flat reply.

Sheila let her gaze sweep the hollow before dismounting, deaf to the plea Laredo was making on her behalf. The gentle Juan appeared at her side, his hat in hand, his dark eyes filled with pain.

"Señora—" he began.

Sheila looked at him, seeing the self-blame in his expression. She allowed her numbed senses to feel for a moment. "This isn't your fault," she assured him quietly. "I am sorry about Arriba. I didn't take very good care of her."

"Señora, please, I—"

But Sheila turned away, shutting him out. Her voice was again chillingly cold as she addressed Ráfaga. "I believe I'm supposed to go to the center of the hollow, aren't I, so they can all see me?"

His features were equally cold as he nodded. "Yes."

She took one step before her path was blocked by Laredo. "I swear I never believed Ráfaga would let this happen, Sheila," he declared huskily. "If I had, I would have knocked his rifle away before he shot the horse out from under you."

There was a regal lift of her chin. "It's too late to think about that now. Please move out of my way."

The boyish look to Laredo's features was obliterated by a haunting grimness. After a split second's hesitation, he stepped to the side. He reached to take her arm, saying tautly, "I'll walk with you."

Sheila drew her arm away, scorning his gesture of support with cold pride. "I'll walk by myself."

Flanked by Laredo and Ráfaga, she walked to the center of the hollow near the two posts. She saw the curious eyes watching her and felt the silent questioning as they wondered how long her self-control would last.

That knowledge stiffened her spine. They expected

her to cringe in terror, this band of criminals and outcasts. It made Sheila more determined not to be an object of amusement and scorn for them.

As Ráfaga stepped forward to state the reason for her punishment, Sheila turned her attention to him. He spoke in the low tone that carried clearly in the silence, devoid of any emotion. Although she couldn't understand his words, she sensed an eloquence in his speech.

When he had finished, there was a quiet murmur of voices instead of the agreeing silence that had followed his explanation of the reason for Juan Ortega's punishment. Sheila permitted a glimmer of hope to shine that perhaps Ráfaga had dissuaded them from seeing her punished for trying to escape.

A voice, a woman's voice, spoke sharply above the indecisive murmurs. Sheila turned, catching sight of Elena. Malevolent dark eyes glared their dislike at Sheila. The brunette's spiteful voice was riddled with condemnation as she viciously argued for Sheila's punishment.

Her malicious words were still ringing in the air when Juan stepped forward to defend Sheila. Laredo stood at his side, signaling by his presence his agreement with all that Juan said. There was a slight constriction of her heart at the sight of her two champions, but Sheila wouldn't permit her feelings to show.

Juan's impassioned plea seemed to have swayed the people to Sheila's side until someone else spoke up. It was a moment before Sheila could locate the jeering Spanish voice. She went cold when she saw Juan Ortega.

His broad face was contorted with the look of vengeance, his lips sneering at her, revealing his yellowed and chipped teeth. His shoulders were stiffly hunched to indicate the pain he still endured from his whipping. There was a sickly pallor about his face, indicating his recovery was not yet complete.

Sheila's slightly widened gaze shifted to Ráfaga, who was listening impassively to Juan Ortega's denouncement. Then it slid to Laredo, who had turned away, a defeated look in his blue eyes. She caught his glance and held it.

"What is he saying?" she whispered, barely moving her lips.

Laredo walked to her side, not looking at her as he answered her question. "He's telling them that it doesn't matter what your reason was for leaving here or the circumstances surrounding it. He's reminding them that he was punished for disobeying an order—an order that he had forgotten in his weakness when you invited him into the house and flaunted your womanhood in front of him. If his reason could not save him from the whip, then neither must yours. And he's reminding them that your flight nearly resulted in allowing a government patrol to find this canyon. If for no other reason, you should be punished for that."

When Juan Ortega stopped talking, there were nods of agreement all around. Some were reluctant, but most heartily endorsed the speech. Sheila didn't need to be told that her last hope to be spared had died.

For several seconds, no one seemed to move. Finally, Ráfaga turned to face her. A muscle was twitching convulsively in his jaw, but there was no other sign that he disagreed with the sentence. A tremor quivered through Sheila's knees, but she steeled them to support herself as she returned Ráfaga's impassive look.

Not waiting for him to issue the command, Sheila turned and walked to the twin posts, standing between them, her head held proudly erect. Ráfaga signaled to one man to tie her up while another brought him the whip. A rope was slipped around her left wrist by the first man and drawn tightly against her flesh.

Laredo was at her side in a flash, his arm barring the man from fastening the hope to the post. He glanced over his shoulder at Ráfaga, his eyes glinting with blue fire.

"Damn it, Ráfaga, you can't do this to her!" he snapped savagely.

"Step aside," Ráfaga ordered, showing complete indifference to the protest.

"For God's sake, man, at least let me take her place!" Laredo hurled desperately, seeking any alternative to spare Sheila.

His demand sliced the thread. Black fury flamed to darken Ráfaga's expression. "Do you think *I* would not stand in her place if I could?" he hurled with savage anger. "Move away from her!"

Electrical currents charged the air between the two men until Laredo finally backed down, lowering his arm to let Sheila be tied to the post. Tortured blue eyes glanced briefly at Sheila before Laredo stepped away, his head bent in frustration.

While her right arm was being tied to the other post, Sheila stared at Ráfaga, icy fear churning her stomach as she tried not to look at the whip in his hand. She wanted to cry, to beg him not to do this despicable, cruel thing. But gazing into his rugged face, again completely devoid of expression, his emotions totally controlled, gave her the strength to keep her fear silent.

Instead of begging for a mercy she would not be shown, Sheila tipped her head with defiant pride to taunt. "Who is going to use the whip on me? You, Ráfaga?"

"No." He said it so quietly that she had to strain to hear it. His dark gaze slid to Laredo, his back turned to them as if trying to shut out the sight of Sheila tied between the two poles. "It will be Laredo who will have the whip in his hand."

Sheila had no difficulty hearing that. Neither did Laredo as he pivoted, a frown of angry disbelief lining his face.

"You can't ask me to do that!" he declared in a tortured breath.

Ráfaga held out the whip, saying quietly, "I would trust the whip in no one else's hand, *amigo*."

There was a moment of indecision as Laredo stared at him. Then he took the whip from Ráfaga's hand and walked around the posts to a spot somewhere behind Sheila. Ráfaga looked at Sheila, meeting her eyes for a

minute. Then he ducked beneath her arm to stand behind her.

Her muscles tensed as she felt the cold metal of a
knife blade slide beneath her blouse, the dull side touching her skin. Then the razor-sharp edge was slashing
through material down the center of her back. He
walked back to Laredo.

"It is time," he said, then gave a faint nod to Laredo.

Beads of perspiration broke out on Sheila's forehead. Behind her the whip cracked three times in rapid
succession. Fear knotted her stomach as she heard the
whir of rawhide whizzing through the air. Sheila braced
herself, curling her fingers around the rope that tied her
wrists to the poles. Nothing could prepare her for the
biting lash of the whip against the bare skin of her back.

A gasping cry of pain escaped from her throat. Gritting her teeth, she tried to swallow the scream, partially
succeeding. Again she heard the snaking whir before
she felt the thousands of needles stab her back in a
whipping line. This time Sheila bit into her lip to
smother the moan of pain.

Tears raced down her cheeks, although she wasn't
aware of crying. There was only the excruciating pain
streaking her back. She knew Ráfaga was standing in
front of her, but she couldn't see him anymore. Her
senses were drowning in pain.

Five or six times—Sheila lost count of the lashes—
she endured the striking whip. The next time, her knees
buckled beneath her and she sagged to the ground, all
of her weight being taken by the ropes. Her arms were
nearly pulled from their sockets, but she didn't feel her
limbs.

Her head lolled forward, hair plastered to her forehead and neck by the sweat running from her pores.
In a stupor of pain, Sheila waited, half-conscious for the
next cutting slash of the whip. Perspiration stung her
eyes and she couldn't see.

There was the salty taste of blood in her mouth, her
own blood seeping from the wound in her lip made by

her teeth. She waited for the bite of the rawhide lash, and waited. When it didn't come, Sheila tried to get her legs beneath her and rise.

Ráfaga's voice came to her. "Stay down," he ordered hoarsely. "I can stop this if you do not get up, *querida*."

Sheila heard him. She even understood him. Somehow she couldn't get his message to her legs. A powerful animal instinct was making her rise, as if to stay down would be to die.

Someone swore savagely in Spanish. Erratic moaning sobs were coming from somewhere close by. Sheila wasn't aware they were being made in her own throat. Then she was standing, swaying unsteadily.

Her heart was pounding like that of a wild rabbit caught in the talons of an eagle. She didn't hear the snake of the whip and her body jerked convulsively as it cracked against her skin. Sheila was nearly driven to her knees again, but the adrenaline being pumped through her veins gave her the strength to stay upright. Again and again the whip lashed her back. Sheila staggered to one knee, nearly unconscious now. She tried to rise.

"No!" It was like a thunderclap, rolling and vibrating through the air, charged with violence.

A pair of hands held her upright. "Don't touch me!" A voice cried out and it sounded demented from pain. This time Sheila realized it was her own voice.

"It is over," Ráfaga promised in a husky murmur.

Her arms dropped to her sides, and the ropes binding her wrists were cut. Sheila sagged against the granite support that was offered, her head resting against something solid. A trembling hand brushed the sweat-dampened hair away from her temple.

A Spanish voice crooned softly near her ear as an iron band slid around her thighs, lifting Sheila so that she seemed to be floating above the ground.

"Is she all right?"

Her dulled brain identified Laredo's voice. Sheila forced her heavy eyelids to open. Her blurring gaze looked into a pair of misty blue eyes, reflecting a pain that seemed equal to her own. It became too much of an effort and she closed her eyes, letting the floating sensation carry her away.

The next conscious moment lasted longer. Sheila was propped in a sitting position on a bed, one strong arm holding her while a hand stripped the slashed blouse from her. Very gently she was shifted to lie on her stomach.

Her lashes fluttered open, recognizing Ráfaga's hand as it lifted the hair away from her cheeks and neck. Beyond him, she could see Consuelo hovering anxiously, her dark eyes rounded and luminous with concern. Her back felt as if it were on fire, but Sheila smiled weakly at the woman.

"I'm all right." Her croaking voice was barely stronger than a whisper.

"Do not talk, *querida*," Ráfaga reprimanded in a gently soothing tone and turned to take something from Consuelo. "We must clean your back. It will hurt you. I am sorry."

At the fiery sting, Sheila turned her face into the pillow to smother her gasping cry of pain. Despite his use of the word "we," she was aware that it was only Ráfaga's hands that touched her, carefully cleansing her back before applying a soothing ointment to her raw skin.

With a coolly moist cloth, he wiped the perspiration from her face and neck. Wrapping the cloth around the rope burns on her wrists, he told her to sleep. Sheila closed her eyes obediently.

When she awakened, Ráfaga was sitting beside the bed in a silent vigil. He was leaning forward in the straight-backed chair, his face buried in his hands. Sheila searched her emotions to find a feeling of hatred for what he had allowed to happen to her, but she found none.

The strong, lean hands moved to rub his jaw, then his neck. As his gaze shifted to the bed where she lay, Sheila saw the raw pain glittering in his ebony-dark eyes. It vanished immediately when he saw she was awake.

"How do you feel?" he asked softly.

Sheila moved slightly and a thousand needles plunged into her back. "It hurts." She kept her voice tight to hold back the gasp of pain.

"It will be painful for some time," Ráfaga told her. "You have Laredo to thank that the marks will heal without leaving scars on your beautiful skin." He hesitated. "Do not hate him for what he did."

"I don't," Sheila assured him.

"That is good." There was a brief curve to his mouth, almost a smile.

"Ráfaga." She studied him silently, then asked, "Would you have used the whip on me if Laredo had refused?"

He stared at his hands, a dark frown lining his forehead. "No, I could not."

Sheila smiled gently. "I think you would have."

His head jerked up at her statement, cold challenge glittering in his eyes that she should call him a liar in a matter such as this.

"I think you would have," she repeated, "rather than give the whip to someone like Juan Ortega."

"Perhaps," he said curtly and started to rise.

Her hand slid across the bed, reaching out to stop him. Ráfaga saw the movement and paused. His hooded gaze flickered questioningly to her face.

"This morning," Sheila began uncertainly, "I hated you and everyone connected with you. Now I don't hate anyone."

Least of all, you, she could have added, but her heart wasn't ready to make a full confession yet. She waited, hoping he would say something that would let her tell all that she felt.

The coldness left his expression. His eyes were like soft, black velvet as they gazed down at her. Her heart quickened its beat. He appeared more compellingly handsome than ever before—strong, masculine, and vital.

But when Ráfaga answered, he said nothing that would prompt Sheila to reveal the true depths of her feelings. "You must have food. I will have Consuelo fix something for you."

Chapter 20

During the days following her recovery, Sheila discovered a new Ráfaga. The old masterful and autocratic man she had once known was gone. His place was taken by a touchingly gentle lover who was considerate and kind while remaining all man. Sheila hadn't believed it was possible to fall more deeply in love with Ráfaga, but she had.

"It's beautiful," she sighed at the wonder of it.

"What is beautiful?" Ráfaga inquired.

Sheila turned with a start, unaware that she had spoken aloud. He was smiling at her in a way that took her breath away, warm and intimate, as if there were only the two of them walking slowly through the tall grasses of the green meadow, leading their horses.

"The day." A hint of pink rouged her cheeks as she lied to him.

"You are tired, I think." His dark eyes studied the faint flush. "We have done too much. Come. Let the horses graze." He took hold of her elbow, guiding her toward a small hillock. "We will rest for a while."

Not arguing, Sheila let go of the reins and the bay horse immediately lowered its head to graze. The cattle and loose horses were grazing not too far in the distance. Where the horses and cattle were, Juan's boy, Pablo, could not be far away. Sheila looked for him, finding him sitting atop a flat rock in the shade. She waved to him and he shyly lifted a hand to return the salute.

"Pablo is a very responsible boy," Ráfaga commented, following the direction of Sheila's gaze.

"Yes, very conscientious," Sheila agreed. "Juan is teaching him English so someday Pablo can go to the States."

"Poor Pablo," Ráfaga chuckled, lowering himself to the ground and drawing Sheila down beside him, "to have Juan teaching him English."

"I should teach Pablo English, and he could teach me Spanish." The thought occurred to her and she said it aloud.

A daisy-like flower was growing in the thick green grasses. Sheila picked it, twirling it absently in her fingers. Ráfaga stretched his length over the green carpet, pulling Sheila into the crook of his arm.

"I think you will not teach Pablo." He turned his face toward her, a bemused smile curving his masculine lips.

"Why not?" Sheila glanced up at him curiously.

"Because he is coming into manhood. I would not like to have him come down with a severe case of calf-love for you," Ráfaga answered, a glittering light dancing in his eyes. "It is an age that is susceptible to such a malady."

"Did you ever suffer from it?" In some ways it was difficult to imagine Ráfaga as a vulnerable young boy.

"All boys do before they become men."

"What was she like?" Sheila stared at the vividly blue sky overhead. The air was startlingly clear and bright, the yellow ball of the sun shining down on the canyon.

"It has been too long ago for me to remember."

"You must remember something," she insisted.

"I remember she had golden hair and didn't know I existed." There was a smile in his voice.

"She was American?"

"I think so, yes," Ráfaga agreed indifferently.

Sheila thought of her own hair, streaked with gold from the sun. A tiny glow of pleasure warmed her. Perhaps Ráfaga was still susceptible to blondes from America. She was considering pursuing the subject when Ráfaga changed it.

"You were right." The hand at her waist tightened slightly. Contentment was in his voice. "It is a beautiful day."

"The mountains look so close. It's almost as if I could reach out and touch them." She gazed at the sharply defined peaks etched against the vibrant blue of the sky. "Have you ever thought about leaving here?" she asked.

"Where would I go?" countered Ráfaga.

Sheila turned on her side, propping an elbow beneath her and resting a hand on the muscled flatness of his stomach. There was a hopeful eagerness to the look she gave him.

"You could go to another country, start a new life, adopt a new name. You are intelligent, resourceful, a natural leader. You could be anything you want," Sheila argued.

"A new country and a new identity would not change the fact that I am wanted, Sheila," he answered patiently. "If I did what you say, there would always be the risk that someday I might be exposed. If I must live by my wits, I prefer to do it here in these mountains. I know them as intimately as I know you."

Her hair had swung forward across a cheek. Ráfaga tucked it behind her ear, his fingertips lightly caressing her skin. Sheila felt the first quiver of desire and tried to ignore it. She had begun something and had to finish it. She couldn't let Ráfaga distract her, no matter how much she would have liked it.

"Ráfaga, I have money," Sheila hurriedly said, then

quickly clarified the statement. "I don't mean money from my parents. I have money of my own. If you—"

A silencing finger touched her lips. "Money buys things, Sheila. It buys things I have no need of. It cannot buy my freedom, not after this much time. The things that I want are here before you." His gaze swept over the canyon. "Friends, the mountains, a place to live, a roof over my head. The only thing money does is buy clothes and whatever food that cannot be raised here."

Irritation flashed that Ráfaga rejected her offer before she even made it. "And when you need money, you just hire yourself out to break some criminal out of prison."

"You find it a contradiction, do you not, *querida?*" His mouth quirked gently. "We go to such lengths to uphold the laws we set for ourselves, then break those of the government for money."

Some of her anger melted at the Spanish endearment. She resented it, wanting to argue, but finding it difficult. "Yes, I do."

"We put ourselves outside the laws that you know and discovered we could not be free without laws. We made our own. It is a contradiction, but we have placed ourselves in this position—in a circle without end," Ráfaga explained.

"But couldn't you leave the circle?" Sheila returned to her original statement.

His hand cupped the side of her neck, his thumb rhythmically caressing the sensitive cord along her neck. "Some living things can be uprooted and transplanted to another terrain to flourish there. You, I think, are one of those." His eyes darkened, looking deeply, it almost seemed, into her soul. "I could not leave the Sierras. There is no reason for me to try. Everything I want is here."

Pressure was applied to her neck, drawing Sheila down. His hard lips tantalizingly brushed the soft curves of hers, teasing them with the promise of a kiss. Yet when Sheila would have moved to accept, his hand tightened on her neck, holding her away.

"Everything I want is here," Ráfaga repeated huskily against her mouth, his breath mingling warmly with hers. "All I could ever want, I have found."

It seemed the time. Her heart was aching with need to give. Sheila whispered softly, "I love you."

In answer, the pressure of his lean fingers along the back of her neck increased, drawing her the half an inch down as his mouth opened over her lips. Her senses were assaulted by the intoxicating mixture of aromatic tobacco smoke clinging to his skin and the musky scent of his masculinity. The deepening kiss touched off the passionate core inside her, spreading a yielding fire through the softness of her body.

With quivering rapture, Sheila swayed onto the solid cushion of his chest, her full curves molding themselves to his muscled contours. Her hands hugged his rib cage, fiercely possessive. His tongue parted her lips to explore the intimate hollows of her mouth. Desire flamed with a golden fire to run molten-hot through her veins.

A hand at her hip shifted her more fully atop of him, then slid up to cup the underside of one breast. Lean fingers tugged the rippling gold of her hair away from her neck as his mouth scorched a fiery trail to the hollow of her throat. Ráfaga retraced the route, pausing at intervals to nibble at the curve of her shoulder, the sensitive cord along her neck, and an earlobe.

Again his hard mouth returned to consume her lips, tasting their sweetness and claiming them as his alone. Sheila could feel the rapid beat of his heart, a wild serenade in tempo with her own racing pulse.

Without warning, Ráfaga rolled Sheila onto her side. His fingers dispensed with the impediments of blouse buttons with an urgency that excited her. A shiver of sensual delight danced over her skin as the material was pushed aside to expose her breasts. The sensation of coolness was brief, dissipating under the warmth of his hand that was closing over the rounded firmness of her breast, swelling at his touch.

Sheila slipped her own hands beneath his shirt, unashamedly glorying in the feel of his hard flesh beneath her fingers. Her nipple hardened to a rosy peak under the manipulation of his fingers. Ráfaga released her lips to investigate the erotic bud with his mouth and tongue. She shuddered with longing. The feeling was intensified as his hand slid over her bare stomach to her aching loins. Her hips moved in response to his suggestive caress.

Pressing her backward to the grass, his strong fingers sought the snap of her Levi's. Sheila moaned softly, unknowingly. Ráfaga immediately hesitated. The sensual fires blazing in his dark gaze swept over her face.

"Does the hard ground against your back cause you pain?" There was the husky rawness of desire to his voice, yet it was a desire that he could control. Sheila had long ago learned that his ability to control himself was a mark of his expertise in making love.

"No." She whispered the shaky denial, sliding a hand behind the strong column of his neck. "Only your teasing causes me pain."

There was a brief flash of white as he smiled in satisfaction and lowered his mouth to her parted lips. "That is the way it should be, *querida*," he said against her lips.

A moment of sanity claimed her as she felt the gliding release of her zipper. Her hands fluttered against his chest in weak protest while she twisted her lips from beneath his.

"Pablo can see us, Ráfaga," she reminded him in a breathless murmur.

He lifted his head. "Do you want me to move away from you?" The glitter in his eyes knew the answer before Sheila gave it.

"No." She rubbed her cheek against his jaw like a kitten wishing to be stroked again.

"You want to stay in my arms, but you don't want me to make love to you." There was the wry inflection of mockery in his tone. "That is not possible for either of us."

"I know." Sheila sighed with the aching need she felt.

Moving away from her, Ráfaga grabbed hold of her wrists, pulling Sheila to her feet as he rose. Her mouth opened to protest, but he fluidly swept her off her feet and into the cradle of his arms. Carrying her as if she weighed no more than thistledown, he walked toward the canyon wall on the other side of the hillock.

"Where are we going?" Sheila glanced around, her view limited.

"There." Ráfaga inclined his head toward a point in front of them.

Their destination was a cave, hollowed out of the rock wall. Part of its entrance was obscured by brush. The angle of the sunlight chased away much of the darkness. Sheila glanced around curiously, noting the man-made marks that widened the entrance.

As if reading the question that was on her mind, Ráfaga said, "A Tarahumura family once lived here."

As he set Sheila on her feet, she forgot all about the past inhabitants of the cave. His hands pushed the blouse from her shoulders. Her arms quickly slipped out of the sleeves. There was a sudden, primitive urgency to her need for him, and Ráfaga seemed to echo it. A shooting fire was in his hard kiss, demanding and possessive. Their passion was a volcanic eruption, the white-hot heat fusing them together.

It was the chill of the setting sun against her nakedness that finally drove Sheila from the wild, sublime peace of his arms much, much later, seeking the covering warmth of her clothes. She was conscious of his dark eyes watching her dress, but she felt no shyness or need for modesty.

There was a sense of pride in the shape of her body, a pride that Ráfaga found beauty in her nakedness and carnal satisfaction in her flesh. She was proud of the translucent creaminess of her skin, the slimness of her hips—as Ráfaga had once described them, wide enough to receive a man—and the ripe roundness of her breasts, their nipples tilting upward.

Dressing with unhurried movements, Sheila heard a rustle of clothing behind her. She slipped into her blouse and turned to see Ráfaga tucking his shirt into the waistband of his denims. He walked to her side, saying nothing, but the dark glow of his eyes was warm and admiring as they gazed into hers. Sheila felt she would be content to bask in that light for the rest of her life.

The back of his fingers lightly stroked her cheek in a feather caress. "I will bring the horses here."

A ghost of a smile curved the male line of his mouth before he walked out of the cave. Sheila watched him leave until he was out of sight. She continued to stare at the place she had last seen him, her hands poised on the buttons of her blouse, fastened a third of the way up the front.

Her fingertip accidentally brushed the curve of her breast and stayed there to lightly trace the hollow formed by her breasts, remembering the way Ráfaga's hands and mouth had stimulated them. Her heart was filled to overflowing with a love that was not just physical.

There was a movement in the thick foliage, but it came from the opposite direction Ráfaga had taken. Still, Sheila turned expectantly, assuming she would see him leading the horses. Her eyes widened in alarm, her fingers curling protectively to clasp the front of her blouse together.

Juan Ortega stood near the entrance, his leering, dark eyes mentally stripping her naked. Sheila wondered how long he had been there. Something in his look told her that he had not just arrived. She felt sickened that he might have witnessed the private interlude. He said something to her in his guttural Spanish and took a step toward her.

From outside the cave, a clipped demand pivoted Juan away from Sheila. Ráfaga had returned. She leaned weakly against the wall, gulping in the air she had been afraid to breathe a moment ago. Her amber-flecked eyes closed in relief as she listened to the low, lashing reprimand issued by Ráfaga and the hurried response from Juan Ortega. She stayed in the shadows even after she heard Juan leave.

"Sheila!" Ráfaga called to her, a harshness remaining in his voice.

"Yes." It was a shaky response, but it enabled him to locate her in the darkened interior of the cave.

His hands seized her shoulders, pulling her from the wall. "What are you doing back here?" It was half-demand and half-question.

"He—he was coming after me. I thought—" She swayed into his arms, trembling with reaction.

"He was looking for me," Ráfaga stated. His arms circled her when he felt the tremors quaking through her. "Pablo had told him that he saw us walking in this direction. Ortega heard a noise in the cave and came to investigate. When he saw you, he said he asked for me. You started going back into the cave and he thought that was where I was."

Sheila drew her head back, trying to see Ráfaga's face in the shadows. "Do you believe him?" she asked with accusation.

"It is possible."

"Yes," Sheila agreed tightly.

The man was cunning and she didn't trust him. Restraining her shattered nerves, she moved out of Ráfaga's arms, quickly buttoning the rest of her blouse. She knew Ráfaga was studying her, but she avoided his eyes.

"Are the horses outside?" She changed the subject, not wanting to talk about Juan Ortega anymore and wanting to get out of the cave that had become contaminated by his invasion.

"Yes, they are outside."

As Sheila hurried into the waning sunlight, Ráfaga's long strides easily kept pace with her. Two horses were ground-hitched near the entrance. A sorrel stood, loose-hipped, an ear indifferently swiveling at their

approach while the bay lifted its head and blew softly.
Sheila walked to the bay, gathering the hanging reins to
loop them over its head. But Ráfaga caught her arm,
stopping her.

"You are frightened of Ortega. Why?" He closely
studied her upturned face.

"I have always been frightened of him—since the
first time I saw him," she answered stiffly, "regardless
of what you think to the contrary."

"What does that mean?" A dark brow arched in a
demanding inquiry.

"It means I did not invite him into the house the
night he tried to rape me, although I know you don't
believe that. My skin crawls every time he's anywhere
near me." A repulsive shiver raced over her flesh as
she said it.

Ráfaga took Sheila by the shoulders and turned her
to face him. "You do not need to fear Ortega. He will
not come near you again. He knows too well what I
would do to him."

He was trying to reassure her and he believed what
he was saying. But Sheila didn't and she didn't know
why. It was just an uneasy feeling she got whenever
she saw Juan Ortega. It was something she couldn't
explain.

Ráfaga's grip tightened when Sheila didn't answer
him. "Do you understand me, Sheila?"

"Yes." She nodded and smiled to conceal the fact
that she couldn't believe him.

The bay horse nuzzled his arm. Sheila used the action
as an excuse to change the subject. "Why don't you ride
him anymore, Ráfaga?"

"Because he is yours."

"Not literally, of course." Sheila smiled more naturally this time, remembering his explanation when she
had been given Arriba.

"The bay is mine to give. It is not a gesture that I
make," Ráfaga corrected. "The bay is yours. I have
told this to Juan. The bay will be the horse he saddles
for you when you wish to ride."

"Because of Arriba," she murmured.

"Yes, because of the mare. I cannot replace the fondness you had for the mare, but I can give you a horse that is her equal." He rubbed the bay's forelock. "The bay is not as fast as your mare," he qualified, "but he can carry you over a hundred mountains and have the stamina to try a hundred more. At night, he has cat eyes that can see the way that is safe."

"But—" Sheila frowned. He himself had proclaimed the bay to be the best horse. Had Ráfaga given him to her as a sign of trust? Sheila didn't have an opportunity to ask.

"We must go." He turned, gathering the reins of the sorrel and mounting. "A rider has come and I must speak with him."

Looping the reins over the bay's head, Sheila swung into the saddle. She could only second-guess his decision as he immediately turned the sorrel toward the house.

Sheila recognized the rider as being the same man who had ridden in during the thunderstorm weeks before. This time the man didn't make any attempt to disguise his interest in her, and she had the impression that he had come because of her.

Whatever information he had brought with him displeased Ráfaga. When she tried to confirm the suspicion that the news was about her, Ráfaga denied it flatly, but he refused to tell her the reason why the man had come—so far and so fast, judging by the weary, lathered horse tied outside the adobe house.

It was one of the few times during the gentle days of her recovery that Sheila remembered Ráfaga shutting her out. And the hours of closeness far outweighed the moment when an invisible barrier came between them.

The change in their relationship was apparent to all who saw them together. In consequence, Sheila found herself receiving the friendly respect of those in the canyon. Even the guards at the door reflected it, no longer snapping to alertness when she stepped outside, but nodding and smiling politely, instead. The adobe house and the canyon were no longer a prison she wanted to escape from, and they seemed to know that.

With soap and a towel in her hand, Sheila walked out of the house. Using a combination of sign language and the smattering of Spanish she had picked up from Consuelo, she explained to the man and guard that she was going to the pool to wash her hair. He nodded his understanding and motioned for her to go. She smiled to herself, remembering when her way would have been barred with a rifle.

Only rarely did she have a twinge of longing to see her parents or reassure them she was all right. It seemed years since she had lived in their house. She felt as though they lived in another world where she no longer belonged. Sheila didn't mind. She was content in this world with Ráfaga.

Humming absently, she knelt beside the pool. She shivered even before she dunked her head into the icy water. Her hair had grown much longer. It floated in the water like a dark gold fan. She rubbed soap into her scalp until it tingled, then worked the subsequent lather through her hair.

Rinsing it, she had the feeling someone was nearby. She turned, half-expecting to see Ráfaga, but there was no one in sight. Shrugging, Sheila lowered her head into the water, closing her eyes against the stinging soap.

The day was too beautiful to return to the house immediately. Sheila moved to a spot near the pool where the sun pierced the thick stand of trees to warm the earth. Unwrapping the towel, she began rubbing the ends of her hair dry.

A faint rustle of grass caused her to turn her gaze to the left. A man stood watching her. Sheila had seen him in the canyon, but she didn't know his name. There was something about him that made her uneasy.

She smiled hesitantly. *"Buenos días."*

The man didn't return her greeting, but he motioned to Sheila to get up. She did so warily, trying to decide whether Ráfaga had sent him to fetch her when she hadn't returned sooner. Somehow she didn't think so.

When the man took a step toward her, Sheila backed up.

An arm circled her waist from behind. A hand over her mouth stifled the scream of alarm. Kicking and clawing, Sheila tried to break free. The first man moved quickly to her, a rope appearing in his hand. Her wrists were bound tightly and she was dragged deep into the woods to a place where three horses were tied.

The smothering hand clamped over her mouth permitted little air for her to breathe. What Sheila could inhale was tainted with the hot odor of the hand. Her nostrils were widely distended, trying to drink in oxygen, but her breathing was labored by fear and exertion.

As the hand was taken away, Sheila screamed, "Ráfa———" A soiled kerchief was roughly jammed into her mouth, nearly gagging her. Another piece of material was bound around her head to hold the gag in place. It was tied tightly at the back of her head, and strands of hair were caught in the knot, adding to the pain in her scalp.

When Sheila was forcibly hoisted onto a saddle, she glimpsed her second kidnapper. It came as no surprise to see Juan Ortega. Somehow it had all been leading up to this since the day he had killed Brad on the road. The terrible sense of inevitability frightened her.

His leering grin seemed to be laughing at the terror in her amber eyes, his chipped and yellowed teeth looking like the fangs of a hungry dog. He tied her hands to the saddle horn, giving her no chance to slide from the horse and run.

Holding the reins, he mounted his own horse. The first man was already in the saddle, waiting. He followed as Ortega led the way. Instead of working their way through the trees to the east, they were heading back toward the pool. Hope glimmered. If they didn't take her out of the canyon, there was a chance she could alert someone.

They were nearly level with the pool, hugging close to the north face of the canyon. Abruptly, Ortega reined in his horse, stiffening. Sheila glanced ahead to see Juan blocking the path, a rifle in his hand. The second man rode quickly to the front, as if to shield Sheila from Juan's sight, but he had already seen her and was making a cold demand in Spanish.

Her heart pounded with relief. There were tears swimming near the edges of her eyes. Juan knew how much she despised and feared Ortega. He would never believe any tale the cunning man might make up. Her gaze shifted to the loathsome animal masquerading as a human. This time, too, he would be stopped.

Then her eyes saw what Juan couldn't see; his view was blocked by the other rider and Ortega's horse. Ortega was slowly and carefully slipping his knife from its sheath. Sheila tried to cry out a warning, but the kerchief muffled the sound. Her attempt shifted Juan's attention to her. It was the moment Ortega had been waiting for—when Juan's sharp eyes were not watching his every move.

With lightning swiftness, he threw the knife. Too late Juan realized his mistake. He tried to bring his rifle to his shoulder, but the knife blade was already plunging into his chest, driving him backward. Sheila's cry of terror got no farther than her throat.

Ortega spurred his horse, yanking on the reins of Sheila's mount. She caught a brief glimpse of Juan's twitching body on the ground as they rode past. Then her horse was turned toward the rocky face of the canyon to climb a faint trail that suddenly appeared behind a moss-covered boulder. A second way out of the canyon. A trail that Sheila hadn't known existed.

Chapter 21

Once out of the canyon, they rode hard and fast to the west. Sheila could feel her mount stumbling with exhaustion, straining against the reins that persistently pulled it along.

She saw the nervous way both men watched the trail in back of them. She knew they were driving the horses to put as much distance between themselves and the canyon as was possible. Whatever their ultimate destination was, Ortega intended to reach it before any pursuers could catch up to them. Sheila could only pray that Ráfaga was on their trail now.

Ortega's horse stumbled and nearly went to its knees. A savage yank on the reins pulled its head up as Ortega cursed the horse violently in Spanish. Sheila saw the flecks of blood in the foam around the horse's mouth and felt a surge of pity for the wounded beast, then decided she should save it for herself. Her time would be coming when she would be on the receiving end of Ortega's abuse, a different and more degrading form of savagery.

In the next rocky clearing they came to, Ortega halted to give the horses a much-needed rest, finally realizing if he pushed them any farther, they would all be afoot. Sheila felt as hot and tired as the horses. Her hands and fingers were numbed by the strangling rope around her wrists. Yet fear made her doubly alert.

The two men dismounted, drinking thirstily from the canteens. Sheila was conscious of how parched her throat was. The gag biting into her mouth made her jaw ache, the material drying her tongue until it felt wooden and rough. Only when they had drunk their fill did they give any water to the horses.

Shifting in the saddle, she tried to ease the cramped muscles in her arms. The leather creaked, drawing Ortega's gaze to her. His lips widened in a lecherous grin as he fastened his gaze on the front of her blouse.

The sun was hot overhead and perspiration ran profusely from her pores. It drenched the blouse, causing the material to cling stickily to her skin. Sheila tensed, aware of the way it boldly outlined her breasts, her nipples jutting against the material.

Her skin felt suddenly clammy with fear as Ortega walked to her horse. She tried to be stoic, knowing he would take delight in seeing her tremble before him. It was hard not to recoil from the touch of his stubby hands as he untied the rope from the saddle horn.

With a yank, he pulled her from the saddle. It was a deliberate tactic to make her fall heavily into his arms. His hand grasped the rounded swell of one breast. He laughed maliciously at her muffled cry of protest. Sheila tried to regain her balance, needing it to have leverage to struggle.

The other man said something in Spanish to Ortega. Sheila understood a few words, enough to know her other kidnapper did not think this was the time or the place to do whatever Ortega had in mind. But Juan Ortega continued to smile as he argued that the horses were resting. Sheila twisted helplessly in his arms, her toes barely touching the ground. The man shook his head and started to walk away.

But Ortega called him back, spinning Sheila around his arms so that she was facing the second man. The hand that had been so roughly kneading her breast reached up to grab the neckline of her blouse, ripping it down before Sheila could try to stop him.

The torn material was pulled to the side, exposing the creamy globes of her breasts, rising and falling rapidly from the panicked breaths she was taking. Ortega's voice seemed to challenge his cohort to ignore the prize they had captured.

Sobbing against the kerchief, Sheila made a superhuman effort and broke free of his hands. She tried to run, but Ortega grabbed at a trailing corner of her blouse, ripping more of it. The second man caught her as she was trying to elude the one she feared most. While he held her fast, Ortega tore the rest of her blouse off. Sheila struggled wildly as he pulled at the waistband of her slacks.

The man had difficulty holding her, but he succeeded. Sheila felt the hard male bulge in his loins pressing against her rump and knew he would rape her when Ortego had finished with her. Her slacks were pulled nearly to her thighs.

Sheila kicked at Ortega, aiming for his groin. He caught her foot before it could deliver its crippling blow and tugged at the leg of her slacks. She was insane with fear now, screaming Ráfaga's name over and over again, but the gagging kerchief made it indistinguishable.

She was being forced to the ground, writhing and twisting frantically like a snake on a bed of hot coals. The man grabbed hold of her bound wrists, drawing them over her head to keep her from rising while Ortega fumbled with his pants.

There was an explosion and suddenly Sheila's arms were no longer being pinned to the ground above her head. She rolled over, trying to rise to her feet. Ortega was already running toward the horses. There was another explosion and Sheila saw him fall.

Her terrorized mind finally realized that the explosion

had been a gunshot. She turned to see Ráfaga striding into the small clearing, cocking the rifle in his hands. Behind him were Laredo and a third man.

Sheila collapsed, sobbing with relief. Her tear-filled eyes saw Ortega desperately trying to crawl. There was another shot and he stopped moving. Then Ráfaga was standing above the body, rolling him onto his back with the toe of a boot, the rifle muzzle pointed at his head.

Then Sheila was aware of Laredo kneeling beside her. He stripped the jacket off his back and laid it over her nakedness. She thanked him with her eyes.

"Thank God you're all right," Laredo murmured and reached to untie the kerchief from around her mouth.

"Do not touch her!" Ráfaga growled the warning. His white teeth were bared in a snarl as he pivoted to bring the rifle muzzle to bear on Laredo.

Laredo, who knew him, stopped instantly, keeping both hands in view as he moved them slowly and carefully away from her head. Sheila, who loved him, felt a cold shaft of fear at the icy savagery etched in the lean features. The steely black look in his eyes was frightening. She couldn't help cringing uncertainly when he walked to her.

Without saying a word, he bent down to untie the gag. His touch was gentle, but it didn't alter the ruthless set of his jaw. A long, sighing sob of relief came from her mouth when the kerchief was removed. Tears slipped from her lashes, but Sheila couldn't cry as she wanted to. Ráfaga slid a knife blade between her wrists, cutting the rope that bound them before he straightened to walk away. She was too numb with shock to rise to her feet.

Neither Laredo nor the other rider dared to make a move to help her. She lay there, not knowing what to do. She wanted the warm comfort of Ráfaga's arms, but he seemed encased in ice, insensitive and hard.

He returned to the clearing, leading three horses and carrying a blanket in his hand. Handing the reins to the third man, Ráfaga walked to where Sheila lay on the ground. After shaking the blanket out to its full length, he crouched beside her, holding it like a screen while he removed the jacket and tossed it in Laredo's direction.

Sheila didn't make an attempt to help him as Ráfaga covered her with the blanket, swaddling Sheila like a baby. And, like a baby, he lifted her into his arms and carried her to his sorrel horse.

Laredo stood at the sorrel's head. "What about them?" He indicated the bodies of the two men.

"Let the scavengers have them." Ráfaga's reply was drawn through clenched teeth. He turned curtly to the third man and ordered him to bring the dead men's horses.

Sheila trembled and his arm tightened around her, crushing her to his chest. She huddled deeper inside the blanket, the only place where she seemed to find warmth. The ride back to the canyon was long and oppressively silent.

At the house, Ráfaga swung agilely from his horse. Still carrying Sheila, he nodded to the man on guard to open the door. Over his shoulder, Sheila saw Laredo start to dismount, but Ráfaga was kicking the door shut the instant he carried her through. He carried her straight to the bedroom and stopped just inside to set her down gently.

His face was a hardened mask, etched in bronze, with steel-black eyes that were emotionless and cold. "Stay here," Ráfaga ordered.

Not knowing how literally he meant it, Sheila didn't move. She doubted if she could have, anyway. She was too numbed by all that had happened. There were sounds of him moving around in the kitchen. Fleetingly, Sheila wondered where Consuelo was, then remembered the knife that had pierced Juan's chest.

When Ráfaga returned, she wanted to ask about Juan, but the question became lodged in her throat. Steam rose from the basin he set in the center of the floor. He spread a towel out beside it and walked to Sheila. Her rounded, unblinking eyes stared at him as he took the blanket from her and tossed it aside. Carrying her to the towel, he let her down to stand on it.

With a bar of soap and the warmed water, Ráfaga began methodically washing every inch of her with the indifference of a physician. Sheila stood silently, like a mannequin, remembering another time when she had been the one to scrub her body clean of Juan Ortega's touch. Perhaps Ráfaga, too, was remembering that time and was washing her now to make up for the fact that there was cause to do it a second time.

When Ráfaga had toweled her dry, he carried her to the bed, laying her down and drawing the blanket over her. He sat on the edge of the bed beside her for a minute. Sheila ached for him to take her in his arms and give her the safety and warmth of his embrace. She gazed helplessly into his dark eyes. Their aloofness was cruel. She wanted to beg him to hold her, but she couldn't say a word.

A tear slipped from her lash, seeming to freeze in a crystal drop on her cheekbone. His fingertip wiped it away, a muscle twitching in his jaw. Without a word he rose and walked from the room. Sheila turned her face to the wall and curled into a tight ball of misery. She heard the closing of the front door and shut her eyes.

After the sun had gone down, Ráfaga returned to the house and brought her food. Sheila tried to refuse it, but he insisted she eat. They were the only words he spoke to her. She managed to down a third of it before pushing the rest away. He took it and left.

In the morning, the procedure was repeated, except that Sheila ate less. She didn't know where Ráfaga had slept, but it hadn't been with her. She retreated into a shell of her own in the face of his remoteness.

Again Ráfaga left the house as soon as she had eaten. Sheila rose, unable to have him find her a third time in bed and look at her as though she was a stranger to him. When she was fully dressed, she walked to the front door. The silence of the empty house was stifling. It made her feel half-sick.

Sheila thought to seek the freshness of the mountain air, but the guard refused to let her leave, shaking his head sadly as he motioned her back into the house. She was a prisoner again, confined to the house.

Restlessly, Sheila paced around the house, pain tearing at her heart and making her nerves raw. She kept watching the shadows outside the window cast by the sun, waiting for noon, when Ráfaga would again bring her food. But it was Laredo who came with the peaking of the sun. The sight of him snapped the thread of Sheila's control.

At his knock, she flung the door open and demanded, "What do you want?"

Laredo shouldered his way into the house, carrying a small tray. "I'm glad to see you're up." His blue eyes swept over her in quick assessment. "I brought you some food. Ráfaga said you haven't been eating much."

"If he's so concerned, why didn't he bring it himself?" Her fingernails curled into the palms of her hands, the intense hurt she felt released in bitterness. Sheila wasn't aware of what she was doing as her arm swung to knock the tray out of his hands, sending it clattering to the floor. "I haven't been eating because I haven't been hungry—and I'm still not! You can tell that to Ráfaga since he obviously can't stand the sight of me anymore!"

"Sheila, it isn't that." Laredo shook his head sadly, his gentle gaze meeting the flaming yellow fire of hers.

"Isn't it?" she said chokingly. "He hasn't spoken a word to me or so much as touched me! He couldn't even sleep in the same house with me last night!"

"You don't understand," he began.

"No, I don't understand!" Sheila cried in frustration and hurt. "Where is he now? What is he doing? Why can't he—"

She was becoming hysterical, sobs cracking her voice. Laredo took hold of her shoulders. "He's with Juan, Sheila," he told her sternly.

Breathing in sharply, she stared at him for an instant, then pivoted away. He didn't try to stop her, but Sheila was aware of his eyes watching her as she hugged her arms around her churning stomach. Waves of nausea swept through her, but she fought them back.

"How is he?" The words came from deep in her throat.

"Still unconscious. He lost a lot of blood," Laredo answered quietly. "The knife missed his lungs, but we don't know how much damage it did internally."

Sheila hung her head, squeezing her eyes tightly shut. "It's all my fault. If I hadn't tried to warn him, he might have seen the knife in Ortega's hand."

He crooked a finger beneath her chin, lifting it. "You can't blame yourself, Sheila. Juan should have known better than to take his eyes off Ortega for even a second."

Something in the way he said the last remark made her look at him. "You know what happened?"

Laredo nodded. "Juan was conscious when we found him. How, I don't know. He managed to crawl to the pool. Ráfaga and I and the guard found him when we went looking for you. Someone had told Juan that they had seen Ortega and Chavez take three horses from the corral. Juan became suspicious and started to trail them. Then he ran into them with you."

She shuddered, remembering. "When they got Juan, I didn't think there was any chance you could catch up to us before they—"

Laredo didn't give her a chance to finish the sentence, drawing her into his arms. "Ráfaga knows these mountains like the back of his hand. Once he saw which trail they were taking, we took shortcuts to intercept them." Her head rested lightly on his shoulder, finding a small measure of comfort in his circling arms. Gently he rocked her. "It's all over now, Sheila," he murmured.

Thinking of Ráfaga's cutting aloofness, Sheila denied it tightly. "Not quite. Ráfaga—"

The front door opened and he walked in, stopping abruptly at the sight of Sheila in Laredo's arms. The bronze mask over his features melted as dark flames of anger blazed in his eyes. Gently, Laredo set Sheila apart from him and met the dark gaze without flinching.

"I told Sheila about Juan," he said in explanation, then walked calmly past Ráfaga and out the door.

Ráfaga continued to stare at Sheila, the black rage slowly being brought under control. His gaze sliced suddenly and pointedly to the tray of food scattered on the floor near his feet.

"The food was prepared to be eaten, not to be thrown on the floor," he informed her icily.

She could have withstood his anger, but this chilling indifference was something she couldn't handle. "Then eat it yourself!" Sheila cried. "I don't want it!"

He seemed to draw himself up to his full height, cold and withdrawn. "We will leave it to the cockroaches, then."

Ráfaga started to walk away, but Sheila couldn't let him go. She caught at his elbow to stop him. He paused, looking down at her while her eyes searched his face for some indication of the reason for his behavior toward her.

"What is it, Ráfaga? What's wrong?" she demanded earnestly. "What have I done? Do you blame me for what happened to Juan? Do you think I went with Ortega willingly at first?"

Sheila remembered how certain she had been that the rider's information had concerned her. His hands drew her shoulders back against him.

"You should berate me for my stupidity, Sheila," Ráfaga said, his breath stirring her hair. "It nearly cost the life of a good man and a loyal friend to you— Juan may yet die; I do not know. It nearly gave you into the hands of a man who would have abused you with his lust." His voice was harsh, with a savage anger that was turned inward. "I deserve your hatred and mistrust for failing to protect you when I have forced you to accept my protection by taking you to my bed. I saw the way you cowered from me out there in the mountains, the fear that was in your eyes when you looked at me."

"I was frightened," Sheila admitted, leaning against him, closing her eyes, "frightened of that cold rage in your eyes. Later I thought you blamed me for what happened. I don't hate you. How could I?"

She would have added, "when I love you so much," but he was turning her around, claiming her lips in a hard, possessive kiss. Sheila wound her arms around his neck as he lifted her off her feet and carried her to the bedroom. The warmth of his embrace made her forget the previous anguish.

Yet there was something missing. Sheila realized that after a few days had passed. They hadn't recaptured that special magic that had linked them before the incident. There was a part of himself that Ráfaga held back. At first, she tried to convince herself that when Juan showed signs of recovery, Ráfaga would return to his old self.

But it hadn't worked that way. Juan was still dangerously weak, but he had begun to respond to the loving ministrations of his wife, Consuelo. And there were still times when Ráfaga would withdraw behind a shuttered look, studying Sheila silently, as if expecting to find something. Those moments troubled her, no matter how much she tried to ignore them.

His side of the bed was empty. Ráfaga was rarely there anymore when Sheila awakened. He rose with the sun, leaving her to sleep. Another dull headache droned at her temples. Sheila frowned and tried to rub away the pain with her fingers.

Light footsteps entered the hall. Sheila turned her head toward the sound, moving too quickly, and a wave of dizziness drained the color from her face.

Consuelo appeared in the bedroom doorway, smiling. "*Buenos días,* Sheila."

"*Buenos días.*" The greeting sounded weak even to Sheila's ears. "How is Juan this morning?"

There was a positive declaration in Spanish that he was much better before Consuelo clicked her tongue at Sheila and teased her about something. Sheila frowned, certain she hadn't understood the woman. She blamed it on the dull headache, deciding it had affected her concentration.

"What did you say, Consuelo?" She asked that the remark be repeated.

A second time didn't improve her comprehension of the Spanish words. Consuelo tried again, combining them with sign language and pantomime. Sheila's mouth opened in shock when Consuelo made a cradle of her arms, rocked an imaginary bundle, pointed at Sheila, and said, *"bebé."*

"It isn't possible," Sheila gasped in protest. But a swift, mental calculation said it was more than possible. It was quite likely true. She was pregnant. Her hand moved across her stomach, as if it might feel the child growing inside her.

It was as flat and smooth as always. For now. How naïve of her not to have suspected, Sheila thought angrily. A month and a half, two months. God, she couldn't even remember.

Immediately, Consuelo recognized that Sheila hadn't known. The gentle woman hurried to assure her that it was wonderful news. Sheila understood more by the woman's tone than her actual words. For a moment, she could feel nothing but shock and confusion. Then she caught the gist of a comment concerning how pleased Ráfaga would be. And Sheila suddenly realized he would have to know she was carrying his child.

Somehow she managed to get Consuelo out of the room so she could be alone to think this discovery through. A part of her glowed with the knowledge that she was carrying Ráfaga's child. But there was fear, too—fear because there were no doctors for miles. She would be bringing a child into the world under conditions that could only be classified as primitive.

As for Ráfaga, he wanted her now, when she was shapely and beautiful. But how long would his desire last when her stomach grew as fat as a melon and her long legs had all the grace of a waddling duck?

Sheila started to cry.

Chapter 22

The silence during the noon meal was heavy. Sheila knew her eyelids were still swollen from crying and her features were drawn with tension. Ráfaga had to have noticed. His alert, yet hooded gaze had continually inspected her face all through the meal.

There were only the two of them in the house; Consuelo was in her own home with Juan. This was the time to tell Ráfaga about the baby. Her hands closed around the empty coffee mug in front of her.

There was no easy way to say it. Trembling, Sheila lifted her chin, a faint challenge in the gesture, and blurted out, "I'm going to have a baby."

Nothing flickered in his dark eyes. "Yes," Ráfaga said, as though he were confirming her statement.

"You knew?" she asked with a slight frown of disbelief.

"Do you think I do not know every inch of you?" There was a cynical lift to one corner of his mouth. "Do you think I would not notice the slightest change in your body?"

271

Her announcement had not brought any pleased light to his dark eyes. There was none of the gladness or pride that Consuelo had suggested would be there when she told him. He didn't want the baby, and Sheila felt something die in her heart.

"What is it you want of me?" Ráfaga inquired, studying her closely, a blandness to his look.

"I want you to be happy about the baby," Sheila wanted to cry. Instead, she shrugged and said, "Nothing," her shoulders hunching forward.

"Do you not want me to arrange for an abortion?"

"An abortion?!!" Her hand moved protectively to her stomach, as if at that moment he could somehow take the life she carried within her.

"Many American women have come to Mexico in the past to rid themselves of babies they did not want. Is that what you wish?" he asked with infuriating calm.

My God she thought, *how could he suggest such a thing?* This was his seed she carried, his baby. How could he believe that she would want to get rid of it?

"No." Her voice was coldly drawn from her throat. "That is not what I wish," Sheila declared, rising from the table. She needed to get away from him before she lost her temper and did something that might ultimately harm their baby.

"Then why have you told me?" Ráfaga's question checked her footsteps as Sheila turned.

"I told you." She held herself rigidly, not looking back. "Because you are the baby's father. I thought you should know."

She was trembling uncontrollably, tears stinging her eyes. There was the scrape of the chair leg as Ráfaga rose from the table. Her heart hammered frantically against her ribs. Every muscle was poised for flight, but he didn't approach her. His striding walk was carrying him to the door.

When Sheila heard it open and close, her hand groped for the chair she had just left, needing its support as her legs threatened to collapse. She found it, sinking quickly into its seat. Burying her face in her hands, she began to cry. She would have Ráfaga's baby, but she would lose him. It wasn't a fair exchange.

The supply of tears ran out. Sheila was numbed to all but her own torment. She didn't hear the door open or the sound of footsteps approaching. She still believed she was alone with her misery when a hand touched her shoulder. Her head jerked, her blurred eyes seeing Ráfaga standing beside her chair.

"Don't touch me!" The chair clattered to the floor as she moved to elude his touch. Sheila faced him rigidly, retreating when he moved toward her. "Don't come near me!" she hissed in bitter anger and hurt, a wounded animal lashing out at the one who had injured her. "Haven't you done enough? Why can't you leave me alone?"

The room was small. Within moments she was cornered against a wall, his hands seizing her arms, refusing to let her go. There was an unrelenting grimness about his mouth.

"Listen to me, Sheila," commanded Ráfaga.

"I don't want to hear anything you have to say!" she cried. Her hands were straining against his chest, but he was making no attempt to draw her closer.

"You will listen," he insisted harshly. "There is a priest I know who will marry us and keep silent. It will not be legal in the eyes of the government, but to the eyes of God we will be man and wife."

"Don't be patronizing!" Sheila rejected his proposal violently. "I wouldn't want to endure the shame of a marriage to you!"

He gave her a hard shake, his teeth bared. "I wish to have our union blessed by the Church and to give you the protection of my name."

"I don't want either one!" Her protest was choked with pain. A surfeit of pride insisted she must deny the offer he made only because of the child she carried. Sheila reinforced her refusal with a lie. "I don't want you!"

For a moment the fire blazing in his dark eyes seemed about to consume her in its raging inferno. Roughly, he pulled Sheila to his chest. The hard fingers digging into her arms lifted her up on tiptoes. The heat between them made it difficult for Sheila to breathe.

"What is it that you want, then?" he demanded savagely. "Do you want me to let you go? Is that it? So you can go to your parents and have the baby there with them? Do you wish to do that and hear him called a bastard?" Ráfaga did not give Sheila the opportunity to make a single response. "I will not let you go! If that is what you hoped, you can wipe it from your mind. I will never permit you to leave me—nor the child that was conceived by our love. We will be married by the priest, and the child, when it is born, will be baptized by a priest! He will be raised here in this house, in this canyon, with whatever brothers and sisters that may follow."

Her heart stopped beating, then soared. "Do you want our baby, Ráfaga?" Sheila sighed.

"It is the flesh of our flesh. Do you think I would deny it?" He frowned angrily.

"I don't know." She closed her eyes, making a small, confused shake of her head. "I thought . . . When I told you, you seemed so—"

His fingers dug into the flesh of her arms in hard demand. "Do you want our baby?" Ráfaga put the same question to Sheila.

"Yes." There was no uncertainty at all in her answer. "Yes, I want the baby." She reaffirmed it more forcefully, although her voice was hardly more than a whisper. "I love you, Ráfaga." She opened her eyes and saw the flicker of doubt in the darkness of his. "You thought I didn't want the baby," she accused in disbelief.

"It was possible." His gaze roamed her face, still not totally convinced. "You were brought to this canyon against your will. I forced you to lie in my bed." One arm was released as his hand moved to her back, faintly caressing while he drew her possessively closer. "I had you punished when you ran away from me. How could I expect you to want a baby conceived with me? When

I saw the redness of your eyes, I knew you had shed bitter tears of regret at the discovery."

"Only because I thought you wouldn't want the baby or me." Her trembling fingertips traced the outline of his carved cheekbone and jaw. "In a few months, I'll be so fat and ugly that—"

"No." His hand covered her lips. "Even when you are heavy with child you will be beautiful." His voice was husky and low, the midnight velvet of his eyes gazing deeply into hers. "Do you remember the time that you tried to escape in the storm and later sat in front of the fire to warm yourself? I watched you then, wrapped in a blanket I put around you. The firelight was dancing in your hair and I imagined you sitting there, your belly swollen with child. At that moment, I knew a desire such as I have never felt before. I thought to satisfy it by taking you. But having you once was like drinking water from the sea. I found I needed to possess more than your body. I wanted your mind and heart and soul. I love you, *querida*, as I have never loved another woman."

Sheila felt her heart would burst with joy. She had waited so long to hear those words, and she had given up hope that he would ever say them, that he would ever feel the love for her he had just professed.

"I love you." It was almost a vow that she uttered softly.

Ráfaga smiled, with his mouth and his eyes. "Soon the baby will begin to swell your belly." His hand moved to her stomach, his fingers spreading over it, igniting a fire within Sheila. "When it does, I will look at you and feel that same surge of desire, *querida*. I will never stop wanting you or loving you." His voice became deeper and huskier as his hand slid beneath her blouse to mold itself around the fullness of her breasts. "Think of the countless hours I will spend watching our child suckle at your breast. Do you now understand the happiness I knew when I realized you were with child?"

"Yes." She laughed with breathless joy, tears shimmering in her eyes. "Yes, I do."

"And you will consent to letting the priest marry us?"

"Yes." Sheila nodded.

His dark brows drew together in a frown. "I regret that I cannot offer you the legality of a government ceremony, but my name is too well known to——"

"I know. I don't mind," she insisted.

Ráfaga breathed in deeply, pain flickering in his eyes. "I have no right to ask you to share this life with me. I can offer you so little, and you give me so much."

"All I want is your love. I have had all the rest. It wouldn't mean anything without you. I know that. You must believe it."

"I only know that I cannot let you go," he declared, roughly crushing her against him as his mouth descended to accept the invitation of her lips.

Three days later the golden light of dawn was spreading across the sky. Ráfaga's hands were gently cupping Sheila's face. His dark gaze shifted beyond her to Laredo, already in the saddle and holding the reins to her horse.

"It is time to leave, *amado*," he told her quietly.

"Please, Ráfaga, come with us now." Sheila asked him to change his mind.

"No." He shook his head, smiling to lessen the hardness of his tone. "It is a long ride. You will need to rest at least a day when you get there, and I cannot risk being that long in a place where I could be recognized—unless," Ráfaga teased mockingly, "you wish to visit me in jail."

"No, of course not." Sheila lowered her head, but she hated being separated from him, even for a few days.

"I will leave tomorrow." He lifted her chin with his thumb. "The next time you see me, we will stand before the priest." His mouth closed over hers in a hard, brief kiss before he firmly guided Sheila to the bay and helped her into the saddle. His hand rested on her thigh as he looked at Laredo. "Remember," Ráfaga told him crisply, "go directly to Father Ramirez.

Speak to no one else. He knows me and will find a place for you to stay that is safe."

Laredo nodded his understanding and handed the bay's reins to Sheila. "I'll take care of her, Ráfaga."

Her eyes were filling with tears as Sheila looked down at Ráfaga. His mouth had thinned into a grim line, but the darkness in his gaze held the smouldering light of his love. Her lips parted to protest again that she didn't want to go without him.

His hand came down hard on the bay's rump. The horse jumped forward in alrm. Sheila checked its flight for an instant, then urged it forward. In seconds, Laredo was riding beside her.

Passing the spring-fed pool, they took the narrow, rocky trail up the north face of the canyon. Single file, they rode with Sheila leading the way up the long, winding trail through a corridor of trees and rocks. Once the sun crested the eastern ridge, the morning blazed with light.

The bay was lunging up the last steep slope of the trail when Sheila heard the rifle shot. She reined the bay in sharply at the top and saw Laredo's head jerk toward the sound. He spurred his horse to the top and dismounted, ignoring Sheila as he ran to a rocky overlook.

"What is it?" She joined him on the ledge.

The clear mountain air carried indistinguishable shouts of alarm. "My God, it's a patrol," Laredo muttered.

A large band of uniformed riders was galloping across the meadow in the direction of the adobe houses. The canyon hideout had been discovered. Her heart leaped into her throat. Ráfaga was down there. Pivoting, Sheila ran back to the bay. But Laredo was there, grabbing a bridle strap to stop her.

"Where the hell do you think you're going?" he demanded, holding the bay's tossing head.

"Ráfaga's down there. I have to go to him."

"Do you think I don't want to?" Laredo snapped. "He knows we're out of danger, that we're safe. All he has to worry about is getting himself out of there. If he can't, then I can damned sure break him out of any prison they put him in. This is no time to be melo-dramatic."

She recognized the logic of his argument, but she wasn't ruled by logic. Digging her heels into the bay's flanks, she whipped the horse with the reins. The bay dragged Laredo for two feet before he was forced to let go and the horse charged back down the trail it had just climbed.

Within seconds Sheila heard the clattering of Laredo's horse behind her. At a wide spot in the trail, he forced his horse alongside hers.

"You can't stop me!" she blazed.

"I realize that!" he flashed angrily. "I know I'm a damned fool, but I promised Ráfaga I'd take care of you, and I could never face him if I let you go down there alone."

He spurred his horse into the lead. Above the scram-bling of horses' hooves could be heard the sound of gunfire in the canyon below. Ráfaga and his men were putting up a fight.

Their reckless descent brought them down the trail in a third of the time. At the pool, Laredo made a pointing gesture in the direction of the adobe house where they had left Ráfaga. The majority of the gunfire was coming from the cluster of houses to the west, but there was the sound of shots being fired near the lone house.

Laredo broke from the trees ahead of Sheila. Im-mediately a volley of shots exploded around him. In-stinct made Sheila stop the bay as she saw him jerk convulsively, sawing on the reins. His chestnut horse was thrown off balance and fell. Laredo stayed on the ground after his horse scrambled to its feet, trotting back into the trees where Sheila waited. She was swing-ing a leg out of the saddle when she heard Laredo call to her.

"Get out of here!" His voice was riddled with pain.

Sheila dismounted, wanting to go to Laredo and

knowing if she stepped out of the trees, she would be forsaking their protection. She grabbed at the trailing reins of his chestnut.

"You can't help me," Laredo told her, grunting with the effort to speak. "I can't move, so get out of here!"

With a sob of anguish, she knew he was right. Her gaze swung to the thatched roof of the house. Sheila turned and mounted the chestnut, leading the bay. She worked her way through the trees away from Laredo to the other side of the adobe house. Ráfaga was trapped inside it.

The clearing from the trees to the house seemed dangerously wide. She had to cross it to reach the house and Ráfaga. Sheila hesitated, then jammed her heels into the chestnut. The bay raced alongside as she whipped the chestnut across the clearing to the temporary protection of the east side of the house.

The patrol had struck first at the cluster of houses. The main force was only just beginning to extend its foray to the isolated adobe building. A rifle barrel glinted from a window at her approach, and Sheila reined in beside it.

"Ráfaga!"

Immediately he appeared in the windowframe. His eyes narrowed angrily at the sight of her, his features hardened and ruthless.

"What are you doing here?" he muttered savagely.

"I had to come back. Hurry!" Sheila urged, but he was already swinging out the window.

"Where is Laredo?" He had a foot in the stirrup and was mounting the bay when he asked the question.

"He's down," she answered simply and saw his mouth tighten.

"We do not have a chance in the meadow. We will try to get into the trees."

Bullets whined around them as they raced the horses back the way Sheila had come. There was no time to dwell on her fear. Sheila simply knew she was afraid. They reached the trees untouched and Ráfaga turned the bay toward the pool and the narrow trail up the north face of the canyon. Almost too late they saw a handful of uniformed riders approaching through the trees, blocking their way.

Without hesitating a second, Ráfaga pivoted the bay. Sheila guessed Ráfaga's alternate plan was to stay within the trees until they reached the east wall, then break for the main trail out of the canyon.

A shout from one of the uniformed riders revealed they had been spotted. To attain speed was next to impossible in the trees, with low-hanging branches whipping at their faces, trying to unseat them.

"Sheila." Ráfaga was behind her. She looked over her shoulder, bending low on the chestnut's neck. "We must try to cross the meadow now before they cut us off."

Her sweeping gaze saw another fragment of the patrol approaching from the meadow side. Pursued from behind and threatened from the side, she knew he was right and nodded her agreement. The narrow canyon suddenly seemed very wide and the sloping trail very far away.

The chestnut burst from the trees ahead of the bay and maintained its lead for a few strides. Both horses were flattened to the ground, running all out, but the bay began inching away. Ráfaga checked the bay's pace to keep the distance between them from widening more.

The riders were bearing down, the angle lessening as Sheila and Ráfaga neared the center of the meadow. Sheila realized there was a slim chance that the bay's speed might enable Ráfaga to make it, but not if he continued to hold back the horse to stay with her. Her decision was made without thinking, purely on the instinct of survival.

"I can't make it!" she shouted to Ráfaga. "Go on without me!"

"No!"

But Sheila was already hauling on the reins of the heavy-mouthed chestnut, turning its head away as Ráfaga tried unsuccessfully to grab for the reins. Aware that Ráfaga was slowing the bay to come back for her, Sheila guided the chestnut directly toward the intercepting patrol.

She began waving her arm and screaming at the top of her lungs, "Help me! I'm an American!" She repeated it over and over again, nearly sobbing as she prayed for Ráfaga to ride on.

The patrol slowed as she galloped the chestnut toward their center. She brought her horse to a plunging halt in front of them. The lead rider made an assessing sweep of her, his attention stopping briefly on the golden color of her hair.

A pointing gesture of his hand separated the majority of the patrol from the rest, sending them after Ráfaga. Finally, Sheila looked behind her and saw the bay racing for the trail. She knew then that she had gained him the time to make it.

Shaking, Sheila tried to dismount, more or less falling from the saddle. Her legs buckling, she went to her knees, relief sobbing from her throat.

A voice made an inquiry in Spanish, but she was too addled to make the translation. It was repeated in accented English.

"Are you all right, *señora?*" The voice was calm, yet very crisp.

Tears matted her lashes together. She wiped them away as she swallowed back the sobs in gasping breaths. At first Sheila was too weak from reaction to reply.

Finally, her nod was accompanied by a shaky, "Yes, I'm all right."

A pair of polished military boots was within her vision, standing near her. Saddle leather creaked close by as a horse stamped restlessly and snorted. Distantly, Sheila could hear the sounds of other activity in the canyon.

"You are Señora Sheila Townsend from Texas?" The accented voice asked for confirmation.

Lifting her head, Sheila held her wind-tangled hair away from her cheek, eyeing the uniformed officer warily. "Yes, I am Sheila Townsend," she admitted.

The man was of medium height, with a hawk nose and piercing brown eyes. "You are the daughter of Señor Elliot Rogers?" At her nod, his thin mouth curved into a polite smile. "We have been looking for you for a very long time, *señora*—since we found your husband's body in the car." With a slight bow and an extension of his gloved hand to help Sheila to her feet, he added, "Please, I am Capitán Ramon Echeverria."

Accepting his assistance, Sheila rose to face the officer. He was watching her alertly, sharply curious and speculating. She was still trembling and shaky inside. It was difficult to contain her resentment toward the officer who had led the raid against Ráfaga.

"How—how did you find me?" Her voice quivered, coming out husky and low as she removed her hand from his grasp.

Again he offered her that thin smile that was polite and nothing more. "As I said, we have been looking for you since we found your husband, *señora*. At first, there were many rumors that you were being held captive by the men who shot your husband. Then there was nothing, as if the mountains had swallowed you up. A few weeks ago a routine patrol was in the vicinity and heard a gunshot. When they went to investigate, they believed they saw a blonde-haired woman with a small group of riders. We have had scouts combing the area since then. That is how we located the canyon," he explained.

"I see," she murmured, then shuddered inwardly that her foolish attempt to escape had led to this.

The Mexican officer's gaze flicked briefly to the sloping trail out of the canyon before returning its piercing attention to Sheila. "It is unfortunate that the man was able to escape when you rode to us. He was the leader of this band, was he not?"

". . . Yes." Sheila hesitated only a second before making the admission, but it was enough to intensify the officer's look.

"His name?" he prompted.

"I don't know his name," she answered quickly. This time it was too quickly.

A dark brow arched immediately. "This is not Ráfaga's band?"

Sheila argued swiftly with herself, debating whether to lie or tell the truth, but there was too much chance of being caught in a lie.

"Yes, that is what they called him, but I don't know his name," she admitted tightly. "I heard him referred to only as Ráfaga, nothing else."

"You say his name oddly, *señora*." The officer's mouth curved briefly, a speculating gleam in his dark brown eyes.

"Do I, Captain?" Sheila tensed instantly, feigning indifference.

"You were here a long time, *señora*." He seemed to choose his words carefully, not releasing her from his pinning gaze. "Yet there was no ransom asked, nor were you sold. You are a very beautiful woman. I do not think this criminal Ráfaga could have been blind to you." Sheila felt herself paling. "I think perhaps he kept you to be his woman. Perhaps, after all this time, *señora*, you were not quite an unwilling captive."

Breathing in sharply, Sheila couldn't let her gaze waver from the astute officer. But the survival instinct was still strong.

"After all I've been through, how do you have the nerve to say that?" she bristled falsely.

"I am sorry, *señora*," he responded insincerely in response to her indignant challenge, "but you must realize how it appears."

"Do you remember the patrol that saw me a few weeks ago?" Crossing her arms, Sheila reached behind her to grasp the hem of her blouse. "I was trying to escape. This is the way Ráfaga punished me." Sheila turned her back to the officer, lifting the blouse to reveal the marks left by the whip. She faced him again with cold challenge. "Do you have any more questions about whether or not I was a willing captive?"

He inclined his head in a deferential nod. "My apologies, *señora*." But suspicion still lurked in his eyes. He was accepting what he saw for the time being, but Sheila sensed that later he would question it. "If the *señora* has recovered, we shall ride to the houses where my men have gathered the prisoners."

Sheila nodded curtly and suffered his assistance to remount the chestnut, aware of his faintly quizzical gaze. She could not read his mind and knew he was wondering if she had been one man's mistress or more. But she pretended not to notice, smiling coolly when he handed her the chestnut's reins. He would receive no information about Ráfaga from her.

Chapter 23

It was an emotional scene that greeted Sheila when they rode between the adobe houses. The captured members of Ráfaga's band had been herded together like cattle to be slaughtered. Their numbers indicated that less than a handful had escaped. Those who were wounded in the skirmish were there, too, moaning with pain. Sheila couldn't see Laredo in the tightly grouped throng and didn't dare ask about him, not yet.

Soldiers standing guard ignored the weeping women pleading to look after their injured men. Frightened children clung to their skirts. The smaller ones wailed their fear of something they didn't understand while the older ones looked around them, their rounded, dark eyes filled with tears.

The officer riding next to Sheila didn't stop where the prisoners were being held, but continued between the houses, where more of his men were systematically going through the crude buildings in search of those who might still be hiding. Sheila steeled herself not to show any emotion at the scene.

She managed to ignore all that she saw until they came upon the last house before the corral. At the sight of Elena on her knees hugging the legs of a man slumped in a chair, Sheila reined the chestnut to a halt. A rifle lay on the ground near his chair. A spreading red stain covered his chest.

When Sheila stopped, the officer turned to see what had attracted her attention. As if sensing their presence, Elena lifted her head. She wiped the tears from her cheeks and rose proudly to face them, a hand resting on her dead husband's shoulder. She began speaking to them in Spanish, her voice low and vibrating with emotion.

"Do you understand Spanish, *señora?*" the officer asked.

"Very little," Sheila murmured, unable to take her eyes away from Elena.

"The woman says she pushed his chair to the doorway when she saw the soldiers coming and put a rifle in his hands. She says the soldiers killed him as if he was a man," the officer translated quietly. "She says now her husband is a man because he is free."

There was a lump in her throat as Sheila nudged the chestnut into a walk. She felt the officer's curious glance and gave him the explanation he sought without looking at him.

"Her husband, César, was paralyzed, a helpless baby who knew nothing and no one."

"You knew this woman?" he questioned.

"As you pointed out, Capitán Echeverria, I have been here a long time," Sheila reminded him grimly and urged the chestnut into a trot .

When they reached the corral, he was there to help her dismount. Sheila was skeptical of his courteous concern for her welfare. She wished he would go away and leave her alone, if only for a little while.

Like a shadow, the officer followed her to a shady spot beneath the overhang, pausing to politely inquire, "May I get you some water?"

"No, thank you," she refused shortly.

He stood beside her. "We will be leaving this place soon. Is there anything you wish to take? I will have my men—"

"Nothing," Sheila broke in smoothly. Her hand was resting on her stomach. Ráfaga's baby was the only thing she was going to take from here.

"No, I do not imagine there is," the officer agreed. "You are no doubt anxious to leave here. You have been through a great deal—seeing your husband murdered and being held by those criminals. You are a very strong woman, Señora Townsend."

"Please"—Sheila found his sympathetic murmurings irritating—"I don't want to think about it."

"I understand," he said, inclining his head in a gesture of deference to her wishes. "You do not wish to speak about these things."

"No, I don't," she agreed sharply.

"If you will excuse me, I must speak to my men."

"Of course." Sheila nodded and looked away as the officer smiled politely and withdrew.

Shutting her eyes to the sights around her, Sheila wanted to close out the sounds, as well. She wished she could cry as the women and children were doing, but she had to keep silent, hiding her grief inside. There was not a trace of any pain in her expression when the officer returned to announce they were leaving.

Again Sheila was separated from the prisoners, riding in the front of the patrol beside the officer. As they moved up the sloping trail, she looked back to the canyon, knowing she would never return to this place, her home.

It was no longer a haven, untouched by the outside world. It had been invaded, and those who had once lived there would never find freedom and safety within its walls again. It was forever lost.

There was sadness in her eyes, but Sheila quickly veiled it when she saw the officer watching her. The handful of soldiers that had given chase to Ráfaga met the patrol at the top of the trail. They reported he had eluded them, vanishing without a trace, as if carried off by his namesake. Her lashes fluttered briefly in relief, but she gave no other sign of gladness.

A mountain breeze touched her cheek, a fleeting caress that seemed to say farewell an instant before they rode into the windbreak of the trees. Sheila was rocked by the sudden realization that she might never see Ráfaga again. She tried to shut out the thought as they started down the mountain.

"Your parents are being notified that we have found you safe and unharmed," the Mexican officer informed her.

"How are my parents?" Sheila asked quickly, anxious to talk and distract her thoughts from Ráfaga.

"They have been very worried about you," he answered.

"Where are they? Are they in Mexico?" She suddenly wanted desperately to see them. It seemed a lifetime since she had been with them.

"*Sí*, your mother has been staying in Chihuahua since your disappearance," he explained. "Your father flies down on the weekends or whenever his business will permit. I have spoken with them often."

"I want to see them." Sheila murmured the wish aloud.

"Of course, and they will wish to see you to assure themselves that you are well, as we have told them." He smiled faintly. "I believe transportation is being arranged so that they might meet us at our night's encampment."

"Thank you." It was a genuine expression of gratitude, accompanied by a tremulous smile as Sheila urged the chestnut into a trot.

The setting of the sun found the patrol still in the Sierras, making camp for the night in one of the valleys. The soldiers were busy picketing the horses and starting a fire. Sheila stood on the fringe of the activity, watching with absent interest.

Her parents arrived with the last streaking rays of a red sun. Sheila rushed into their arms, laughing and crying, hugging and kissing, with all three of them talking at the same time. Yet her joy at being reunited with them was bittersweet.

Regaining control of her emotions, Sheila finally stepped back to look at them, holding their hands tightly. She gazed at them through a blur of tears and smiled at the sight of them. Her father managed to look the part of the powerful, influential businessman despite the denim Levi's and jacket he wore. And her mother, dressed in a pantsuit of rugged khaki, still possessed that aura of elegance that was so much a part of her.

"Are you sure you're all right, honey?" Her father squeezed her hand.

"Yes, I'm fine," she assured him.

"All these months with no word." He shook his head briefly, his voice choked with emotion. "Your mother never stopped believing that you were alive and well." He curved an arm around his wife's shoulders. "Even when things looked darkest, she never would let me give up hope."

Sheila looked at her mother, knowing the iron strength contained within that feminine shell. She felt the searching inspection of the almond-brown eyes as they probed beneath Sheila's expression.

"What happened, Sheila? Did they—" Constance Rogers paused, delicately.

And Sheila smiled faintly. "Are you trying to ask if I was raped, Mother?" she questioned gently. "I wasn't." There was no reason to hide the truth from her parents. Sooner or later she would tell them about Ráfaga, and she preferred to do it now. "Ráfaga made love to me, but he didn't rape me."

Her father was instantly outraged. "You mean the leader of that band—"

"Strangely enough, Dad," she interrupted gently, "if you ever had the opportunity to meet Ráfaga, you would have liked him."

An odd look passed over her mother's face. "I always believed it was nonsense, but I can see it in your face. You are pregnant, aren't you, Sheila?" she murmured.

"Yes, I am," she admitted with a glow of serenity in her eyes. "Ráfaga and I were to be married tomorrow by a village priest on the other side of the mountains."

"My little girl marrying a criminal?" He stared at Sheila incredulously.

"It doesn't matter, E.J." her mother soothed. "She's with us now. Once we have her back home, all of this will be behind her and forgotten."

Sheila frowned. "I hadn't thought about going back to Texas." She brushed her fingers across her forehead in confusion. Her thoughts hadn't gone as far as the future.

"Well, of course, you will, honey," her mother insisted with a smile. "You have the baby to think about. I presume you do want to keep it?"

"Of course," Sheila retorted and pressed a protective hand against her stomach.

"You need a place to live, medical attention for you and the baby," her mother reasoned. "What is more natural than for you to come home?"

"I suppose so," she conceded hesitantly.

"There isn't any reason to inform others that the baby isn't Brad's," her father added.

"Dad—" Sheila laughed softly— "when the baby is born with black hair and dark eyes, nobody is going to believe that Brad fathered it."

"After the baby is born," Constance Rogers inserted, "you will want to go back to college and obtain your degree. After all, you now have the baby's future to consider, as well as your own."

"Yes." Sheila nodded, but somehow her parents' references to material things and social status didn't seem important anymore.

As if her mother sensed her lack of total agreement, she changed the subject. "We can make plans later about what you want to do, Sheila. Right now your father and I are just relieved that you are here."

A mist of tears drifted across her vision. "It seems so long since I've seen you," Sheila said.

"For us, too, baby." Her father hugged her close, pressing a moist kiss on the top of her head.

"Ah, Señor and Señora Rogers," the Mexican officer's voice intruded on their reunion, "it is good to see your daughter again, is it not?"

"Very good," her father answered, releasing Sheila from his embrace. "We can't thank you enough for finding her, Captain."

"It is nothing." He shrugged. "The prisoners are being fed. Our meal will be ready shortly. If you would care for some coffee—" His arm started to swing toward the campfire in invitation.

The rest of his words were cut off by a strident American voice. "Son-of-a-bitch, if you expect me to eat this garbage, you'd better untie my hands!" There was a ring of pain in the tone as the same voice repeated the demand in Spanish.

"Laredo," Sheila gasped and took an instinctive step toward the sound.

The officer moved to bar her way. *"Señora,* I—" He started to deny her passage.

"Please, he was kind to me," Sheila explained hurriedly. "May I speak to him for a few minutes?"

The officer was about to refuse when her father stepped forward to champion her cause. "Surely it wouldn't do any harm, Captain."

The request was considered thoughtfully before the officer acceded. "I will come with you."

There was little enough conversation among the prisoners, but when Sheila appeared with the Mexican officer, there was an unearthly silence. Several looked at her with open resentment for associating with the enemy. The others coldly ignored her.

Laredo's gaze was deliberately averted as she stopped beside him. He was lying on the ground, partially propped up. The white of a bandage was wrapped around his right thigh. Blood soaked the shirt on his left side. A plate of food was on his lap, but his wrists were shackled.

"Hello, Laredo," Sheila finally said in a quest for his attention.

He looked up, his cold blue eyes briefly glancing at the man with her before focusing on Sheila. "I don't care for the company you're keeping, Mrs. Townsend."

She knelt beside him, murmuring very low, "Neither do I." In a louder voice, she asked, "Are you hurt very badly?"

"They tell me I'll live."

At closer quarters, Sheila could see the grayness beneath his tanned features. "You're not eating," she said, observing the untouched food on his plate.

"I have a little problem with my left arm. I can't seem to move it," he explained sarcastically. "So unless they pour this slop down my throat, I guess I'll have to go hungry."

Sheila glanced sideways at the officer. "Can't you untie his hands long enough to let him eat?" she requested politely.

There was hesitation before the order was given to one of the soldiers to free Laredo's hands. Sheila could see it was a tremendous effort for him to eat. After three spoonfuls, he stopped.

"It certainly doesn't taste like Consuelo's cooking." Laredo smiled wanly.

"It doesn't look like it, either." Sheila picked up the spoon and began feeding him. One of the soldiers from the campfire approached the captain. He stepped to the side to talk to the man.

As Sheila lifted the spoon to Laredo's mouth, he murmured lowly, "Was Ráfaga hurt?"

"No, he got away," she whispered. "He didn't have a scratch. Where will he go, Laredo?"

"Only Ráfaga knows that." He tried to lift himself higher and winced with pain. "What about you, Sheila?" he asked in the same low tone that couldn't be overheard. "Where are you going? Back to Texas with your parents?"

"I don't know—maybe at least until after the baby

is born. Or I might stay here. Maybe I'll be able to find Rá——" She stopped the statement abruptly, realizing it was Ráfaga the soldiers had hoped to capture.

If she stayed in Mexico, they would be waiting to see if she contacted him or vice versa. For his sake, she had to leave. If she thought with her head instead of her heart, Sheila knew it would be best if she never came back to Mexico.

His was an impermanent existence. He could never offer a future for her or their baby. Their unborn child was entitled to some kind of a decent life, the freedom that Ráfaga yearned for and could never have. In America, Sheila could give their child that, plus the advantage of money.

Perhaps by sacrificing her life for their child, she was discovering the true meaning of love. Was she being noble? Or was she simply scared of running and hiding if she lived the rest of her life with Ráfaga? She was really too confused to know.

"If you go to the States, would you . . ."—there was an odd catch in Laredo's voice— ". . . could you take a trip to Alamagordo?"

Her chin trembled slightly in understanding. "To see your parents?"

"Their name is Ludlow—Scott Ludlow, Sr. Don't tell them about me, but—"

"I will make sure that they are all right and get word back to you somehow," Sheila promised softly. "In the meantime, I will do what I can for you and the others. I've heard money helps."

There was only silence as she fed him a few more spoonfuls. Laredo eyed her thoughtfully. When he finally spoke, it was so low that Sheila had to bend closer to hear what he was saying.

"If you really want to help," he murmured, "you can start some kind of distraction. Two of the guards watching us are in their teens. There's a chance we could overpower them and get their guns. Hopefully, in the confusion, a few of us could get away."

"You could be killed," Sheila gasped in protest, but Laredo just looked at her silently. "I'll try," she agreed with a reluctant sigh. Stealing a glance over her shoulder, she saw the officer concluding his talk with a subordinate. She quickly turned back, asking Laredo, "Where's Juan? I haven't seen him with the others."

"He's over there," Laredo answered with a sideways nod, "under the blanket." Sheila looked, seeing a long shape wrapped completely in a brightly colored blanket. Her throat constricted painfully. "His wound opened up. He died," Laredo announced flatly.

"*Señora.*" The officer was standing beside her.

Swallowing to ease the tightness in her throat, Sheila straightened up from Laredo. The plate was empty. She had no more reason to remain with him, and the officer was reminding her of that. She turned away as a soldier put the shackles back on Laredo's wrists. Her face was pale with the shock of Juan's death. She kept it averted from the officer's watchful gaze as they started toward her parents, near the campfire.

"Thank you for letting me speak to him," she said, needing to break the silence.

"You have an affection for this man?" he inquired.

"He is a friend," Sheila answered simply. "He was from home, someone I could talk to."

"I understand." He nodded, but she doubted he understood it. "Pardon me, *señora,* but I could not help observing that you seem a bit upset. Are you not happy to be with your parents?"

"Of course I am." Her response was brittle.

He gave her a brief, quizzical glance, then allowed silence to dominate their walk to the fire. Sheila stopped barely within its circle of light. Her parents were seated off to the side, talking together, as yet unaware of her return. The officer signaled to one of his men to bring them coffee, then turned to contemplate Sheila. She knew she should go to her parents, but she also knew they were talking about her—and Ráfaga and the baby. So she stayed where she was.

"We rode far today," the officer commented absently.

"Yes," Sheila agreed.

"I had time to think while we were riding," he continued. "I am convinced that you are Ráfaga's woman. Although I cannot prove it, I believe that you belonged to him willingly. Your eyes and your face do not hold the expression of a woman who has been forced to accept a man's attentions. Sometimes I see your eyes gazing upon the mountains and there is a special glow in them, as if you know he is out there somewhere. Perhaps you think he will come for you." His eyebrow lifted, light dawning in his eyes. "Yes," he remarked positively as Sheila stiffened, "yes, he will come for you."

The officer turned away, snapping sharp orders to several of the soldiers around the fire. There was instant activity. A complacent smile was on his face when he looked back to Sheila.

"I am posting extra sentries. We will be ready for him—your Ráfaga—when he comes," he declared.

"You are wrong," Sheila denied desperately. "He won't come."

A shot rang out, then a second and a third. The officer grabbed at Sheila's arm, shouting to his men. More shots were fired before the soldiers answered with gunfire of their own. Sheila struggled against the hand that restricted her movements.

Scuffling noises came from where Laredo and the others were held. In the chaos, they were making their bid for freedom. A bullet whined by her ear, striking the officer. His grip loosened instantly and she twisted free.

"Sheila, over here!" Ráfaga's achingly familiar voice called to her and she turned toward the sound.

Her eyes scanned the shadowy darkness of the trees surrounding the camp. She started to run, uncertain of the direction.

"Sheila, no!" her mother cried. "Don't go!"

But her choice was made. There was nothing the civilized world could offer her or their baby that would equal one moment in Ráfaga's arms, no matter what the circumstances. Ráfaga stepped from behind a tree. The rifle at his hip sprayed a cover-fire for Sheila. She ran to him.